BEHIND THE LENS

CASSIDY STEPHENS

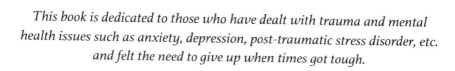

This book is dedicated to those who have dealt with trauma and mental health issues such as anxiety, depression, post-traumatic stress disorder, etc. and felt the need to give up when times got tough.

You all have your own story to tell, so make sure you're around to tell it.

Keep going. Tell your story.

Never give up.

DISCLAIMER

This book deals with trauma, mentions of domestic abuse, anxiety, depression, flashbacks of PTSD nature, and panic attacks. Please read at your own discretion.

PREFACE

Hello, everyone, and welcome to "Behind the Lens!"

This is my third published book and the start of my second Teen Fiction/Young Adult series: "Behind."

I cannot believe that my writing journey has gotten me this far. I have God to thank as well as all of you. Thank you to my friends and family for supporting me while I guide myself through the last of my teenage years and document the stories that touch my heart and fill my mind so that it never runs dry.

"Behind the Lens" is one of the most vulnerable books I have ever written. This book dives deep into my struggles with anxiety and depression during my teenage years.

Even though my characters' and I's mental health dilemmas were caused by different things, the general outlook is the same.

Sharing my emotions that I have hidden behind my walls with the world around me is terrifying, but I know that a lot of people around me have the same struggles.

This book is for all of you. Everyone deserves to tell their story, and - in a way - this is mine.

"Behind the Lens" is a realistic look into the life of a traumatized seventeen-year-old girl. Why is she afraid of living the life that was meant for her? For now, I don't know, and frankly, she doesn't either.

What does a silly pair of glasses have to do with the situation at hand? What will happen when a strange boy is brought into the mix?

Follow along in the footsteps of Abigail Bartley as she navigates through her final year of high school with a fake smile on her face.

Even though she has three of her best friends, a kind therapist, and her parents by her side, nothing can help her anxieties evaporate for good...or can it?

You are not alone.

You are strong.

Tell your story.

I love you.

PROLOGUE

THE HUMAN BODY OFTEN FUNCTIONS LIKE A TIMEPIECE. BEFORE THIS rather obscure observation is shot down, some explanation is in order.

Both the human mind and a timepiece can distinguish the concept of time from reality. Every hour, every minute, and every second that passes indicates that the lifespan of each of these things are approaching their demise. Both the human body and a timepiece possess hands. As time goes on, the pair of hands for each of these beings gradually slows down until eventually, the hourglass has run out of sand to spill.

There is one crucial difference between the human body and a timepiece, though: a timepiece can be restored on this planet with the simple usage of a battery. Once a human grows old after experiencing the gift of life, it comes to their attention that their time has run out; hence the saying: "Time is free, but it is priceless."

That was exactly how Abigail Bartley felt whilst seated on a comfortable couch that seemed to take up over half of the suffocating room. A clock on the wall to her right ticked in perfect rhythm with her heart pounding in her chest. Across her sat a woman who could not have been older than thirty. The curls of her honey blonde hair bounced each time she shifted her position on the chair she was seated in. Despite the friendliness and compassion of this woman, Abigail was picking at her nails and avoiding eye contact with her.

The ticking of the small clock grew louder as each second passed. The young woman was beginning to feel uncomfortable—a deep contrast from the kind smile on her face. Neither of them said a word. The silence grew thicker with every tension-filled moment.

Eventually, the woman spoke. "Abigail, are you sure there's nothing else you'd like to talk about in the last remaining minutes of our session?" she asked gently. Her intention was nothing but sincere, but Abigail interpreted it as demeaning—as if the woman was looking down on her from above.

"No. I told you that before," Abigail snipped just above the ticking of the wall clock.

Silence ensued once more. Abigail's head was bent towards her lap. She gnawed at a hangnail on her right hand, wincing as she accidentally pulled it off. The teenager resorted to picking at a loose thread surrounding a hole in the knee of her light jeans. A long tendril of straight ebony hair hung between her eyes and down to the upper half of her stomach.

A clearing of the woman's throat jostled Abigail from her trance. "Your senior year starts on Monday; right?"

"It does," Abigail crossly mumbled. "What does that have to do with anything?"

"Abigail, during our time together over the summer, I've noticed a lot of things about you and your body language. Something I've learned about you is that when you're experiencing anxiety, you tend to become bitter," the woman explained. "Could this be because you're not looking forward to your senior year?"

The teenager slammed her fist down on the arm of the couch. "Miss Cullen, you know full well what happened to me last year. Isn't that what *this*-" she paused to wildly gesture around the small room that was suffocating her, "-is all about? I've spent hours in this office telling you about all of my problems and now you have the nerve to ask me if I'm anxious about my senior year?"

"You don't need to call me Miss Cullen. Kristy will do," Kristy soothed the troubled girl who refused to look her in the eyes. "As your therapist, it's my job to create a safe space for you to discover what's bothering you and to figure out solutions to those problems. If you feel more at ease in a quiet room where you can embrace your thoughts on your own, then that's what I can provide. If you want to speak about it, then I will be happy to listen."

"Thank you...Kristy...but frankly, I hate school. My mental health has drained more in this past school year than the rest of my life combined. I can't go back there." Abigail felt a stab of guilt rush through her.

Kristy gave her a sad but understanding smile. "That's something I've been hearing from several of my clients. School has gotten more stressful and work-inducing throughout the past years. From what you've expressed to me, school is where you feel the least bit safe. Correct?"

"Yeah." Abigail succeeded in tearing the loose thread off her jeans. She tossed it down on the thin gray carpet beneath her shoes.

"Do you remember what I told you to do when you start to feel unsafe?" inquired Kristy.

Abigail hesitated, racking her brain for an immediate answer. "Surround myself with my friends, voice my problem to someone I trust, and take deep breaths to calm myself?"

"That's right." Kristy smiled encouragingly. "You mentioned to me a couple of weeks ago that you haven't seen your friends all summer, yet they're the people you trust the most other than your parents. Is there a reason for that?"

"Yes, there is," Abigail huffed while picking at her nails again.

"And what is that?"

"I wanted to improve for them before I reunited with them on the first day back to school," she confessed. "They know what I've been through. They've seen me cry, lash out, and scream about it countless times, but do they deserve any of it? No. I'm doing this for them."

The pencil in the therapist's hand scribbled quietly on the paper in her clipboard. "I see. That's a very valid reason, but the most important thing you need to be doing is taking care of yourself. You don't need to be happy and carefree all the time. Nobody expects that of you, especially your friends. You're all going through this journey of life together."

"They have their own lives, you know. I can't just waltz in and expect them to take care of me whenever I'm upset," reasoned Abigail.

"How come you don't feel that way with me? Could you consider me a friend?"

"Yes, but isn't it your job?"

"It is, but it's also a pleasure to listen to what you have to say," Kristy informed her of something she already knew.

Abigail released a sigh through her lips that were void of makeup. "I don't understand how it's a "pleasure" to listen to me complain."

"Listen, Abigail." Kristy set her clipboard on the table to her left. "Everyone needs an outlet to release their feelings onto, whether it be through words to a safe person or just having a safe place. It's my passion to provide that safe place for those who need it. Does that at least make a little bit of sense?"

"Yes, Kristy, it does," Abigail replied more genuinely than before.

Kristy stood from her chair, beckoning for Abigail to do the same. "Thank you for coming in today, Abigail," she kindly expressed. "I know it's hard to talk to me sometimes, but you did it and I'm proud of you."

Abigail reluctantly offered her a partial smile. "Thank you."

"Absolutely. I hope your first day of school goes well. If you need anything, you can call me anytime. It doesn't matter whether it's in the middle of the night or while I'm working. I'll get back to you as soon as you can."

"You don't have to bother."

Kristy cocked her head to the side with a friendly smile. "It's never a bother," she assured her. "I'm here for you whenever you need it. If we need another session between today and Tuesday, I'm sure I can squeeze you in."

"Thank you." Abigail fiddled around with a thick strand of her long dark hair.

"You're most welcome," Kristy concluded, opening the door to her office for her young client. "Have a great weekend."

"You too."

Abigail gave her therapist a small and fake smile as she walked past her and down the hallway she had walked countless times before. It seemed like routine to her as she walked by the front desk and gave a polite wave to the receptionist before leaving the building itself. The words "Journey to Joy: Counseling and Wellness Center" were written in delicate cursive lettering over the front door she passed through.

"Journey to Joy," Abigail sarcastically thought. *"My journey to joy is a complete waste of time since I'm literally going nowhere with it."*

Her mind left her sour as she fished her keys out of her pocket and unlocked a gray Honda Civic that was sitting in front of her in the parking lot. Abigail slid onto the driver's seat and shut herself inside the comfort of her car. She inserted her key into the ignition and turned it sideways. The moment Abigail plugged her phone into the charging port, music continuing on from her previous drive began blaring through the speakers. It hardly took any time at all for her to adjust the gear to reverse and skid out of her parking spot.

The roads were vacant and would have been silent if it weren't for the loud bass rumbling through the car's tires and onto the weathered asphalt. Abigail's knuckles grew an even lighter shade of pale as they forcefully gripped the steering wheel. Her nails ached with the throbbing of her heart in her fingers from gnawing on them. Anxiety was a very troublesome thing.

The sun hung towards the left in the partly cloudy sky. At a red light, Abigail pushed open the ceiling compartment that contained her gold-tinted sunglasses and unfolded the accessory. She slid them on her face and continued onward once the stoplight switched from red to green. Her gray car sped at about six miles per hour over the stated speed limit. The sunlight from behind a particularly large cloud ricocheted off the lens of her sunglasses.

Abigail released a sigh the very moment Kristy's words took effect on her mind. Her senior year was truly starting in three days' time. The realization hit her like a dump truck. She needed to get herself together in time for the first day in almost three months.

Time was ticking, and it was valuable.

1

"THIS IS GONNA BE FUN."

THE SUBURBAN TOWN OF HILLWELL WAS A PETITE ONE. IT WAS LESS than the size of a grain of sand on any sort of map. Hardly anyone was aware of Hillwell's existence in the Midwest region of the United States except for those who lived there. There was no reason for that, though. Hillwell had every quality that a small town would need.

Tucked between an obscure range of mountains, Hillwell resided in an elongated plateau of relatively flat land. The town was isolated from many others in the county. Despite its appearance, Hillwell was generously populated. Along with the miniscule number of tourists arriving each summer, there were few who chose Hillwell as their home. Among these few were the Bartleys—Abigail, and her parents: Lillian and Harold.

Hillwell was a peaceful place. Birds chirped softly whilst on power lines threading through the small neighborhoods. The sun rose with grace over the horizon, making way for a clear blue sky overhead. Every so often, a vehicle would glide down the slow, but well-used streets. Being in a small town had its perks. The environment in the valley surrounding a certain moderately-sized house was nothing but tranquil.

That was...until an alarm from the house of twenty-three Little Creek Landing began to blare through Abigail's ears.

A hand shot out from underneath the thick comforter that laid over her. Five fingers felt around on the nightstand to the hand's left until they grasped a small, flat object that was the source of the loud sound - a phone - and yanked it under the comforter. At once, the ruthless alarm was shut off and the calmness of the prior domain returned.

Abigail forced the comforter off her along with the sheets and pried her eyes open. The ceiling was not the most entertaining to look at. The sole thing that Abigail found at least remotely fascinating was the ceiling fan slowly turning overhead. When the fan began to bore her, she forced herself out of the comfort of her bed and groggily stood on her two bare feet. She toddled over to her closet across the room and decided on an outfit to begin the dratted day.

As Abigail entered the bathroom that was conveniently next to her bedroom, she grimaced at her fatigued reflection in the mirror. Her pajamas were nothing but an oversized t-shirt and a pair of soft shorts. Loose tendrils falling from the bird's nest of a bun on top of Abigail's head framed her heart-shaped face. A pair of deep brown eyes stared back at her, complimenting her lightly tanned skin. Abigail was not focusing on her most attractive features, though—they were tainted by the dark circles protruding from under her eyes and the anxiety behind them.

She forced herself to take a decent shower and blow dry her hair afterwards. About thirty minutes later, she was dressed in her outfit of choice, which consisted of a white fitted tank top under a black Adidas jacket with white stripes on the sleeves paired with medium blue jeans sporting a hole in the right knee. Abigail put a faux diamond earring in each ear after dressing her face in foundation, concealer, powder, and mascara.

The sound of her parents bustling around on the downstairs floor along with the smell of freshly baked pancakes coaxed Abigail down the stairs and into the kitchen. Her guess was correct since she discovered her father dashing around the house to search for his dress shoes for work and her mother in the kitchen cooking up a fresh breakfast consisting of pancakes and quite possibly, bacon.

Echoes of her daughter hopping down onto the bottom floor caused Lillian to turn and greet her with a friendly smile. "Morning, Abigail!" she chirped. "How'd you sleep?"

"Fine." Abigail sat down at the kitchen table, setting her clasped hands on the wooden surface in front of her.

"Are you excited for your senior year?"

Her daughter was blunt with her response: "No."

"Honey..." Lillian's tone dropped to a soft one. "You're going to do great this year. Last year was exceptionally awful for reasons that won't repeat."

"You don't know that," grumbled Abigail with her head tilted downwards.

Lillian approached the kitchen table with a plate of two chocolate chip pancakes and three strips of bacon. "He left town, though, didn't he?"

Abigail's fist hit the table with a thud, startling her mother out of her two-inch high heels. Lillian nearly dropped the pancakes and resorted to setting them down in front of her daughter, who was now quite frustrated on the exterior. Abigail's mother gave her an apologetic look as the girl herself returned it with a glare.

"I'm sorry for bringing it up, Honey," she apologized sincerely. "I know he's the person you're worried about, but he's out of Hillwell now and therefore, out of your life."

"There's more people like him."

"That doesn't mean it'll happen again."

Lillian appeared as if she was about to counter Abigail's statement when her husband triumphantly shouted from the living room. "Aha! I found my work shoes!"

"Good for you, Harold," Lillian half-heartedly called back. "Are you going to eat your breakfast?"

"Probably not. I'm sorry, Dear, but I'm already late for work."

Harold awkwardly waddled into the kitchen, hopping on one foot while tying the shoe on his other foot's laces.

Lillian offered him a grin. "Alright, Honey. Have a good day at work."

"Thank you, Darling." Abigail cringed at her father's attempt at creating pet names. The man gave his wife a gentle kiss on the lips before moving to do the same to the top of his daughter's head of black hair. "Have a great day at school, Sweetie. If you need anything, please text or call me. I'll be there as quick as a whistle."

Abigail laughed quietly at the gesture and attempted to hug back when he gave her one over her shoulders. "Thanks, Dad. I will."

"Toodaloo!" he called while exiting the house, which made his wife and daughter smile. That was his goal every morning before he left for work.

Once Harold had shut the front door, Lillian turned to Abigail and softly encouraged her. "You'll do better than you expect this year. Your father and I have your back with every step of the way. Like he said, you can text or call if you need anything."

"I will." Abigail shoveled another bite of her pancakes into her mouth. "Thanks, Mom."

"I love you, Honey."

"I love you too."

The teenage girl did not have too much time in the morning before she needed to leave the house in her father's footsteps. After finishing the entirety of her breakfast, double-checking her backpack, and giving her mother a farewell kiss on the cheek along with a hug, she was out the door. Her gray vehicle was sitting in the driveway and waiting for her. Abigail entered her car and listened to the engine roar to life. At once, the music - her safe space - started to play over the speakers as she backed out of the driveway and onto the main road of her neighborhood.

Hillwell High School was the only one of its kind in several square miles. The small town only had a need for one high school, which resulted in students from all over the plateau enrolling in this singular building of education. The one-story building with an exterior of pale coral brick was directly in front of one of the larger mountains in the range surrounding the town. There were no football, soccer, or football fields in sight—there was no demand for them in an isolated place. Instead, a large gymnasium was located on the far right of the school. A sign with the words "Hillwell High School" in bold lettering welcomed the new and returning students.

Abigail gave up on fighting the frown on her face that appeared the moment she passed by the familiar white sign. Cars and busses littered the large parking lot to the point where she needed to snake her way in. Abigail received one of the last parking spots available despite the fact she had arrived at eight o'clock in the morning, or fifteen minutes before her first class. Anxiety filled her and she began gnawing on her nails the very second that her car was switched off and her music stopped.

"Well," she said to herself, *"It's now or never. Put on your poker face."*

Beams of light from the rising sun reflected the sunglasses upon Abigail's face as she slung her black backpack over her shoulders. She stuffed her hands into her jacket pockets to prevent any more of her vicious nail biting induced by her pounding heart. Like it was second nature, Abigail threaded herself into the seamless crowd of the student body. Why wouldn't it be natural for her? She had done this very thing three times before starting in freshman year.

Unlike the previous years, Abigail held her head lower than she was used to. Being well-known had its perks, but also its disadvantages. She learned that lesson the difficult way; it was never going to happen again. Abigail kept her eyes from behind the lens of her sunglasses trained on nothing but the double doors that were straight ahead.

"Well, if it isn't Abigail Bartley!" a voice trilled from behind the girl herself. Of course, there was an interruption. That was bound to happen.

Abigail froze and spun around on her heel, lifting her sunglasses from her face and setting them on her forehead. The previous expression of fear that was enlisted on her face quickly faded into a cool smile. "Jade Summers," she drawled. "It's been a long time; hasn't it?"

"Good God, I haven't seen you all summer," Jade expressed breathlessly. "How've you been? It's been so long!"

"I've been doing the best I can. How about you?" Well, Abigail's response was not exactly a fib. She truly was treading through life to the best of her ability.

"Honestly, so am I." Jade tucked a small piece of her hair behind her left ear.

Jade's shoulder-length platinum blonde hair was almost white in the sunlight. She stood at least two inches taller than Abigail, or, in fact, four with her blue heels in contrast to her friend's black high tops. The girl across from Abigail wore a long navy blue cardigan - the same shade as her heels - along with gray jeans and a white top with a gray floral design on it. Abigail determined her friend's outfit to be slightly formal for school, but who was she to judge?

Abigail was not about to begin a conversation with someone she failed to do so over the past three months, so Jade happily filled the void. "So, what classes do you have? I assume you got the email with your schedule last week like I did."

"Oh, yeah. One second." Abigail reached into her back pocket and revealed her phone. She scrolled on it and tapped the screen a couple of times until she came across the email from Hillwell High's admissions office. "I have British Literature, Precalculus, AP Chemistry, AP Government, and PE; all in that order."

"I think we might share a class." Jade did the same with her phone. Excitement gleamed in her cyan eyes at her new discovery. "We have AP Chemistry together!"

Abigail grinned, but her smile stalled to reach her eyes. "Oh, that's great! I'm surprised I got into two AP classes this year," she expressed semi-gleefully.

"You'd think that with a limited number of students, we'd be able to have more than just one class together."

"Then again, there's only five blocks excluding lunch."

Jade shrugged, causing the gray backpack on her back to slightly bounce up and down. "That's very true. We should probably get inside before we get stepped on."

"That's easy for you to say," Abigail snickered as the two started walking side by side. "You're a giant next to me, especially in those heels. Why are you wearing those anyway?"

"They were fifty percent off! I couldn't pass them up and I thought they looked nice with this cardigan." Jade defended herself.

"Point noted."

Abigail and Jade passed through the double doors that had been propped open, probably to welcome the returning and first-time students to Hillwell High. At once, Abigail felt her anxiety return. This place was overwhelmingly familiar for her with too many poor memories. Deja vu haunted her each time she walked down the halls of the building she knew for an upwards of three years. Abigail brought her index finger's nail to her mouth and began to nibble at it, but promptly shoved her hand back into her pocket when Jade turned her way.

"Are you okay?" she asked with concern.

The smaller of the two nodded. "Yeah. I guess I'm just nervous since it's the first day."

"Oh, that's understandable," Jade sympathized, her concern withering away as quickly as it arrived. "You'll be alright. It's just school, after all."

"Yeah...just school." Abigail attempted to keep her thoughts in order. *"Okay. Remember what Kristy said. When you're feeling unsafe, surround yourself with friends? Check. Voice your problem? Kinda check. Take deep breaths? In progress."*

Another familiar voice nearly scared her out of her skin. If it wasn't for the voice's tender and sweet tone, she would have been very startled. "Hi, Abigail. Hi, Jade."

Abigail and Jade whirled to the side to discover another of their friends. "Brielle!" the two of them chorused.

Brielle O'Brian was the sensible one of the group. She had long, straight auburn hair that reached to a few inches below her shoulders. Freckles delicately dotted her cheeks and matched her chestnut brown eyes. She was dressed in an oversized faded purple hoodie and a pair of old jeans that Abigail recognized from last year. Brielle's round glasses looked like she had stolen them from Harry Potter himself. All her friends agreed that the glasses looked more adorable on her than the fictional character.

"Hi, guys," Brielle repeated shyly. She hugged a thick textbook to her chest. "How was your summer?"

"It was pretty good," Jade replied.

"Mine was okay," answered Abigail with faux enthusiasm. "How was yours?"

"Oh, it was great!" Brielle authentically beamed. "I started going to a book club and met some new friends. Thank you for asking."

"No problem." Abigail checked the time on her phone. "Should we get to class?"

"Probably wouldn't be the worst idea," Jade confirmed with another shrug.

The three friends parted ways to their lockers - the number of which contained in the same email as the class schedules - and prepared for their first classes of the day. Abigail eventually found her locker in one of the many endless hallways of Hillwell High. She began to unlock the combination lock on the handle - the combination also being in the email - and the door opened to reveal an empty locker. Abigail placed her textbooks on a shelf near her eye level and stuffed her backpack on top. She kept her British Literature textbook with her along with supplies.

Abigail propped her phone on the top of her pile of stationary supplies as she walked to find her first classroom. It turned out that her British Literature classroom was a short walk from her locker. She slid into the classroom and away from the large mobs of people swarming the hallways. To her relief, there were only a few people in the classroom already.

The very second that Abigail plopped down at her desk near the middle of the classroom, her sense of calmness withered away. At least fifteen to twenty people barreled into the classroom as if they had been following her. She watched as everyone took their seats, recognizing a couple of faces, but most of them were foreign to her.

There was one face that seemed familiar, but she somehow could not put her finger on it.

Abigail's gaze studied the person near the very back of the group who was dashing in like her life depended on it. The pale young woman was very petite - barely reaching the "intimidating" height of four feet, eleven inches - and was, to put it simply, structured like a twig. Her black hair was shaggy and styled into a short pixie cut with drastically contrasting neon green roots. The most familiar feature of hers was her gray eyes that pierced through Abigail's with an enthusiastic and welcoming glow. *That* was how Abigail recognized her.

"Oh, my God—*Keagan*? Is that you?" Abigail's jaw dropped at the sight of her friend.

"In the flesh!" Keagan Lopez, the ever-so spontaneous female, quickly claimed the desk next to Abigail's. "How've you been, Abi? It's been *forever* since I've seen you."

"I've been okay, but...woah...look at you! You look so... so..." Abigail trailed off. She was searching for just the right word to describe it.

Keagan's smile was more than contagious. "Different? Unique? Awesome?" she suggested. When Abigail nodded, her eyes sparkled. "Thank you! Over the summer, I decided to do something new, so I chopped off all my hair and dyed it. I've had to redo the green roots, though, so I hope it looks alright."

"It looks amazing. I can't believe you used to be blonde," Abigail complimented her. She felt the urge to gnaw on her nails again, so she kept her hands clasped tightly in her lap.

"Thank you, Abi!" The girl next to her was ecstatic. "You're not looking so bad yourself. What's different? Did you get a haircut? New makeup routine?"

"Hopefully more self-confidence," she blurted out before she could stop herself.

"That's my girl!"

Abigail discovered her cheeks to be heating up from Keagan's support. She averted her gaze towards the textbook laying dully on her desk, but it quickly darted upwards when another set of footsteps entered the classroom. Abigail had to do a double take at the young man who had to take one of the last remaining seats in the room that was in the front row. It was not because of his physical appearance. In fact, it was due to his attire. She bit her lip to keep herself from gawking at the thickly rimmed black glasses on the boy's face.

She fell silent when she heard the whispers and rumors instantaneously beginning to circulate the classroom. Nobody seemed to be keeping to themselves except for she and Keagan. A sense of dread began to fill her and throb through her tightly wound fingers at the thought of the room around her being filled with people of her age group. It never used to bother her...not before her junior year. The classroom seemed to be growing smaller and smaller.

Abigail felt well-grounded when she noticed her phone screen light up with a notification. She picked it up and clenched it tightly in her jittery hands. The message was from Keagan, and it reflected her very thoughts. Abigail deemed it a satisfactory idea to get her mind off of the overwhelming amount of people surrounding her.

"*Get a load of that guy a few rows in front of you,*" Keagan's message read. "*Did you see the size of those glasses on his face? What an interesting fashion choice.*"

Abigail eagerly typed back. "*I noticed. What the hell was he thinking? Out of all the styles of glasses that the ophthalmologist could offer, he picked those?*"

Not even fifteen seconds later, another message appeared in the text thread. "*I noticed you staring.*"

"*I was curious. Didn't recognize him and those huge things.*" Abigail's reply was blunt.

"*Oh. Are you sure it wasn't for another reason? ;)*"

"*Yes, I'm sure. They're weird.*"

Abigail glanced at Keagan out of the corner of her eye, who was smirking maniacally at her phone while texting her an answer. "*Uh huh,*" the text said, "*I see what you mean.*"

"*What do I mean?*" Abigail furiously typed at her phone.

"*Don't tell me you fancy him already.*"

Abigail harshly set her phone down on the desk and glared at Keagan, who offered her an innocent smile in return. She was about to deliver a thoroughly thought-out retort when the classroom door was opened and a man in his fifties entered. He wore a plaid shirt with khaki pants and dress shoes, carrying his own textbook and supplies. Abigail fought back a scoff at the sight of the man in front of her. Merely looking at him was boring.

"Good morning, class, and welcome to British Literature," the teacher greeted monotonously to Abigail's dismay. "My name is Mr. Wright, and no, I'm not always right," - that earned a half-hearted laugh from about three students - "but I do my best. Let's get started with our daily roll call, shall we?"

Since Abigail's last name began with a "B", Mr. Wright called on her name near the beginning of his list of attendance. After she replied with a simple "here" to her name, she looked over at Keagan again. It took a couple of seconds for her friend to catch her gaze, with her cheeky grin but when she did, Abigail mouthed two simple words: "You jerk."

Abigail looked back towards her lap afterwards in order to avoid a reprimand from her new teacher who appeared to be more interesting than watching paint dry. She did not want to risk receiving a punishment less than five minutes into the school year. Not even a second after her brown eyes left Keagan's, her phone's screen lit up with another notification. Curiosity getting the best of her, she peered at the device sitting on her desk and grimaced at the text from Keagan.

"This is gonna be fun."

2

"ABIGAIL BARTLEY, ARE YOU FLIRTING WITH ME?"

Much like the cramped office belonging to her therapist, Abigail felt like she was wasting valuable time by spending most of her Monday morning in classrooms.

At first, she thought that five minutes between every single class was a generous amount of time, but she soon discovered that was far from the truth. Abigail darted from classroom to classroom, nose in her phone for her room numbers and schedule while she did so. Having three blocks of one seventy-five-minute class each took a toll on Abigail's confidence that morning. She had British Literature with Keagan, Precalculus with no one she knew other than vaguely familiar faces, and AP Chemistry with Jade. At least the majority was with people she trusted.

Now, Abigail found herself wandering into the school's lunch-room. Hillwell High's cafeteria was not the ordinary slummy place where poor quality food was served. Instead, it acted as more of a restaurant, except without the waiters. Students had the ability to wait in a line that eventually led to a clean counter and reception area where they would purchase food from a limited menu. Of course, there were special days for discounted food, such as "Taco Tuesday" and "Fried Chicken Friday," but Abigail usually resorted to the chicken tenders and fries.

Abigail reserved her spot in the back of the line, which was growing longer by the minute. She watched as people around her flooded the large cafeteria and claimed tables all over the room. Her hands lightly trembled in her pockets. She never used to be bothered by a lot of people in a large space. Abigail clenched her left hand in a fist around her wallet and her right hand doing the same, but with her keys.

A tap on the shoulder along with a loud "Hey Abi!" originally startled her, but once she realized it was Keagan greeting her, she settled down.

"Hi, Keagan," Abigail replied, forcing a smile onto her face. She then noticed her two other friends who were standing on either side of Keagan. "Hi, Jade and Brielle."

"Hi!" the three of them chirped at once.

Abigail blinked at their synchronization. "...How were your classes?" she asked to bring the subject off the entire student body around them.

The three of them shrugged and murmured answers that were meshed together. Abigail guessed that they consisted of "They're alright" or "Boring." Then, she perked up at Brielle's question of "How were yours?"

"They were okay. Thank you for asking." Abigail nonchalantly gave them a vague response.

The group of four moved ahead in line quicker than they originally had thought. Soon enough, they were at the front counter. Abigail removed her wallet from her pocket and recited her order to the lady who grabbed an already-prepared tray of chicken tenders and fries from a shelf behind her and placed it in front of Abigail. She placed a few dollar bills on the counter along with a couple extra for a bottle of water before picking up her tray.

Jade purchased her lunch next, which was a cheeseburger and fries. That left Keagan and Brielle; the latter of which was fingering through her old leather wallet for a couple of bills for her lunch.

Keagan decided on a rather large chicken salad and Brielle chose the same, but in a smaller size. It was a cheaper item on the menu. Before Brielle was about to empty her wallet out on the counter, Keagan pet her gently on the shoulder, grasping her attention.

"Would you like me to pay? You can get a bigger size—my treat," she whispered just loud enough for Abigail and Jade to make out.

Brielle shook her head and pushed the five-dollar bill and one single towards the lady behind the counter. "No, thank you. I'll have something later at home," she softly insisted.

"Are you sure?" Keagan frowned and paid for her own meal after Brielle nodded. She then snapped her fingers with an idea. "I got it!" She glanced at the menu and held out two more dollar bills to the lunch lady. "Excuse me. Could I get an order of mozzarella sticks on the side?" she asked politely.

The lunch lady nodded and took the two outstretched bills, replacing them with a side of fresh mozzarella sticks. Brielle frowned with confusion until Keagan explained, "We'll share. Does that sound good?"

"Um...sure. Thank you." A smile reluctantly grew on Brielle's face, which caused Keagan's to appear once again. "Should I pay you back for them?"

"Absolutely not." It was Keagan's turn to insist.

Abigail and Jade smiled to themselves due to Keagan's gesture and Brielle's reaction. The four of them regrouped at the condiments table and picked out either their sauces or dressings before embarking on a journey to find a table. Abigail and Jade both hoarded the ketchup and mustard packets while Keagan decided on ranch dressing. Brielle picked the caesar.

Unfortunately, the situation consisting of Brielle often lacking money in her wallet was quite common. The O'Brians weren't very well off when it came to money despite having stable jobs and a loving family environment. Brielle hated when any of her friends offered to pay for her meal, but sometimes, it was inevitable. She knew deep down that regular grocery store visits for packed lunches were too expensive for her family at that time.

Abigail, Jade, Keagan, and Brielle claimed a table of their own near the condiments table just in case they ran out of what the table itself provided. Once the four of them sat down, it was like their own personal bubble was created. Abigail felt a wave of calm wash over her when she saw her most trusted friends around her.

Directly after a mouthful of her salad, Keagan piped up, "Hey! Does anyone want to play truth or dare?"

"Um, why?" Abigail cocked her head to the side with suspicion.

"Well, we haven't really been a group for the whole summer, so there may or may not be some new "truths." We'll just have to see," Keagan elaborated gleefully.

"That sounds fun," Jade agreed at the same time Brielle nodded. "I'm in. How about you, Abigail?"

Abigail forced down a bite of one of her chicken tenders due to the thought. "Sure. I'll play, but do I have to ask any questions?"

"Not if you don't want to," Brielle offered to the relief of Abigail. "Can I go first?"

"Yeah, of course," Keagan answered, happily munching on a piece of chicken in her salad.

She turned to Jade, who had been quiet. "Jade, truth or dare?"

"Truth," Jade bluntly decided.

"Um, let me think." Brielle paused to consider a question. She then proceeded to ask one of the most stereotypical - and possibly safe - questions for this game: "Do you have any crushes at the moment? If so, who is it?"

Something flickered in Jade's cyan eyes, but it went away as hurriedly as it arrived. "I actually don't." She shrugged off the question and moved on. "Abigail, truth or dare?"

"Dare," determined Abigail before she could stop herself. It was her go-to response to any question regarding that game.

Jade swore under her breath. "Great. Now, I need to think of a good dare. Does anyone have any ideas?"

Abigail stayed quiet, Brielle shook her head, and Keagan pondered out loud. "I don't have any right now. Sorry, Jade," the latter apologized sheepishly. Her gray eyes appeared sorrowful, but they quickly flashed in entertainment at the sight of something behind Abigail. "Oh, Abi! There's the guy with the big glasses."

Four pairs of eyes - only Brielle's being discreet - followed the boy with the particularly thick black frames around his glasses. For the first time since a glimpse during her first block of the day, Abigail was able to see his face. Other than the obnoxious eyewear, he had dark brown eyes, a slightly round face, a head of medium, voluminous brown hair and a slight undercut. He held himself at a decent, but not a demeaning stature as he sat down at a table lacking more occupants. Abigail quickly turned back to her own table.

"How's that relevant?" Abigail questioned, but she was curious anyway.

"It's not," Keagan beamed innocently. "I just thought I'd bring it up since you were staring at the back of his head during the entirety of Brit Lit."

"Okay," Abigail sighed and began listing reasons, "One: He's taller than me by at least half a foot. I was trying to see the board. Two: I was trying to figure out why he'd wear those stupid things in the first place."

Keagan's eyebrows wiggled suggestively. "You blushed when I mentioned the fact you were fancying him."

"I was embarrassed that you'd think such a thing," she snipped before eating a fry from her half-full container.

"So, you *don't* fancy him?" Keagan continued to interrogate.

"No!"

A moment of silence made its way to the table until Jade thoughtfully proclaimed, "Prove it."

"Excuse me?" Abigail questioned in disbelief.

"Keagan just gave me a great idea for a dare," Jade sneered with a sense of triumph. "I dare you to walk over to him and steal the glasses right off of his face."

Abigail suddenly found her food very interesting...or at least more interesting than it already was. "That's a stupid dare."

"But it's one that's making you nervous!" sung Keagan.

"I'm not nervous," she reasoned, resisting the urge to bite her nails again. "I just don't want to do something so incredibly pointless."

"Oh, please?" Jade asked her again with puppy dog eyes. "I can't think of any other dare."

Abigail heaved a sigh, abandoning an undeserving chicken tender with the gesture. "Can it wait until after lunch? I'm starving and want to finish my meal."

"As long as we can stalk you." Jade had a teasing grin on her face.

"Deal."

The rest of the lunch period ticked by quicker than Abigail wanted it to. Abigail had stared at her phone, which was face-up on the table for the majority of lunch. She half-heartedly took part in the rest of the girls' truth or dare game, which only lasted for about five more minutes until Keagan and Jade started talking about something or another. Brielle, the ever-so quiet soul that she was, said hardly anything, but the seldom words she used were merely to ask about Abigail's well-being. She asked about three times, but each time, Abigail waved off her anxiety and lied.

Before Abigail knew it, the cafeteria was flowing into the hallways and dispersing into the classrooms required for classes in the fourth block of the day. The four friends were planning on waiting until most of the crowd was emptied out of the large room before venturing forward, but Keagan suddenly grasped onto Abigail's hand and pulled her forward. The remaining two girls followed suit while Abigail attempted to keep her hand that was in Keagan's from trembling.

"Do you spot him anywhere?" Keagan asked her playfully as the four of them walked down a hall further away from the cafeteria.

Abigail shook her head. "Nope. I guess this was all just a stupid idea and I missed him. I'll see you guys later," she rambled, beginning to walk off, but Keagan grabbed her arm again.

"Don't leave yet. I see him." Keagan pointed to someone standing by a wall of lockers. "His glasses made it really easy."

"Oh." Abigail let her arm in her friend's grasp become limp.

Brielle gently tapped Abigail on the shoulder. "You know, you don't have to do this if you don't want to," she offered seriously.

"It's okay." She smiled at her three friends. "I've got this. It's a dare, after all."

"Then, go on!" Jade playfully pushed her towards the boy with glasses.

Abigail tried her best to hide the faux qualities of the grin on her face. "Fine, but no recording, no interrupting, and - Keagan - no laughing hysterically. Got it?"

The three of them nodded and hid behind a wall of lockers. Abigail turned towards them one last time to notice three heads on top of each other like a totem pole, peeking out from behind the lockers. She rolled her eyes and stuffed her hands into the pockets of her Adidas jacket. Abigail straightened her posture and adjusted the part in her hair before walking over to the certain young man of whom happened to be the center of Jade's dare.

Abigail watched as he sifted through his locker in search of what appeared to be a certain textbook. Tufts of brown hair fell over his forehead and nearly into his eyes. He finally picked out a textbook and held it under his arm. The boy was about to walk off and away from Abigail, who cleared her throat just loud enough for him to hear. He abruptly turned towards her with his brown eyes filled with confusion.

"Uh, yes?" he quizzically inquired to the girl who was leaning against the wall two lockers away.

She gave him no time to escape. "Hi, I'm Abigail Bartley," she greeted him hurriedly. "Are you new here? I haven't seen you around before."

"...I'm Noah Howell, and yeah. This is my first day," he awkwardly replied. Nevertheless, he outstretched his hand for Abigail to shake.

Abigail forced away the urge to flinch. "Oh, that's nice." She slowly extended her own arm as if she was afraid he'd chop it off and returned the gesture. At the same time, her free hand surged upwards and attempted to grab the right temple of his eyewear.

To her dismay, Noah darted out of the way. He adjusted his glasses, which nearly fell off. "Wait...what the hell?"

"I was doing you a favor," Abigail retorted without an ounce of self-doubt. "Those glasses make you look like an idiot."

"Thanks?" Noah's eyebrows scrunched together.

"Why do you wear those things? In fact, why do you even *own* them?" she pressed. Abigail cocked her head to the side like a puzzled dog.

Noah glanced down at the floor before letting his eyes land on Abigail. He appeared to be the slightest bit offended. "Uh, to see?"

"They still look atrocious. Why not try contacts?" Abigail sweetly asked him.

"Hey—what if I like how I look in these?" Noah clapped back, crossing his arms over his chest. "At least I don't approach people I've never seen before and criticize them about their appearance or attire. I could make a comment about your makeup, but I choose not to."

Abigail's jaw nearly dropped, but her lips curved upwards into a surprised, unamused smile instead. A breathy chortle echoed through her teeth. "For your information, I know how to apply my makeup satisfactorily each morning. You just slap on a pair of glasses and call it a day."

"Woah, okay. Just chill. Don't shoot lasers out of your eyes." Noah held his hands out in front of him in a position that resembled surrender. "I never said that the makeup looked bad on you. It's your choice whether to wear it or not. I was merely using it as an example to explain to you how your comment made me feel. I don't appreciate it."

"I'm just saying...you could enhance your appearance more without them," she mused thoughtfully before her eyes rested on Noah again. "You might even look cute."

At this, Noah lifted an eyebrow, smiled, and filtrated a snarky remark, "Abigail Bartley, are you flirting with me?"

Abigail's tongue decided it would be a good time to tie itself in a knot. She never meant to come across as flirtatious. She was simply fulfilling a dare from one of her closest friends, which happened to include a boy. Abigail did not act like herself around boys...not at least after what the previous school year brought. Her lips were pressed together in a tight line. Abigail noticed that her hands were clenched into shaking fists, and she quickly stuffed them into her pockets.

"Absolutely not," she quipped stoically. "Stop being such a jerk to someone who's only trying to look out for your social status. Hillwell isn't exactly tame when it comes to ridiculing."

"I can see that," countered Noah with that innocent grin still on his face. "Are you finished?"

"One more question."

"Shoot."

Abigail eyed the boy who had just shut his locker door, set the combination lock on the handle, and leaned against the metal with his textbook still under his left arm. "Why do you wear those particular glasses?" she questioned inquisitively. "Wouldn't you want another pair?"

"Nope," Noah replied with a cheeky smile. "I wouldn't wear any other pair."

With that, he sauntered off, leaving Abigail to stand by his locked locker with an expression of dumbfoundedness. Jade, Keagan, and Brielle took it as their cue to reveal themselves from their hiding place and approach their friend who was still attempting to keep herself calm. She whirled around at the sound of three sets of footsteps behind her.

"Holy...," Keagan trailed off and muttered a swear word relating to excrement. "I had no idea he had such a spine. He looked like a wuss to me."

Abigail rolled her eyes. "Oh, shut up."

"Are you okay?" Brielle asked timidly. Her pink lips were positioned in a sympathetic pout.

"Yeah, I'm okay."

"That was pretty funny, to be honest," Jade snickered with a smile. "I didn't think it would get *that* interesting."

"Yeah, whatever. I need to get to class," Abigail mumbled.

"Can we go together?" inquired Brielle. "I believe we both have AP Government."

Abigail shrugged. She was not about to say no to a kind offer. "Yeah, sure," she complied, which caused Brielle to reveal one of her rare smiles. She turned to the group. "See you guys later."

"Bye!" Keagan and Jade exclaimed. The former enthusiastically waved to them.

The group of four parted ways and made their next journey towards their respected classes for the fourth block. Despite Brielle's desperate attempts to start a conversation in order to help Abigail feel better about her recent experience, her friend stayed quiet or gave blunt replies. The shy girl hated seeing her friends upset, but she knew not to overstep her own boundaries. Brielle felt safe around Abigail, therefore she did everything she could to ease her nerves.

Abigail's nerves refused to be eased for the next few hours. During her last two class periods, her mind continued to remind her of her uncomfortable encounter with Noah. Her thoughts were like a broken record, being put on loop repeatedly for at least two hours. Throughout the afternoon, Abigail took every chance she received to bite at her nails--a nervous habit that she desperately wanted to get rid of. By the time she reached her fifth block class, the tips of her fingers were throbbing and raw.

Now, she found herself in PE, which she hated more than Precalculus. Math was not her strong suit whatsoever, so saying such about a Physical Education course was quite dramatic. Abigail quickly discovered that her PE teacher was a short woman in her forties. She was ruthless. Rather than slowly introducing the class of twenty-one to her rules of the gymnasium and what she expected, Mrs. Watson immediately instructed them to perform numerous types of stretches and exercises for the entire seventy-five-minute block.

For the last five to ten minutes of her class, Mrs. Watson had the students run laps around the gymnasium. The room with a high ceiling and skylights was not small. It accommodated a basketball court with two hoops and a few sets of bleachers off to the side. The locker rooms that were located near the back of the gym were segregated by gender, the boys' on the left and the girls' on the right.

Since it was the last block of the day, Abigail took extra time to change into her workout clothes, - which she would have needed to do anyway - remove her makeup and pull her long hair into a high ponytail. Her oversized t-shirt covered her figure and reached down to her upper thigh, where she was sporting a pair of black cropped leggings. She swapped her high tops for some exercise shoes she had stuffed into her backpack that morning.

Abigail huffed and puffed with each step she took as she jogged. She clutched her metal water bottle in her right hand and took a much-needed sip from it. The water cooled her throat while she continued to run at a light pace. Every single stride burned in her lungs to the point where she found it difficult to breathe. Running was not her favorite thing to do.

"C'mon, Abigail—you can finish this," she encouraged herself and pedaled forward.

Sure enough, Mrs. Watson blew her whistle a couple of minutes later. The twenty-one students skidded to a halt a mere millisecond later. Abigail rested her left hand on her thigh and bent over in an attempt to catch her breath. Her black hair fell in her face as she breathed heavily. Abigail's heart pounded too quickly for her to handle, so she decided to sit down where she was and rest her trembling legs. She set her water bottle to the side after taking another sip.

"Okay, class—great hustle!" Mrs. Watson complimented the class to her students' relief. "Tomorrow, we'll be starting to uncover and identify the benefits through sports. We'll begin each class with at least three laps around the gymnasium starting then, so be prepared."

Abigail bit back a loud sigh. Everyone around her assumed they were dismissed and made their ways to their assigned locker rooms. Abigail hesitated for a moment or two to keep her breathing under control before following behind her peers. She took at least a few extra minutes in the girls' locker room changing back into her regular clothes and getting herself together before leaving the gymnasium itself. She had the obscure feeling she was forgetting something.

By the time she returned to "civilization," the hallways were nearly deserted. Abigail decided she would be far from surprised if she saw a tumbleweed blow through the vicinity. She let out a small sigh at the fact her friends had most likely returned home. She didn't blame them one bit. Hillwell High was not the best environment to be. The day had been a long one and Abigail determined there was no more room for any more surprises.

Abigail quickly discarded that thought once she reached her locker. There, by the foot of it, was her metal water bottle with a slip of paper beneath it. She grasped the paper in her hands and read the few words that had been left for her in elegant handwriting.

Just wanted *to be clear that I didn't mean to criticize you with my comment earlier. You look nice in makeup, so do what you want. I didn't appreciate your criticism in regard to me doing the same.*

-Noah

P.S.: You forgot your water bottle in PE.

Scratch that. Abigail needed to be equipped for many more surprises. This was only the beginning.

3

"IT'S NOT A BIG DEAL."

ABIGAIL HAD NEVER EXPERIENCED SUCH A QUICK FIRST WEEK OF SCHOOL. The five days consisting of the beginning of the year were over before she knew it. Abigail found herself swamped with work from each one of her classes. After returning home from Hillwell High each day when she did not have her therapy sessions, she did her homework for quite a while. Abigail couldn't remember a time when she had so much work.

Needless to say, she was grateful for the weekend. In a perfect world, she would have taken those days off. Unfortunately, Abigail's life was far from a perfect world, which meant nearly the entirety of her Saturday and Sunday were taken up due to school. Abigail failed to remember a time where she had been so exhausted and emotionally drained. It hardly took her long to do so, though. Junior year was tough enough for her.

Abigail had struggled to complete every single assignment in her possession before returning to school the next Monday. It was quite a task, but she completed every word, every problem, and every reading assignment over the week. It left her physically and emotionally exhausted, but at least she was temporarily keeping her grades at the maximum level.

The table rocking slightly from Jade accidentally kicking the leg of it nearest to her jostled Abigail out of her minimal daydream. Her brown eyes darted up from her blurred image of the chicken tenders and fries on the table in front of her and returned to her three friends, who were having a conversation about something Abigail had forgotten. She picked up a fry and raised it to her mouth before eventually taking a bite.

"So, then I was saying – "No, I've had this hair the whole time!" - to my mom who literally didn't notice I chopped it off and dyed it until a week later," Keagan exclaimed with more laughter than Abigail deemed necessary.

"No way," Jade chortled, nearly choking on a bite of her lunch. "Your hair was literally just a shade darker than mine. It's such a drastic difference that I'm still getting used to."

"But a pretty one," Brielle cut in with a smile.

Keagan beamed in the auburn-haired girl's direction. "Aw, thank you! You're so sweet."

"Thank you."

Abigail remained silent for longer than she thought possible. Usually, she would take part in the daily ritual of lunchroom conversations, but this time, she failed to do so. Instead, she picked around at her food like it was something foreign and not as generic as the chicken tenders were. Her appetite had faded away from breakfast, where her mother made her French toast. Where her love of food went, Abigail had no idea.

"Hey, Abi," Keagan hissed to the girl on her right. "Are you okay?"

Her head snapped in Keagan's direction and she shrugged nonchalantly. "Yeah, I'm okay. Thanks, though."

"Is something wrong?" Jade asked, completely dropping the humor she experienced from mere seconds earlier.

"Nope," Abigail retorted. She took a bite out of one of her chicken tenders. "I've just had a lot of work and didn't get time to rest this weekend."

"Me either, to be honest. It's a lot more work than I was expecting," commented Brielle.

Keagan proudly declared, "Well, I procrastinated until Sunday night and got everything done in about two hours. I'm not sure how much my grades would like that, but whatever."

"Good for you," Abigail and Jade monotonously cheered.

"Thank you!"

Brielle turned back to Abigail with a compassionate smile. "You know, if you want a study buddy or someone to work with, my door's always open."

"Thank you, Brielle," Abigail expressed. Brielle's smile was contagious.

The rest of the lunch period - which was only about five more minutes - passed by in a boring blur. Exiting the cafeteria was not as overwhelming as it was the first week of school, but it still caused Abigail to be on the top of her guard. Her friends noticed this, however, so they kept to a group until they were required to split their separate ways and retrieve their things from their lockers.

Abigail pretended to feel at ease as she took her books out of her locker. She had something else on her mind that refused to go away for the entirety of the week. The slip of paper seemed to have burnt through her jacket pocket with each step she took. In fact, the words written on it were what prompted Abigail to action.

I didn't appreciate your criticism in regard to me doing the same.

That simple sentence spurred a sprout of guilt to grow and flourish in Abigail's chest. She was so overcome by her relentless anxiety that she failed to notice the words spewing out of her mouth. Noah did nothing wrong to deserve the remarks regarding his glasses. Why did Abigail's friends - minus Brielle - think it was such a good idea for a dare? Abigail had no idea. She did have an idea of what her next move would be. Her therapist advised her to do so last Friday.

She was going to apologize to Noah.

Abigail formulated such a plan while her brain refused to circulate around schoolwork during portions of the week. She was going to find Noah at his locker, apologize for his glasses, and maybe give him a compliment or two. Abigail refused to sugarcoat things too terribly much. She hated being around those of the male gender more than she found distaste for her PE class.

Despite her mind screaming against her not to do so, Abigail walked in the direction of Noah's locker, which was not too far away from hers. She gripped her AP Government textbook tight to her chest, as if it would fall through the floor if she let go. Abigail felt her hands begin to tremble, so she clenched onto the textbook tighter to force them to still. She was quite worked up over having to talk to someone far outside of her comfort zone...again.

Sure enough, Noah was at his locker just like he was on the first day of school. He filed through his textbooks and picked out the necessary supplies for his next class. The teenage boy did not think much of his walk to AP Calculus before he shut the door to his locker, turned to his left, and was abruptly met with two brown eyes belonging to Abigail.

"Holy—God, you startled me," Noah spluttered when he noticed the girl only a couple of feet away. When Abigail didn't say anything, his brows furrowed. "Um...can I help you?"

Abigail blinked with a blank expression and then got herself together. "Oh, sorry," she sheepishly replied. "I just wanted to apologize for what I said to you last week."

"Oh, you did; did you?" Noah rhetorically inquired, a small grin on his face.

"I did," she confirmed almost with sarcasm. "It wasn't the nicest thing for me to say, and" - *"Come on, Abigail—be honest. Just like Kristy said."* - "it was a dare from one of my friends. I don't know what kind of crack she was on, but she noticed your glasses and dared me to steal them off your face."

Noah's smirk grew to be a little larger. "Is that so?"

"Yes, it's *so*," Abigail scoffed and let her annoyance of the situation get to her. "I'd hate to break it to you, but those glasses don't exactly make you invisible."

"I'll keep that in mind," he assured her.

There was an awkward pause that made the tension in the building so thick it could only be cut with a knife meant for steak.

Abigail held her book against her while Noah did the same. She noticed him pretending to check the time on his wrist, but he was not even wearing a watch. Abigail almost laughed at the boy's attempt to keep the conversation flowing. It looked as if he was not going to speak or do anything to keep her there, so Abigail assumed that role.

"So, I got your note last Monday," she hesitantly spoke up.

"Oh, you did?" Noah perked up. When Abigail nodded, he continued, "I'm glad. That's a nice water bottle and it'd be a shame if it got lost."

"Yeah. Thanks for bringing it back to my locker. It's one of my favorite ones...wait." Abigail paused with a moment of realization. "How'd you know where my locker was? I get we're in the same PE class, but the fact you know the location of my locker makes no sense."

Noah shrugged in a carefree manner. "Well, I'd like to consider myself an observer. Last Monday, when I was walking to PE, I saw you at your locker since it's on the way to the gym. I just remembered where it was."

"Oh. Thank you, then."

"No problem." He offered her another small smile. "I'll see you around."

"You too."

The two of them parted ways, but the tension in the hallway refused to leave them alone. Abigail only had one thing on her mind, and that was to get through the rest of the school day; the same was relevant to Noah, who was walking in the opposite direction. Abigail and Noah were still in earshot when suddenly, Noah lost his balance by tripping over someone's foot. He would have landed flat on his face if he had not stuttered forward a couple steps and caught himself with his hands.

Abigail heard a thud of a textbook and the yelp of a person followed by a clatter from behind her. It was a normality to hear certain sounds in the hallways of Hillwell High, but something told her to turn on her heel and see what the matter was. So, that was exactly what she did. The sight of Noah on the floor with his textbook opened and pages bent caught her off guard. He appeared to be quite disoriented since he was currently feeling around for his belongings on the dirty school floor.

When Abigail did not hear a single apology from whoever had tripped him, she tentatively approached. "Uh, are you good?" she asked just loud enough to be heard.

"Huh?" Noah whirled around and clutched his textbook, prying himself to his feet. "Oh, yeah. Just a bit startled...again." His brown eyes darted around a couple of times in confusion. "Wait a minute..."

"What is it?"

"My glasses," he fumbled for coherent words to use. "They're gone. Do you see them anywhere?"

How did Abigail manage to miss the fact his glasses - the object that started this entire debacle - were missing from his face? He looked very different without them. "Oh, um..." Abigail searched the floor of the hallway that was quickly clearing out but did not find what the two were looking for. "No, I don't see them anywhere."

"Oh, God." Noah clasped his hands over his face and stressfully raked his fingers down his cheeks. "This is bad...really bad."

Abigail cocked her head to the side. "...Don't you have a spare?"

"At home."

"Contacts?" She tried again.

"In my locker, but I hate them."

"Okay, great!" Abigail cheered almost dully. "So, you can wear those until the end of the day and then replace them for your spare glasses. It's not a big deal."

Noah blinked at her blurry figure in disbelief. "You don't understand," he stated anxiously.

"I don't. Enlighten me?"

"Those glasses that you find oh-so eye-catching are quite important to me," Noah wheezed, waving his arms around like a penguin's flippers. "It's a big deal."

"Why can't you just use your spare and then if you can't find your old ones, you can get a new pair?" Abigail suggested. Noah's anxiety was going right over her head.

Noah shook his head. "No. I want *this* pair."

"Why?"

"Because...," he faltered. His river of words had finally run dry. "It's hard to explain. That particular pair is very special to me, and I'd like them back."

Abigail puzzledly frowned. "...Okay."

"Yeah." Noah opened his locker again, which he thankfully had left unlocked, and began searching for a pair of contacts.

"You know," Abigail offered cautiously, "I could maybe keep an eye out for them...I mean, if you want me to. If they're *that* important."

Noah placed a contact in his left eye and recoiled when he did so. "Do you mean that?" he questioned with uncertainty.

"Yeah, I do." Even Abigail was unsure of what she was saying. "It sounds like it's life or death at this point, so...yeah."

"Thank you. Seriously—I owe you," Noah expressed his gratitude after completely inserting his contacts.

Abigail gave him a quizzical expression. "You do?"

"Yeah." Noah checked the time on his phone, blinking to get adjusted to his new annoying eyewear. "I'm sorry, but I really need to go this time. I'm late."

"Oh, okay. I guess I am too," Abigail joked to lighten the mood.

Noah forced a smile. "See you."

"You too."

For the second time in about five minutes, the two separated at Noah's locker and walked towards their classes for the fourth block. Although this time, there were no interruptions. Abigail successfully returned to her AP Government class while Noah dashed towards his AP Calculus room. His teacher was not happy with his tardiness, but it was a seldom and out of habit occurrence for Noah. The teacher let it slide just that once.

Throughout the next seventy-five minutes, Noah kept blinking to ensure his contacts were indeed not falling out of his eyes. The plastic material made his eyes water uncomfortably and it felt as if he was very out of place. Noah hated how his teacher was so fast paced, but there was nothing he was able to do about it except attempt to keep up. He was smart, but that did not mean he was lightning quick with learning.

Once his AP Calculus was finished, Noah wanted to leave. He clutched his textbook along with his other supplies under one arm and attempted to exit the domain belonging to such an advanced math course. Despite Noah being a self-claimed "smart person", he was human as well, which meant he did not necessarily have to like math.

Noah failed to notice the sound of quick footsteps from behind him followed by a voice that seemed friendly. "Hey, wait up!"

He stopped in his tracks and looked over his shoulder. "Uh, me?" he asked with uncertainty.

"Yes, you," the male's voice confirmed Noah's confusion.

Standing in front of Noah was a boy about two inches taller than him. His dark auburn hair was a bit shaggy and cut just short enough to run his fingers through. He sported an olive green sweatshirt which made his brown eyes look more hazel in the lighting of the hallway along with a pair of jeans and high tops similar to what Noah was currently wearing. The boy had a confident stance, not slouched, but imperfect as well.

Noah opened his mouth to reply with an unanswered question, but no words came out. The boy who was now next to him spoke up, "So, two things. One: you left your phone on your desk," He handed Noah his phone, "and two: I saw you take a bit of a tumble in the hallway after lunch. I was going to ask if you were okay, but there was someone else there with you. Are you alright?"

"Oh, thank you." Noah took his phone back and put it in his pocket. "I'm okay. Thanks for asking, though."

"You're welcome," the young man replied with a smile. "I'm Ryder, by the way."

"Noah. Thanks for checking in on me," he returned the introduction by outstretching his hand. Ryder shook it.

Ryder offered him a contagious smile. "No problem. I couldn't help but notice that you looked a little stressed last period. Everything alright?"

"Yeah, everything's fine" Noah fibbed like it was second nature.

"If you say so." Ryder shrugged, dropping the subject. "So, how do you like the school so far? I don't remember seeing you around before this year."

It was Noah's turn to shrug. The two started walking side by side. "It's okay. I moved here recently, so everything's been chaotic."

"You moved right before the school year?" Ryder questioned in bewilderment.

"Yeah," Noah sighed. "It was a last-minute decision, but I'm glad I'm here. It'll be a chance to make some friends."

Ryder patted Noah's shoulder welcomingly. "Well, now you have one friend to add to the growing list. You'll consider this place a second home before you know it."

"Is it that easy?" he asked with a nervous chuckle.

"Yep," Ryder confirmed, emphasizing the "P." "It's that easy."

Noah grew peacefully silent at the realization he made his first friend at Hillwell High. He did not consider Abigail a friend...not yet, but there was an alluring sensation in his mind that drew him to want that. His heart thudded in his chest with relief. He was not as alone as he thought he was. All Noah needed to do was feel comfortable in Hillwell.

But...would it really be as simple as Ryder said?

4

"BREATHE. WHAT IS HAPPENING?"

Homework done? Check.

Reuniting with friends? Check.

Two weeks of school completed? That would be a work in progress.

Abigail scribbled furiously at the sheet of notebook paper underneath her pencil. She had lost track of how many times she tucked her long black hair behind her ear while she worked. The British Literature assignment was torturing her with each word she had to write. Abigail let out a sigh when her hand convulsed with a cramp. She had no need to educate herself with the knowledge pertaining to Shakespeare's *Macbeth*.

What was the point of a literary analysis anyway? Abigail saw none applicable. Instead, she was scribbling down nonsense from the plot summary she had searched on her phone. Her hand was throbbing as she wrote down each letter, each word, and each sentence. It was worse than her chronic habit of biting her nails. Abigail kept one hand in a fist pressing against her forehead with an elbow on the table while her other hand was writing. She inhaled deeply before continuing on with the assignment.

Around her were the four walls of a small café that was not quite a hole-in-the-wall establishment, but it wasn't the poshest place around. It was cozy with hardly any customers for breakfast. Abigail had left her house early in order to conceal her unfinished Literature homework from her unsuspecting parents. That was not the sole reason she escaped her humble abode, though. She also wanted coffee.

So, there she was, working on her British Literature homework in a miniscule cafe with the aid of a caramel macchiato. The Express-O Café was along her route to Hillwell High, so Abigail deemed it the perfect place to complete her work. Other than the occasional shiver at a chill making its way into the establishment when the glass front door was opened, Abigail was comfortable.

When the time on her phone hit ten minutes after eight, she took her caramel macchiato "to-go", stuffed her supplies into her backpack, and raced out of the café. Abigail was lucky to have her keys in her full hands, so she was able to unlock her gray vehicle and slide inside without hesitation. Mere moments after she had her caffeinated drink in the cupholder between the two front seats and slipped her sunglasses on her face, she sped off with her music pulsating through the car's speakers.

The parking lot of Hillwell High was not as flooded as it was on the first day of school two weeks ago that day, but it was close. Abigail snaked into one of the last available parking spots near the double doors leading into the intimidating building. Abigail would have been lying if she said she was not nervous for her third week of school to begin. Even though there had been no monumental disruptions to her well-being, her anxiety never ceased.

Abigail forced her hands to remain in the pockets of her light-washed denim jacket that complimented her black leggings, black high tops, and the gray Nirvana tee she was wearing with it. She watched the world around her through gold-tinted sunglasses as she walked towards the double doors for the eleventh time that year.

"Okay, Abigail," she muttered to herself. *"You've done this before and you can do it again."*

She strutted into the building like it was the easiest thing she had ever done. Abigail had no room in her mind to worry about what came next in her monotonous schedule. She lifted her sunglasses off her face and let them rest on the top of her head just like she did every other school day. Abigail twirled her keyring around her finger briefly before placing it in the pocket of her denim jacket.

Unbeknownst to Abigail until a noise was made, another person - who was quite petite - filed in next to her. "Hey, girl!" they announced cheerfully.

Abigail flinched at the sudden noise, but she calmed quickly when she realized exactly who it was. "Hi, Keagan."

"By the way, Jade and Brielle already went to their first classes," Keagan supplied the answer to an unasked question. "How are you, Abi?"

"Oh. I'm okay; how are you?" Abigail stopped at her locker to hurriedly unpack her backpack. Keagan stopped and waited next to her.

"Pretty good." The small girl's short hair flopped as she moved to lean against the locker next to her friend's. "Did you ever get that Brit Lit homework done?"

"Yeah. I stopped by the Express-O Café on the way here to get it done. My parents would kill me if they knew I didn't finish all my work by last night. You?"

"Nope."

Abigail stifled a laugh. This behavior was normal from Keagan. "I don't blame you," she snickered. "Answering questions to complete an analysis of *Macbeth* isn't my strong suit."

"School isn't my strong suit," Keagan casually disclosed.

"Agreed."

Keagan and Abigail eventually made it to their British Literature classroom. They were two of the last students who arrived, which gave them a lot of unnecessary attention. Not everyone was perfect— Abigail knew that for a long shot. Her gaze was cast downwards like a puppy who had just gotten scolded as she and her friend entered the classroom and took their seats directly after Mr. Wright had taken a roll call.

Mr. Wright gave them a pointed look of annoyance. "Miss Bartley and Miss Lopez, I appreciate you attending my class in general, but it would be preferable if you arrived on time," he stated bluntly.

"I was only finishing an assignment for this blessed class. You give a ridiculous amount of homework." Abigail bit her tongue from speaking her mind. Instead, she gave him a polite nod. "Yes, Sir."

"Sorry, Sir," Keagan apologized directly after.

"It's okay, you two," Mr. Wright replied, a smile returning to his boring face. "Now, we'll be continuing our discussion regarding Shakespeare's *Macbeth*. Does anyone have any comments about the reading and analysis which was required to be completed this weekend?"

Abigail blew a piece of her hair out of her face while a couple of students around her raised their hands and commented about their own work. She had her scribbled mess of an analysis on her desk with the papers bent and possessing some tears. She had tried her best, but her homework still managed to be an abomination. Luckily for her, Keagan was not far behind. She had begun her analysis but did just enough to get by.

A notification from her phone nearly startled Abigail out of her shoes. Tentatively, she grasped her phone from her desk and kept it hidden in her lap. *"I'm bored already,"* the message from Keagan read.

"Me too," Abigail texted back.

Not even a second later, another text popped up in the thread. *"Did you notice how the big glasses guy looked at you?"*

"No?" Abigail's breath caught in her throat. *"By the way, I don't know if you've noticed, but he doesn't have the big glasses anymore,"* she added, referring to the spare pair of glasses that Noah resorted to a week ago.

Keagan attempted to sneak a glance at Noah, who was a couple rows in front and diagonal to her. She was successful. *"Wait, you're right! Do you think it was because of the dare? Because if it was, I feel really bad now."*

"No, it wasn't," Abigail clarified. *"He actually lost his glasses last*

Monday and has to use a spare. It wasn't because of the dare. I was honest with him and told him."

"You did?!" Keagan's head snapped over to Abigail's, which was harboring a discreet smile. When Abigail nodded, she mouthed, *What the fu-*

"Miss Lopez," Mr. Wright exclaimed, which caused Keagan to nearly fall out of her flimsy chair. "Are you trying to talk to and distract the other diligent students of this class?"

Keagan's eyes darted away from Abigail's and returned to her desk. "Sorry, Sir. I was asking Abigail if she knew the answer to one of the analytical questions for the assignment."

"And why didn't you complete the question on your own?"

"I didn't have time," she confessed, and it was true.

Mr. Wright's eyebrows lowered in suspicion, but he decided not to probe any further. "Very well, then. Please refrain from speaking to your classmates until the end of class. Understood?"

"Understood."

Once Mr. Wright returned to speaking about Shakespeare, Abigail looked at Keagan again. Her friend subtly winked at Abigail and motioned towards her phone. Abigail, having no idea where this was going, looked down at her phone in her lap and saw another notification.

"One more thing, though," Keagan's message read.

Abigail lifted an eyebrow in confusion and typed: *"What?"*

"I ship it. ;)"

She dropped her phone out of her lap. It landed on the floor with a thud loud enough to cause over half the classroom to turn.

"Miss Bartley," Mr. Wright sighed when he discovered exactly where and what the sound came from. "Were you using your phone during class? You should be aware of our no-phones policy."

"No, Sir. It fell out of my pocket," she easily lied. Her leggings didn't even have pockets.

Mr. Wright nodded. "Alright, then. Be careful not to use your phone or I'll have to take it from you until the end of class. Is that clear?"

"Yes, Sir. Very clear."

For a second time, Abigail felt a sense of guilt overtake her. She hated being called out in the middle of class. Ever since Abigail's debacle in the past, she hated having attention drawn to herself. It was a huge no-no in her book, so whenever she could avoid it, she would.

As Abigail began searching through her analysis homework on her desk, she noticed another pair of eyes discreetly watching her. She blinked once, and then twice until she realized brief eye contact was made with someone she had not spoken to in about a week. Things with this person were quite awkward since they had practically been ignoring each other for the past week or so. Abigail averted her eyes at the same time Noah did.

A gut feeling spurred her to glance over at Keagan, who was grinning at her. A silent giggle and another wink later, Abigail knew she was in big trouble.

That thought followed her to the end of her British Literature class. Keagan had not mentioned anything about it, but Abigail knew it was at the front of her mind. Keagan was *that* sort of friend who relished in the reactions of her friends' mere seconds after leaving an amusing comment. Abigail felt that aura along with the compassionate heart of Keagan's on the day she met her years ago.

Abigail and Keagan were unable to meet the rest of their friends between classes since the five minutes between them ticked by quicker than Abigail could say so. Before she knew it, she and Keagan had split up to their respective classes--Abigail to Precalculus and Keagan to Algebra II. To their distaste, math was a required course to take up until their graduation.

Once the clock hit nine thirty-three, or two minutes before the second block of the day began, Abigail sat down at her usual desk near the back of the classroom. No one that she personally knew accompanied her in this class, so she asked herself "Why bother?" when it came to making new friends. She had Jade, Keagan, and Brielle and they were not going anywhere any time soon.

She opened her math book and nearly scraped her finger on the page as she turned it to the chapter her class was currently discussing. In truth, Abigail had no idea what was going on in the world of Precalculus. The letters, numbers, and functions blurred together into one giant, jumbled disaster. Abigail was lucky she was passing. If there were no disruptions to her mental health, she had a wonderful chance at passing sufficiently.

Unfortunately, that never seemed to be the case for Abigail.

Among the several pairs of footsteps parading into the classroom, there was one that stuck out above the others. There was an aspect that was familiar when it came to that set of footsteps as Abigail listened. It created a pit of fear in her stomach even though she somehow could not put her finger on what exactly it was that was frightening her. Once her gaze snapped up and met the haunting pair of brown eyes, she knew she was in for a lot more than she bargained for.

Her heart abruptly stopped beating in her chest as she took in the appearance of the young man entering the classroom. She hated how his sandy brown hair rested perfectly on his head. She despised the prideful glint in his dark eyes. She resented the flawless stature of how he held himself as he passed through the doorway. The thing Abigail hated the most, however, was how he arrogantly smirked when he caught her gaze.

Abigail pulled her denim jacket tighter around her as her breath hitched in her throat. Then, her heart began to pound uncontrollably. Rather than time ticking too hastily, it was too slow for her taste. Each step of his appeared to be blurred and in slow motion. The walls of the already cramped classroom started to close in. Abigail's breathing began to be tight and quick. She felt herself begin to panic just at the sight of him. The memories were horrid enough. The fact he was less than twenty feet away from her was too much for her to bear.

So, she decided she didn't have to.

She lurched from her seat and clasped her phone tightly in her pocket. Abigail wasted no time leaving the classroom even though it caused her to accidentally bump into the Precalculus teacher. Abigail had nothing on her mind other than to get away from him as quickly as her short legs could take her. She left the room so quickly that she left her Precalculus textbook behind.

Abigail ignored the weird stares she received from the occasional student at their locker or walking to the restroom. She held her keys firmly in one hand and her phone in the other. The very second that she opened the double doors of Hillwell High, she tapped on a familiar contact in her phone and held it up to her ear.

On the second ring, the person on the other line picked up. *"Abigail? Honey? Shouldn't you be in class right now?"* her mother asked.

"Mom, can you do two things for me?" Abigail hurriedly gasped.

"Honey, what's wrong?" Lillian's voice was worried.

Abigail unlocked her car and shut herself inside. "Just do these two things. Please."

"Okay, Abigail. Breathe. What is happening?"

"I need you to try to set up a session with Kristy right now. I need to talk to her about something. Now," she desperately blubbered. "I also need you to *please* call the school and tell them I won't be there for the rest of my classes."

There was a pause on the other line. *"Okay, okay,"* Lillian gushed out. *"What's going on, Abigail? You can talk to me. Why can't you stay at school?"*

"I just can't. *Please*, Mom," Abigail unleashed a strangled beg. She was already beginning to floor it out of the parking lot.

"Alright, Honey. It's okay. Can you tell me what's going on?"

Abigail felt herself begin to hyperventilate as she drove at least ten miles per hour over the speed limit. *"It's okay, Abigail. Take some deep breaths. Remember what Kristy said to do when you feel unsafe,"* she internally fretted. Abigail's knuckles turned a lighter shade of pale as her hands gripped onto the steering wheel like her life depended on it.

"What's going on, Abigail?" her mother repeated quietly.

The teenage girl's eyes began to fill with unshed tears at the realization. Once she said it out loud, it was going to be true. After another moment of hesitation, she finally choked it out:

"He's back."

5

"MATH ISN'T MY BEST SUBJECT."

ABIGAIL'S IMAGINATION COULD EASILY HAVE BEEN COMPARED TO A SNOW globe. The scenery inside of the snow globe, whether it be a building, a snowman, or something else, was always beautiful and tranquil. Specks of snow lightly dusted the ground around whatever object was in the middle. In the snow globe was pure peace, but that pure peace never lasted forever. Every so often, there was an outside force grasping the globe and shaking it wildly, creating chaos within the glass sphere. This chaos did not persist, though. Eventually, the snow floated down and blissfully blanketed the surface again.

This was an endless cycle. Her mind's snow globe was shaken up on her first day of senior year, where she needed to reunite with her friends and feel more comfortable. Ever since then, her globe's snowflakes were resting calmly on the ground until the previous day's events shook it up again. Abigail felt like she was amid that very globe, carelessly being shaken and tossed about during a confined blizzard.

She had voiced that exact comparison to her therapist the previous morning. Even though Kristy's hours did not begin until noon, she was able to take Abigail at ten o'clock sharp with a heavily discounted price. Many tears were shed during the sixty minutes

Kristy and Abigail shared in the cramped office. The latter had lost count of how many shuddering breaths she took as she recollected every memory that compressed in her brain. She hadn't forgotten a single detail of what the young man had done to her.

The moment Abigail returned home after her therapy session, she noticed her father dropping his work equipment on the ground by the front door. He immediately embraced her in a hug which only triggered another breakdown after Abigail had just recovered from one. Despite his work being very important to him, Harold never failed to put his family first.

The Bartleys spent the rest of the day watching comedies and playing board games to distract Abigail from her debilitating flashbacks.

Abigail's mind was spinning by the time she landed herself right where she was the previous day: in the same building, the same room, and even the same desk that she was yesterday. She was barely present as she answered worried questions from Keagan, Brielle, and Jade regarding her leave of absence for most of the school day. She thought a simple "I got overwhelmed" would suffice, but unfortunately, her friends knew there was something more behind her mask of serenity and confidence.

So, she told them. By the time Abigail explained what exactly had happened, she was a blubbering, trembling mess, but she was surrounded by her friends. Before she knew it, she was embraced in a comforting group hug, protected by the three girls who kept her sane over the past year. The comfort from Jade, Keagan, and Brielle caused the four of them to be late for their first classes of the day.

Abigail didn't notice the worried expression on a certain boy with glasses' face in the front row as she walked into her British Literature classroom tardy with a crack in the glass making up her poker face.

Now, she was waiting for her Precalculus class to begin with her head bowed and hands clasped in her lap. She picked at the fragile skin around her fingertips, which reddened more with every tug. Abigail's lower lip was caught tightly between her teeth. Maybe focusing on one pain would draw her mind away from the other - more overbearing - task at hand? She was about to find out.

A sickeningly familiar aura drug her gaze from her lap to the doorway. There he was for the second time in two days. Abigail's blood grew cold at the sight of him in all his glory. When before, he was a blurred mess of a human to her eyes, now, he was crystal clear. His brown eyes pierced deep into her soul, enough to cause her to want to squirm out of her seat and dash out of the school just like the day before. Abigail's eyes darted away once his dashing, yet haunting smirk appeared on his face once more.

"Just ignore it. Ignore his presence but be on your guard like Kristy said."

Abigail refused to move her eyes from her lap as the young man sat down at his desk a row behind the front. She did her best to distance herself, being almost on the opposite side of the classroom, but she could not move again. No more seats were available for her use, so Abigail needed to remain at her desk.

She nearly failed to do so when a thud on her desk caused Abigail to flinch so hard that she almost tipped out of the seat. "Oh, I'm so sorry, Dear," the woman in her thirties exclaimed frantically. "I didn't mean to startle you. You forgot your textbook at your desk yesterday."

"Oh, thank you," Abigail sheepishly muttered, eyeing the blasted textbook.

She was barely able to meet the woman's eyes. Mrs. Harris always proved to be one of the kindest teachers at Hillwell High. She even looked friendly with her dark brown hair that was as neat as a pin framing her thin face. Mrs. Harris' gaze was filled with apology as a gentle smile graced her flawless milky complexion. Abigail decided to take the risk and offer Mrs. Harris a grateful, but small grin in return directly before she returned to the whiteboard at the front of the classroom.

"Good morning, class!" She greeted the twenty-five students. "I hope you're all ready for today's lecture on polar functions."

Some of Abigail's classmates groaned. Abigail remained silent, pretending to look through her textbook with genuine interest.

Despite the unenthusiastic aura of the class, Mrs. Harris smiled and began writing down the fundamentals of polar functions for her students to read, utilize, and memorize before the class period was over.

Of course, Abigail did none of that. Despite the endless scribbles in her notebook that she would have to piece together later that day, she digested none of the learning material. Her eyes were glued to the paper on her desk and the textbook opened underneath it, but her actual field of vision seemed to drift over to the head of perfect brown hair across the room. Her mind resembled a hamster wheel with the small rodent turning it in circles for the next seventy-five minutes. Rather than render her brain completely useless, she formulated a plan to escape.

The very second that the young man Abigail desperately desired to avoid left the room when class was over, she sprung from her seat. She messily gathered her things and dashed towards Mrs. Harris' desk, bumping into several people and students' desks in the process. Abigail ignored any reactions she was given as she approached her teacher, who was filing through a small pile of papers.

Abigail cleared her throat. "Excuse me," she stated just over a whisper.

"What?" Mrs. Harris abruptly turned around. Her eyes softened when they landed on her student. "Oh! Hello, Abigail. Is there something I can do for you?"

"I need some help," replied Abigail as if she was afraid to say a word.

The older woman frowned at the nervous look atop Abigail's face. "What is it, Dear?" Mrs. Harris inquired softly.

"Is there another Precalculus class that I can switch to?" she asked in a rushed tone.

"Oh, um," the teacher faltered and began typing on her laptop that was on the desk. "I'm looking right now, but is there a big problem with this one? Are you okay?"

"Yes, Ma'am. I'm fine," Abigail lied between her teeth. "My schedule in the morning is just too hectic and I feel like an afternoon session with a free period in the morning to complete any necessary homework would work better for me. Are there any available?"

Mrs. Harris skimmed the screen of her computer. "There's a Precalculus class that I teach in the fifth period block, but all twenty-five spots are filled. I can put you on a waiting list just in case a seat is opened, though."

"No, I need to be out of this specific class *now*. It doesn't matter what time," Abigail fretted insistently.

"I'm not sure if that would be possible, but let me see...," Mrs. Harris trailed off. She typed a few letters into her laptop while Abigail waited impatiently across from her. "There is an Algebra II class available during this block, but from your record, you took it last year. Repeating it would be unnecessary. Now, I do have an AP Calculus class with a couple of seats open, but it's during the second block."

"Okay. I'd like to be enrolled in that class, please."

"You didn't let me finish," Mrs. Harris asserted to her student's despair. "I cannot enroll you in AP Calculus just like *that*," she snapped her fingers to emphasize the last word, "You'll have to finish Precalculus with a sufficient grade, but there's the option for you to take a placement test by the end of the month, which is when the add/drop deadline for classes is. If you get higher than an eighty-five percent on the test, I can speak with the principal and we'll determine your enrollment status. This would be a quicker route than the waiting list."

Abigail clutched her book tighter to her chest. Her teeth clenched with worry. *"Great—now I have something else to be nervous about,"* she cursed to herself, but she forced a smile onto her face. "Okay. I'd like to do that, please."

"Are you sure, Dear? The test would have to be taken by a week from Friday at the latest."

"Yes, I'm sure," Abigail cautiously replied. Her faux confidence bled through her perfect teeth. "Thank you for your help, Mrs. Harris."

Mrs. Harris gave Abigail an unsure smile in return. "You're

welcome, Abigail. Please email me if you have any questions regarding the placement test."

"I will."

Abigail wasted no time leaving the Precalculus classroom and rushing to her locker. She attempted to ignore the occasional odd look from a peer or two. Instead, she concentrated on the new task at hand: getting into another math class and distancing herself further away from the very person she wanted to avoid. He terrorized her enough to study her britches off for a placement test that would have been completely unnecessary if he ceased to exist.

She fumbled around with the combination lock on her locker until the metal door flung open and she was able to access it. Abigail filed through her books, exchanging her Precalculus book for her AP Chemistry textbook in the process. Since Abigail was doing so at a quick pace, she hardly noticed the small slip of paper slowly floating down from inside her locker until it landed on the toe of her left high top.

Abigail's eyebrows furrowed together at the note someone must have left for her. She cautiously bent down and unfolded the petite piece of paper. Her eyes widened when she noticed the familiar elegant handwriting.

ARE YOU OKAY? *I don't mean to be a creep, but you looked upset in British Literature.*

-Noah

SHE BLINKED at the note once, twice, and then three times before it registered. Someone other than her three friends *actually* cared about her well-being. She pretended she truly didn't care that a person she hardly knew wanted to check up on her. Abigail never thought enough about it to care before, but why now? The gesture warmed her cracked heart just a little...just enough that she wanted to express her gratitude.

Gripping a stray pen from her locker, she clicked it and flipped the piece of paper over. She hastily scribbled a response to Noah that merely took a couple of seconds, but it was enough to get her point across. Of course, she did not want to disclose any unnecessary information. She hardly knew Noah, but it was a start.

I'm okay. Something happened yesterday that made me upset, but I'm better now. Thank you for asking.

-Abigail

"Making her upset" was an understatement, but Noah didn't have to know that.

Abigail folded the slip of paper the opposite way so her note was on the inside and shut her locker door. Since Noah's locker was in transit between hers and the AP Chemistry classroom, she dropped it off then, slipping it through the top slot of his locker. She felt an anxious pang in her chest once she did so. Would Noah judge her for writing a response? Surely not, since he initiated the conversation between the two.

That snippet of a thought stalked her from the AP Chemistry room to the cafeteria. Every so often, Abigail thought as if she was being followed, but, in reality, it was her imagination playing tricks on her. She remained on her guard, just like Kristy instructed her to do. Abigail had another task on her plate that she needed to swallow down before feeling relatively calm again.

Everywhere she looked, Abigail thought she saw *him*. After Precalculus, he seemed to vanish off the school premises. It almost seemed to Abigail that she was dreaming, the young man being a vision of her worst nightmares. She told herself it was time to wake up, but what if the nightmare was truly her reality? Abigail refused to live through his reign for a second time. Once was more than enough.

For the second time in three minutes, Abigail willed herself to exit Dreamland and enter Hillwell High's cafeteria once again. She was surrounded by friends. It was the ideal place for her to reside while she recovered from the damage that was caused. For a while, Abigail thought she was safe from his mental clutches. Once again, her mind deceived her into believing everything was going to be alright, because there he was—a couple tables over from her, Keagan, Jade, and Brielle. His eyes darted over to her. For a split second, the smirk that Abigail hated rested on his handsome face, but she blinked and it was gone.

This simple facial expression spurred Abigail into action. Her fist collided with the wooden surface of the table and nearly startled all her friends out of their seats. Three pairs of eyes - one brown, one gray, and one hazel - bore into Abigail's with a look of bewilderment seeping through them. Half of a fry fell from Keagan's mouth, Brielle dropped a forkful of salad on the table, and Jade's hair was now messed up. Abigail's outburst satisfactorily did its job: getting their attention.

"Does anyone here know the entirety of Precalculus?" Abigail's river of words spluttered out of her mouth like a sudden waterfall.

Keagan looked like she was about to perform an award-winning spit-take. "I'm sorry, what?" she slowly asked. "You slammed your fist on the table and scared the crap out of all of us for that?"

Abigail hesitated for a moment and then nodded. "...Yes."

"Why's that?" Jade inquired with pure curiosity.

"Are you okay?" Brielle was concerned.

"Honestly, no. I'm not okay," Abigail replied truthfully. She swallowed back a lump of anxiety forming in her throat. "Like I told you, *he's* in my Precalculus class. So, I want to get out of there as soon as possible."

Keagan cocked her head to the side. "Is there another class in a different block that you could take instead?" she suggested.

"I asked my teacher about that and yes, there is, but I'd need to be put on a waiting list," Abigail explained. Suddenly, the food in front of her refused to look appetizing. "My only other option is to take AP Calculus during my second block since I don't want to repeat Algebra II. There's a placement test that I need to take by the end of the month if I want to be *considered* for that class. I need to get an eighty-five or above."

Keagan blinked a couple of times before answering, "Oh... Do you want some help with studying? I'm in Algebra II, so I don't know any Precalculus, but I can try."

"So can I," Brielle offered between taking two bites of her salad. "I'm taking Precalculus during the fifth block, so I know just about as much as you. I can look ahead and try to help you study, though."

"I'm in Precalculus with Brielle, so count me in!" Jade chirped positively. "I'm not promising anything, though. Math isn't my best subject."

If Abigail's eyes widened any more, they would have fallen out of the sockets and rolled across the cafeteria floor. "You guys mean that?" she stammered shakily.

All three of her friends nodded. Keagan's was most enthusiastic, Jade's was neutral, and Brielle's was subtle, but all of them agreed on one thing: to help Abigail get away from *him* as quickly and effectively as possible. If Abigail was not in the lunchroom - the heart of Hillwell High School - she would have begun tearing up at the gesture. Abigail awkwardly rocked back and forth in her seat to keep herself in check. The last thing Abigail needed was a nervous breakdown in front of everyone in the cafeteria.

Abigail glanced over towards *his* table once again. There he was. She grimaced at how carefree his smile was as he talked with his friends who knew nothing about him. Abigail hated how he could live his life with no problems while she suffered through hers because of him. She despised every smile the boy exhibited on his face. Every laugh he exhaled sounded maniacal to her ears. It vibrated in her brain. How could he play pretend and act like absolutely nothing happened? *He* was the cause of her pain. *He* was the reason she was so paranoid.

She turned back to Jade, Brielle, and Keagan, who were quietly looking in her direction. Once they noticed who she was looking at, small frowns appeared on their faces. Brielle averted her eyes politely towards her salad, Keagan pretended to occupy herself with more fries, and Jade simply appeared concerned. Abigail took a hearty bite out of one of her chicken tenders and swallowed it down. She had no idea how hungry she really was after skipping breakfast that morning.

"Okay," Abigail eventually agreed, "Let's learn an entire year's worth of Precalculus in two weeks. How hard can it be?" she added on with sarcasm.

6

"IT COULD BE VERY ENTERTAINING."

SCIENCE CLASSROOMS COULD HAVE BEEN DESCRIBED WITH ONE WORD: stuffy.

Noah twirled his poor excuse for a pencil around in one hand while the other's elbow rested on the desk in front of him. His balding AP Biology teacher was droning on and on about the fundamentals of a flower's anatomy. He let out a shameless, yet silent yawn while his teacher was writing a few things down on the whiteboard at the front of the class. Almost everyone around Noah was drifting off to sleep, already asleep, or just bored.

He wrote down a form of organized notes in his notebook dedicated simply to AP Biology. Noah figured out soon enough that if he did not write notes on absolutely everything that his teacher - Mr. Murphy - said in each seventy-five-minute period, he would have a much better chance at failing the frequent tests which were distributed once a week. Despite Noah being a straight-A student, he failed to care less about his dratted AP Biology class.

Even the classroom around him was boring. With beige walls and no windows, the room seemed smaller than it was. Noah had no idea how twenty-five students were able to fit in such a tight space. He felt very constricted as it was without students in the room. If it were just him and the teacher, he would have felt like the room was closing in on him at every second.

The clock on the wall ticked agonizingly slow. Noah thought this class was never going to end so he and his peers could escape into the sanctuary known as the cafeteria. His eyes darted towards the clock that hung directly over top of the whiteboard. With each letter that Mr. Murphy wrote on the said board, his marker squeaked. Noah desperately fought the urge to cringe at the horrendous sound. Why did the clock seem to be ticking backwards?

Mr. Murphy spun around on his heel. He inspected the class one by one while he spoke about the diagram of a flower he had just drawn. Noah instinctively straightened his posture. Despite not caring less about his teacher's view of him, he wanted to be a good student, no matter how "nerdy" or dumb it sounded. He relished in making good impressions.

From the looks of it, someone a couple of seats away from Noah did not have the same mindset as he did. The very petite young woman was slouched in her chair with her neck craned to make her face look towards the ceiling. Her short black hair with green roots almost had an unruly status. Some of it covered her pale face, some of it did not. The girl's feet dangled at least two inches over the ground since they could not reach it. Her eyes were closed and soft snores emitted from her mouth. Noah vaguely recognized her as Keagan, one of Abigail's friends.

The AP Biology teacher frowned and smacked his marker against his desk. "Miss Lopez!" he called out. "No sleeping in my class!"

"Huh? What?" Keagan snorted and sat up as straight as a ruler. She offered him a cooky and sheepish smile. "Oh! I'm sorry, Mr. Murphy. I guess your presentation was so exhilarating that I passed out from the whiplash," she joked.

"It mustn't happen again, or you'll receive a detention," Mr. Murphy firmly instructed her. "I've had enough people fall asleep in my class for me to not fix the error."

"That says a lot about your teaching style," Noah thought silently.

Keagan shrugged and pretended to flip through her textbook. "I'll keep that in mind," she replied without making eye contact.

"Thank you *very* much, Miss Lopez," Mr. Murphy grumbled and addressed the sleepy class once more. "Now, hopefully we'll have enough time to finish today's lecture."

If the class was in some sort of teen fiction movie, a collective groan would have sounded throughout the room. Noah continued writing down notes that were necessary for him to complete his homework while the rest of the class pretended to pay attention. AP Biology was a class that was hated by the majority of Hillwell High, which meant students either took it as early as possible or procrastinated until the very last year since it was required to graduate.

Thankfully, the class concluded before Noah would deem himself driven insane. The entirety of the twenty-five students filed out of the room as quickly as possible. None of them gave Mr. Murphy a second glance. All of them were looking forward to the hour of freedom bestowed upon them by the fateful lunch period. All Noah knew was that he was relieved to be out of his AP Biology course and walking towards the cafeteria.

Noah clutched his textbook under his arm while he walked towards his locker. The hallways were overwhelmingly crowded. Trying to find a path where he would not be jostled around was an impossibility. He hated how many people were crammed into such a small hallway. Having lockers so close together was counterproductive. Noah despised being shoulder-to-shoulder with a complete stranger who shared his wall of lockers. All he wanted to do was get out of there.

His journey halted once he unlocked his locker and a small, folded piece of paper fell out, landing on the floor near the tip of his left shoe. Noah blinked at it in confusion. No one had ever left him a note before. Why would someone waste valuable seconds ticking away at their life to scribble a few words down on a small slip of paper?

Noah hesitated at the realization he may or may not be a hypocrite according to that statement.

Rather than letting curiosity get to him, Noah bent down and picked up the note after he put his school supplies back into his locker. He recognized his own handwriting on the outside. When he took a closer look, Noah's eyes slightly widened and he adjusted his glasses - his spare that he hated - in order to determine if what he spectated was true. Sure enough, it was his note that he wrote to Abigail earlier that day.

Noah flipped the note around and read the slightly sloppy handwriting on the back of the note with an expression of confusion and surprise. The last thing he was expecting was a response to his note, even though it asked a question. The words from Abigail were much more polite than when they were during his first encounter with her. Honestly, Noah realized he had no idea what he was expecting - if anything - from her.

I'M OKAY. Something happened yesterday that made me upset, but I'm better now. Thank you for asking.

-ABIGAIL

HE FOUND himself reading the note for a second and third time. The words sunk in quickly. What could have upset her? Noah tried not to overanalyze anything or come to any sort of crazy conclusions, but what if something serious was going on with her? A family issue? A friend issue? Maybe it was something worse than he thought? Noah wanted to find out, but he also did not want to invade her privacy. Besides, he hardly knew her.

Noah considered writing her another note and putting it in her locker, but before the thought could fully cross his mind, a hand landed firmly on his shoulder. He nearly flinched out of his shoes until he whirled around and noticed it was one of his - scratch that - his *only* friend at Hillwell High. The dark auburn hair gave it away.

"Hey, Noah!" Ryder exclaimed with his usual friendly tone. "What's up?"

"Hey, Ryder. Nothing much," Noah replied, messily shoving the note from Abigail into the pocket of his jeans. "How about you?"

"Same here. It's been a long morning. I'm glad to be just over halfway done today," exhaled Ryder with a relieved grin.

"You're telling me," Noah sarcastically agreed.

"Is something wrong?"

Noah shrugged. "No, I don't think so," he fibbed easily. "Why do you ask?"

"Just wondering," Ryder countered. It was his turn to shrug since he had nothing else valuable to say.

So, the two resorted to listening. Neither of them considered themselves as fluent in gossip, but they preferred to be informed of what exactly was occurring at Hillwell High. This was something that the two friends did together while in transit to the cafeteria, or the heart of the entire school. Neither Noah, nor Ryder, liked to talk to many people. That would explain Ryder's lack of friends until the two crossed paths. He had close to none, but he didn't seem to mind.

Noah and Ryder retrieved their lunches from the exceedingly long line and attempted to find a vacant table. The cafeteria was flooded with so many teenagers that even the Ark belonging to Noah's namesake would have been impressed. Eventually, the two of them discovered a table that was free of any of their peers. Ryder rushed over in a sprint and claimed one of the chairs, causing it to skid slightly across the floor. Noah cringed and sat across from him.

Ryder took a bite out of his cheeseburger and set it back down on a napkin. "So, who are you pulling for in the MLB game tonight?" he asked to make conversation.

Noah pondered about it for a solid second before replying, "Yankees."

"The Yankees aren't even playing tonight," Ryder deadpanned. He somehow kept a neutral expression on his face.

"You know I don't watch baseball," he protested with a small chuckle.

"I know," Ryder clarified nonchalantly. "You need to, though. One of these days, you're coming over to my house and watching a game with me."

Noah blinked with surprise. "Is that an invitation?"

"Why not?"

It was a well-known fact by then that Ryder enjoyed baseball. He watched it, he used to play it, and it was one of the only things he could effectively talk about. Ryder knew all the stats from nearly every team, player, or even specific game. He was able to name almost every World Series winner by heart, the best players from each winner's team, and the list goes on. It was a good thing that Noah was a good listener. He was already informed of the baseball stats from the previous ten years despite knowing nothing about the game except the basic rules.

"Well, um," Noah hesitated, thinking it over. "I've never had the best luck with making friends, especially since I just moved."

"That's okay. Me neither, and I've been going to this school ever since sophomore year. It gets better," Ryder consoled him.

"It doesn't sound like it," he muttered too quietly to be intelligible.

Ryder tilted his head to the side. "What'd you say?"

"Nothing."

The table drifted into an awkward silence. Neither of them had anything to say, so Noah and Ryder said nothing at all. That led to Noah's gaze shifting around the lunchroom to entertain himself effectively. Noah continued to assure himself that he was not a stalker, but rather an observer of the public. Keeping himself aware was better than being completely and utterly gullible when it came to other people. Often, a person's outer shell was not who they were on the inside. Only actions spoke louder than the complexity of faux words.

Noah's line of sight drifted to a table that was relatively close to his and Ryder's. At least three tables sat in between his own and the one that drew his eye. Sure enough, he was able to see the side profile of Abigail Bartley at that table with three other girls—one of which being the girl - Keagan - from his AP Biology class. Abigail looked as perfect as ever, with her black hair neatly parted to the right side and her eyelashes coated with just the slightest bit of mascara. Her gold-tinted sunglasses rested flawlessly on the top of her head. He noticed something different about the tint to those eyes, though. They seemed fearful.

He took a closer look and noticed Abigail's gaze shoot over towards another table. Noah was unable to pinpoint where exactly she was looking, but her eyes fixated on a certain thing. He watched as they widened for a split second, but then they snapped away and back towards Abigail's own table where her friends were speaking about something he was unable to properly distinguish. Noah nearly jumped like the three of her friends did when she slammed her fist on the table.

"Noah, are you okay?" Ryder asked. It distracted him from whatever was occurring out of his earshot.

Noah blinked and adjusted his glasses so they would not fall off his face. "Uh, yeah," he fumbled for a proper response. "I'm fine. Why?"

"You looked like you zoned out or something."

"I was just thinking," he admitted, which was not completely a lie. Noah paused, considering the outcome of whether he said what was on his mind was a good idea or not. Eventually, he decided it was worth a shot. "Can I ask you something?"

"Yeah, go for it," Ryder replied, turning his attention from his food to his friend.

"How do you know if you like a girl?"

Noah froze right after he blurted it out. He had no idea he said it out loud until Ryder's eyes grew the slightest bit larger. The confusion lasted for a split second until Ryder ate one of his fries and digested the question for a short time. Noah was impatient. Part of him wanted to get up and sprint out of the room as quickly as possible, but the other part desired a sincere answer and possibly closure.

"Well," Ryder began mid-chew and then he swallowed, "Let me ask you a few questions and then we'll go from there. Do you think about them a lot?"

"In what way?" Noah tentatively questioned.

"Any."

"Then, probably. Yeah."

Ryder chuckled quietly at that. "Okay, how about this? Have you found any flaws about them that really stand out to you, or does everything about them seem as close to perfect as it could get?"

"Uh...," Noah trailed off to think. "The second one."

"Then, I think it's a likely possibility that you like someone," he concluded to Noah's knowing dismay. "Who's the lucky girl?"

Noah scoffed, "Lucky? Why do you want to know?"

"Because I'm curious," he insisted with a cheesy grin. "You don't have to tell me, but it won't leave this table. I promise."

Noah was unsure. He had known Ryder for over a week at that point. Was he able to trust him? Well, Noah was about to find out. "Okay... If you really want to know, it's Abigail Bartley."

"Oh, my God." Ryder's jaw dropped with the realization.

"...What?"

"Abigail and I used to date."

Noah was unfortunately taking a sip of his water at that very second. Long story short, quite a bit of it clogged his nose and spurred him into a coughing fit. Ryder instinctively held his hands out. He had an apologetic look on his face as he watched his friend practically choke to death on a few drops of water.

"You...*what*?" Noah spluttered once he got his breath back.

"Woah, I'm sorry. I didn't realize it would be such a shock, but yeah," Ryder awkwardly clarified. "But it was during sophomore year. She was pretty, I was a hopeless idiot, and it only lasted for maybe a couple months at the most. I'm not a threat—I promise. In fact, I could help you if you want."

Noah blinked, being caught off-guard. "Oh, uh...thank you. I just don't know what to do since this is the first time I've really..."

"Had a crush?" Ryder supplied.

"No, it's more like...anxiety over someone who's the opposite gender," Noah finished, which made him cringe due to his wording.

Ryder snickered knowingly, "Makes sense."

"Leave me alone," he groaned with a frustrated sigh afterwards.

Noah fought the urge to tug at his hair due to the stress of someone else knowing about his worries.

"Oh, come on." Ryder prodded his shoulder. "It could be very entertaining."

"How on God's green earth would this be entertaining?"

"I can be your wingman or something. I used to know her, so it might work out. Then again, she's most likely changed in the past two years. Let's give it a shot," he pridefully proposed.

Noah glared at his fries. "I don't know if this is such a good idea."

"It's better than doing absolutely nothing about it," he reasoned.

"I don't know," repeated the nervous teenage boy who was fixing his glasses for the umpteenth time that day.

"Let's do something about it, then." Ryder outstretched his arm with a smirk. "Shall we?"

Noah stopped short. He glanced down at Ryder's hand, and then back at his face. His expression was cautious, but he eventually caved and allowed his semi-new friend to aid him in furthering his hopes of getting to know the girl who had captured his interest in just a couple of short weeks. Noah firmly shook his hand.

"...Let's give it a shot."

7

"I'M NOT DUMB; I PROMISE."

"THIS IS A DISASTER!" KEAGAN DRAMATICALLY WAILED.

The librarian across the room, who was sitting at her desk, replied distastefully, "Shh! This is a library and you will treat it as such."

Keagan cringed at the fact she was being reprimanded. "Sorry," she sheepishly apologized.

Jade fought the urge to hold back her snicker while Keagan pouted. Abigail and Brielle were hard at work on the other side of the table. Textbooks, papers, pencils, protractors, rulers, calculators, and other stationary supplies used with the core subject of math were littered all over the spruce surface of the table. Abigail was scribbling out a problem from what appeared to be the middle of the book while Brielle flipped through the pages of formulas to offer aid. Abigail fought the urge to smack the poor sheet of paper and snap the pencil that produced yet another incorrect answer in half.

"This'll never work," Abigail muttered with frustration.

"Not necessarily," Brielle quietly comforted her. "Once we figure out exactly which formula to use for this chapter section, it'll be easier."

"But we've been trying to do that for the past thirty minutes!"

"Shh!" the librarian expressed once again.

Abigail gripped her pencil so tightly that it really did snap this time. Brielle flinched from next to her and awkwardly handed her another one. Abigail took it and started to silently doodle a cartoon dog on the corner of her sheet of notebook paper. All three of her friends were deathly silent while Abigail let her confidence in herself slip right between her fingers and shatter on the dusty library floor beneath their feet.

Jade skeptically peered over at Abigail's paper. "That looks like an interesting math problem," she commented regarding the dog drawing.

"Gee, thanks," Abigail stiffly snipped as she began shading in the dog's face.

Keagan took a small bite out of a chocolate chip cookie that she snuck into the library. There was a "no food" policy, but she could not find enough effort to care. "Maybe we should take a break and try again sometime after school?" she suggested mid-chew.

"We've done that for the past three days," Abigail retorted and resumed her dog drawing. "Spoiler alert: we've gotten nowhere."

Sure enough, the past seventy-two hours had been filled with nothing but math, frustration, and lowering self-confidence. Abigail lost a lot of sleep for the past two nights, staying up until the wee hours of the morning in order to study until her eyeballs felt like they were going to scale over. She felt as if she did not spend as much of her waking hours as she could on studying, she would fail the placement test and land herself right back at square one.

"We still have over a week to learn the material. We're already on chapter four out of fifteen. We'll get there," Brielle reasoned calmly.

Abigail responded by letting her head drop on top of her open textbook with a thud. All three of her friends jumped. Keagan extended two of her fingers and used them to pry Abigail's face off of the pages so she was sitting upright. Abigail blinked a couple of times to let her eyes become readjusted with her surroundings, which consisted of a dusty library that hardly anyone used. Shelves of books neatly lined the large room. The Hillwell High School Library was of exceptionally good quality—it simply needed a good cleaning.

"Shh!" the librarian once again yelled, being hypocritical of her rules.

Jade mumbled several profanities in response. The one that stuck out the most was the word that rhymes with "duck." Keagan snorted but said nothing to agree with her. Abigail and Brielle continued looking through their textbooks until Abigail slammed hers shut. The librarian shushed them for a fourth time, but she ignored them.

"I've had it," Abigail declared in an annoyed whisper. "Thank you all for trying to help, but it's useless. I'll never learn all of this in time."

Keagan protested, "Don't say that! If we put all our heads together, we'll figure it out in no time. Just wait and see."

"No, I can't do it," she persisted firmly. "It's way too much."

"Yes, you can. It sucks right now, but when you pass that placement test, you'll feel so much better," Jade encouraged her with optimism.

"But then, I'll have to learn AP Calculus a year ahead than I thought I would. I can't do it. Is it even worth it just to get away from him?"

"Sure, it is," Keagan confirmed, smiling softly. "He's a prick, so you're doing what needs to be done and getting away from him. If it'll make you feel safer, then it's more than worth it. Your mental health is much more important than a silly class."

"What if the class is affecting your mental health? This is making me feel *so* much better about the situation." Abigail spat sarcastically.

Abigail whirled around at a tap on her shoulder. It was Brielle, who quietly spoke up, "Maybe it would be more helpful if you could get someone who already knows Precalculus to teach you," she offered another solution. "You know...since none of us know all of it. I can keep working on this if you want, but I don't know it all already."

"I don't know anyone who knows all of Precalculus," Abigail noted with a pout.

The table grew silent. It was even quieter than what a library was supposed to be. Silence ensued so intensely that a pin dropping could have been heard. The words in the textbook in front of Abigail grew to be blurry as her mind began to wander. Brielle continued flipping through her own Precalculus textbook while Jade scrolled on her phone. Keagan was oddly quiet and staring at the ceiling as if she was pondering something.

Abigail's head flew towards Keagan when she snapped her fingers. "I've got it!"

"What?" she asked almost nervously.

"What about the guy with the big glasses? He seems smart and you kinda know him." Keagan's face was beaming with pride.

Abigail tensed. She hadn't thought of that. With everything going on, she truthfully forgot about Noah and his glasses debacle. "Noah? Why him?"

"Oh, *that's* his name!" Keagan finally came to a conclusion.

All four of the teenage girls ignored the librarian who shushed them yet again.

Brielle smiled at the suggestion. "That sounds like a good idea. I mean, if you're comfortable with it, then it sounds good," she clarified.

"Yeah!" Keagan agreed quite loudly. "Let's go find him and see!"

The librarian stood from her desk, her tight blonde curls bouncing as she did so. "That's it!" she boomed angrily. "Out! Out— all of you or I'll give you four a detention each!"

"Can a librarian do that?" Jade whispered to her friends. The three of them shrugged.

Abigail, Jade, Brielle, and Keagan were then forced to gather their belongings and exit the library. The table was as neat as a pin once the four were completed. The librarian did as much as shooing them out of the premises with a ruler in her right hand. Keagan was tempted to dare the librarian to hit her with it, but Brielle clamped a hand over her mouth once she began her proposition and dragged her out behind the others.

The four of them walked in a row towards their lockers one at a time to return their respected items to their holding spaces. Abigail appeared to be hesitant for the entire journey between the library and the cafeteria. Once her hands were free, her left index finger's nail was being gnawed at due to the anxiety she felt unsteadily pound in her chest. When one of her friends - Jade - looked her way out of concern, she quickly removed her nail from her mouth and played it off as messing around with her long black hair, which was worn down like it usually was.

The foursome purchased their usual meals in Hillwell High's lunchroom. Like the very unfortunate normality of Brielle's, she barely had enough to purchase lunch, so Keagan persuaded her to let her treat her to lunch. It took at least five minutes of holding up the lunch line, but Brielle eventually caved and Keagan bought her not just a salad, but fries as well. Even though Brielle wanted to let her shattering pride get in the way, she was grateful.

"So, when are you gonna talk to him?" Keagan eagerly questioned Abigail once the four of them sat down.

Abigail shrugged unenthusiastically. "Maybe after lunch. I honestly don't know."

"You know," Jade proposed between two bites of her burger, "We could continue to work on it together. We already got four chapters done and have eleven to go. It'll easily get done in a week if we do it together and by ourselves."

"But none of us know the material and we're BS-ing our way through it," Keagan reasoned with her. "If we keep doing this nonsense, Abi will end up learning nothing and have a better chance of failing the test rather than passing it."

"Gee. Thanks, Keagan." Abigail's brows furrowed at her friend.

Brielle frowned and looked at Keagan. "You could've said that in a tamer way."

"I know." Keagan cringed at her word choice. "I guess I could've. Sorry, Abi."

"It's fine. I'm going to fail the placement test anyway, so why bother?" Abigail grumbled at near unintelligence.

"Not necessarily," Brielle assured her. "I'm sure you'll do just fine, especially if you get some assistance from someone who actually knows what they're doing."

Keagan grinned with a fry in her mouth. "Yeah! When are you going to ask the glasses dude about helping you?"

"I was thinking about doing it after lunch." Abigail shrugged. She practically inhaled half of a chicken tender a second later.

"Why do you always get chicken tenders?"

"Why do you always get the chicken salad?" countered Abigail swiftly.

"Touché," Keagan pointed out in a matter-of-fact tone.

Neither of them noticed the slight remnant of a sour expression on Jade's face. The blonde who wore her hair in light, wavy curls kept to herself for most of the conversation. Brielle gave her a quick glance, noticing Jade's unfamiliar attitude. Once she did so, Jade instantly smiled like it was with the flip of a switch. Brielle found it scary how Jade switched her demeanor so quickly and effectively.

"Are you okay?" Brielle timidly asked Jade, who was munching away at her fries.

"Huh?" Jade blinked at her and then recollected herself. "Yeah, I'm perfectly fine. Why?"

"Just making sure."

Brielle decided that that moment, there was something off with Jade. Was she going to interrogate her about it? Likely not. Was it a problem that she was planning on speaking with the rest of the girls about later? Quite possibly. Brielle figured it was none of her business when it came to Jade's decision to say anything about whatever was bothering her. So, she kept it to herself. Jade silently appreciated Brielle's effort, but Brielle did not know about that.

The rest of the lunch period passed by both quickly and agonizingly slowly. Abigail caught herself checking the time on her phone a countless number of times. With each minute that passed, she was closer to retrieving her last resort—her final cry for help. Abigail had no idea what else to do with the awful hand that had been dealt to her of the deck of cards called life. Her five cards were enough to make any gambler cry out in frustration. The last thing Abigail wanted to do was fold and let whatever fortune she previously had yanked away from her.

From the second the lunch hour ended to the moment Abigail was exiting the cafeteria with the four of her friends, anxiety was crawling up her throat. Abigail felt as if she was going to be sick from the amount of pressure she had put on herself. Rather than her mind being filled with the principles of Precalculus - like it was supposed to, according to her - it was swarmed with every single possible outcome of what would happen if she spoke to Noah about her ambition. She thought that he would think it was an absurd idea. Truthfully, her line of thought was quite flawed, but there was no time to correct her error now.

Abigail felt her hands begin to shake relentlessly, so she shoved them into the pockets of her oversized unzipped gray jacket. She resisted the urge to gnaw at her poor nails which had received enough of a beating throughout the past few weeks. Anxiety filled her from her shell to her core. It was enough to add an uncertainty to each step. Abigail grimaced as her black high tops squeaked against the tiled floor as she walked.

Her friends had all left to their respective classes after questioning Abigail's well-being, which she lied about. With all honesty, she was not completely alright. In fact, she was not okay at all. The last thing Abigail wanted was to learn more math than she ever needed to in order to avoid someone who instilled such fear in her. She thought she had escaped. Unfortunately, that was far from the case. *He* was right under her nose this entire time. For months, Abigail believed she was away from his wrath over her mind. Now, she needed to work extra hard to make sure that was true.

Abigail took the now-familiar route towards Noah's locker with her AP Government textbook in hand. The boy in question was at his locker in search of his AP Calculus textbook, which Abigail noticed he had been becoming quicker at doing so. She caught herself hesitating before approaching him, which was what she expected. What kind of person would walk over to a boy they barely knew to enlist them into tutoring them on the entirety of Precalculus?

"Keep it together. If he says no, it's not the end of the world. You have three friends who love you enough to suffer through it with you."

The teenage girl then put on her poker face and wished sunglasses were allowed in the premises of Hillwell High. It was a ridiculous rule, and one Abigail did not understand. Why was a harmless accessory banned to be worn over someone's eyes while indoors? It surely helped with her anxiety to cover her wide, worried eyes and leave her as a seemingly emotionless mess. Abigail shrugged off her unnecessary thoughts and focused on her task at hand.

When she deemed it the right time, Abigail cleared her throat from a couple lockers away from Noah. At the sound, he abruptly turned towards her and shut his locker door. The combination lock clicked as he adjusted it. Noah eyed her with a confused expression, but there was a bit of nervousness in his eyes that quickly flickered away.

"Oh—hey, Abigail," he greeted her, attempting to be as composed as possible, which was not hard for him.

"Hey, Noah," Abigail quietly replied. Her eyes flitted towards the floor, but then back at him as she contemplated what to say. "You're smart, right?"

"Seriously? You blurt that out? It's not like he'll respond with "No, I'm an effing idiot." You're such a moron." Abigail could have slapped herself due to that statement.

Noah was unequipped to answer that question. He was tongue-tied until he stuttered out an uncertain answer, "...I'd hope so? Why?"

"Well...um...," Abigail stammered over her thoughts. After an uncomfortable amount of time passed, she added on sheepishly, "I'm not dumb; I promise."

"You're fine. Take your time."

Why was Noah so patient with her? Abigail saw herself as a stumbling fool who could not even generate a short sentence out of her lightly chapped lips. She glanced up at Noah for a short second, who was quietly waiting for whatever she had to say. What *did* Abigail have to say? She had no idea, even though she rehearsed it in the depths of her mind for the entirety of the lunch period and on her trek to his locker. Then, a realization hit her. She had an advantage.

"So, Noah...," Abigail timidly began.

His eyes darted to hers again at the sound of his name. "Yeah?"

"Do you remember when you said you owed me or something?"

Abigail's question caught Noah by surprise. He had to think back to when he lost his glasses in the first place, which was when he professed that statement to her without even thinking twice about it. "Uh, yeah," he tentatively responded. "Last Monday, right?"

"Yeah." Abigail nodded with uncertainty. "Well...I was thinking, and I've been having a little problem with math."

"Really? Which math are you in?" Noah asked her. He was a bit astonished to say the least.

"I'm in Precalculus," she supplied. "Do you happen to be good at math?"

Noah briefly pondered over it and then offered her a small smile. "Well, I've somehow made my way up to AP Calculus, so I'd hope so."

"You're in AP Calculus?" Abigail questioned with a slight eager undertone.

"Does that surprise you?"

"Actually, no, it doesn't." She shifted her weight from one foot to the other. "Nerds are smart. Right?"

One of Noah's eyebrows raised. "Oh. So, I'm a nerd now?" he inquired playfully. Abigail nodded. "What gave it away? The glasses?"

"Yep! Any luck on finding them, by the way?"

"Nope." Noah's demeanor appeared to completely change as he frowned slightly.

"Oh." Abigail felt a rush of guilt pulsate through her. "They'll show up."

"I know. What was it that you were initially going to say?"

Abigail blinked blankly at the sudden change in subject. It took her brain a couple of seconds to register. "Oh, um...this is a really weird favor to ask, and it's a lot to explain, but basically I need to get into an AP Calculus class as soon as possible. The only way to do that is to take a placement test a week from tomorrow and get at least an eighty-five on it. I was wondering if maybe...you'd be able to help me learn the rest of Precalculus before I take it? My friends tried to help me, but none of them knew more than I did and it was awful."

Silence ensued, which made Abigail's heart drop. Then...

"Okay."

"Wait...*really*? Are you serious?" Abigail choked out.

"If I wasn't, I wouldn't have agreed." Noah shrugged calmly. "It may be a little confusing, but it's not my place to ask what's going on. It sounds like you really need it, so why not?"

A small smile grew across Abigail's reluctant face. "Oh, my God. Thank you so much," she exhaled with relief. "You have no idea how important this is to me."

"It's not a problem." Abigail's grin was soon discovered to be contagious by Noah. "So, when were you thinking? Is tomorrow afternoon after school okay for studying?"

Abigail opened her mouth to confirm, but she remembered what occurred every Tuesday and Friday afternoon. She couldn't afford missing a therapy session with Kristy, even if it was only one. They helped keep her sane. "Uh, can we do it tonight?" she blurted out without thinking. "I can't do Fridays...or Tuesdays for that matter."

"Oh, okay." Noah's eyebrows scrunched together in a quizzical nature. "Did you want to do it at my house or something? I recently moved to the Highland Heights neighborhood."

She stopped in her mental tracks. Abigail was not about to mention the fact that she and Noah were apparently neighbors. "Actually, I know a place near school that would be nice. I go there in the mornings sometimes to finish extra work. It's called the Express-O Café and if you go straight down the road on your way home, it's to your left at the second streetlight. You can't miss it."

"That's alright with me. What time would work for you?"

"Uh, seven?" Abigail suggested a random time. "It closes at like ten."

Noah nodded to confirm. "Yeah, that's okay with me," he replied, but then thought of something else important. "Um, should I get your number just in case I get lost and need directions there?"

Abigail was at a standstill. She did not want to share her number with anyone, especially a person of the opposite gender. It did not matter that Noah seemed trustworthy. So did *he*. Abigail refused to take any chances with Noah like she did for *him*. She realized she was in a bit of an awkward spot, so she shook her head.

"You can look it up no problem," she muttered hastily.

"Oh, uh-" Noah started, puzzled.

"I'm sorry," Abigail interrupted before he was able to conclude, "I have to go to class now, but I'll see you tonight. Thank you, again!"

Noah watched as she whirled around him to arrive at her next class. "...See you tonight."

Abigail was silently apologetic as she walked away. She did not mean to rush so quickly out of Noah's line of sight. Her anxiety got the best of her and she needed to make an escape. She brought her finger up to her mouth and began chewing on the nail but stopped when a throb of pain throttled through it. Abigail forced herself to look on the bright side. Her plan to avoid *him* was flowing swimmingly. All she needed to do was pass the placement test, and with Noah's help, hopefully it would be better the second time around.

Speaking of the boy, Abigail narrowly missed the lingering smile on his face as she strode down the hall and away from him.

8

"ARE YOU SURE YOU'RE OKAY?"

"I can't do this, Keagan," Abigail confessed hurriedly into the phone.

"Sure, you can, Abi!" Keagan's clear voice chirped from the other line. *"I'm sure doing math with the big glasses dude will be fine, and if it's not, you only have to do it for just over a week. It'll be over before you know it."*

Abigail furiously typed at her laptop while she sat at her desk. Her phone was set to her left face-up with Keagan's contact on the screen while the two talked on speakerphone. The call had lasted for about seventeen minutes at that point. Abigail was attempting to complete a British Literature assignment before she was to embark on her first studying adventure with Noah. She wished she was able to say she was looking forward to it. In all honesty, she was terrified.

"I don't know," she shakily exhaled. "This is probably a really, *really* bad idea. I hardly know him and now I'm meeting him somewhere? Especially after what happened?"

Keagan hesitated, which only made Abigail type louder out of spite. She knew her friend could easily hear her. *"You're meeting in a public place, right?"* she finally asked.

"Yeah—we're meeting at the Express-O Café in fifteen minutes, but I'm not sure if I want to go anymore."

"Do you have his number? You can always reschedule."

"I actually refused to give him my number," Abigail admitted. She felt like smacking herself due to how stupid her decision sounded.

"You what?!"

"I know; I know," she sighed and saved her assignment to her laptop, closing out the program a second later. Abigail couldn't be bothered by schoolwork at that moment. "It sounds really stupid, but I didn't feel safe with him having my number."

A soft melody was being fingerpicked on the other line. It sounded as if Keagan was playing the acoustic guitar while she spoke, *"Oh, I'm sorry for overreacting. It doesn't sound stupid at all. I understand. You could just...not go."*

"I don't want to stand him up, though," Abigail wailed as she leaned far back in her rolling chair with her eyes shut.

"You know, Abi," Keagan reasoned carefully, *"You need to put yourself first. You can always explain it to him at school tomorrow."*

"It would still be rude of me."

"Maybe a little bit, but like you said, you hardly know him."

Abigail groaned in frustration. "Wasn't it your idea to ask him in the first place?" she snapped unintentionally.

"It was, but you know I'm not the sharpest knife in the drawer." Keagan's voice was very calm. The acoustic guitar in the background reflected her tone harmoniously. *"Your safety and well-being come first and foremost."*

"It's too late to back out now."

She heard Keagan stop playing her guitar. *"Would you like me to come with you?"* she offered genuinely.

Abigail sat back up in her chair and took the phone in her hands. "I think I'm okay, but thank you, Keagan. That means a lot to me."

"No problem!"

"Thanks for listening to me freak out for the past twenty minutes, but I should probably get ready and leave now," she expressed with a slight change in attitude for the better.

"You're welcome," Keagan beamed brightly. *"Text me if you need anything. I'll just be suffering from this Brit Lit assignment for the next three hours."*

"Okay, I will," Abigail laughed. "Bye, Keagan."

"Bye, Abi!"

Abigail hung up the phone and stuffed it into the center pocket of her faded red hoodie. Her brown eyes were almost glossy as they stared up at the ceiling. The fan overhead slowly turned to create just the slightest amount of noise to keep her sane from dead silence. She watched as each blade quivered as it seemed to grow more gradual by the second. Abigail compared the fan blades to her overall emotions at that moment. It was very fragile, but still moving. She clenched her hands into fists

She reluctantly got to her feet and pulled on her black high-top shoes along with grabbing her math textbook on the way out. Abigail attempted to hide the woozy feeling her body hindered whilst the anxiety throttled through her veins. It was almost too much to handle. She wobbled out of her room as if she had drunk too much after switching the light off and giving it one last look. That room was her safe space, where she was able to be comforted whenever she needed. Now, she was leaving it.

Her keys jingled in her hands after she grabbed them from their place on a hook on the wall when she reached the first floor of her home. Abigail put her sunglasses on top of her head and was about to open the front door, but a voice stopped her in her tracks.

"Hey, Abigail!" her mother called out from the kitchen. "Where are you off to?"

"Oh, uh...I'm going to a friend's so we can study for a Precalculus quiz on Monday," she miserably faltered.

Lillian turned off the sink. She was washing the dishes from dinner not long beforehand. "That sounds very nice, Honey. Which friend?"

"Jade," Abigail blurted out the first name that came to mind.

"Oh, she's a nice girl," Lillian commented with a smile. "Drive safe and be careful. Okay?"

"Text when you get there!" Abigail's father reminded her from the living room where he was watching television.

Lillian turned towards her husband on the couch. "Harold—she knows."

"I just thought I'd remind her," he said with a shrug.

"I'll text," Abigail told them reassuringly, laughing softly. "Bye, Mom. Bye, Dad."

"Love you!" Lillian exclaimed as her daughter opened the front door.

"Love you too."

Abigail could not have shut the front door quickly enough. She already felt guilty about lying to her parents, especially after what had happened before. Instead of dwelling on it for the entire evening, though, she decided to get a move on with her life and not let it bother her. Her racing mind was relentless as she unlocked her gray car and sat in the driver's seat. Abigail did not move a single muscle when her vehicle was turned on and her usual music blared through the speakers.

Despite the sun nearly concealed under the horizon, she briskly removed her sunglasses from on top of her head and placed them on her face. Abigail hesitated and took them off, wiping them off on her sweatshirt sleeve before putting them on again. Her heart pounded ruthlessly in her chest, nearly over the sound of the engine as she drove off. Abigail ignored the fact she nearly left skid marks in her poor parents' driveway.

Even though Abigail was dreading meeting Noah at the Express-O Café, she found herself driving three to five miles per hour over the speed limit. Her foot was pushed further down on the gas pedal than it needed to be. Abigail thought she was holding her breath for the entire time she was driving towards the cafe, which was no more than five minutes from her home. The very second that she peeled into the parking lot, she exhaled deeply and the dizziness poking her forehead faded away.

After sending the promised text announcing her arrival to her father, she forced her jittery legs to move as she exited her car and held her textbook to her abdomen like it was some sort of protective chestplate. Abigail locked the gray vehicle and grasped her keys in her hands. She had no idea if it was instinct or pure coincidence that she was holding her key with the point between her knuckles for protection. Abigail dreaded the thought of her past repeating itself. She grimaced when she noticed her hand gripping her keys was visibly shaking.

Abigail carefully pushed open the door to the Express-O Café directly after removing her sunglasses and placing them on top of her head. The building was a homey one with a white exterior and a pale pink and brown sign with a coffee mug and the café's name on it. Despite its interior, Abigail knew to never judge a book by its cover. She did that before and refused to do it again, especially with a boy she hardly knew.

"God, Abigail—you're such an idiot," she reprimanded herself.

The door shut behind her with an abrupt slam. Abigail attempted to suppress her jump when it did so. She was already on her toes. The last thing she needed was something to catch her completely off-guard.

"Hey, Abigail. Are you okay? I didn't mean to startle you." Noah's voice from a couple yards away startled her out of her pinkened skin.

Abigail slowly turned to view Noah, who was leaning against a wall near the front door. He was sporting a white graphic t-shirt and dark jeans along with a pair of high tops. She determined he was scrolling on his phone with one hand and holding a notebook while waiting for her to arrive. A mechanical pencil was resting behind his left ear. A wave of embarrassment washed over her at the realization she almost tipped over due to her unfortunate footing. Her eyes darted towards the floor, which looked to be recently cleaned, before they reached him again.

"Hi, uh, yeah...sorry," Abigail stammered with an awkward smile. "I didn't mean to keep you waiting. Have you been here long?"

Noah shook his head and put his phone in his jacket pocket. "I just got here about two minutes ago, actually. Don't worry about it," he explained coolly.

"Oh, okay." She rocked herself back and forth on her heels.

"...So, did you want to get some drinks or something?" Noah asked after a moment of hesitation from the both of them.

Abigail mentally smacked herself back to reality. "Oh, I'm okay for now. It's probably too late to have caffeine or I'll be up really late."

"Yeah, that's probably the best idea," Noah agreed.

"Where'd you want to sit?" questioned Abigail while her eyes scanned the interior of the building.

Noah shrugged. There were plenty of places to choose from since hardly anyone was in the restaurant. Only about three tables were occupied, mostly with college students or adults. "How about that one?" He pointed out a table near one of the windows.

"That's fine."

The two of them walked over towards that table and sat down across from each other. Abigail set down her textbook on the table. She removed several sheets of notebook paper covered with her messy handwriting that she had stuffed in there while studying with Jade, Brielle, and Keagan along with a pencil. Meanwhile, Noah opened his notebook and retrieved his own mechanical pencil from behind his ear, clicking the top of it to view the lead.

"Could you explain to me what exactly you want to work on?" Noah dated the top of the page of his notebook that he flipped to.

Abigail blankly stared down at her previous work. "As I said earlier, I need to learn all of Precalculus...and I need to know it all before next Friday for a placement test," her voice wavered as she explained. "I've already learned the first two chapters in class and my friends tried to go over chapters three and four with me, but I don't remember much. I looked at it before coming over here, but I don't think I understand it."

"Can I see your book?"

Abigail nodded and passed it over to him. She uncomfortably waited while he flipped through the beginning pages of her textbook. Noah skimmed the first two chapters of the book and then turned to the third, the fourth following after that. While he did so, he scribbled down bits and pieces of each chapter section, which made

Abigail impatient since it took at least five minutes. Before long, Noah slid the textbook back over to her and looked down at his full page of notes.

"Sorry, I was just making sure I knew exactly what's going on," he apologized. "I took Precalculus last year, but it's good to have a recap."

"Yeah, that's true," Abigail replied half-heartedly.

Noah glanced at his notes and began to read. "So, do you understand the first two chapters comprehensively?"

"...I guess so. I got 'A's on the quizzes in class."

"That's good." Noah gave her one of his genuine smiles. "How about chapters three and four?"

"That's complicated," Abigail pointed out cheekily.

He tilted his head slightly. "Elaborate?" he requested.

"Well...," Abigail considered. The tension in the room was so thick that it was suffocating her from the inside out. She decided to lighten the mood. "If you give me a sample problem from anywhere other than chapters one and two, I guarantee you that I won't be able to solve it."

"Oh, I see," chuckled Noah with amusement. "Let's start with the basics of chapter three, then. Shall we?"

Abigail nodded, a reddish tinge of embarrassment flooding her cheeks. "Okay."

She brushed her hair out of her face and tucked it in place with her sunglasses. Noah started to explain the fundamentals of the third chapter in her textbook. Abigail wished she had brought more paper to take notes with, but she simply decided to listen instead. Despite despising the subject, she had a motive to follow and a plan in place. It was too late to back out now, especially when she had someone willing and capable to come to her aid.

Abigail listened carefully while Noah walked her through the main concept of the third and fourth chapters before moving onto the fifth, the end of which being where Abigail drew the fine line. She caught herself beginning to understand the material due to the way Noah was explaining it thoroughly and patiently with her and had been for at least a couple of hours. Abigail hated to admit she was bored, but that was all math was to her: boring.

Noah let out a frustrated sigh when a small snap of lead breaking off of his pencil was heard. He glanced down at his mechanical pencil and clicked the top of it several times, but none of the lead popped out. Abigail was too busy reading her textbook to notice him glaring at the poor pencil and searching through his pockets for any more containers of lead for it.

"Why didn't I bring another pencil?" Noah asked himself.

He then looked at Abigail, who was distracted and decided to inquire, "Hey, can I borrow your pencil for a second so I can finish writing this down?" As he did so, he abruptly reached over the table for the very object, which was a bad idea.

Once Abigail saw his hand quickly heading towards her, she flinched away from it. Her own pencil crashed down onto the floor. Her textbook would have followed, but Abigail caught it before it was able to slide off the surface of the table. It only took a second to realize what exactly she had done. Abigail was vulnerable around someone she hardly knew. She recoiled and grabbed her pencil from off the floor, attempting to ignore what had just happened.

She hated it.

"Here's the pencil," she mumbled and flung the thin object at him.

Noah attempted to catch it, but it inevitably hit him in the face. He fixed his spare glasses from where they moved due to the pencil hitting it. He awkwardly caught the pencil in his lap and held it in his hand before quickly finishing the last word of the bullet point. Noah set the pencil back in front of her and refused to meet her eyes for at least ten seconds. When he looked up, a sharp breath caught in his throat as he noticed the exact emotion flooding her brown irises.

Fear.

Abigail was afraid.

A thought instantly rushed through his mind when it came to why such a strong feeling was embedded in her system. Noah pretended not to let it affect him, but it seemed as if he had already figured it out. He kept it to himself. Once again, Noah determined what Abigail was going through was none of his business. If she wanted to say anything, she would say anything, but then again, she hardly knew him.

Noah cleared his throat, which caused Abigail's gaze to snap up to meet his. "I'm sorry if I startled you," he sincerely apologized. "I didn't mean to. Are you okay?"

"Yeah, I'm okay," Abigail muttered in an attempt to keep her cool. She shook her head and the fear from her eyes was gone. "Can we finish for tonight, though?"

"That's fine. When did you want to meet again to go over the next few chapters?"

"When are you free?" she inquired while gathering her things.

"Whenever's fine. We can talk tomorrow at school." Noah ripped out the page including his notes out of his notebook and handed it to her. The paper nearly tore at least twice, but it was still functional. "Here you go; these will be helpful as you study. I'll write more for you at our next session."

Abigail chewed on her lip guiltily. "Thank you, but...should I be paying you for this?" she squeaked. "You really don't have to help me this much."

"That's not necessary. You look like you already have enough on your plate," Noah assured her.

"But...," she started to protest helplessly.

"How about you buy me a drink next time and then we'll be even?"

"Deal."

By the time Abigail and Noah exited the Express-O Cafe, the sky was a midnight blue. The half-moon illuminated the sky along with the streetlights making the newly paved asphalt beneath them glow and sparkle minimalistically. The parking lot was nearly empty other than Abigail's gray vehicle sitting close to the front of the lot and the desolate cars parked near the back that belonged to employees.

Abigail pulled her keys out of her pocket and pressed the "unlock" button. The gray car's headlights flashed before resting on their normal setting. Her eyes darted over to Noah, who held his notebook under his arm. He was awkwardly standing on the curb with his nondominant hand in the pocket of his jeans. Abigail's eyebrows furrowed at the sight. Why was he not approaching his own vehicle?

Unless...

"Did you walk here?" Abigail carefully asked him.

Noah shrugged nonchalantly. "Yeah, I did," he replied. "We only have one car and my mom was at work when I left, so it was the most convenient."

"Oh, um...," she faltered over the situation. Eventually, she spat out an offer before she was able to think about it. "Would you like a ride home? It's the least I could do."

"I can't ask you to go out of your way like that," he argued in surprise.

"I live in the Highland Heights neighborhood as well. It wouldn't be more than a couple minutes out of my way. Then, we'd *really* be even."

Noah pointed an incredulous look in her direction. "Are you sure?"

"I'm sure."

With several unasked questions floating around in his head, Noah chose not to argue and got into the passenger's seat while Abigail did the same with the driver's side. She plugged her phone into the charging port and shut the door behind him at the same time Noah executed the latter. Abigail inserted her key into the ignition and turned it sideways. At once, the music she was used to played at a loud volume through the car's speakers. Abigail felt a sense of dread surge through her when she noticed Noah almost fall out of his seat and cover his ears.

"Holy sh-" he began to swear, but he covered it up once Abigail turned the volume knob almost to mute. "...That's loud."

"I'm sorry. I'm not used to driving people around," Abigail cringed, clenching her teeth together.

"Do you usually listen to stuff this loud? That's bad for your ears," Noah stated. He slowly removed his hands from over his ears.

Abigail looked at him with a blank expression. "What?" she questioned innocently.

When Noah didn't respond, a small smile graced her lips. "I'm joking, Noah. My ears are just fine."

"Oh," he sheepishly responded and averted eye contact.

Abigail switched the gear to reverse and backed out of her parking spot after looking behind her to ensure herself it was safe. Then, she drove off down the familiar route towards her house that she had lived in longer than she was able to remember. Even though her eyes were glazed over with anxiety due to what she was doing, she kept her gaze on the road. Abigail tried to ignore the fact that a boy she hardly knew was inches away from her. Her knuckles clenched the wheel so tightly that they turned paler than they already were.

Noah couldn't help but notice her tense demeanor. He kept his fingers knotted together in his lap and his eyes facing in front of him, but every so often, he glanced over at her. He knew there was something serious going on with her. First, the flinch from his sudden movement and then this. Noah didn't want her to be frightened of him. The pieces of the puzzle were slowly falling into place. He refused to become one of the missing additions.

Instead of creating thicker tension, Noah decided to change the subject. "Thank you again for driving me home." He tensed up when he noticed the tiniest of winces from Abigail because of his sudden voice over the quiet music. "Since I recently moved, I don't know the town well and it'd be even worse at night."

"It's not a problem." Her voice was clipped. "What's your address?"

"Uh, two fifty-three Precipice Way." Noah had to think over it for a second.

Abigail bit her tongue. She was not about to tell him she lived on the adjacent street. "I know exactly where that is," she commented quietly.

"Alright."

The silence between them was quite awkward. Abigail gripped the wheel as tightly as possible as she drove through the neighborhood she knew and loved. Noah remained quiet for the rest of the drive. He had nothing to say to her and she had nothing to say to him. Even though the quiet was undesirable, it was peaceful at the same time. Abigail slowly felt herself begin to calm down while she approached the Howells' household.

She eventually pulled into the driveway in front of Noah's modest home, which appeared perfect on the outside, but who knew what was on the inside? Abigail switched the gear to park, which caused Noah to snap out of whatever trance he was in while looking out his window. Fatigue mixed with worry and guilt was very draining. He looked over to Abigail, whose gaze landed on her lap.

"Are you sure you're okay?" Noah's voice was a whisper.

Abigail paused before nodding. "Yeah, I'm okay. Thank you," she confirmed.

"No problem."

"No, I mean it," Abigail firmly insisted. "Seriously, thank you. For everything. You have no clue how much this means to me."

Noah offered her one of his smiles that she was slowly growing to find contagious. "You're welcome, Abigail."

"So...I'll see you in class tomorrow?" Abigail had nothing else to say. She internally berated herself for seeming so dismissal.

Instead of appearing offended, Noah nodded. "Yeah. See you then."

With that, Noah exited Abigail's car and walked around the hood. Abigail watched as he stepped onto the porch and turned around to her surprise. He gave her a small wave, which she timidly returned. Abigail felt uncomfortable enough being parked in his driveway, so she quickly backed out of the concrete runway and sped off towards her own street.

Once again, Abigail failed to notice Noah discreetly watching her as she departed.

9

"YOU SHOVED ME OFF THE TOILET."

FEAR.

To some people, fear was a foreign concept. Said people lived in the luxury of not having to worry about every single aspect of their lives. Every breath did not have to make them anxious. Every person failed to cause them terror. Not everyone lived in fear. A lot of people still wonder today how a portion of the population can physically exist without that very emotion strangling them at each turn.

Fear revealed itself to its victims in many ways. For some, it tended to be gradual, slowly beginning with desolate worry. Later, it transitioned to nervosity, followed by anxiety. On rare occasions, the anxiety would turn into terror. Sometimes, the last stage came into existence without any warning or eventual buildup. That - terror - was the worst type of fear. Luckily, it was seldom brought to the surface for most of the world's humans.

However, to a poor unfortunate soul, the seldom moment was thoroughly divulged.

Slivers of light peeped through the blinds covering a window facing the sun, which was slowly rising in the east. The modestly sized bedroom was at a low level of light. Other than the miniscule amount of sunlight creeping its way into the room, there were no other sources. Darkness crowded every nook and cranny, including the bed in one of the dimmest corners where a young teenager laid.

Sweat trickled down the adolescent boy's head, wetting his hair and dripping onto the pillow underneath it. The small droplets glistened, reflecting the little sunlight that gained access to the room. On the outside, everything was peaceful. Fan blades turned agonizingly slow from the ceiling. A slight breeze rustled itself across the carpet before wafting up into the above air vent. Everything in that room was peaceful, or at least peaceful on the exterior.

Then, he woke up.

Noah lurched upright out of bed as a heavy gasp inflated his lungs. His eyes flung open to that peaceful room, which was not so tranquil after all. The empty room was suddenly filled with the sound of his heart pounding in his ears. Noah held his hand against his chest and began to take slow, deep breaths. His head throbbed with each inhale and exhale. It felt as if his lungs were stretching further than their capacity.

His vision appeared to lag as he turned his head towards his phone that was resting - unlike him - on the nightstand next to his bed. Noah glared at the blurry alarm screen on his phone and aggressively turned it off. He fumbled around for his glasses which were formerly next to his phone and slid them on his face. Despite having the correct prescription, they didn't feel the same as his old, missing pair.

Noah fought to keep his eyes open while he prepared for the long day ahead of him. After a shower, a change of clothes, brushing his teeth, washing his face, and making sure his hair did not resemble a bird's nest, he approached his backpack that rested near his bedroom door. Noah sifted through the contents to ensure he had all his textbooks, stationary supplies, and homework for that day. It was the last time he needed to do so before the weekend, but Noah still cared just as much as he would on a Monday morning.

After at least three minutes of filing through his work, he slung the right arm of his backpack over his shoulder. Noah's jaw rattled in a near-silent yawn while he walked down the stairs towards the first floor. He took each step carefully while his backpack slightly wobbled with every movement. Noah let his hand hover over the handrail.

When he was about halfway down, not one, but two heads of wavy light blonde hair pushed past him to race downstairs. Noah attempted to catch himself, wobbling and clinging onto the handrail as he watched the two small humans fight for the leading position for the floor. He shook his head when the two lookalike girls bumped into each other and instantly started to argue.

"Lucy!" the shorter one by one inch yelled. "I was here first!"

The taller one - Lucy - folded her arms over her chest and frowned. "Lacy, you started this whole thing by pushing me out of the bathroom."

"But you continued it!" Lacy dramatically whined.

"You shoved me off the toilet."

"Girls," Noah started to calmly protest, but the waves of the sibling argument washed over his words.

"Yeah, and it was really funny too!" Lacy giggled like her action was the punchline of the most hilarious joke in the entire world.

Lucy frowned bitterly. "I have a bruise on my bottom now."

"Girls," Noah repeated a little bit louder.

Now, the two of them were fighting on the floor in front of the stairwell. "You shouldn't have spent twenty minutes in there when we *both* need to go to school soon," Lacy retorted.

"We have three bathrooms: one downstairs, the master bathroom, and the other upstairs bathroom," Lucy reminded her. "You could've just used the master."

"Noah was taking a shower in there."

"So? There's one downstairs too, and I was almost done."

"The downstairs one doesn't have a shower."

"You took one last night."

"Girls!" Noah's voice finally retrieved their attention. Both girls stared at him with two pairs of identical brown eyes. Their older brother sighed. "Does this really have to happen every single morning?"

"Yes!" Lacy shouted at the same time Lucy mumbled, "No."

Noah stifled another tired sigh. "Please try not to argue. It gets really tiring," he informed them yet again. He looked at Lacy. "Don't push your sister off the toilet. You know better than that. Wait your turn."

If Noah was not so exhausted, he would have found the situation quite amusing.

"Sorry, Noah," Lacy reluctantly apologized to which Lucy nodded.

Noah paused for a second. When Lucy said nothing in response to her sister, he urged her, "What do you say when someone apologizes to you?"

"It's okay," Lucy forced out under her breath.

"That's better," Noah told them. He ruffled Lacy's hair and then moved onto Lucy's. "Thank you both. That wasn't so hard, was it?"

"Yes," Lucy replied at the same time Lacy said, "No."

Noah was unable to prevent a chuckle at that. "Alright—how about we get you two some breakfast. Is Mom making anything?"

"I think she's making eggs and bacon!" Lacy excitedly exclaimed.

"Oh, that sounds good."

Lacy clasped onto Noah's hand and dragged her older brother into the kitchen so quickly that his backpack nearly fell off his arm. Lucy followed behind quietly. The pink skirt she was wearing bounced slightly while she walked, revealing the white shorts she wore underneath. Lacy's fern green dress reached halfway between her knee and her ankle. Noah suddenly felt underdressed with his black Van Halen hoodie and blue jeans with a hole in the knee.

For some reason, his sisters loved to wear dresses and skirts to school despite being in the fifth grade. Other than the fact their mother loved to dress them up, Noah had no idea why his younger siblings would wear such clothing. When he was younger, he never let his mom pick out his outfits and dress him up. Instead, he was very independent and still was today. Perhaps Noah's wardrobe full of hoodies, t-shirts, and jeans was self-explanatory.

A crackling sound of breakfast cooking welcomed the three siblings. The footsteps entering the kitchen instantly caused their mother - Jennifer "Jenny" Howell - to turn around. "Good morning, everyone!" She warmly greeted her children. "Who's ready for some eggs and bacon?"

"Me!" the twins chorused.

Noah watched as the two girls raced towards the kitchen table and sat in seats across from one another. Instead of waiting like his sisters did, he turned to his mother. "Do you want any help?" he asked her.

"That'd actually be great; thank you," Jenny replied from the stove.

Noah approached his mother and gave her a quick peck on the cheek like he did every morning before that. "No problem. What can I do?"

"Can you set the plates and I'll clean up everything else?" requested Jenny with a genuine smile. "It's all ready."

"Sure." Noah took four plates out of the cabinet at his eye level closest to the stove and set them on the counter. He started putting together everyone's breakfast.

"Thank you, Hun," she responded, beginning to clean off the stove.

"No problem."

"When can we get breakfast?" Lucy questioned impatiently.

Noah sighed once again and purposefully prepared her plate slowly. "You'll have to be patient or I'll take even longer to get breakfast ready."

"You heard him." Lucy smacked her sister from across the table. "Be quiet."

"No hitting," Noah instructed firmly.

Jenny looked at her son with a weary expression once her twin daughters paid them no attention again. "You seem to be doing my job better than me," she joked, but Noah saw the truth behind her eyes.

"I really don't mind," Noah assured her. "They're...quite a handful, though."

"You're one to talk—you were difficult at their age."

"I prefer the term "independent,"" he informed his mother.

Jenny offered him an amused laugh while cleaning off a pan. "Yeah, as in the fact you refused to do anything if it wasn't by yourself. Let's just say you weren't the cleanest while folding laundry."

"Mom."

"Or putting the dishes in the dishwasher."

"Mom."

"Or making your bed."

"*Mom,*" Noah firmly countered, but he was unable to hide his own chuckle. "I've been getting better with that stuff...right?"

"Yes, you have," Jenny confirmed amusedly.

Noah walked over to the table and set a plate in front of his two sisters and the remaining seats for himself and his mother. "I'm glad to hear it."

The family of four consumed their breakfast without much hesitation. Mornings in the Howells' household were fast paced with Noah needing to attend Hillwell High in the early hours of the day at the same time Lucy and Lacy were required to be at their elementary school. Jenny was under quite a lot of stress when it came to her children. She never attempted to put any child over the other. She simply did not have time for everything.

After breakfast, Noah aided his mother in helping his younger sisters ensure they were prepared for a long day at elementary school. Both of his siblings' backpacks were packed to the brim with textbooks, a binder, plenty of pencils, and other stationary supplies to get them through their classes. Afterwards, he watched as the twins pulled on their shoes—each being a pair of identical sandals. Meanwhile, Noah's backpack was already packed and slung over his shoulder for a second time that morning.

Lacy and Lucy fought to be the first to exit the house while Noah and Jenny waited amusedly for the two to fit through the front door at the same time. Their mother unlocked their car, which was a more-than vintage maroon station wagon. The twins climbed into their seats in the back of the car directly after tossing their backpacks and packed lunches in the passenger's seat. Noah was last in the effort to walk down the driveway. He patiently stood by the station wagon's hood.

Jenny placed her purse in the passenger's seat and then turned back to Noah. "Are you sure you want to walk? It looks like it's going to rain any minute."

"My school's across town from the twins'," Noah countered with a shrug.

"I can drop you off on the way."

Noah adjusted his glasses to angle them away from the expected rainfall. "I'm fine walking. Besides, you're already running late as it is."

"Are you sure?" she asked, uncertainty in her eyes.

"I'm sure."

"Alright, well...," Jenny trailed off before engulfing her son with one of her hugs that seemed to make all the world's problems go away, "Be safe. Let me know if you need anything."

"I will, Mom." Noah hugged her back with the same energy.

"Are you sure you don't want a ride?" Jenny repeated flusteredly.

Noah shook his head. "I'm sure. Thank you, though."

The teenager stood back while his mother got into the driver's seat of their car and gave him one last wave, which he returned. Noah watched as the maroon station wagon backed out of the driveway and turned in the opposite direction of Hillwell High. Noah waved once again at his sisters, who eagerly waved back with their faces pressed against the window.

A small droplet of rain landed on his nose a second later. Noah sighed and tugged the hood of his black sweatshirt over his head. It was a good thing Noah decided on wearing a pair of his older shoes. He fitted his hands into his pockets and began on the now-familiar trek towards the controversial building of Hillwell High. Noah was thankful that Hillwell rested on a flat plateau rather than a hilly scape. He would have been out of breath in the first ten seconds of walking.

The rain began to torment Hillwell along with the slight gust of wind that snaked through the streets every so often. Noah had to continuously remove his spare pair of glasses every couple of minutes and clean them off because of the fog that clouded the lenses. On about the fourth time he did so, Noah noticed a slight rumble in the concrete of the sidewalk beneath his shoes. He slowed his pace in the slightest as the rumbling grew more intense and was determined to be some sort of music.

Noah stuttered to a near-halt when he noticed a car drive by. Since his glasses were off, it was merely a gray blur, but once he put them back on his face, there was no mistake as to who was in that particular vehicle. Sure enough, it was the girl known for her deafeningly loud music, which - unbeknownst to Noah - was a stress reliever. Abigail was seated in the driver's seat with one hand on the top of the wheel and her sunglasses, despite the fact there was no sunlight, on her face. The windshield wipers were on the intermittent setting and flicked a couple of raindrops onto Noah as the vehicle passed. Abigail kept her eyes on the road.

"I wonder why she's in such a hurry," Noah noted due to her slightly accelerated speeds. Little did he know that it was a normality to her. *"She might get a ticket for that."*

Little did Noah know that Hillwell was such a small town that tickets were hardly ever distributed by police officers.

He didn't bother wiping the droplets of water off the sleeve of his jacket since he was covered in them anyway. Noah was getting tired of cleaning off his glasses, so he decided not to bother with that either. Instead, he kept walking down his usual route. By that point, he had memorized every crack, blemish, and even the occasional pebble that someone had failed to kick off the sidewalk. Every house blended into one billboard-worthy neighborhood. Everything about Hillwell seemed to be perfect.

In fact, Hillwell *was* perfect as far as the eye could see. Noah thought it was *too* perfect--way too perfect to be true. He knew there was something going on in the premises of Hillwell High that was quite serious. Noah was busy putting the puzzle pieces together, but the image was still too disassembled to distinguish. He was mere moves away from solving the Rubik's Cube of the situation known as Abigail Bartley and whatever was going on with her.

There was only one more hand to be dealt. Noah needed to figure out why it was not yet in the deck with the other playing cards.

10

"WHAT'D YOU SAY? SPEAK UP."

ABIGAIL'S FINGERS WERE IN AGONY.

Approximately every five seconds, Abigail discovered she had subconsciously lifted one of her fingertips to her mouth and was gnawing on one of her nails. The skin around the tip had successfully developed into an irritated pink tint that throbbed each time the appendage moved in the slightest. When Abigail was not biting at her nails, she was clawing at the skin around them, which only made the situation worse.

The clock seemed to be ticking further away from a quarter after three rather than towards it. Abigail paced back and forth in front of the door to her Precalculus classroom, which was still closed. Little to no movement occurred in that room. Mrs. Harris was at her desk, typing at her laptop to complete any work she needed to accomplish for the rest of the week.

Everyone around Abigail seemed to be very thankful that it was Friday. She, however, was not. Abigail resisted the urge to scream as soon as another relieved person came into view. She wished she was able to become one of them, but that was not possible. Abigail had something on her agenda that she needed to cross off. It was something she had been worrying about for what appeared to be forever. Forever quickly turned to a couple of minutes.

Abigail stopped in her tracks and watched one of the clocks in the hallway. With each short tick, she felt her nerves worsen. She knew the sooner this was over, the better she would feel, but unfortunately that did not help the preliminary anxiety that occurred anyway. Abigail knotted her fingers together to prevent herself from chewing on them. It was a gross habit in her opinion, but she was unable to find it in herself to stop.

She almost jumped right out of her high tops when a hand petted her on the shoulder. Abigail whirled around to discover Jade, Brielle, and Keagan, the latter who had pet her, with encouraging smiles on their faces. She awkwardly waved, but that was not enough to satisfy the ever-so energetic Keagan, who stood up on her tiptoes and tackled her in a hug.

"Woah...uh, what's all this for?" Abigail spluttered out, carefully returning her comforting embrace.

Keagan only hugged tighter. "It's a good luck hug!" she explained cheekily. "You didn't think you were going to be here alone, did you?"

"It's a test."

"A test that you'll do great on," Jade asserted, patting Abigail on the head.

Abigail grunted at her friend's hand on her sunglasses. "You don't know that. I could bomb it and make an embarrassment out of myself. This all would've been for nothing."

"But you studied so hard," commented Brielle, which was true. "There's no reason why you'd fail it. You did great with those flash-cards I brought you earlier."

"I know, but my mind might go blank as soon as the pieces of paper are put in front of me." she retorted. Despite receiving a one hundred percent on the flashcard quiz Brielle performed, she felt completely unprepared.

"That's not true. I'm sure you'll do well," Brielle continued to assure her.

"I don't know..."

Keagan gently smacked her on the back. "You'll do great! Get yourself some confidence."

"Yeah, you'll ace it," Jade added on confidently.

"I really don't know," Abigail protested once again. "I could fail."

"Oh—come on, Abi!" Keagan refused to take "I don't know" as an answer. "You spent all week studying with the glasses dude-"

"Noah," Abigail corrected.

"-right, Noah, and from what you've told me, you're doing great. You said yourself that he was a lifesaver. Right?"

"...Right."

Jade frowned a bit in the slightest, but it quickly morphed into a kind smile once Abigail looked her way. "You'll do well," the blonde encouraged her. "I know you will."

"Thanks, Jade." Abigail reluctantly smiled.

Before the four of them were able to say anything else, the door to the Precalculus classroom opened with a small *creak*. The soles of Abigail's high tops were glued to the tiled floor beneath them. A pair of short heels that Abigail distinguished to be Mrs. Harris' clicked against the floor. Despite the sweet smile on her teacher's face, Abigail's nerves intensified. She felt her hands tremble harder with each step Mrs. Harris took.

"Hi, Abigail," the Precalculus teacher exclaimed with a gentle tone. "Are you ready?"

"*No*," Abigail's mind screamed, but she choked out a "Yes" instead.

"Okay. Come on in. Mrs. Harris opened the classroom door the rest of the way for her student to pass through.

As Abigail started to walk through the doorway, motivating comments and pats on the back commenced from her three friends. She briefly glanced behind her and gave them a half-hearted grin before the teacher shut the door behind her, offering Abigail's friends a kind wave. Abigail walked toward a random desk in the front row of twenty-five total and sat down. Her hands remained in her pockets as they tensed and shook in intermittent spasms.

Mrs. Harris sifted through a small pile of papers and stapled the top few of them together. She set a mechanical pencil, a protractor, and a cheap portable calculator on top of the pile and brought it over to Abigail, who looked at her apologetically. As the teacher set the stack of supplies in front of her, the teenager smiled sheepishly.

"I'm sorry—I forgot to bring my things," she apologized.

"I knew you were stressed, so I figured I'd help you out a little bit," Mrs. Harris responded authentically. She tapped the page on the top of the pile. "Now, there's no time limit for this placement test. I'll be grading papers for a long while anyway, so I can remain here to proctor your test. If you have any questions about the instructions or something you don't understand, you can ask me, but I can't provide too much assistance. Does that make sense?"

"Yes, Ma'am," Abigail swallowed down the nervousness bubbling in her throat.

"You don't need to take this test if you don't want to, though. Precalculus is much more than satisfactory for your graduation requirement."

"I know."

"Good luck, then," Mrs. Harris reiterated, offering Abigail a gentle pat on the shoulder.

Abigail watched as her teacher returned to her desk and sat down, beginning to get to work on grading her papers. The thought of Abigail's being one of them gave her several more nerves to worry about, especially since she knew her Precalculus grade mattered more now than ever before. Her gaze slowly traveled down to her test. She moved the supplies her teacher provided for her to the side, grasping the mechanical pencil in her right hand and clicking the top to reveal the lead.

She looked at the first sheet of paper that glared back at her. Other than her name and date at the top, Abigail's test was completely blank. She gripped her pencil tightly and held it over the answer line for the first problem. The text next to her pencil began to grow blurry. How was she supposed to survive a test that depended on her mental stability when the test itself was affecting her sanity in the first place?

As her pencil quivered in her hand, she thought back to all her sessions with Noah, which totaled to seven in nine days. Noah had even used his valuable Sunday night, which could have been utilized in sleeping and rejuvenating his energy for the week ahead - since he always completed his homework earlier than the weekend - to help her study while freaking out over the placement test being the following Friday. That Friday was now today, and Abigail couldn't thank him enough. She would not even be in that classroom without him.

Despite her debilitating nerves, she forced herself to work through the first problem. Abigail was unsure if it was her imagination or if she was going crazy, but she thought she noticed Mrs. Harris look up and briefly smile at the sound of her pencil hitting the paper. Before she knew it, Abigail was flying through the first page of the test when the echoes of supportive comments and gestures from her friends flowed through her ears.

Abigail let her mind wander as she scribbled down an answer for each question. Her brain collected bits and pieces from every tutoring session she had with Noah. Noah had been so patient and kind with her as she learned the entirety of Precalculus in less than two weeks. She remembered nearly every detail regarding each problem, however, her mind kept doubting her, whispering in her ear that she was failing the placement test as she took it. Abigail dismissed those thoughts immediately.

By the time she was finished, her head was spinning. Abigail dizzily collected her test and borrowed supplies and rushed over to Mrs. Harris' desk. The teacher jumped in her seat when Abigail accidentally slammed her pile of belongings onto the desk surface, but she smiled nevertheless and took her test from the bottom of the pile.

"How'd it go?" she asked, looking Abigail in the eye.

Abigail shrugged and shifted her weight from foot to foot. "I don't know," she admitted. "I understood most things, though."

"That's good." Mrs. Harris glanced at the first page of the test. "Would you like to wait for me to grade it or not? It shouldn't take me long—maybe twenty minutes."

"I'll wait," Abigail replied before she could stop herself.

"Alright. I'll let you know when I'm done."

Abigail nodded and took her leave from the classroom, which had quickly become stuffy with the stress weighing upon her. Her hands feebly pushed the door shut. She let out a long sigh of relief and leaned against a nearby set of lockers to stabilize her throbbing heart. Abigail held two fingers up to her neck to check her pulse, which was almost unnoticeable with the velocity of which it was beating.

"How'd it go?" Brielle's soft voice quickly brought Abigail out of her thoughts.

"...I don't know."

"Abi, I told you—no more of the "I don't know" crap," Keagan repeated her earlier words with a cheeky smile. "I'm sure you did great."

"Yeah, I bet you did awesome," Jade added on truthfully.

Abigail averted eye contact from all three of them and said nothing to argue or agree with either of them. Jade and Brielle had no words to say when Keagan was the one to break the silence between them.

"When you want to do something, you do so and succeed with flying colors," she stated. "Why would it be any different now, especially when you have such a valid motive?"

"Because not everything works out for everyone."

"You'll see," Keagan mused thoughtfully. "When do you get your grade back?"

"In about twenty minutes," mumbled Abigail.

"Wow. That's much sooner than I thought."

Abigail decided to shift the subject as far away from her nerves as she could get. "How come you three are still here, anyways? It's been at least an hour."

"Simple," Jade replied, holding up a red box of cards. "We played Uno. Brielle's winning with six games, Keagan has five, and I also have five."

"Oh, that's cool." Abigail longingly stared at the game in Jade's hand.

"Do you want to play until you get your grade back? It might help get your mind off the stress," Brielle offered kindly.

Abigail nodded and the four of them sat down in a circle near a wall of lockers. "Sure. As long as the janitor doesn't come by and try to shoo us away."

"Oh, he did...twice." Keagan nonchalantly shrugged. "I offered him a crisp five-dollar bill to go away and not report us loitering after school hours and what do you know? He actually took it."

"You *bribed* the janitor?" Abigail spat in complete shock.

"Yeah, of course. Are we playing Uno or not?"

Brielle began shuffling the large deck of cards, which was difficult for anyone - especially someone with small hands - but she somehow managed to do so. "I thought we were," she supplied.

"Yes, please," Abigail confirmed with a relieved smile.

Brielle finished shuffling and dealt seven cards to each person. She set the rest of the deck in the center along with a card face-up as the starting point. Starting with Abigail, who was on Brielle's left, the four of them rotated through the circle and either set down a card or drew however many they needed to. With each card being set down next to the draw pile, Abigail felt her nerves begin to chip away a little bit. She was having genuine *fun* for the first time in over a week —nearly two at that point.

Seventeen minutes passed and now, the leader in the tally of wins for each player was Brielle with seven, followed by Keagan with six, Jade still with five, and Abigail with two. The very second that the fourth game in that timeframe ended, the door to the Precalculus classroom cracked open and Mrs. Harris' face popped through the opening. Abigail froze. Maybe the smile on her face was a sorrowful and compassionate one rather than an encouraging one.

"I finished grading your test," she informed her gently. "Would you like to hear your grade privately or right here?"

Abigail swallowed a nervous lump back down her throat. "...Did I do badly? That's all I want to know, and you can say it right here."

"No." Mrs. Harris shook her head, "In fact, you did quite the opposite."

The black-haired girl's eyes widened at Mrs. Harris' statement, which seemed to be more positive than negative. Her voice shook as she asked after a moment of silence, "Does that mean I passed and can move up to Calculus?"

Mrs. Harris nodded and held out the graded test for her to take. "Yes, Abigail. You passed with a grade of eighty-six percent, which is very impressive for someone learning Precalculus so quickly. That means you're free to attend the AP Calculus class during the second block rather than Precalculus. Congratulations!"

"Are you serious?" Abigail's voice was clipped with disbelief. She looked at the large red "86%" on the top right corner of her test.

"Of course," Mrs. Harris elaborated. "I wouldn't have written a fake grade."

It took a moment for reality to register for Abigail. Her smile widened to reach her ecstatic brown eyes. "Oh, my God! That's amazing!"

At once, Keagan, Brielle, and Jade tackled Abigail in one of the biggest hugs she had ever received. Abigail attempted to hug the three of them at once in response, but all four of them were hopping up and down with the most genuine happiness that could have been generated at that moment. Cheers and giggles commenced from the foursome along with hair-ruffles, pats on the back, and smiles all around.

Mrs. Harris was smiling quietly while the four cheered. "It *is* amazing," she replied once they had settled down. "Why don't you girls go celebrate?"

"You heard her!" Keagan's voice rang out above the others. "How does ice cream sound?"

"Fine by me!" Abigail gushed in a relieved tone. She turned to Mrs. Harris with an authentic grin plastered on her face. "Thank you, Mrs. Harris. It means a lot."

"No problem. If you have any questions or need any help with AP Calculus, please email me. I'll try to help." The kind teacher reciprocated Abigail's gesture.

"I will."

Mrs. Harris waved and shut the door. Abigail waved back, but Keagan grasped onto her free hand and led her down the vacant school hallways. Jade and Brielle walked on either side of them like a row of geese, but horizontal rather than vertical. Abigail stopped by her locker to retrieve her things - her friends already had their items with them and Brielle had put away the Uno game - before they left the building entirely.

Abigail thought she saw Keagan glance over towards the end of the hall. Her gaze followed her friend's to notice the janitor standing on a chair. He was facing the opposite direction and appeared to be installing or adjusting something. Abigail thought about taking a better look, but she changed her mind. She was on too much of a high.

The sun shone bright overhead while the four embarked on their journey to the local ice cream parlor. Abigail and Keagan drove themselves in separate vehicles while Jade offered Brielle a ride across town. Rather than anxiety clawing at her throat, Abigail felt truly free for the first time in several days. She already had a plan to call Kristy, who was currently out of town, or she would have had a session that day, about her success and let herself be happy—to relish the moment that was surprisingly given to her.

Fifteen minutes later, Abigail, Jade, Brielle, and Keagan were standing in front of the only ice cream parlor in town. The words "Ice Ice Baby" were written in pink calligraphy above the glass entryway. Abigail scoffed at the name just like she did every time she went there. She knew that the parlor was named as such only because of the pun. Everyone knew that the song itself was a ripoff of another classic. Here, however, the ice cream was not. It was the best - and the only - in the small town of Hillwell.

"So, what kind of ice cream is everyone getting?" Jade asked the group.

"Vanilla with rainbow sprinkles," Brielle answered after a second of thought.

"Probably chocolate," Abigail replied.

"I'm getting a triple scoop mint chocolate chip in a waffle cone bowl with chocolate syrup and a cherry on top," Keagan concluded proudly.

The three girls looked at her skeptically. Only Abigail had the guts to comment, "That's really specific. Did you look up the menu just now?"

"Can't blame a girl for being prepared." Keagan shrugged and held up her phone.

"You know what?" Abigail expressed, "I think I'm going to look up the menu too. Chocolate can be boring."

"Okay, but how about we go in? It's getting cold out here," Jade suggested. It was her own fault for wearing a borderline crop top and jeans that had more holes than denim while it was approximately fifty degrees outside.

Abigail had no idea how Jade didn't get dress coded, but she refused to complain. Dress codes were ridiculous anyway.

"Sounds good," Keagan agreed. She pulled the heavy glass door open and held it there for her three friends to enter.

After Brielle and Jade walked into the parlor, Abigail shuffled in blindly. Her eyes were glued to her phone as she took small strides and slowly scrolled through the menu. Keagan walked behind her and attempted to help her decide, but Abigail was insistent on finding something herself. Despite the menu being over the counter and easily legible, Abigail found her phone much more convenient.

"Ooh, the peanut butter cup sounds good," Abigail eagerly thought out loud. Her eyes finally left her phone and landed on her friends, who were waiting in line. "Hey guys, I think I finally know what I..."

Abigail trailed off as her eyes drifted over towards the counter and more specifically next to the cash register. Her phone slipped through her fingers and fell onto the floor with an excruciating crack. She knew her phone screen had cracked, but she couldn't find it in herself to care. Her mood had completely changed from relieved to terrorized. Abigail's lips were parted and suddenly dried as if a drought had overcome them. She knew she needed to breathe, but her brain refused to communicate with her lungs, allowing her to do so.

Her friends were completely oblivious until they heard her phone fall and hit the white tiled floor. Keagan looked as if she was about to ask what was wrong, but all it took was following Abigail's gaze and locking onto her targeted point of vision. Jade and Brielle were close behind, and once they realized, the group fell silent.

After a sickening moment of nothingness, Jade tentatively spoke up, "Is that..."

"It is," Abigail quavered before Jade could finish.

There, behind the counter, was a seemingly innocent human being serving the customer in front of the four friends. He sported a tall stature, well above average by at least two or three inches, dusty brown hair, brown eyes, light skin, and the tan and pink uniform required by all employees of the ice cream parlor. At first glance, it appeared as if he was simply a teenage boy who needed extra money and did not mind pink in every direction. To Abigail, it was a completely different story.

"It's *him*."

Keagan's head whirled around to face the trembling teenager. She picked up her phone and set it gently in her hands. "Abi, we don't have to get ice cream here. We can go somewhere else and forget this ever happened."

"This is the only place in town to get it," Abigail retorted sourly.

"We can come another day, then."

"No, it's fine."

Brielle set a gentle hand on her shoulder, which Abigail flinched away from. "We can do whatever you feel comfortable with. If that's leaving, it's okay."

"I said it's *fine*," Abigail snapped. Brielle went mute and Keagan and Jade shot her sympathetic looks. She knew it was not Abigail's fault, but it was still harmful. "I'm sorry," Abigail apologized. "How about we get the ice cream and go?"

Her friends nodded, and just in time too. It was their turn at the counter. Keagan, Jade, and Brielle let Abigail stand behind them as if the three of them were a shield. Abigail refused to meet *him* in the eyes while the three gave him their orders. She was silently suffocating, especially since the human shield broke apart ever-so slightly to allow Abigail to pass through. Abigail let her black hair fall in her face while she attempted to build up her confidence.

"Come on, Abigail. Just recite your damn order," she lectured herself. Abigail eventually mumbled, "One peanut butter cup with two scoops in a waffle bowl."

"Sorry, I can't hear you," the familiar voice that Abigail hated grunted. "What'd you say? Speak up."

Abigail knew there was a smirk on his face from the tone of his voice without even looking at him. Before she could think twice, her eyes snapped up to meet his own. Her breath caught in her throat. *He* looked the same as he had before with his gorgeous eyes, handsome face, and overall perfect demeanor. If only others knew what was on the inside.

"I said I wanted a peanut butter cup, two scoops, in a waffle bowl," Abigail snapped without avoiding his piercing gaze this time.

"Woah. Feisty, aren't you? You haven't changed a bit," he drawled cockily.

Keagan looked as if she was contemplating strangling him over the counter. "Listen, Pal. We came here for ice cream, not stupid remarks. Now, you'll get us the ice cream and we'll be on our way. Got it?"

"First and foremost, my name's Landon; not "Pal,"" he calmly mentioned. "Secondly, that goes for you as well. I was only making an innocent comment to an old friend."

"Landon is a wussy name. We'd like our ice cream now." Keagan removed her credit card from her wallet and inserted it in the card reader to pay for all four of their orders. Brielle looked as if she was about to protest, but Keagan shook her head in her direction.

Landon arrogantly crossed his arms over his chest. "Oh, really? Are we not going to talk about the fact I could literally step on you?"

"If you go get our ice cream, we won't even have to talk about it." Keagan looked utterly unfazed about the fact Landon towered over her by at least a foot. "Besides, you wouldn't want me to report this place for bad customer service and a rude cashier; would you?" Keagan batted her eyelashes at him.

He hesitated but agreed "Alright. Fair enough."

Landon decided not to argue. He tore the receipt from the machine and roughly handed it to Keagan. The small girl gave the crumpled piece of paper a pointed look but said nothing and led the group over towards the side of the counter where customers were to wait for their ice cream or whatever else they ordered from the stupidly named parlor. Jade and Brielle stood on either side of Abigail while Keagan paced back and forth in the waiting area. Abigail frowned in dismay when she discovered Landon to be the one delivering their ice cream to the counter.

The four of them stepped up to the counter and took their respective ice cream bowls off the surface. When Abigail retrieved hers, Landon's smirk returned, and he cleared his throat to get her attention. Abigail slowly turned to face the young man who she had grown to be devastatingly afraid of. She looked him directly in the eyes.

"Hey, Abigail—you might want a napkin. The peanut butter cup's kinda messy," he informed her, handing her a napkin.

Abigail cautiously took the napkin and noticed Landon's handwriting near the top left corner of the pale papery material. Landon did not wait for her to read it. He returned to the cash register to attend to the next set of customers. Her hand was trembling too much to hold the napkin steady, so reading the small letters was quite a task.

"I've missed you. Call me and let's hang out sometime. It can be just like old times. :)"

Below the note was his phone number. Abigail did not need it, though. She had already blocked his contact on her phone and labeled it with a plethora of middle finger emojis and profanities.

"Wait, what is it?" Keagan strained to look over Abigail's shoulder. She nearly dropped her spoon full of mint chocolate chip ice cream when she finished reading the note. "Oh, my God. What a prick."

When Keagan began listing several obscenities off the tip of her tongue to insult Landon, Jade desperately attempted to stop her. "Keagan, let's just get out of here."

"I want to violently murder that-"

Jade grabbed Keagan's wrist and dragged her out of the shop amid her second cursing spree. Brielle and Abigail quickly followed in tow with their ice cream in hand. Abigail briefly set hers down on a table and looked at the napkin she had carried outside with her. Without another thought, she began tearing it into the smallest of pieces before throwing it in the nearest trash can. Brielle nodded approvingly when she caught Abigail's eye.

"I'm proud of you," Brielle complimented sincerely.

Abigail's eyes never left her ice cream that was freezing her hands, but she did not care about that anymore. She was numb. "Thank you."

"I know that was scary, but you don't have to deal with him anymore." Brielle picked at her ice cream with her spoon and collected some of the sprinkles on the tip.

"I hope so," Abigail wistfully murmured.

Keagan rejoined the two with Jade and boomed, "Brielle's right. You won't have to deal with him since I'm planning an anonymous assassination."

"Keagan." Brielle attempted to stop her.

"I'll "accidentally" run him over with my car-" Keagan began, but she was cut off.

"That thing?" Jade snickered jokingly, pointing to the black Volkswagen Beetle a few spaces away from where the group was conversing. "He could jump over it."

"Not if I'm going eighty miles an hour."

Abigail's face slowly broke out into a tiny smile and a laugh at that. "You don't have to execute an assassination attempt-"

"Ha! Execute—nice one, Abi," Keagan interrupted with a chuckle because of the unintentional pun.

"Thank you, but what I was going to say was that it'll be fine," Abigail finished. "Since I'm in AP Calculus now and am surrounded by you guys otherwise, I have nothing to worry about."

"Yeah, that's true," Jade agreed. "We'll still keep a close eye out, though. It'll be okay."

Abigail hesitated, bile rising in her throat from a memory that surfaced abruptly, but she swallowed it down. She nodded with a neutral look on her face. Suddenly, her ice cream did not look so appetizing anymore because Landon held it and quite possibly prepared it. Abigail felt the same way about herself. When he had "prepared" her in any way, shape, or form, she was unappetizing to herself too. In fact, she felt disgusting. Abigail hoped with all of her heart that she would not have that same viewpoint of herself forever.

Not after what he did.

11

"WHO THE HELL'S TOM BOMBADIL?"

"CLASS, IT'S NOW TIME TO REVEAL YOUR CHOICE FOR THIS MONTH'S novel," Mr. Wright exclaimed, somehow boringly. "I have the tallies on the board, but the titles of the books in the lineup are covered."

"We have eyes, Mr. Wright," Abigail sarcastically commented in her mind. It looked as if Keagan was trying her hardest not to laugh at the ridiculousness of the situation.

Throughout the month of September, the British Literature class of twenty-five were busy doing pointless assignments and analysis on certain literary works that would not matter one single bit in the future. Abigail had completely forgotten about the vote for the first novel the class was to read and write a paper on due to everything that had gone on during the past four weeks. October snuck up on her before she knew it and that morning, Abigail cast her vote for a random novel out of the three options.

"Now, without further ado, the novel in third place with five votes is," Mr. Wright announced while removing the sheet of paper taped over the third-place winner, "*Lord of the Flies* by William Golding."

The class was silent other than a few half-hearted hands clapping together.

Mr. Wright paid no mind to the unenthusiastic class and revealed the novel who won the figurative silver medal. "The runner up in second place with seven votes is *Pride and Prejudice* by Jane Austen."

A couple of girls frowned, Keagan being one of them. She leaned over towards Abigail and whispered, "That's the one I voted for. It's a great book."

"I think that's the one I voted for too," Abigail quietly replied. "Though, I just picked a random one. I remember the 'P's."

Keagan snickered. The two of them faced the board once again and waited patiently as Mr. Jones continued with his monotonous presentation of the Olympic gold medal. Abigail had never seen such a dumb announcement before that would only lead to more time wasted by reading a book that she knew nothing about.

"Now, the winner with nine votes, and the novel we will read this month is," Mr. Wright paused for dramatic effect, "*The Lord of the Rings: The Fellowship of the Ring* by J.R.R. Tolkien."

The class was silent. Abigail and Keagan looked at each other like their teacher had gone crazy. Then again, it was not the teacher who decided on the books to be voted upon—it was a class effort. Abigail thought she would have been reading a book like Pride and Prejudice which was a stand-alone, but now, it looked as if the situation took a wide turn towards the road of utter destruction.

Mr. Wright gave the class an almost wicked smile. "As most of you should know, *The Lord of the Rings* is a trilogy, not a stand-alone novel. If we read the first book, we should be inclined to read the entirety of the story, which means there's a change in plans for our reading assignments for the next couple months," he gleefully informed his students. "Instead of voting on books for November and December, we will be reading the rest of the trilogy: *The Two Towers* and *The Return of the King*. Each of these novels is separated into two "books," and I expect you to read both "books" of *The Fellowship of the Ring* by the end of the month. Because of the length of these novels, this will be your only assignment for October. I encourage you to take notes on each chapter of the key points because in December, you are to write your paper on all three of these novels. More information will be sent out as the deadline gets closer."

Abigail had no idea her jaw had dropped until Keagan put her index finger underneath it and gently pushed her mouth closed. She fought to blink at the absurd amount of homework she had just been given. Just looking at books made her begin to convulse at the waste of valuable time she would be enduring while staring at words on a piece of paper. A muffled sound tried to jump into her thoughts, but Abigail pushed it away. It wasn't until Keagan tapped her on the shoulder that she realized she was being spoken to.

"Are you okay, Abi?" she asked soothingly.

"No," snipped Abigail. "I'm not okay. I'm starting AP Calculus a year early today and now I have this huge project looming over me that I have to worry about along with my other classes."

Keagan rubbed calming circles on her back. "Shh, Abi, it's going to be okay. We can do it together." She stopped, noticing the back of a familiar brown-haired head a couple of rows in front of Abigail. A smile spread across her face. "Glasses dude can help you too."

"No, he's done too much."

"All you have to do is ask him...if that's what you want."

Abigail shook her head again. "No, I can do this on my own."

"Okay, but he's an option for you if you'd like that."

"I'll do it myself," Abigail insisted before raking her eyes back towards the dull Mr. Wright.

"It looks as if our time's up for today," the balding teacher concluded to the entire classroom's relief. "Please make sure to have your copies of the book by the end of the week. You can find it in the library to borrow or at any bookstore. I guess you could buy it online as well. It's a story you'll want to remember. Don't forget that you have a substitute for the rest of the week."

The classroom suddenly became a madhouse as all twenty-five students were a hustle and bustle on their way out of it to attend their class directly afterwards. Abigail and Keagan stood up from their desks and collected their belongings in their arms. Abigail unleashed a defeated sigh as she and Keagan began to walk. Despite her hatred for the teacher for more stress added onto her schedule, she gave him a nod as a "thank you" as she passed by. Before she was able to walk through the doorway, though, an unexpected voice stopped her.

"Hey, Abigail," Noah greeted her while pushing his glasses back up the bridge of his nose. He was walking a bit quicker than normal to catch up with her.

Abigail stopped in her tracks at the sound of his voice. Keagan took a hold of her arm and yanked her out of the classroom and out of the walkway. Noah followed and stood next to the two of them. Abigail had no idea what to think. She hardly spoke to him outside of tutoring sessions. The guilt of having him teach her almost every day of the week for nearly two weeks was weighing heavy on her shoulders, so she did what she thought was right.

She avoided him.

Keagan cleared her throat to get Abigail's attention. She quickly made eye contact with Noah again and composed herself. "Hey, Noah."

"Sorry, I didn't mean to startle you—I was just wondering how the placement test went," Noah clarified politely.

"It's okay." Abigail offered him a sheepish look. "I passed and am going to AP Calculus now, so I'd hope it went well."

Noah's apologetic expression quickly became a smile. "No way—that's awesome! Great job."

"I couldn't have done it without you."

"Oh, uh, I'm sure you could," Noah faltered, scratching the back of his neck with his free hand, "But it's not a problem. I'm glad it worked out."

Keagan chuckled almost silently, to which Abigail elbowed her in the arm. Abigail awkwardly grinned at Noah. "Yeah, me too," she agreed.

"So, what do you think of the reading project?" Noah asked to make the topic a bit more casual rather than timid.

"I don't know." Abigail was caught off-guard. "It seems like an awful lot of reading, so that won't be fun. It's just a waste of time."

Noah frowned at that. "You think reading is a waste of time?"

"Yes, that's what I think."

"I think you'll come around to the story. Have you ever seen the movies? The books are even better," Noah commented truthfully.

Keagan shrugged when Abigail didn't answer. "I'll have to admit that the movies were pretty good. Very long, though."

"See?" Noah grinned his trademark smile. "It won't be so bad."

"Don't use me as an alibi—I voted for *Pride and Prejudice!*" Keagan retorted. "And I watched the extended editions. Totally worth it, but it took the whole day to watch all three in one sitting."

"This is going to be a disaster." Abigail buried her face in her unoccupied hand.

"Do you want some help with it? It won't be that bad."

Abigail slowly peeked through her fingers at Noah's offer. "No, I'm okay," she dismissed as kindly as she was able. "Thank you, though."

"Oh, are you sure?" Noah cocked his head to the side.

"Yeah."

"Alright, then," Noah responded a bit awkwardly. "I guess I'll see you later."

Abigail grasped her Literature textbook tightly in her arms. "Yeah, I'll see you later."

As soon as Noah disappeared into the crowd of students, Keagan smirked in Abigail's general direction. The girl in question rolled her eyes and the two of them vanished into the crowd as well. Abigail shrunk as she took each step, afraid she was going to bump into a particular someone, but Keagan led her straight to her locker and to her next class, so she was able to feel safer. Abigail knew Keagan was a good friend, but she had never realized how great she was since she hadn't got to know her as well as she did then.

Abigail grasped her AP Calculus textbook that she had rented from the school's library earlier that morning. Her new classroom was relatively near Keagan's Algebra II class, so the two of them did not have to separate until they were almost to their respective classes. Abigail hesitated a second or two before entering the AP Calculus room and taking one of the last seats available by one of the windows. She set her textbook down on the desk along with her other supplies and let out a breath of relief.

"He's not here."

When her teacher - Mr. Russell - entered, despite his strict appearance, Abigail felt much better about the room itself. With his firm stare, short black hair with flecks of gray, and slightly stout structure, Abigail knew this class would be a difficult one. She already preferred Mrs. Harris, but he would have to do for the time being. Abigail listened as he began his lecture for the morning, which meant she needed to rush to take notes so she would understand.

Seventy-five minutes, six pages front and back of notes, and a cramping hand later, Abigail wobbled out of her first session of AP Calculus. The rest of the morning blurred into one huge wave of monotonous stress. Abigail barely was able to stay awake during her AP Chemistry class. Jade kept having to poke her to keep her conscious while her teacher spoke about various equations. All of Abigail's energy was used on AP Calculus and worrying about her newest project in British Literature.

Abigail was relieved to have a container of chicken tenders and fries in front of her during lunch while her friends conversed. She knew she was being oddly quiet, but rather than discomfort, Abigail was fatigued. She yawned for the umpteenth time while Jade was speaking about how the black and pink floral shirt that she was wearing was found at the thrift store. Brielle and Keagan appeared genuinely interested while Abigail was picking at her food.

Keagan snapped her fingers in Abigail's face to get her attention. "Hey, Abi? Are you okay?" she inquired. "You look like you're about to use your fries as a pillow."

"No, I'm not," Abigail feebly chuckled. "I'm just really tired."

"I can tell. Was Calculus okay? Maybe that's it."

Abigail shrugged and eyed her right hand, which was still sore. "I took several pages of notes, so my hand was cramping and I could barely keep up, but I think I understand what's going on."

"Have you been getting enough sleep?" Brielle timidly asked her.

"I think so."

Jade brushed her blonde hair out of her face. "Give yourself time to relax," she advised. "It's barely October and you're burning out."

Abigail hated to admit how right she was...so she didn't. She stuffed half of a chicken tender in her mouth to excuse herself from speaking.

"Well, the Brit Lit project certainly isn't going to help," Keagan mumbled. "All the guys in the class picked the *Lord of the Rings* trilogy just because they saw the movies and thought they were awesome. The whole series together is over four hundred thousand words!"

"You've got to be kidding, right?" Jade scoffed in disbelief.

"Do either of you want any help?" Brielle offered.

Abigail shrugged. "I just need to figure out where it is in the library since I don't feel like buying the books."

"I have the books." Brielle's face lit up. "Would either of you like to borrow them?"

"I was going to just watch the movies a couple days before it's due anyway so I can have more free time," the girl with the pixie cut expressed, kicking her small feet up onto the surface of the table. Her checkered Vans were in clear view.

All three of her friends rolled their eyes. Typical Keagan.

"What? I was going to watch the extended editions so I can get more information for the paper in December!"

"Um, you do realize that the books and the movies have some differences, right?" Brielle inquired, soft-spoken while in between two bites of her salad. "For example, Tom Bombadil isn't in *The Fellowship of the Ring* movie at all."

Keagan offered her a blank look. "Who the hell's Tom Bombadil?"

Despite Brielle being the only one in the group who knew about Tom Bombadil, she, Jade, and Abigail laughed at Keagan's dumbfounded reaction. Eventually, Keagan joined in, laughing at her own uneducated question. That was something about the four of them that Abigail loved: any of them were able to produce laughter in almost any situation. Laughter was just what Abigail needed at that moment, especially after what had happened.

The last few minutes of the lunch period flew by quickly and before any of them knew it, Abigail, Keagan, Jade, and Brielle had thrown away their trash, returned their trays to the stack near the trash can, and were on their way to their fourth classes of the school day. Keagan and Jade split from the group while Abigail and Brielle stopped by their lockers one at a time and began to walk to their class that they shared: AP Government. Neither of them said much of anything as they walked. Brielle was a quiet soul who only spoke when she had something important to say.

When the two of them were a few yards away from their classroom's door, Abigail stopped in her tracks. Brielle took a couple more steps before she realized Abigail was not next to her anymore. She turned around and walked towards her with a concerned expression on her face. Abigail was staring down at her textbook and sifting through the supplies she had brought to use in that class.

"Abigail, is something wrong?" Brielle questioned.

"No, I just realized I forgot my notebook," Abigail replied honestly. "I'll be right back—just let me get it real quick."

"Oh, okay. I'll save you a seat."

"Thank you!"

Abigail dashed off in a half-jog, half-sprint to her locker down the nearly empty halls. The thought of being alone, even if it was only for a minute unnerved her, so she decided she would be in a hurry to return to class. What was the worst that could happen in a minute anyway?

"Come on, Abigail—you're safe. Just get the notebook and go."

She fumbled with the combination lock until it popped open. Abigail had stuffed it under her arm while she sifted through her many textbooks and miscellaneous items in her locker. While trying to keep herself calm, Abigail eventually discovered her notebook buried under her AP Chemistry textbook. Abigail quickly grasped it and shut her locker door. What she was not expecting was there to be a certain boy waiting on the other side of the open metal door.

"...I stand corrected."

Abigail flinched hard when she met his eyes; those brown eyes she would never see the same again. "Since you were so rude to me at the ice cream parlor last Friday, I figured we'd have a proper chat," his voice snarkily proposed.

"What do you want?" Abigail stammered in a frozen state.

"Aw, don't be like that," Landon cooed with his smirk still on his face. "What happened in the past few months? You were always over-the-moon to see me."

Abigail avoided his question and gritted, "You're not supposed to be here."

"Sweetheart, parole exists for a reason. You couldn't have expected me to be in jail for most of the summer and then some."

"Then why weren't you here the first couple weeks of school?" The question slipped out before she could stop herself.

Landon smiled innocently. "Oh, I was on vacation with my family. It was very nice to visit the beach before having to return to the monotonous routine...don't you think?"

"So, while I was terrified to even leave my house, you were on a damn vacation?" Abigail's teeth ground together in fury, but she kept her wavering cool and said nothing.

Meanwhile, the hallways were not exactly empty. The occasional student walked past to attend their class either right on time or a minute or two late. Two of those occasional students - one with brown hair, brown eyes, and a certain pair of spare glasses and the other with auburn hair, strong stature, and a more talkative nature - were doing just that. Noah and Ryder were on their way to their AP Calculus class, slowly walking and talking.

"So, how's it going with your little crush?" Ryder inquired cheekily.

Noah stumbled over what he was about to say, tongue-tied. "It's not a crush, it's just-"

"Anxiety over someone who's the opposite gender," Ryder finished before Noah was able to.

"Yeah, sure." Noah rolled his eyes and kept walking. "I guess it's going okay. I talked to her earlier today and she said that the help with math got her in AP Calculus. I'm not sure why it was so important to her, but she was very happy about it."

Ryder smiled at that. "Hey—that's good! So, she definitely doesn't dislike you."

"I'd hope not."

"So, what's next? You could maybe ask her ou-" Ryder began, however, he was interrupted by Noah pulling him to a stop just after they rounded the corner.

"Shh," Noah firmly hushed him.

Ryder gave him a pointed look. "Huh?" His eyes then widened. "Wait, is she close by or something? Sorry, I didn't mean to-"

"Shut up," Noah elaborated and yanked him back behind the corner. He slowly peeked around the corner just enough to be hidden by a wall of lockers. "She's there...and there's someone talking to her —big guy."

"That's admittedly a bit weird," Ryder commented a bit too casually for the conversation. "She hasn't been around guys since-"

"Since when?" He interrupted his friend for a third time.

Ryder looked around the corner. The two of their heads stacked on top of each other, Noah's at the bottom and Ryder's at the top, looked like a small totem pole. This time, it was Ryder's turn to pull Noah back out of sight. The force was so sudden that his spare glasses fell off and nearly hit the floor, but he caught them in the nick of time.

"Oh, shit," Ryder swore under his breath.

By this point, Noah looked very concerned. "What? What is it?" he interrogated in a near-panic.

"That's Landon Woods she's talking to," Ryder hurriedly explained. Noah appeared more confused than ever. "Last year, something happened between them. They used to date, and now there's occasional rumors going around. Nobody knows what happened, but it seemed awful because Abigail was terrified to go near him until school got out."

At that moment, the last piece of the puzzle fell into place for Noah.

It was Noah's turn to swear almost silently. He glanced around the corner and then back at Ryder. "What do we do?" His tone was almost frantic. "She can't be okay."

Ryder hesitated, but then snapped his fingers quietly. "I've got it."

"...What?"

"Follow my lead."

"What?" Noah spluttered at that. "Ryder, you need to tell me what you're planning."

"I told you to follow my lead," Ryder simply repeated.

"No, we don't have time for this."

"If you'd be quiet and trust me, we would," he countered barely over a whisper. "Just follow my lead and act natural—okay?"

Noah paused but nodded. He realized his argument was only going to backfire and leave more room for whoever this "Landon" person was planning to do. Ryder gently pushed them forward and the two walked down the hall, pretending to have a conversation led by Ryder. Noah's heart quickened as they slowly approached. Landon was still speaking to Abigail and the latter looked as if she wanted to be anywhere but there. Noah attempted to listen.

"What's the matter?" Landon took a step closer, which caused Abigail to take a step back until her spine was against the rigid metal wall. "Are you afraid?"

Abigail gulped down an anxious breath and shook her head firmly.

"You look like you're scared of me. We can't have that, now, can we?" He put a hand against the wall of lockers and towered over her, boxing her in.

"Just remember what Kristy said when you don't feel safe. Surround myself with friends? Can't check that off. Voice my problem to someone I trust? Can't check that off either. Take deep breaths to calm myself? That's not likely." Abigail attempted the third option anyway and kept her eyes locked firmly on his own. "Landon, you need to leave."

"But we just started talking," Landon pouted sarcastically. "Do you want me to leave that much?"

"I didn't say want; I said *need*," Abigail seethed whilst her entire body shook. "Landon, you need to go away and leave me alone."

Landon frowned. "Not gonna happen, Sweetheart. You have no idea what you're missi-"

The ridiculously tall boy's statement was cut off by a slightly shorter body slamming into his own. Abigail thought she had seen a flash of auburn on the other side of the collision, but she blinked and it was gone. In front of her was a disoriented Landon and a startled and quite anxious Noah. Abigail had no idea what had happened, but seconds earlier, while Noah and Ryder were walking by, the latter pushed the former into Landon. The confrontation between him and Abigail was successfully disrupted.

"What the hell, man?!" Landon retaliated, shoving Noah to the side. "Watch where you're going. I'm standing here."

"Leave her alone," Noah blurted out as he stumbled to a halt, his voice nearly as shaky as Abigail's. It was more put-together and thick, though.

Out of the corner of his eye, Noah noticed Abigail's eyes widen and her stepping away from the two much taller people. It pained him to know she was afraid, possibly of him too, but he knew he was doing the right thing. From what Ryder said - and the plan he executed - Landon was not a good guy. There was something very off about him and there was from the very second Noah laid eyes on him. He was bad news.

"Excuse me?" the boy himself inquired.

"I think you heard me," Noah quipped. "I told you to leave her alone."

"I never said I couldn't hear you. I just don't care."

"Wow, Ryder—some plan that you have here. You shoved me into a jerk and then fled," Noah grumbled to himself. Despite this, he stood taller and was almost at Landon's eye level. "You're going to leave right now and not come back. Do you understand?"

Landon folded his arms over his chest. A sly smirk danced among his face. "Okay. Whatever. I can't make any promises. Abigail should know that. Right?" He looked in Abigail's direction and winked, which made her cower her head lower into her textbook.

"Go away," Noah asserted. He even went as much as to push him away from Abigail.

"Alright, alright. I'm going," Landon spat and disappeared down the hallway.

Once Landon vanished around the corner, Noah's gaze darted to Abigail. She was frozen with her hands trembling as they clutched her AP Government textbook. Her eyes were cast downward, watching her shoes as her weight shifted from one foot to the other. Abigail's breaths came out in quickened, silent puffs in through her nose and out through her mouth. Noah felt like a dummy for standing there without a word, so he decided to change that.

"Hey, uh," his words startled Abigail enough that her brown, glazed eyes darted up to his own the second a letter was echoed. "Are you okay?"

Abigail swallowed down another lump in her throat and forced herself to nod. "Yeah," she choked out. "I'm fine."

"Are you sure? You don't look like it," Noah persisted gently.

"Yeah. I'm okay. Thank you, Noah."

"Don't worry about it," he replied. "It wasn't a problem and he looked...not good."

Abigail laughed quietly while Noah cringed at his choice of phrasing. He smiled a bit at the sound of her small chortle. "Yeah, he wasn't."

"I'm sorry about him...really, I am," Noah apologized when he clearly did not need to.

"It's not your fault," Abigail assured him with a small grin. It quickly vanished when she noticed one of the clocks on the wall, though. "Oh, no. I'm late. I'm really late."

Noah did not seem phased to her surprise. "It happens. Would you like me to walk you to class?" He fumbled when he realized what he offered. "I mean, if it'd make you feel better."

Abigail laughed once again. "I'd actually really like that. Thank you."

"No problem."

The two of them walked in silence down the hall which was completely vacant by then. Neither of them felt the need to talk--the quietness between them was peaceful. Abigail felt a sense of peace slowly wash over her, but her anxiety quickly let it wither away, always keeping her on her guard. Despite knowing Noah better than she did a couple of weeks ago, Abigail could have never been sure.

Abigail led Noah towards her AP Government classroom and Noah followed suit. She stopped in front of the door and gave him a quiet nod, to which he replied with the same gesture. In Noah's line of sight, he noticed Brielle, one of Abigail's friends, next to an empty desk. She smiled and gave him a kind wave. He waved back and watched Abigail awkwardly attend to her seat. Her teacher didn't seem to mind her tardiness, he realized as he shut the door.

Noah's face paled and he stopped in his tracks on his way to his locker when he had another realization. He begrudgingly remembered back to when his AP Calculus teacher first lectured him about the concept of lateness:

"You're late," Mr. Russell stated the obvious as Noah hurriedly entered the classroom.

Noah let out a sigh and responded genuinely, "I'm really sorry, Sir. I got held up. It won't happen again--I promise."

"You'd better make sure it doesn't," Mr. Russell instructed firmly, "Or it'll land you in detention the next time it occurs."

"I understand. Sorry again."

Noah let his face drop into his hands and his fingers rake down his flushed cheeks. He unleashed a sigh and knew exactly what was coming for him.

"Oh, fu-"

12

"IT LOOKS LIKE GIBBERISH TO ME."

ABIGAIL NEVER THOUGHT OF HER LOCKER AS A DANGEROUS SPACE...NOT until what had happened the previous day. It was simply a metal box with a door that creaked and a combination lock that she almost always forgot the code for. She never expected for someone to be hiding behind the squeaky door that was slightly beginning to rust. For being the only high school that Hillwell had, the faculty needed to step up their game just a tad.

With that information in hand, Abigail jumped at least two feet back when she shut her locker door, British Literature textbook in hand, and was met with Keagan's anticipating gray eyes on the other side of the metal. Once she realized it was not a mortal enemy, Abigail put a hand over her chest to calm her racing pulse.

"Oh, God—Keagan, don't do that," she wheezed.

"Oh, I'm sorry, Abi," Keagan instantly apologized. "I didn't mean to scare you, but I'd like to inform you that I did it."

Abigail hesitated, her mind blanking. "...Did what?"

"Don't tell me you forgot why we arrived at school extra early this morning." Keagan's jaw was a gaping hole.

"I remembered," Abigail clarified. "I just didn't think you were serious."

Keagan frowned and began to instruct her, "Okay, so when the sub calls out the name at the bottom of the list, we'll yell out...*you know* in unison."

"I feel like we'll get in trouble for this."

"Nah, we won't," Keagan dismissed the idea. "It's not like we're putting a whoopie cushion on the sub's chair."

"You're right. We did that last year," another approaching voice exclaimed over the murmurs of conversations from other students crowding the halls.

The two of them turned to see Jade walking towards Abigail's locker with Brielle hot on her heels. "Hi, Jade! Hi, Brielle!" Keagan welcomed both.

"Hey, Keagan—hi, Abigail," Jade replied while Brielle waved. Her cyan eyes focused on them. "What are you doing *this* time?"

"We're pranking the Brit Lit sub." Keagan then leaned over and whispered in Jade's ear and then Brielle's.

Jade's eyes instantly lit up with the idea while Brielle appeared indifferent. She wanted to be supportive of her friends, but pranking teachers, especially unexpecting substitutes, was against her morals. Her other friends - mostly the spontaneous and sometimes reckless Keagan - did not pay as much attention to morals. Pranking teachers was something that happened every so often since not many students did so.

Sure enough, Brielle offered her two cents, "Are you sure this is safe?" she asked. "I mean, you two might get in trouble for that."

"It'll be fine, Brielle!" Keagan refuted the idea. She gently nudged Abigail above the elbow. "And it'll help you feel better because it'll be funny—right, Abi?"

Abigail nodded, a grin appearing on her face this time. "Yeah."

"Okay, but don't come complaining to us when you get your butts thrown in detention," Jade snickered teasingly. If her friends didn't know her, it would have sounded cruel.

Keagan shrugged. "We won't," she beamed and took a careful hold of Abigail's wrist. "Come on, Abi--let's go have some fun."

"Okay—see you guys," Abigail fumbled over her words with a smile and a wave as she let Keagan pull her away.

The two of them stopped by Keagan's locker before racing towards the British Literature classroom. Keagan dragged Abigail in tow behind her as she rushed towards the very room where the "fun" would occur. Abigail was most uncertain about Keagan's idea at first, but she had quickly warmed up to it after hearing rumors from her British Literature classmates that the substitute needed a bit of "warming up" when it came to teaching.

Ever since Abigail informed the group of what had happened with Landon the previous day, her three friends had been eager to lift her spirits. Neither Jade, nor Brielle had any ideas that seemed to spark interest in their friend's eyes, but Keagan snapped her fingers in approximately three seconds with an idea. Only she and Abigail were completely in on the scheme to prank the substitute teacher, and it was most likely dangerous when it came to perfect school records, but Keagan was far from caring. She never did. Abigail, on the other hand, just wanted to get through her senior year with minimal hiccups and escape as soon as possible.

By the time Abigail and Keagan made it to their seats, the British Literature classroom was nearly full. Abigail noticed Noah while on her way in. He gave her a small nod to which she returned as a bit of an awkward greeting while she walked past. Abigail did not miss the telltale smirk on Keagan's face. Instead of drawing light to it, she rolled her eyes and sat down in her usual seat near the center of the classroom.

A couple of minutes later, a middle-aged woman with tightly curled black hair and a generous height above average entered the classroom. She could have only been the substitute, which sent Keagan into a fit of silent laughter. Abigail had no idea what to think. The teacher herself looked to be completely innocent, and for a second, a stab of guilt throbbed in her chest, but it was not a big deal to prank someone. Pranks were harmless most of the time.

"Good morning, everyone," the substitute teacher addressed the bumbling class. "My name is Mrs. Atkinson. I assume Mr. Wright notified you of my presence for the rest of the week."

Murmurs echoed around the classroom. Abigail was silent while Keagan attempted not to burst out into a fit of laughter no matter how dumb her idea of a prank sounded.

Mrs. Atkinson paid no mind to the twenty-five students' chit chat. "Alright, then. I'll get started with the roll and then we'll begin with our class."

Keagan clamped a hand over her mouth while Mrs. Atkinson went over the first few names—Abigail's being one of them. Once the black-haired girl said "Present," she looked over at her friend who was about to burst at the seams. Abigail rolled her eyes and brought her eyes back towards the front of the classroom as the substitute continued to read each name off the handwritten list.

Mrs. Atkinson paused when she reached the bottom of the list, though. She squinted and adjusted her glasses to see if she was reading the word correctly. "Um, I'm not sure if I should be allowed to say this last name," she slowly commented.

Keagan almost snorted, but she held it back. Abigail's gaze snapped over to hers. The petite girl with her feet several inches off the ground mouthed "Ready?" to her. Abigail nodded and was unable to keep the small smirk off her face. She let her mind focus on an amusing topic rather than a terrifying one.

"This name is at an interesting place on the roll and the spelling is quite controversial," Mrs. Atkinson continued.

By then, the entire class except for Abigail and Keagan were confused. Keagan bit the inside of her cheek to keep herself from laughing and Abigail picked at her nails to create a distraction from the amusement that lay ahead. Mrs. Atkinson scanned the name at the very bottom of the list several times. Her eyebrows furrowed together, but she eventually decided to speak up.

"Um, is Maya B-...Butreiks here?" the poor substitute enunciated.

Keagan couldn't take it anymore and slammed her hands down on the desk. At the same time as Abigail, the two of them burst out into contagious laughter. Both of them forgot about what they were supposed to yell, but it didn't matter anyway.

The whole class exploded into a laughing fit. For the first time in a long time, Abigail found herself laughing freely and without having to care about a certain someone being in her paranoid life. She felt safe, especially with Keagan at her side. The sensation of laughter after a drought consisting of nothing but fear and anxiety was wonderful. Unfortunately, that feeling did not last for more than twenty seconds.

"Quiet!" Mrs. Atkinson boomed. The class instantaneously hushed. Both Abigail and Keagan were caught off-guard when the substitute glared at them. "Miss Bartley and Miss Lopez, is it?" She didn't even wait for an answer. "I'm assuming that you two were behind this "prank" or whatever you'd call it. Is that right?"

"Yes, Ma'am," Abigail shamefully replied.

Keagan said nothing until Abigail harshly elbowed her in the arm. Her gaze snapped towards Mrs. Atkinson as she rubbed the point of contact. "It was my idea. I'm sorry."

"I don't care whose idea it was," Mrs. Atkinson asserted. She reached into a drawer and grabbed two objects before she started walking towards their desks. "All I care about is that the two of you partook in it. Both of you will be receiving an hour's detention after school. Come up to me after class so I can fill out your slips."

Abigail said nothing when the red detention slip was shoved into her hands, but Keagan was not having it. Her eyes narrowed slightly, and she was about to open her mouth to protest, but the substitute was clear with her words.

"If you try to argue with me, you both will have a second detention the day after. Is that clear?"

"Yes, Ma'am," Abigail muttered for the two of them. Keagan was seething, but she offered the substitute teacher a curt nod.

Abigail glared down at her red detention slip that she gripped tightly in her hands. That was the last thing she needed. She glanced over towards Keagan, who had set her detention slip on the surface of her desk and was typing vigorously on her phone. Abigail rolled her

eyes for the second time that morning. This was typical of Keagan—
when she wanted to break the rules, she broke them well.

"*Thank God Kristy's still out of town,*" Abigail thought. She knew if
she had to miss a session, she needed to pay a fee. Kristy was very
kind about the whole situation and tried to lower the prices as much
as she could, but Abigail still did not want to burden her parents by
having them spend more money on her.

She was about to start actually paying attention to the class in
session when her phone silently pinged with a notification. Abigail
quickly took it out of her pocket and hid it in her lap while she
looked at the text from the girl next to her.

"*I'm really sorry I dragged you into this mess.*"

Abigail typed back: "*It's okay. The prank really made me smile.*"

"*Should we wreak havoc in detention later?*" Keagan texted back.

"*Probably wouldn't be the best idea, but it'd be fun.*"

Abigail noticed Keagan grin out of the corner of her eye. "*Is that a
yes?*" the girl in the pixie cut asked enthusiastically.

"*No.*"

Keagan bit back another laugh and the two of them listened to
Mrs. Atkinson's lecture. She was somehow worse than Mr. Wright,
who most definitely was not always right. Abigail found herself
glaring at the detention slip for most of the class period. Keagan
seemed indifferent about the whole situation. She had received
detention several times for the stupidest things. Abigail was relieved
when her first class period of the day was finished. Once Mrs.
Atkinson dismissed the students, the entire room became chaotic.

Since the two of them needed to stay behind so Mrs. Atkinson
could fill out their detention forms, neither Abigail, nor Keagan
noticed Noah secretly slide out of the classroom before everyone
else.

Abigail and Keagan walked to the latter's locker first to retrieve
her Algebra II books before they began walking towards Abigail's to
obtain her AP Calculus ones. Neither of them said much while on the
journey between the two lockers and through the blustering sea of
people. Both Abigail and Keagan kept themselves on their guard in

hopes to avoid a certain person. Luckily, the two made it safely to Abigail's locker.

The last thing Abigail was expecting was a small slip of paper to be floating onto her shoe once she opened her locker door. Abigail immediately discarded the idea of retrieving her textbook and bent down to pick the note up off her shoe. Once she unfolded it and briefly read what was on it, she had to refold it due to Keagan's searching eyes.

"Abi, what's that?" she probed once she saw what Abigail was looking at.

Abigail stuffed her British Literature textbook into her locker and picked up her AP Calculus book. "Nothing, Keagan. Probably just a loose slip of paper."

"Why were you reading it with doe-eyes?" Keagan started to interrogate with waggling eyebrows.

"I was *not!*" Abigail retorted harshly. "I just wasn't expecting a random piece of paper to fall on my foot.

Keagan smirked. "What'd it say?"

"Nothing."

"Can I see?"

"Absolutely not."

"Why not?"

"Because I said so."

"You sound like my mom."

"So?"

"That's not a valid reason."

"Yes, it is."

"Can I read it?"

"No."

"Pretty please?"

Abigail rolled her eyes, groaned dramatically, and finally surrendered the paper over to Keagan, who eagerly took it from her. She unfolded the small slip of notebook paper and began to read the note with elegant handwriting.

. . .

Just wanted to ask if you were okay again, especially after what happened yesterday. I know it's none of my business, but I hope you're doing alright, and if you need anything, don't hesitate to let me know. I know you said you didn't want it before, but here it is just in case.

-Noah

P.S.: The prank in British Literature was funny. Sorry you and your friend got detention for it.

Next to his signature was his phone number.

Keagan's jaw dropped. She thrust the piece of paper towards Abigail, who struggled to catch it, but she succeeded right before it hit her shoe once again. "Abi!" she screeched. "Do you know what this means?!"

"...What?" Abigail cautiously answered her question with one of her own.

"You scored his phone number!"

"I know."

"Wait...," Keagan trailed off with another realization. "That's right —you declined it in the first place. Why'd you do that?"

"I don't trust him. I don't want to take any chances, especially after what happened," Abigail quipped simply.

"Is this the first time you've gotten a note from him?"

Abigail's hesitation did all the replying for her.

Keagan's knowing smirk grew into a huge, genuine smile. "That's actually one of the most adorable things I've ever seen."

"No, it's not."

"It is!"

"Can we just drop it, Keagan?" Abigail requested. The expression on her face was pleading. "Please?"

"Okay, I'm sorry," Keagan apologized sincerely. She offered her a small grin. "But you should consider saving his number."

Abigail shut her locker door and locked it. "You know how I am about saving numbers."

"I know, but he literally tutored you almost every night for over a week so you could pass that placement test while having no idea why you wanted to do that in the first place," Keagan reasoned with her. "It's not every day you find a guy like that."

"I'll think about it," she caved quicker than she thought.

Keagan smiled and patted her on the shoulder. "Good thinking."

The words of her friend resonated with Abigail for the rest of the school day. Abigail was unable to focus during many of her classes. She knew Noah was nothing like Landon ever was, but Abigail still had a strong sense of uncertainty in her bones. Abigail trusted Landon with all her soul, though. She refused to let herself do the same with someone she had known for barely a month.

Her nails were ground down to the rim by the time she was in PE class —her last of five. Mrs. Watson, like usual, had the class run laps around the large gymnasium. Abigail had lost count of how many times she ran around the room that was able to hold an entire basketball court. She struggled to catch her breath while she returned to the girls' locker room and changed back into her regular clothes. Abigail could not be bothered to take a shower when she already had detention in a short amount of time. She did not want to be in any more trouble than she currently was.

Abigail trudged towards her locker, her legs aching and throat burning with each step, to return her empty water bottle to her locker and pack up her things so she did not have to attend to it after detention. She took her time - fingers throbbing from irritation - placing her textbooks and other supplies in her backpack. Abigail nearly fell over when she slung the heavy bag over her shoulders, but she proceeded down the hallway, red detention slip in hand.

Keagan filed in next to her with her own red detention slip. Her neon green drawstring bag with the Vans logo on it was draped over her back. The piece of paper in her hand was crumpled and folded several times over as if she was trying to hide it. Abigail almost winced at the number of creases in the small slip. It seemed like Jade and Brielle did the same as they approached their two friends. Jade eyed the detention slips while Brielle carried a small stack of books in her small hands.

"I guess the prank in Brit Lit didn't work out, huh?" the platinum blonde assumed.

Keagan and Abigail looked at each other. They both had failed to mention their detention to Jade and Brielle during the lunch period. "No, but it was really funny," Keagan countered.

"I can concur," agreed Abigail. She and Keagan fist bumped.

"I'm sorry you two got detention," Brielle sympathized kindly. She gestured down to the books she was holding. "I forgot to bring this up earlier, but I have the *Lord of the Rings* trilogy if either of you would like to borrow them for your project. I recently finished reading them for my book club."

"You're in a book club?" Jade, Keagan, and Abigail asked at the same time.

Brielle nodded with a smile. "Yeah! It meets every Tuesday at the Express-O Café, so I have one tonight. Would any of you like to join? I can invite friends."

"No thank you," Abigail politely responded. "I think I have too much on my plate with that project and AP Calculus, but maybe some other time."

"I'm with Abi on this one. I'm sorry, but I have a lot of work to catch up on and extra reading would probably distract me," Keagan agreed as sweetly as she was able.

Jade shrugged. "Maybe another time but thank you. That's very kind of you."

"That's fine," Brielle replied, unfazed. She held out the three books towards Abigail and Keagan. "If either of you want to borrow these books, they're in very good condition."

"I'm planning on watching the movies, but Abi can have them if she wants," Keagan offered, which made Brielle roll her eyes.

Abigail grinned softly in Brielle's direction. "Yeah, that'd be great."

Brielle handed her the books and she took them, holding them against her chest. "Thanks, Brielle."

"No problem." Brielle was nothing but genuine.

Keagan took Abigail's sunglasses off her head, ruffled her hair, and then put them back on, which made the girl fumble with them before they were adjusted. "Ready to go serve our time in prison?" Keagan teased.

"I guess so." Abigail looked at her two friends apologetically. "I'll see you guys tomorrow, and thank you for the books, Brielle."

"You're welcome." The auburn-haired girl's eyes were shining behind her glasses. "Good luck with detention."

"Yeah, good luck," Jade added on.

Abigail and Keagan thanked them before departing on their way. The detention room happened to be their British Literature class-room, which they both grew to hate. From the sound of it, Abigail determined there were a few more people in detention, so it would not have been just her and Keagan. She was pleasantly surprised to see Mrs. Harris - her kindhearted and helpful former Precalculus teacher - overseeing detention for that day. Abigail and Keagan walked over to her desk and set their detention slips on the surface.

Mrs. Harris looked up from her laptop at the sound of paper sliding onto her desk. Her eyebrows furrowed when she noticed Abigail, who had always been a good student. "Hello, you two," she greeted them politely despite the situation they were in. "Please take a seat anywhere in the room. You're allowed to talk, but please be quiet and respectful of the other people in the room. When your time is up, I'll be letting you know."

"Thank you, Mrs. Harris," Abigail responded a bit awkwardly. Keagan followed behind with the same amount of discomfort.

Mrs. Harris frowned at their answers. "Is everything alright?" she asked them.

"Oh, no—everything's fine," Abigail clarified for the both of them.

"Alright...well, if you need to talk to me about anything, I'm here. Just come up to my desk anytime and I'll be willing to listen."

The two of them uttered a "Thank you" and then turned towards

the classroom of students who were serving punishment just like
Abigail and Keagan. Abigail noticed several people who were not
unlikely to end up in detention - thankfully none of them being
Landon - but one person in the very back corner caught her eye. The
young man with brown hair had papers all over his desk with a
particularly thick textbook opened in the corner. He was studying it
intently before scribbling down something. The cycle rotated at least
twice before Abigail noticed exactly who it was by the pair of glasses
slowly sliding down his nose.

Keagan tapped Abigail on the shoulder as they walked towards a
pair of desks in the middle of the classroom. "Dude, is that Noah?"
she whispered in her ear.

"Yeah, it is." Abigail kept her eyes on the studious teenager who
looked very out of place.

"I wonder why they tossed him in the joint," Keagan wondered
aloud.

Abigail's lips became a thin line as they sat down. "If you're so
intrigued, why don't you ask him yourself?"

"Hm," pondered Keagan amusedly. "I just might."

"No!" she quickly retorted as Keagan started to stand from her
seat.

"Why not?"

Abigail rolled her eyes at the innocence on Keagan's face. "It's
none of our business."

"But you told me to ask him myself," she countered.

"...Fine, but I'm coming too," Abigail caved to Keagan's delight.

"I thought you would."

Abigail decided not to ask what that meant. Instead, she led
Keagan towards the empty desks near the back of the classroom.
Keagan sat in a desk diagonally to Noah's, and Abigail sat in the desk
to Noah's right and behind Keagan's. Despite the noise of footsteps
and small snickers from Keagan, Noah neglected to pay attention to
the two girls who were now surrounding him. There was no escape
due to him being in the corner of the room.

It wasn't until Abigail cleared her throat and sarcastically questioned like she was rooming with a prisoner in a jail cell, "What are you in here for?" Keagan's nod of approval afterward almost made Abigail drop her face in her hands.

Noah flinched just enough to drop his pencil on the surface of the desk. "I could ask you the same thing." He went along with Abigail's tone. A small, playful, and somehow kind smirk was on his face. "But, if you're so intrigued, I was late to AP Calculus one too many times. I wouldn't recommend swearing in front of the teacher either. This is my second day of detention in a row because of mouthing the f-bomb."

He "forgot" to mention his reasoning for being late was to help with Abigail's situation the previous day. Guilt was the last thing Abigail needed. She said nothing about it, but she had a sinking feeling that she was the reason for his punishment.

"Oh, I'm sorry—I'll keep note of that," Abigail promised him sympathetically. "As you know, Keagan and I are here because of the Brit Lit prank."

Keagan casually waved above her head to Noah without giving him a glance. She was busy scrolling on her phone with her high tops resting on the top of her desk.

"Yeah, that sucks. It was honestly crummy of her to give you both a detention right in front of the class," Noah expressed after waving back to Keagan, who pretended not to see it.

"I understand it, though." Abigail shrugged. She felt intimidated by the classroom's walls beginning to close in on her, so she fought to keep her tone level.

Noah was no mind reader, but he somehow picked up the anxious aura from the girl sitting next to him. "Are you okay?"

"Yeah." She pointed to the work that was on his desk to redirect. "What's that?"

"That would be our Calculus homework due Friday."

"It looks like gibberish to me."

His brows scrunched together at that. "Do you want some help with it? I mean...*are* you doing okay in Calculus?"

"Oh, yeah—I'm doing fine," Abigail stated confidently. "It's a lot of work, but I'm getting used to it. I got some of the work done already for Friday."

"That's good. I'm glad to hear it." Noah's grin was back on his face.

Keagan snorted but did not look their way. Abigail glared at her. "Go back to your scrolling, Keagan," she muttered.

"Righty-O!" Keagan decreed and continued scrolling on her phone.

"Shh," Mrs. Harris shushed Keagan politely. "Please treat this space as if it were a library. There are other students concentrating here."

Keagan slumped down in her seat. "Sorry."

"It's okay. Thank you."

Abigail forced down a chuckle at Keagan being reprimanded. Noah went back to doing his work, but he did not become silent. "Is everything okay with...," he broke off the end of his question when Abigail deeply frowned in the corner of his vision.

"I think so." Abigail nearly had to choke out the words. "Thanks for yesterday."

"Like I said, it's not a problem." Noah discarded the idea of doing his work and gave his full attention to the girl sitting next to him. "Don't worry about it."

"I wonder why he won't mention the fact he gave me his number earlier today," Abigail thought to herself. *"Maybe he's giving me time...?"*

Noah appeared to determine a general comprehension of Abigail's imagination, because he hurriedly said afterward, "You know, if you need anything, I'm here for you. I just want you to know that."

Abigail's breath hitched in her throat. She knew Keagan was listening with keen ears, but for once, she couldn't care less. The glint in her brown eyes gradually morphed from one of fear and angst to an unfamiliar warmth. Before, she refused to let in any sort of that comforting sensation. The fear of it turning ice cold against the depths of her pulsating heart was too much for her to ever be able to bear.

If Abigail was so hesitant to allow such kindness from someone a little more than a stranger to affect her, why did their sunlight begin seeping through the cracks of the weathering wall guarding her soul?

The answer was simple: there were none; at least none to describe how her walls were slowly tearing themselves apart brick by brick for a boy she hardly knew.

She let the smallest, but most authentic of smiles slowly crawl upon her face. "Thank you. Really, thank you."

Noah nodded in reply and went back to doing his Calculus homework. There was nothing else to say—or at least nothing Abigail could think of. Instead, she took her phone out of her jacket's left pocket and a small slip of paper from her right. Abigail opened the contacts app on her phone and created a new contact. Afterwards, she unfolded the small paper and typed in ten specific digits before clicking the save button.

On the top of the contact, Noah's name was displayed.

13

"THEY'RE COUSINS SIXTY-THREE TIMES REMOVED."

IN FRONT OF NOAH WAS A VERY MODEST HOUSE. BEHIND HIM WAS A frigid twenty-minute walk.

Noah pulled his zipped jacket tighter around him when another gust of wind jostled his shivering body. It was almost as if his face was frozen solid from the journey between his house and the one in front of him Noah's teeth chattered silently as he stepped down the cracked and weathered driveway.

Everything about the house in front of him screamed modesty. The house, which barely topped twelve hundred square feet, had a single story, gray shutters, and a matching roof that needed to be replaced years beforehand. No cars rested on the driveway. It seemed as if the house was completely deserted. Noah knew that was far from the truth, though. He had been invited earlier that day at a certain time.

Noah cautiously made his way up the porch steps. Despite being invited, Noah was uncertain about the whole idea. He had hardly known the person he was preparing to visit. It had barely been a month since the two of them crossed paths. Why was he being invited to their house so soon? Was he going to get kidnapped? Murdered? Both?

He shook his head dismissively. Those ideas were ridiculous. Besides, they were his friend and Noah trusted them...at least more than he did initially.

Before he was able to turn back and let his nerves get the best of him, Noah rang the doorbell and stepped back. The toe of his left high top tapped rhythmically on the wood beneath it while he waited. Maybe civilization had died out in the twenty minutes it took for him to walk from one neighborhood to the next and a zombie apocalypse happened? Noah internally smacked himself. He needed to get those absurd ideas out of his head.

Fortunately, Noah had done exactly that mere milliseconds after the front door opened a smidge. A familiar head of auburn hair peeked through the crack. "Hey, Noah!" Ryder exclaimed and opened the door all the way. "Glad you could make it."

"Me too," Noah stammered from the cold. "Sorry I'm a little late—I forgot my mom had the car for work tonight, so I walked."

Ryder's lips curved downwards at that. "In this wind? Come in before you catch pneumonia."

"You don't have to ask me twice." Noah shuffled into the house just before Ryder shut the front door. He took his glasses off of his face and cleaned them from the fog that had developed from his warm breaths against the cold exterior wind. "Who's playing?"

"You don't know?"

"I told you I don't watch baseball."

"I've heard you say that *way* too many times," Ryder joked amusedly. "But, for your information, the Yankees actually are playing tonight. They're playing the Phillies."

Noah lifted an eyebrow at both the recurring joke from when he pretended to know about baseball and the peculiar name. "What kind of a name is the "Phillies"?"

"A name that the team from Philadelphia uses," Ryder countered.

The brown-haired boy drew his lips in an "O" shape. While speaking about foreign sports terms, Noah had not realized he entered the main portion of Ryder's home and his friend had ventured to the kitchen. His eyes darted around once his glasses were adjusted. The living room and kitchen were nearly an open concept, but with a small wall separating the two rooms just enough. It was clear that Ryder's family was not very wealthy, but there was just enough stuff in the building to make the house seem like a home. Family pictures littered the walls and shelves. Noah thought he recognized who looked to be Ryder's sister with auburn hair, a short stature, and round glasses that resembled Harry Potter's.

Before he could question it, though, Ryder reentered the living room with a large bowl of cheddar flavored chips. "Sorry it's not much," he stated out of nowhere. "If you haven't noticed, my family isn't exactly...you know."

"What?" Noah smiled with disbelief that he was even apologizing for his home life. "No, don't worry about it. Why would I care about that?"

Ryder exhaled a relieved sigh. "Oh, okay. That's good. It's just that a lot of people are judgmental when it comes to how much wealth a family has."

"My family isn't the most well-off either. I get it," explained Noah. "We've been through a lot and my mom works all the time. We always have to get a sitter for my little sisters."

"Oh, I'm sorry."

"It's okay. I'm happy we've had a fresh start in Hillwell."

"So am I." Ryder placed the bowl of chips on the coffee table and the two of them sat down on the couch to face the slightly small television. "So, who are you rooting for in this game? Looks like it already started."

Noah shrugged, grabbing a chip and popping it in his mouth. "I'm not sure. How about you?"

"It doesn't really matter. The Cubs are my favorite team, and they aren't playing, so I'm not rooting for either of these teams."

"Oh, that's understandable."

"I hope you know this means that you're a Cubs fan now or I'm kicking you out right this second," Ryder teased.

"Woah." Noah held his hands in front of him protectively. "They just won the World Series. What more do you want?"

"They hadn't won in a hundred and eight years before then!"

"So?"

"That's a long time!" Ryder screeched.

Noah almost dropped a chip on the floor. "Well, you don't need to yell about it."

"Sorry."

Ryder was indeed not sorry.

The two fell into silence as the second inning of the game began. The score was tied at zero runs apiece. All Noah knew about the sport was that a player needed to circle the three bases and touch home plate to constitute a home run. Ryder personally couldn't be bothered to explain anything, so he refrained from doing so. Instead, he amused himself by watching Noah watch the game with confusion in his eyes and clap awkwardly when a home run was scored by either team.

After at least forty-five minutes of purely watching the game and occasional commentary from Ryder regarding it, the unacquainted silence in the living room was broken by the baseball fanatic. "So," he began, "how's it going with Abigail Bartley?"

Noah promptly choked on a chip. Ryder's eyes bulged out of their sockets. He jumped up and dashed towards the kitchen. Noah heard a cabinet door being thrust open, a clinking of two glasses, and the sink turning on and running. Not even five seconds later, Noah heard Ryder's footsteps bolt into the living room. A glass of water was carefully handed to him, and he took a long sip. The cool water cascading down the walls of his throat soothed his irritated esophagus.

"Woah. Sorry about that, Noah." Ryder's eyes were apologetic. "I didn't mean to catch you off-guard like that. Are you okay?"

Noah nodded and took another sip of his saving grace from the ill-fated chip. "No, it's okay," he composed himself. "I'd hope it's going well, especially if I gave her my number today."

"You did *what*?" It was Ryder's turn to be caught off-guard.

"I gave her my number. I'm not sure if that was the right decision or not since she hasn't texted yet, but she has it."

Ryder's shock morphed into a smile. "I'm sure it was a good decision. Give her time, though. She's been through a lot."

"I know," Noah replied quietly.

"Don't be harsh to yourself about it. If she didn't want anything to do with you, then she wouldn't have wanted you to tutor her so much. What was that for, anyways?"

Noah shrugged. "I don't know, but it's none of my business."

"That's why she should cherish you—and I think she does: you don't pry into her business," Ryder determined without a doubt.

"I don't know about that but thank you."

"You need to stop doubting yourself." Ryder poked a finger at his chest. "Okay?"

Noah hesitated, but reluctantly agreed. "Okay."

A car's high-pitched beep to signal the vehicle being locked sounded from outside. Noah listened through the thin walls - while keeping his eyes focused on the game - as at least two pairs of footsteps walked up the driveway and up the porch steps. When the door handle had a key inserted into it and began to turn, Noah felt uneasiness creep up his throat. At once, more ridiculous thoughts ran through his head.

"Is this where I'm killed off like in a cliche fiction novel?" he questioned himself. Instead, Noah smacked himself in the face. *"Shut up."*

"...Did you just slap yourself and say, "Shut up?"" Ryder asked with furrowed brows.

Noah blinked once, then twice, and then realized he said that out loud. "Oh, sorry. I was just thinking and I guess it slipped out."

"Is everything okay?"

"Yeah, I'm good," Noah confirmed. He gestured to the door. "Is that your-"

Before he was able to finish, three pairs of footsteps entered the house. His question had been answered as two females - one adult and one adolescent - along with one adult male walked into the foyer. Their voices filled the house and from the tone of them, a positive conversation was being executed. Noah couldn't help but listen to the three of them.

"And then I told the group that the three elven rings, Nenya, Narya, and Vilya, weren't actually made by Sauron, but by an elf-lord named Celebrimbor. He helped Sauron with the rings for the dwarves and men, but he didn't trust him, so he forged the elves' rings in secrecy. That's why Sauron, the giant eye in Mordor, had no idea what the elves were doing during the course of the story— because he never had the same power over the elven rings as he did the ringwraiths. I explained that this information seals up the plot hole of Elrond and Galadriel communicating through telepathy about where the One Ring was without Sauron knowing this whole time!" the voice of the teenage girl exclaimed enthusiastically in almost one breath. "Everybody was really impressed!"

The older male's voice replied, "I'm so proud of you, Honey! I bet the whole book club learned a lot from you tonight."

"I agree," the elder female inputted her own two cents. "That's so interesting. I never would've thought of that."

It was clear that neither of the girl's parents knew what she was talking about. Noah, on the other hand, completely understood her logic. He leaned over to Ryder, who had turned the volume of the television down.

"Is that your..."

"Sister," Ryder supplied with a happy grin. "She's really smart. I can't remember the last time she came home from her book club without telling all of us how she knocked the socks off of her friends."

"I can tell." Noah returned the gesture. "She seems very intelligent."

"She is. In fact, she's over two years younger than me, but she's in the same grade as me—a senior. She skipped the ninth grade and I had to repeat my freshman year because I failed so many classes, so she'll be graduating at sixteen and I will at eighteen."

"That's very impressive."

As if it was on cue, Brielle entered the living room with her parents in tow, a proud smile on her face. "Hey, Ryder! Want to hear a cool fact I told everybody at book club?"

"I heard as you came in!" Ryder replied with just as much energy. "It was the one about the elven rings, right?"

"Yep!"

Noah decided to apply some of his own knowledge of Middle-earth. "I've never heard that fact before, but it makes perfect sense."

"It does!" Brielle beamed and then noticed the voice was not her brother's. "Oh, hi. Noah, right? Ryder told me he invited you over, but I wasn't sure if I'd see you. I'm Brielle."

"That's me. It's nice to meet you, Brielle." Noah held out his hand and Brielle shook it. At that moment, he recognized her to be one of Abigail's close friends.

Brielle fixed her "Harry Potter" glasses so they were not crooked. "So, you like *The Lord of the Rings* too?" she asked fondly.

"Yep." Noah wracked his brain to think of a fact for her that she did not know. "Did you know Aragorn and Arwen are actually cousins?"

He almost smacked himself for a second time when Brielle's nose scrunched in disgust, but she perked up again almost immediately. "They're cousins sixty-three times removed. It's because Aragorn is a descendant of Elros, who was Elrond's brother. They were both part of the half-elves race, which I assume you know about. Elros picked a mortal human life while Elrond picked the opposite. That's also probably why Elrond let Aragorn grow up in Rivendell."

"...I guess you did know that. Never mind." Noah blinked blankly at her thorough explanation.

Brielle nodded eagerly. Ryder found the situation quite amusing since he had almost fallen off of the couch laughing. In the meantime, the entirety of the O'Brian family was currently in the living room. Noah caught a glimpse of their parents. Bailey O'Brian had light, straight blonde hair that reached to her shoulder. Her pale complexion caused her brown eyes to stand out. Her husband - Richard O'Brian - possessed auburn hair just like his two children, but it had more similarities to Ryder's. In fact, Ryder was the spitting image of Richard, but in a younger format. Noah discovered that the O'Brians were close-knit from their first impressions alone.

Noah caught Bailey's eye. She gave him a warm smile. "Hello!" She turned her attention to him. "I heard you're Ryder's friend. It's very nice to meet you. I'm Bailey."

"You too." Noah shook her outstretched hand. "I'm Noah."

"And I'm Richard. It's nice to meet you, Noah." Richard held out his hand and Noah shook it directly after Bailey's.

"You too."

Bailey spoke up, "Ryder, Honey, we'll leave you be to finish watching the game. If you need anything, just yell. Okay?"

"Okay, Mom. Thanks." Ryder smiled in his mother's direction.

Ryder's parents left the room, and so did Brielle a couple seconds after. Noah was about to continue watching the baseball game, but Ryder had other ideas. Once everyone was out of earshot, he tapped him on the shoulder.

"Noah, I have a great idea."

"... Should I be scared?"

"No."

Noah narrowed his eyes at the smirk on Ryder's face. "I think I should be."

"No," Ryder once again retorted. "I have an idea that could help you get closer to Abigail. I mean, if that's what you want."

"What's your idea?" Noah was unsure.

"We could ask Bri. She's good friends with her." When Noah didn't say anything, Ryder elaborated, "She's how I met Abigail in the first place, actually. If you don't want to, that's fine, but it might work out in your favor."

"...I don't know."

"Would you like to just ask?" Ryder inquired.

Noah paused to consider it. *"For the love of God, don't mess this up."* He nodded slowly. "It might help, so fine. Let's do it."

"Bri!" Ryder shouted. Noah fought the urge to cover his ears. "Can you come down here for a minute?"

"Coming!" she yelled in response.

At once, a pair of footsteps stomped down the stairs. Noah felt his heart pound quicker than the rhythm of Brielle's socks hitting the wooden steps. Was he really doing this? Noah felt like an idiot for even agreeing to Ryder's idea. He was quite embarrassed about the fact he was going to ask one of Abigail's friends how to get closer to her. Was that weird? Noah certainly thought it was weird.

Brielle already had a wide smile on her face. It almost frightened him how different Ryder's sister was at school from at home. "What is it?"

"Well," Ryder began, placing a hand on Noah's tense shoulder. "Noah wanted to ask you about something, and it might be a little weird, but he's having some girl trouble. You're a member of the female species, so you're the first person I'd talk to."

"Girl trouble?" Brielle asked with a lifted eyebrow. "You mean like a crush?"

"Not a crush. He prefers to call it "anxiety over someone who's the opposite gender,"" Ryder clarified.

Brielle was unable to hide the grin rising on her face. "So, basically a crush."

"Yes."

"I'm right here!" Noah deadpanned quite loudly.

"We know," Ryder and Brielle chorused. The latter quizzically questioned, "What does this have to do with me, though?"

"You kinda know her," Noah spit out despite his heart about to leap up his throat.

Brielle's eyes seemed slightly enlarged from behind her glasses. "I do? I don't know many people at school except for three."

"I know." The brown-haired boy swallowed down the anxiety exiting his lungs before he spluttered it out, "I've narrowed it down to three options and now I'll narrow it down to one. It's Abigail Bartley."

Even Ryder looked surprised at Noah's sudden confession. Brielle's mouth barely parted, lips dry and eyes frozen, but it took hardly any time at all for the smile to return to her face. "No way. No way! That's amazing! You two would be so great together. I'm so happy for you! Don't even get me started on-"

"Okay, don't freak him out, Bri," Ryder interrupted. He noticed the embarrassed pink hue to his friend's face. "We were wondering if you had any ideas on how Noah could get to know Abigail better. Do you have any suggestions?"

Brielle thought for a moment. She snapped her fingers with an idea, something Noah noticed her brother did as well. "I've got it! You could sit with us at lunch starting tomorrow."

"You wouldn't mind?" Noah asked unsurely.

"Nope," chirped Brielle. "I'm sure everybody else wouldn't mind either."

"Even if I sit with you guys too?" Ryder butted in jokingly.

Brielle released a faux sigh of frustration. "I guess we could make an exception."

"If you *must*."

The two of them started laughing, but Noah kept to himself. He fiddled around with the zipper of his jacket and shifted his weight to the other foot. The anxiety he felt slowly began to fade away, but it remained intact. Noah knew the core of it was not going anywhere. He found it in himself to smile along with the two siblings. Having a crush, or "anxiety over someone who's the opposite gender," did not have to be debilitating...right?

Noah decided to ask again, "Are you sure you don't mind?"

"I don't mind at all," Brielle confirmed authentically. "It'll turn out great. You'll get to talk to Abigail, I'll get to have some bonding time with my brother, and we'll have some fun."

"I hope so."

He really did.

14

"YOU THROW A KILLER PUNCH."

"I don't think this is a good idea," Noah confessed once he reached the open doors to the Hillwell High cafeteria.

"Oh, come on," Ryder whined, practically dragging him through the doorway. "It'll be just fine. Remember how you were so willing last night?"

"I remember being really anxious if that's what you mean."

Ryder led him to the line where most of Hillwell High's students were waiting to purchase their lunches. "You'll be okay. How come you tutored her several times and were completely fine with that. That makes no sense."

"That was different," Noah defended himself.

"It still doesn't make sense." Ryder looked at the menu hung over the counter. "What are you getting?" he asked.

Noah sighed in relief at the shift in topic. "Probably the tacos. It's Taco Tuesday, after all, so that's discounted. How about you?"

"The same, actually."

Noah and Ryder made it to the front of the line quicker than they thought. Both of them recited their orders, which were the exact same thing. While the two of them waited for their food, Ryder checked his phone and looked at his texts between him and his sister,

Brielle, regarding their "secret" plan to combine their lunch tables in order to help Noah feel more confident about talking to Abigail.

"Are you still okay with us sitting with you guys?" Ryder's text that he sent to his sister a couple of minutes ago had read.

Brielle had replied to him a minute later. *"Yep! That's fine with me. I'm excited."*

"Me too." Ryder responded.

Noah gave Ryder a sideways look. "Is everything okay?" he inquired out of concern.

"Yeah, I was just double-checking with Bri if it's still okay for us to sit with them," Ryder explained. When Noah frowned, he offered encouragement, "Buck up, Noah. It's going to be more than okay. You might even have a good time over there."

"You know...maybe you're right," Noah reluctantly agreed.

"See? Now you're getting it."

Ryder scoffed at the eye roll he received from someone he could possibly consider his best friend. "Don't roll your eyes at me," he playfully instructed.

"Too bad. I just did." Noah smirked because of that.

"Here you are!" the lunch lady chirped, grabbed their attention. "Two orders of two hard shell beef tacos with extra cheese along with two medium sodas."

"Oh, thank you," Ryder replied to the cheerful woman behind the counter. Noah followed suit with a nod and a similar expression of gratitude.

The two of them grabbed their trays of food and walked over to the condiments table. They collected whatever sauces they wanted before beginning to head over to the table Noah had been dreading ever since the idea was pitched the previous night. Despite Ryder's silent question regarding his well-being through a simple look, he felt like he was being trapped in a lose-lose situation. Noah nodded in response. When he took his eyes off the tray, his drink began to slip off. Noah stumbled and Ryder caught his drink before it was able to fall. Noah grunted at the fact his glasses were sliding down his nose.

"You good?" Ryder asked out loud this time.

Noah nodded again, but awkwardly as he answered Ryder's question with his own, "Could you maybe fix my glasses? Probably wouldn't be good if they fell in a taco."

"Oh, yeah, sure." Ryder balanced his tray in one hand while he pushed Noah's glasses back up his nose and into place.

"Thanks."

Ryder and Noah continued their short walk to the table Abigail and her friends usually claimed in the lunchroom. With each step, Noah's heart hammered harder against his ribcage. The sensation was agonizing, and at times, Noah found it difficult to breathe. He knew it was all mental, but he couldn't help but think something was wrong with him. Noah was extremely paranoid about that very subject, however, he needed to shove it away before he panicked in the middle of the cafeteria.

Abigail and company did not seem to notice the two foreigners approaching their table. What they did notice, though, was Ryder clearing his throat to obtain their attention. At once, four pairs of eyes - two brown, one gray, and one cyan - darted towards them. Noah wanted to crawl into a hole and disappear, never to be seen again.

"Hi, ladies," Ryder exclaimed with an almost teasing tone. "I was wondering if Noah and I could sit with you four. Is that okay?"

Noah took a step back, but Ryder yanked him forward again. The former glanced up at them and noticed Brielle's smile was bright enough to light up the whole room. Keagan had a small, but growing smirk on her face. Jade had a neutral look on her face, however, it disappeared into a smile that looked as fake as a cheap spray tan. Out of the four of them, Abigail looked to be the most confused. Her brown eyes were glazed over with a sheen of nervousness, but she kept blinking it away to make way for kindness. She knew Noah, as well as the boy next to him, but she hadn't spoken to the latter in years.

Noah wondered what was up with Jade.

Keagan glanced across the table at Abigail. Noah thought she was telepathically asking for the go-ahead to allow him and Ryder to sit with them. When Abigail nodded, Keagan turned her eager eyes back to the two boys. She smiled welcomingly and gestured to a couple of the extra chairs at the table—one being next to Abigail on one side, and the second being next to Brielle on the opposite side of the table.

"Sure! What a nice surprise," Keagan expressed gleefully.

Ryder - not surprisingly - took the seat next to Brielle. "Thanks!" He set his tray down on the table and offered Brielle a mischievous grin. "Hey, Bri."

"Hey, Ryder," she monotonously replied. A smile was clearly behind her tone.

Noah sat down next to Abigail, who suddenly appeared quite distant. She stared down at her food like it was the most interesting thing in the world. Noah hoped he was not the source of her anxiety, but knowing him, he probably was. He had done everything he could when it came to helping her, even though he did not know the exact reason why he was drawn to her. Noah had put the pieces of the puzzle together, but the picture was still a bit blurry.

Keagan decided to start a conversation with Abigail due to the silence growing more intimidating over the six of them. "So, Abi, have you started reading the first book for Brit Lit yet?"

"I read the prologue last night," Abigail replied, finally taking her eyes off her food. "It took me over an hour because it kept going on and on."

"That's why I'm watching the movies," Keagan beamed. "The introduction monologue takes less than ten minutes."

"I told you that the movies were different from the books," Brielle reminded her.

Keagan shrugged nonchalantly. "They can't be too different."

"There's several differences, like Tom Bombadil not being in the first movie at all. He has a large part in the first book."

"Who the hell's Tom Bombadil?"

"You asked that already."

"Well, who is he?" Keagan continued to question in a state of confusion.

Brielle began to explain, to which Keagan, Ryder, and even Jade listened. None of them knew she enjoyed speaking so much about a fictional world other than her older brother. He often got a mouthful of it. Noah witnessed an example of that last night.

To Noah's surprise, after Abigail ate a few bites of her food, she carefully looked up to meet his eye and asked him, "Have you started reading the book yet?"

"I actually haven't, but I'll start it tonight. It's something I've already read a few times," Noah answered. "I know the prologue is long, but it gets a lot better."

A petite smile slowly grew on Abigail's face. "I'll take your word for it."

"Trust me on this. It starts slow, but I think you'll enjoy it," Noah assured her, which made her smile grow. "Your friend over there knows a lot about the series."

"Who? Brielle?"

"Yeah," he responded. "I was over at Ryder's watching baseball with him and she came in talking all about it. Ask her if you want. I'm sure she'd be helpful with the project."

Abigail shrugged, popping a fry in her mouth. "I might ask."

"Can I have one of those?" Noah inquired.

"Knock yourself out." She turned the fry container towards him.

Noah eagerly took a particularly big fry from the container and put it in his mouth. "Thanks," he said with a grin.

"You're welcome."

Keagan noticed the table grow deafeningly quiet again, so she changed the subject for a second time. "You know, maybe we should have a *Lord of the Rings* movie night sometime soon. It seems like we all are at least somewhat interested in them. The movies are great, and I was planning on watching them for my project anyway!"

"I think that's a good idea," Brielle quickly contributed her thoughts.

"Me too," Noah was second.

Ryder was third. "Me three."

"I wouldn't mind," Abigail added to the pile of agreements.

Jade, the only one of the group who hadn't spoken for the majority of the time Noah and Ryder had been at the table, reluctantly agreed, "I've never been interested, but I'd be happy to watch the movies with you all."

"It's settled, then!" Keagan declared cheerfully. "How would you guys like to come over on Friday and we can watch the first movie? It can be a weekly thing until we finish the trilogy. Then, we could move on to *The Hobbit*."

"Good God, we're a bunch of nerds." Jade facepalmed herself with a smile. "But that sounds good to me. Sure!"

"Me too!" Brielle cheered.

"Me three." Noah was third.

"Me four." Ryder was the fourth.

Finally, Abigail was the fifth to confirm, "Fine with me. Let's do it."

"Great! My address is forty-four Mistyfoot Trail."

The whole table erupted in chatter - except for Abigail and Noah - about the event that was being mentally added to their schedules. Despite being surrounded by friends, Abigail did not quite feel as if she was in the safe bubble filled with trust around them as she usually did. She noticed something off with one of them, and that one happened to have platinum blonde hair and a pair of cyan eyes. Abigail wondered what was wrong or if anything was going on with her, but it was not something she was able to worry about for long.

Before anyone knew it, the lunch period ended, which led to clusters of students exiting the lunchroom. The group of six remained close and waited until most of the large group of their peers had left the room so none of them would get separated. After they had done so, the six walked over towards the trash can and threw away what was left on their trays, stacking them near the bin with the others afterwards. None of them said much of anything since whatever words spilled out of their mouths were absorbed with the loud hustle and bustle of the crowds around them. High school was a very, very overwhelming place to be.

The six teenagers subconsciously walked towards Abigail's locker. The black-haired girl somehow was positioned in the front with Keagan, followed by Noah, then Brielle, Jade, and Ryder. They all were in the midst of differing conversations while Abigail remained quiet. She had nothing to say, so why would she try to talk? Instead, she focused on arriving at her next class on time and without any problems.

Abigail unlocked her locker and began filing through her textbooks until she found the one she needed for her class. While she collected her supplies, she felt a tap on her shoulder. Abigail glanced over at Keagan but paid it no mind as she kept searching for her things. The taps became more aggressive until Abigail snapped her head towards her.

"What?" she snipped more harshly than she meant to.

Keagan gestured with her eyes towards something behind her locker door. "Wussy-named jerk alert," she sputtered out. "He's coming this way."

Abigail instantly froze. She knew exactly who she was talking about without a name being mentioned. She shut her locker door and slung the lock on it, shutting it with a click. Abigail held her textbook close to her chest as if it were a shield. No one else seemed to be paying attention except for Noah, who remained quiet. He had no idea what to say in a situation like this. Last time, Ryder had set him up without him knowing, but it worked out.

Sure enough, the boy Abigail grew to hate, with his dusty brown hair tousled in the small breeze that whisked by as he walked, approached and stopped a couple yards away. "What's this?" he innocently questioned. "Do you have a posse now?"

"What's it to you?" Keagan challenged when Abigail said nothing.

"I wasn't talking to you," Landon asserted. His eyes landed on the nervous girl. "I was talking to Abigail."

Abigail took a shuffling step back. At the same time, Noah took an unexpected step forward. "Does she look like she wants to talk to you?" he questioned to his own surprise.

"And who are you supposed to be? Superman?" Landon cockily retaliated.

"Who are you supposed to be?" Noah retorted with just as much sarcasm. "If I was, would that make you Lex Luthor?"

Landon rolled his eyes. "Good one, but once again, I wasn't talking to you. I was talking to Abigail."

"Well, we're telling you to shut up and leave," Keagan spoke up. She was standing directly in front of Landon, having to crane her neck upwards to look him in the eyes.

"It's a free country," Landon defended himself. "I can be wherever I want and *talk* to whoever I want. Unless you want to breach my rights as a citizen, you should leave me alone to talk to Abigail like I wanted to."

"That's the stupidest thing I've ever heard. You need to leave," Keagan spat venomously.

"What? Court taught me something. I'm sure it taught you something too." Landon shrugged, easily spilling what Abigail did not want anyone other than her close friends to know. "Right, *Abi*?"

Abigail shrank back into her jacket. She felt tears begin to brim behind her eyes, but she forced them down. Abigail swallowed a shaky sob straining to break free. The boy in front of her had ruined her. Abigail knew she would have been so much better off without him ever being in her life, and there he was: stepping back through the doorway like he had an invitation.

She looked around at the group of five around her. Keagan was standing directly in front. Jade remained near Abigail. Abigail hadn't a clue where Ryder and Brielle went, but the two had disappeared. Little did she know that Ryder had taken his frightened sister away from the conflict and towards comfort. What Abigail did not expect was Noah almost next to Keagan, using part of his body as a shield-like protection for her. Abigail expected it of Keagan, but most definitely not of Noah.

Before she was able to comprehend what was happening, Keagan raised a hand in a fist and a loud *smack* followed by a startled yelp reverberated across the hall. Landon stumbled back with his right hand over his nose. Everyone flinched at the sound of bones hitting unblemished skin. He slowly removed it to reveal a thin trail of blood spilling from his nostrils. His brown eyes were sickeningly glazed over with anger, but Keagan stood firm. She shook her hand to get rid of the pins and needles sensation from the punch she delivered.

"Listen here, you warthog-faced buffoon," Keagan gritted out. "Abi's my nickname for her, and I'll be damned before you even think of using it. Stay the hell away from her. Got it?"

"You don't have the jurisdiction to tell me wha-"

Keagan kneed him between the legs before he could finish. "*Got it?*" she emphasized.

"Fine, fine—whatever," Landon rushed out without thinking.

"Good." Keagan stood over the collapsed figure on the ground. "Now, *beat it.*"

The four remaining members of the group watched as Landon scrambled to his feet and scurried down the hall. Keagan had her lip between her teeth in laughter. Noah and Jade were both chuckling quietly. Even Abigail had a small smile on her face. The petite girl put her hands in the pocket of her oversized hoodie with a satisfied smile.

"Well, then," Keagan beamed, turning around to face the group. "That problem took care of itself. Now, did it?"

"You throw a killer punch," complimented Noah.

"Why, thank you." Keagan leaned over and whispered in Abigail's ear. "He's a good one."

Abigail felt the tips of her ears turn a rosy shade of pink. She pulled her hair over them to cover the hot and apparent sensation. "Thanks for sticking up for me, you guys," she redirected.

Keagan flashed Abigail a bright smile. "You're welcome, Abi."

"No problem," Noah replied a little nervously.

"Sorry I didn't say anything," Jade apologized sincerely. "I didn't know what to do, but Keagan really took charge."

"It's okay." Abigail looked around and noticed two auburn-haired absences. "Where'd Brielle and her brother disappear to?"

As if it was on cue, Abigail's phone pinged with a notification. She pulled it out of her pocket and read the text: "*Sorry we left before things were resolved. My brother took me away since I was a little scared. Are you okay?*"

"*I'm okay, thank you. See you in AP Gov.*" Abigail typed and sent.

She looked at the three people standing in a circle along with her. "...We should probably get to class."

"Yeah, good idea," Noah agreed, trying to lighten the mood. "I don't want another detention from Mr. Russell. You know how he is."

Noah's goal was accomplished when a tiny smile appeared on Abigail's face. "Yeah, I do." Abigail paused like she just realized what was going on. "I'll see you guys later." She began to walk away but stopped. Abigail eyed Keagan playfully. "Hey, Keagan?"

"Yes?" the girl questioned innocently. Her short hair flopped lazily to the side when her head cocked to the right.

"A *Princess Bride* reference? Really?" Abigail asked her. "Can you *not* do that before you absolutely obliterate somebody? It's embarrassing."

Keagan winked at her friend, her gray eyes shining with knowing.

"As you wish."

15

"THAT JERK DESERVED IT, THOUGH."

ABIGAIL'S HEAD WAS STILL SPINNING WITH THE WHIPLASH OF THE events from two days ago. The last thing she was expecting was for Keagan to punch the person she feared the most directly in the face along with kicking him in the nether region. Why would her friend put her well-being in jeopardy just to help her out? Was Abigail really that important to her?

She hated the fact that she was so easily approachable by the "wussy-named jerk" as determined in Keagan's words. Even with five people around her, he still had the guts to waltz up to her and attempt to make her uncomfortable. Despite the extremely polite undertone to his words, Abigail knew Landon was seething inside when he noticed she was completely guarded by people she trusted...or almost trusted.

Abigail's mind traveled back to the amount of confidence her friend displayed with someone who was towering over her as the enemy. She had a plethora of questions for the spontaneous girl she called one of her best friends. How was she even able to do such a thing off a whim? Abigail would never have the confidence to stand up for herself or someone else like that. Did Keagan do those sorts of things often? How was her confidence so high?

She quickly scratched those thoughts. Anything was possible with Keagan.

Even now, as Abigail watched the girl herself sit at her desk, legs swinging without a care as she doodled in her wrinkled notebook, she knew Keagan had a lot more going for her than she thought, especially if she was able to defend herself so well. The hoodie she wore seemed to swallow her up. Abigail eyed the drawing in Keagan's notebook of a specific dog. When she looked closer, she noticed the breed to be a Yorkshire Terrier.

Abigail gently tapped Keagan on the shoulder when she was sure Mr. Wright was not paying attention to his class that was supposed to be doing busy work. "Is that Flynn?" she asked.

"Yeah," Keagan whispered happily. "This is just a freehand, though. I'll get the real thing to pose for me when I get home so I can make a better portrait."

"Do you think he'll sit still?"

Keagan thought about it for a moment before determining, "Not a chance."

"Even if you offer him a treat?" Abigail suggested.

"He'd attack me."

Abigail frowned at that. "Not if he's not hungry."

"Girls, your conversation should be about the work in front of you and nothing else," Mr. Wright firmly reminded them. "If not, it must be something that would be shared with the class. Is that clear?"

"Yes, Sir." Abigail cringed due to being reprimanded. "Sorry, Mr. Wright."

Keagan gave Mr. Wright nothing more than a glance before returning to her drawing. "Sorry, Teach."

Mr. Wright blatantly rolled his eyes. "With that being said, everyone please return to your work. I don't want to hear or see any disruptions from any of you. Understood?"

The classroom fell silent once again. Abigail already completed the busy work that Mr. Wright had assigned the class at the beginning of class that day, so she resorted to watching Keagan lovingly sketch her best friend in her notebook. She admired how Keagan paid such exquisite attention to detail. Even if it was only a lead sketch, Abigail wouldn't have been able to tell the difference between the beloved dog and a drawing.

Keagan continued drawing in her notebook while Abigail watched until there was an abrupt knock on the door. It was as if time froze in the classroom. Each scribbling pencil stopped writing. Mr. Wright stopped grading papers. Even the clock seemed to stop ticking for a couple of seconds until Mr. Wright put down his pen and walked towards the door. The door opened and a woman stood. Abigail recognized her as the Vice Principal: Mrs. Coleman.

"Keagan Lopez, you're requested in the Principal's office," Mrs. Coleman announced louder than she should have.

The girl stopped in her tracks. Her legs stopped swinging. Her eyes stopped blinking. Keagan timidly asked, "Right now?"

"Yes, right now. It's urgent," she asserted.

"...But, Mrs. Coleman, I didn't do anythi-"

Mrs. Coleman interrupted, "Miss Lopez. Now."

Abigail's breath hitched in her throat as she watched Keagan stiffly stand to her full height. She stuffed her phone in the back pocket of her mom style jeans. Keagan took her battered notebook off of her desk and put it on the surface of Abigail's.

"For safekeeping," Keagan answered an unasked question.

Abigail nodded and carefully shut the cover. "Good luck with...whatever this is."

"Miss Lopez," Mrs. Coleman continued to talk over the silent class. "Don't dawdle. We're all waiting on you."

Keagan gritted her teeth together and left the rest of her things behind. Abigail waved to her, but unfortunately, she did not see it since she followed the irritable Mrs. Coleman out of the room and down the hall. She hated the fact that as soon as she left the room, the entire class went back to exactly what it was doing before. It was almost like she was never even there. Keagan knew she was tiny, but she did not think she was completely invisible.

One of her goals was to leave a lasting impression on the lives of others, whether by being a good friend, diligent in her studies when she was able, or even playing a harmless prank to make the class laugh. Keagan easily identified as a people pleaser, but unfortunately, the phrase "You can't please everyone" applied to her as well. She always tried to do the right thing. When Brielle was unable to afford her lunch in the cafeteria, she insisted on buying it for her. When Jade felt left out sometimes during conversations, she offered her attention.

Now, she was walking behind the obnoxiously clicking heeled shoes of Mrs. Coleman's because she thought she did what was right. Keagan knew exactly what had happened with Abigail the previous school year. She had lost count of how many times her close friend had cried on her shoulder or screeched through the phone in emotional agony. It was exhausting, but worth it at the same time. Keagan went to drastic lengths to protect and defend the ones she loved, but it sometimes landed her in trouble.

She knew it was unethical to physically attack someone, but what *he* did to one of her best friends was even more so. Keagan decided once she landed her eyes on him for the first time during her senior year, any punishment held against her for defending Abigail would be worth it a thousand times over.

Keagan almost allowed that very thought to fly out of her head once the door to the Principal's office was opened. Principal Bryant was intimidating enough by herself. Keagan's eyes widened at the fact a man in his thirties was sitting in a chair next to the Principal's desk. His dark blue uniform was what caught Keagan off-guard. She stopped in her tracks once she entered the door. Mrs. Coleman almost slammed the door behind her.

"Good morning, Keagan," Principal Bryant greeted her kindly despite the awkward situation the room of four people were put in. "I'm sorry for disrupting your first block class."

Keagan slowly scooted into the room with a neutral, but admittedly nervous expression. "It's okay, but what is this all about?"

"We should've explained earlier, but this is Officer Henry. He's here to ask you some questions about an incident in the hall on Wednesday. It was reported that evening at about five o'clock."

"To the police?" Keagan asked in disbelief. She took a seat in the chair across from the Principal's desk.

"He believed it to be serious enough," Principal Bryant elaborated. She looked at the officer next to her. "Officer Henry, would you like to take it from here?"

The man cleared his throat. "Yes, thank you." He turned to Keagan. "Now, Miss Lopez. Two days ago, around ten minutes after twelve, you allegedly physically assaulted a young man by the name of Landon Woods. Could you run through the events that led up to this?"

"Wait...," Keagan trailed off, her legs slowing to a stop from swinging, "he said that I *assaulted* him? He had it coming."

"Could you elaborate?"

"He's not a good person. With all due respect, Sir, Landon deserved it, and I'll tell you why. Landon has harassed one of my best friends - Abigail Bartley - more times than I can count. It got so bad that...well, just look at his criminal record! He was on trial for it a few months back."

"We'll be taking a look at his record, but *please*, can you recount the exact events that occurred before the alleged assault took place?" Officer Henry requested again.

"Me and my other friends, Abigail, Jade, Brielle, Noah, and Ryder, were walking towards Abigail's locker," Keagan explained. "He approached us and started being rude to Abigail, taunting her and making her uncomfortable. Then, he crossed the line. That's when I couldn't take it anymore and punched him. I kneed him in the balls too."

"What exactly did he say to you that got you riled up?"

Keagan hesitated, but she spoke anyway. "He mentioned a court case which was very scary and uncomfortable for Abi-...Abigail. He spoke to her like the two of them were the best of friends. He's manipulative and cruel. I needed to defend her and protect her from him."

"I see," Officer Henry stated neutrally. "Are you aware that the Hillwell High School campus has been monitored by video surveillance for the past week?"

"What? No," Keagan spluttered out.

"It hasn't yet been announced to the student body," Principal Bryant clarified to satisfy Keagan's bewildered remark. "We've reviewed the footage from one of the cameras pointing in your direction and your alibi checks out. The cameras enabled us to partially hear the conversation between you two and from what Landon claimed, everything fits."

"Okay, good," the teenager exhaled in relief. "Does that mean I'm okay?"

"Not exactly," Officer Henry countered stiffly.

"...What do you mean?"

"Landon Woods has requested and been granted a restraining order against you."

It took a moment or two for the officer's statement to click in her mind, but when it did, she was outraged. "A restraining order? In under forty-eight hours? How is that even possible?!"

"Mister Woods' lawyer is a talented one at best," replied Officer Henry. "The court granted his restraining order very quickly after the assault took place."

"But...aren't I supposed to know about this order before it's granted to him? Isn't it illegal to grant a restraining order to someone without the other party knowing about it" Keagan desperately questioned, her hands flailing in front of her.

"Since you're a minor, you're treated as such. Your legal guardian, Christine Lopez, has been notified and she attended the official hearing that occurred yesterday at two o'clock."

"What?! Why did you ask me any of those questions, then? My birthday's on the thirty-first. Why couldn't you treat me like an adult?'"

"To get confirmation from you, and the court didn't make an exception." Principal Bryant somberly looked in Keagan's direction. "I'm very sorry this is all so sudden and that you seem to be uninformed of this decision, but I must be the bearer of more bad news."

"This can't get much worse," Keagan almost chuckled with a fake grin on her face. It quickly disappeared when two pairs of eyes firmly locked onto her. "...Can it?"

"Landon Woods' restraining order against you states that you cannot be or remain in the same residence or occupation as him. Since he's a minor, school is one of his occupations."

Keagan felt like tearing her hair right out of her head from the roots. "Does that mean what I think it means, Principal Bryant?" she squeaked.

"It seems like it, and I'm sorry," Principal Bryant blandly confirmed. "Keagan Lopez, due to the nature of the restraining order requested and granted against you, we have no choice but to expel you from Hillwell High School until further notice. Officer Henry will escort you off the campus grounds."

"What?!" Keagan asked frantically, shooting up from her seat. "That's not fair! Can't I get my things first? My mother didn't even tell me about the restraining order or the hearing! How was I supposed to know?"

"The law states that the restraining order has been put into place at the end of the hearing, so you're already violating it," Officer Henry quipped. He stood from his seat. "Come on. You're lucky that Mister Woods didn't press additional charges against you."

"But-"

"Miss Lopez. You need to leave the grounds immediately." The officer's brown eyes were dull, but somehow a little bit menacing at the same time.

"I understand why you're doing this, but I was not aware of anything that occurred in the past two days. Not the hearing, the restraining order...nothing." Keagan gazed up at him with her lip slightly quivering. "At least let me get my wallet from my locker so I can drive home," she pleaded.

The officer paused. "...Go ahead, but you have five minutes. I expect to see you at the front doors by then."

Keagan did not waste any time. She turned on her heels and sprinted out of the Principal's office. She passed by the Vice Principal, who was rudely waiting outside and attempting to listen in, and ran as quickly as she could down the endless hallways. Class had let out a couple of minutes prior, so Keagan weaved in and out of the large groups of people. Rather than racing to her locker, Keagan was on the search for her friends, whether they were new or old.

Meanwhile, Abigail and Noah had met up with Jade and Brielle near Abigail's locker while between classes. Since Keagan was absent for the last remaining minutes of class, Noah decided to walk her to her locker so she would not be alone. Neither of them said a word. Abigail was too nervous about the situation one of her best friends was in. She instinctively gnawed at her poor nails until the rest of her friends arrived.

"Hey, Abigail! Hi...Noah." Jade waved to her once they were within earshot. Her tone wavered slightly when she noticed Noah's presence, but it faded away as soon as it appeared.

Noah waved awkwardly while Abigail's voice trembled, "Hey, Jade."

"Wait, what's wrong?" inquired the blonde. Her mood completely dropped from positive to well-below negative.

Brielle quietly asked, "Where's Keagan?"

"She got sent to the Principal's office," Noah supplied. "We don't know why but I bet it has something to do with what happened Wednesday with Landon."

Sure enough, Keagan was hot on her friends' heels as she dashed at her full speed down the hall. Her shoes squeaked as they rubbed against the tiled floor of the building. Keagan accidentally pushed and shoved many of her peers as she ran, but no apologies were uttered through her chapped lips. Her chest heaved and her heart pulsated long after she skidded to a stop, nearly knocking her friends over like bowling pins.

"They expelled me!" Keagan screeched as she approached the four of them. "That piece of trash reported me to the police and there was an officer there interrogating me along with the Principal."

"What?!" Abigail, Jade, Brielle, and Noah shouted at the same time.

Keagan took deep, quick breaths as she rushed out, "Landon requested a restraining order against me and apparently he has a really good lawyer, so it was granted yesterday. My mom went to the hearing yesterday because they notified her and not me since I'm a minor even though my birthday's literally on the thirty-first. My mom never told me and then they dragged me down to the Principal's office and Principal Bryant expelled me because of the restraining order against me."

"Oh, my God—I'm so sorry," Jade expressed. "That jerk deserved it, though."

"He did," Noah added truthfully.

Brielle was concerned. "What will you do in place of school? You need to graduate."

"I don't know, but I-...I'll figure it out," Keagan stuttered out. Everyone noticed the scarce tears building behind her eyes. "I have to leave before I get in trouble."

"Wait, um...take your sketchbook, at least," Abigail mumbled, passing her friend the notebook that she willingly received.

"Thank you, Abi," Keagan replied sympathetically. "Are you okay?"

Abigail said nothing in response to her question. Instead, she wrapped her arms around Keagan's small frame and hugged her tightly. Abigail was not one for physical contact, but in times like these, she deemed it completely necessary. Keagan returned the loving embrace and rested her head against Abigail's shoulder. Abigail's guilt seeped through her skin and into Keagan's mind. Once the two separated, Keagan decided to assure her.

"You know I would've done it regardless of the repercussions. If you think it's your fault, then I'll whack you with my notebook."

Keagan turned to the group and offered them a lopsided smile despite her eyes desperately wanting their tears to spill. "See you all tonight for the movie if I'm somehow not grounded."

The group bid farewell to Keagan, who attempted to hide her

salty tears until she was out of their sight. The five remaining - including Ryder, but who was not present - were forced to go along with their school routine, but this time, without their spontaneous and most eager aspect of the group. When the group finally separated, one thought ran through Abigail's mind.

"I don't care if you say it's not, Keagan. It's my fault."

16

"KEAGAN, MUST I REPEAT THAT YOU'RE GROUNDED?"

"*ABIGAIL, I KNOW THAT IT SEEMS LIKE THE MOST APPROPRIATE EMOTION TO feel right now is guilt, but you have nothing to feel guilty about. Your friend was trying to protect you, and she would've done that no matter what you said or did. Try not to blame yourself for something you didn't do. That's something you can work on this week. Whenever you feel guilty about the situation, remind yourself that it wasn't your doing. Okay?*"

The black-haired girl was motionless while seated on the couch she grew to know so well at that point. At first, she said nothing. Abigail's eyes brimmed with unshed tears, for she knew Keagan's had shed many that day. No matter what Kristy told her, the sensation of self-hatred chewed her up and spit her out whenever it was given a chance. The small room felt more cramped than ever.

Regardless, she choked out the only word Kristy needed to hear:

"*Okay.*"

Abigail thought back to the session she had with her therapist merely ten minutes before. Throughout the entire hour, she had hardly said a word. Once Kristy asked her the question "What happened?", she spilled everything very expressively. Despite her long explanation regarding Landon's restraining order and Keagan getting expelled, Abigail did not let any teardrops fall down her cheeks.

She felt bad for not telling her parents about the entire situation, but venting to her therapist gradually more and more each session instead helped her immensely. Abigail, of course, had notified them once she discovered Landon's return back in September, but other than that, not a word had been peeped except for the occasional "I'm fine" or "I'm staying away from him." She promised her mom and dad that she had not spoken a single word to him, which she had not. Instead, he initiated the unwanted conversations between the two of them.

Now, Abigail was seated in the driver's seat in her car with one hand on top of the steering wheel as she drove through a neighborhood she had neglected to visit in months. She saw her world through the gold-tinted lenses in her sunglasses, shielding her eyes from the slowly setting sun. One of her favorite playlists blared in her ears as her vehicle cruised at exactly thirty-one miles an hour down the familiar street.

Houses blurred together into one straight line as Abigail parked her car on the curb in front of the Lopez family's house. It was larger than she remembered, being at least three thousand square feet at the minimum along with two stories, a large backyard, and plenty of space for only two residents. Abigail recalled that Keagan's mother was very well off, a factor she had forgotten about over the difficult events of the summer.

Abigail sent a quick text to her parents, notifying them of her arrival, and removed her key from the ignition. When she got out of her car, she shivered a little bit despite wearing an oversized hoodie to protect herself from the weather. She wriggled the sleeves over her hands and shut the vehicle's door, locking it behind her.

Mistyfoot Trail was relatively peaceful. Keagan's family lived in a rather large and high-end neighborhood, which was something she kept low on her radar about. Not many cars drove down the main street since not many families in the town of Hillwell were able to afford such lavish properties to call home. There was an exception for the "many cars" statement, though, when two of them drove down the road and parked near Abigail's.

The teenager watched as Jade got out of her own car while Ryder and Brielle, followed by Noah, exited the car she recognized as the O'Brians'. Abigail felt a pang of apologetic emotions when she realized she could have easily given Noah a ride to the Lopezes' house since the two were neighbors. Abigail pulled her hoodie tighter around herself with her hands in the front pouch. When her friends approached, she removed a hand from the pocket and gave them a small, but genuine wave.

"Hi, guys." Abigail's tone was almost neutral, but there was still a glimmer of hope within it.

"Hey, Abigail." Noah was the first to reply. He frowned when he noticed the leftover guilt swimming in her brown irises. "Are you okay?"

She nodded and responded in a hushed whisper, "Yeah, uh, I'm sorry for not offering to give you a ride here or anything. I feel bad for Ryder and Brielle going out of their way when I live right down the street."

"What? Don't worry about it," Noah assured her. "They offered anyway."

"Oh, okay."

Ryder stepped up to stand next to Noah, which caught Abigail by surprise. "Hey—I know we haven't talked lately or anything, but I just wanted to say I hope you're okay. Bri told me vaguely what's going on with the restraining order issue and I want you to know you've got me on your side."

"Oh...um, thank you, Ryder" Abigail was unsure, but when she saw Brielle's encouraging nod and a bright smile, she spat out the words.

"It's not a problem."

Abigail recognized that charming smile of his and dark auburn hair, but it felt nothing like it used to back when she was fifteen. In fact, she hadn't properly spoken to him since the two split apart during their sophomore year. It was not something she minded.

Abigail was wary around those of the opposite sex, especially after what had happened.

She continued to swim in her thoughts for a brief second until she noticed one of her friends had not said a single word since their arrival. When her eyes met Jade, who appeared gold from her eyewear, she noticed the slight frown on her face. Abigail knew there was something off with her blonde friend. She was always willing to speak her mind once the opportunity offered itself to her. Now, for the past few weeks, she had been wary about mumbling a word.

"Jade, are you alright?" Abigail asked her.

Jade seemed to snap out of a trance her brain had her in. "Yeah, I'm good. Sorry. I didn't sleep well last night, and today's been a hell of a day."

"Agreed."

"Should we go inside?" Jade changed the subject.

"Uh, sure," Abigail fumbled, but she grinned anyway.

The five of them approached the large house and walked up the rounded porch steps towards the front door. Abigail was in the front, followed by Noah, Jade, Brielle, and then Ryder. She pressed a finger against the button of the doorbell and rang it. Abigail listened to the sound of it echo throughout the interior walls of the house. Along with the ringing, she also heard yelling from the inside.

"Mom, I told you that they're coming over and they're already here!" Footsteps followed the harsh statement. "Look, I gotta go—you told me they could come!"

The voice on the other line was so loud that Abigail could hear gibberish. The teenager on the other side of the door was livid. "No, don't pull that BS with me, Mom! You said it was okay for them to come over when you *knew* about all this shit that's going on. Don't even try it. Bye."

The front door abruptly opened with a heavily breathing Keagan on the other side. She stuffed her phone into the back pocket of her jeans and stood aside for the group of friends to enter her home. Keagan had a smile on her face like nothing had even happened.

"Hey, guys!" she beamed even though her smile didn't reach her eyes. "Come on in—I've gotten everything ready in the lounge."

"Lounge?" Noah questioned.

Ryder shrugged in response.

Abigail rolled her eyes and walked into the house. "You'll see," she briefly explained.

Keagan led the five people through her large house. The inside was eerily quiet except for the six total pairs of footsteps roaming through the inside until they reached a staircase. Keagan remained oddly silent as she walked up the stairs, down a hallway and into a room straight down the center. All five of her friends appeared confused by her unusual quietness until she opened the door and revealed the room inside.

Abigail had seen "the lounge" before a couple of times. It was just how she remembered, with a long black sectional sofa in the far corner of the room. A seventy-inch flatscreen television was hung on the wall across from the sofa. A glass coffee table sat in front of the sectional sofa with four two-liter bottles of different sodas along with several party sized bags of chips ranging from Doritos to spicy Cheetos. Pillows and blankets littered the couch. Abigail looked at the flatscreen television and noticed the first *Lord of the Rings* movie's main menu to be displayed. It was clear that Keagan had been prepared.

"Woah," Ryder exhaled, clearly impressed. "You thought of everything."

"It's very nice," complimented Noah with a genuine smile.

"Thank you!" Keagan chirped. She dashed over and threw herself onto the couch cushion in the corner. "Come on in! The movie's about to start!"

Abigail took a seat to Keagan's left and Brielle did to her small friend's right. Ryder sat down on the opposite side of his sister. That left Jade and Noah with a spot directly next to Abigail. The black-haired girl eyed them both with uncertainty. She would not have minded if either of them sat next to her, but it appeared to be a competition to Jade. Abigail watched as Jade plopped herself down next to Abigail with a satisfied smile on her face. She frowned when she noticed Noah's face fall slightly. He sat on the opposite side of Jade at the end of the couch.

"Did...did she do that on purpose?" Abigail asked herself.

She was unable to answer her own question because Keagan held the remote in her hands and was about to click the button that read "play" on the television. She sat criss-cross applesauce in the corner of the couch with her gray eyes wide with anticipation. Even though she had seen the trilogy many times, it was like watching it for the first time.

"Everybody ready?" Keagan grinned when she received nods and several confirmations containing "yes" and "sure" from her friends. "Okay, this one's a long one—three hours and forty-eight minutes."

Abigail thought she heard Jade groan quietly when everyone else seemed excited. "Good thing we're getting the movie started early," she noted to look on the bright side.

"I can point out differences between the movie and the book if you'd like," Brielle offered politely. She sat next to Keagan with an enthusiastic expression on her face.

"That'd be great!" replied Keagan happily. Her eyes then widened with a sudden realization slapping her in the face. "Wait a minute."

Everyone was confused until she screeched, "Flynn!"

At once, the scurrying of paws approached, climbing up the stairs at a speed that could break a world record. Keagan was ecstatic when her small black and brown Yorkshire terrier with bright brown eyes came into view. She coaxed the small dog towards her, and he obeyed. Flynn jumped up onto the couch and wedged himself between Keagan and Abigail

Keagan pressed "play" and scratched Flynn behind the ears. "Alright, now we're ready."

The movie began - enhanced with the surround sound speakers placed in each corner of the room - and the six friends grew quiet. Nobody spoke as the first scene unfolded. Other than the movie itself, everyone was silent except for the occasional crunching of chips and the guzzling of soda. Every so often, Brielle made a comment about a certain factor of the movie that was different from the novel, which was very helpful to Abigail. Abigail suggested that Keagan take notes since she refused to read the book for her project, but she declined, stating that she would simply binge the series again.

After quite a large chunk of the movie had passed, Keagan was frowning at the screen. "Why can't Frodo just shut up and quit complaining?" she whined, which was quite hypocritical.

Jade's head snapped over to meet Keagan's eyes. "He literally just got stabbed by that huge ghost thing."

"Nazgûl," Brielle politely corrected.

"Bless you," Keagan exclaimed, which made the three girls laugh.

"For simplicity's sake, they're also called the Ringwraiths."

"Gotcha," Jade stated.

The three of them returned to the movie. Abigail had been quiet along with one other person in the group—besides Flynn, who was asleep. Her field of vision gradually shifted over to her left to view Noah, who was watching the movie without saying a word. Abigail frowned when she noticed the tired, yet sad expression on his face. She was unable to read his thoughts, but she knew someone was down in the dumps when she saw them.

Abigail removed her phone from her pocket and opened her contacts app. Fingers trembling, she found the contact she made for Noah, which had been untouched until that point. She remembered when he gave her his number. He told her to use it if she needed something, and she had not. The thought of texting someone new, especially a male, unnerved her, but she wanted to be a good friend. Abigail was getting to know him better, after all.

"Should I...?" Abigail briefly contemplated, but she got her answer quickly. Instead of thinking twice, she created up a new text thread and typed out a message.

"Hey, this is Abigail. You okay?"

She sent it, but then added another message down below.

"And yes, I saved your number from when you gave it to me a few days ago."

A second later, Noah's phone dinged with Abigail's message. She watched as he took it out of his jeans pocket and looked at the two notifications that were now on his screen. Noah's eyebrows shot up, but he did not meet Abigail's eye. Instead, he unlocked his phone and saved her contact. He sent her a message.

"Yeah, I'm okay. I'm just a little down. Thanks for asking."

Abigail texted back quickly. *"Can I ask why?"*

"I feel like I upset Jade somehow. She glared at me before sitting down next to you. I'm not sure what I did."

"You didn't do anything wrong. I don't know why she'd do that." Noah's response surprised Abigail. *"She did tell me that she didn't sleep well and it's been a long day today, though."*

Noah seemed to overanalyze Abigail's reply, but he concealed it wonderfully well. *"Oh, okay. That makes sense."*

Little did both of them know that Keagan subtly looked over Abigail's shoulder. She noticed Noah's name on the top of her phone and smirked wickedly. She pondered over an idea and quickly put it into action.

"Hey, Jade, could you switch places with Abigail?" Keagan requested. "I'd like to talk to you about something real quick and it'd be easier if we weren't leaning over her."

Jade hesitated and then argued, "Why can't you move?"

"I'm comfy!"

"...Fine." Jade rolled her eyes and stood up. Abigail scooted over and they switched places. "What'd you want to talk to me about?"

Keagan began talking about something unintelligible since she knew exactly what was going on. Her head was swimming through the thought of Keagan setting her and Noah up. Abigail knew it was completely possible. In fact, Keagan often offered her advice on how to talk to Noah and how to get to know him more by remaining within her boundaries.

Harmony commenced in the room, but not for long. The sound of the front door abruptly opening and closing within two seconds interrupted the movie for the second time in under five minutes. At once, Keagan's happy expression became solemn. She knew it was her mother who had come home, but from the sound of it, there was another set of footsteps along with the older woman's. Keagan abruptly stood up and started to walk out of the room.

"I'll be right back," she notified her friends before leaving and shutting the door behind her.

"Are you okay?" Jade asks after her.

Keagan mustered up a fake smile. "I'm fine. I just want to talk to my mom."

With that, Keagan shut the door behind her. Brielle leaned over and obtained the television remote from the coffee table. She pressed the pause button and turned to her friends with a concerned look on her face, light red hair falling in her eyes. Brielle adjusted her glasses before they fell off, which reminded Abigail of Noah's. Has he found them yet? That was a stupid question to her—if he found them, he would have been wearing them.

"Do you guys think everything's okay?" Brielle's soft question got everyone's attention, including Abigail's.

Jade shook her head. "I don't think so... Did everyone hear her yelling on the phone with her mom when we got here?"

Everyone nodded at that.

"Do you know if this happens often?" Ryder asked the group.

"It seems like it," Jade supplied.

Abigail, surprising everyone, stood up from the couch and put her phone in the pouch of her hoodie. "I'm going to go check on her," she told them.

"Are you sure that's a good idea?" inquired Jade with furrowed brows.

Abigail nodded. "She needs a friend."

"Be careful."

That statement was not from Jade like she had expected. Instead, it was from Noah.

Abigail turned around to face Noah, who was eyeing her with a worried look. She offered him a small smile. "I will," she assured him.

Abigail abruptly walked towards the door, opening it and shutting it behind her. She creeped down the stairs and remained on them when yelling commenced. Below was the living room, where Keagan, her mother, and another person were standing. Abigail quickly discovered that the third person was a man she had never seen before, and from the looks of it, Keagan had not either. Her friend was enraged.

"Mom, you have no right to tell me my friends have to leave when you bring some random man over!" Keagan seethed menacingly.

"Keagan, must I repeat that you're grounded?" Christine retorted with just as much volume as her daughter. "It's none of your business whether I bring someone over. Vincent is a very nice man. Plus, it's my house and you will respect that."

Keagan stomped her small foot on the hardwood floor hard enough to shake the room. "You didn't tell me I was grounded until *just now*. How was I supposed to know?"

"I thought it would be assumed, given the circumstances."

"Circumstances of what?" Keagan interrogated. "Like the circumstances of you - I don't know - going to a hearing to pass a restraining order against me without me knowing? I was interrogated by a cop, Mom. A *cop*! Right there in the Principal's office because you didn't bother to tell me you were in court all afternoon."

Christine glared at Keagan. "Because you punched a young man in the face on school property. He could've pressed charges."

"Well, you could've been proud of me for defending my best friend, but *no*. You're never proud of me no matter what I do. I always try to get good grades for you. I try to be polite to whichever men you invite over without me knowing. I try to be a good person, but it's never enough for you."

"Keagan," Christine attempted to counter.

"Save it." Keagan backed up towards the stairs. "Enjoy your night with...whoever this guy is because I sure as hell don't know."

"Keagan." Her mother tried again.

She whirled around from her position on the stairs. "I'll send my friends home when the movie's over, but I'm going back up there to hang out with them. Goodnight."

Without waiting for another word, Keagan stormed up the stairs only to come face to face with Abigail, who had forgotten Keagan was going to be there. Keagan fought back the embarrassed tears building up behind her eyes. She gave Abigail a concealing grin.

"Everything okay?" she asked innocently.

"I was just going to check on you," Abigail timidly admitted. "I heard part of the conversation. Are you okay?"

Keagan's smile faltered, but it strengthened a second later. "Yeah, I'm fine. Just the usual."

"Are you sure?"

"Yeah," she said too quickly for Abigail's liking.

Abigail immediately disagreed with Keagan's statement. She was not one to begin an argument, though. She knew what it was like to need space. "Okay, but if you need someone to talk to, I'm here for you."

"Thank you." Keagan's eyes glittered at that. She embraced Abigail in one of her tight bear hugs. "Same for you. Always."

"Thanks, Keagan." Abigail returned the gesture eagerly.

"Anytime, Abi."

The two of them remained there for a moment longer and then finished climbing the flight of stairs. Abigail opened the door and let Keagan in first before shutting it behind her. The remaining four people eyed Abigail with similar expressions of anxiousness until she assured them with a thumbs up when Keagan was not looking. Everyone's faces softened when Abigail's genuine grin came into view. Keagan skipped back to the couch and reclaimed her seat, sitting crisscross applesauce next to Flynn. She grabbed the remote and pressed play.

"Intermission is over!"

17

"I DON'T EVER WANT TO SEE YOU AGAIN."

THE NEXT TWELVE DAYS WERE QUIET.

Too quiet.

Abigail knew it was because Keagan had been absent from school due to her expulsion that nobody in her group of friends thought was fair. She felt alone in British Literature every morning with the empty desk next to her. Noah caught her by surprise by adjusting his seating arrangement to be next to her rather than closer to the front of the room.

She was touched by Noah's gesture, but she was unable to shake the fact that school would never be the same again without Keagan. Her laughter and spontaneous nature lit up the room without fail every time she was in it. Abigail missed one of her best friends since the group was not like it used to be. Abigail, Jade, Brielle, Ryder, and Noah still sat together at lunch every day, but they all missed Keagan. It was obvious.

The entirety of Hillwell High was quieter without her. Keagan's positive and encouraging aura always brightened up Abigail's high school experience. Now that it was gone, the hallways were gloomy and dark. Abigail would not have been surprised if a rain cloud magically appeared in the building. Anything was possible with Keagan.

There, in the middle of the British Literature classroom that she grew to know so well, Abigail sat deathly still. Her legs were tightly crossed at the ankles with her high tops barely grazing the floor beneath them. The maroon hoodie Abigail wore nearly swallowed her up. Her nails were chewed to the brim and pulsating with each heartbeat threatening to shove the organ out of her chest. Abigail missed Keagan's reassuring smile and huge gray eyes. They made her feel at home in a place she considered hell.

Noah was seated at the desk next to Abigail's with his nose stuffed in his own copy of *The Fellowship of the Ring*. Every couple of page turns, he pushed his spare glasses back up his nose and into place. Abigail did not even realize she was watching him until he glanced over at her out of the corner of his eye. She snapped her head back to her open textbook before she seemed suspicious.

He frowned a bit and put his bookmark, which was a ripped piece of notebook paper, in his place. Noah shut the book and took his phone off the surface of the desk. He opened it and sent a quick text to the girl sitting next to him. Noah briefly looked at the thread of conversations they had over the phone through texting, which was relatively long by that point.

Abigail almost flinched when she saw her phone light up on the desk. Quite a few things had been startling her lately. She picked it up and read the text after making sure her brightness was down enough so Mr. Wright would not notice her disobeying his rules.

"You alright? You look jumpy."

She blinked at the message in the little gray bubble on her screen. Noah had been checking in on her often, which she appreciated, but she needed to be accustomed to it. As discreetly as possible, she typed out a sufficient reply. It was not exactly the truth, but not a lie either.

"I'm fine; thank you. It's been a long two weeks."

Noah's reply popped up quickly as she expected from experience.

"Do you want to talk about it? I know it's hard without Keagan."

"I just wish everything worked out."

"Me too. I'm here if you need anything."

Abigail felt a smile grow on her reluctant face. *"Thank you."*

"Okay, class," Mr. Wright exclaimed. Abigail fumbled to put her phone away at the same time as Noah. Both of them were successful. "Since the October deadline for The Fellowship of the Ring is next week, I'll be revealing what your assignment is that you can be working on. Due in mid-January, all of you will be expected to write an essay of your desired length - it must include an introduction, a three-paragraph body, and conclusion - about the series, and compare it to an event you've experienced in your life. It can be from whatever stage of life you choose, but it must relate to the *Lord of the Rings* trilogy."

The class murmured and conversed amongst themselves regarding the new project. Rather than be excited about it, Abigail was dreading the assignment ahead. Even though she did not have to worry about it until January, it was something else on her plate along with the other unappetizing entrées.

Mr. Wright grinned at his classroom. "That concludes today's lecture. I'll see you all tomorrow," he announced, walking over to the classroom door and propping it open.

At once, the classroom turned into a madhouse. Abigail stood in place along with Noah while the rest of their peers fought their way out of the room. She clutched her British Literature book and her borrowed copy - from Brielle - of *The Fellowship of the Ring* tightly against her chest. She felt as if the walls were closing in on her and the room was growing smaller. Abigail hated the feeling of being alone, but it turned out that she was not alone after all.

"Are you sure you're alright?" Noah asked her again.

Abigail blinked up at him. "I think so. It's just been hard lately."

"I understand," Noah sympathized while the two walked towards the classroom's exit. "It's especially difficult with everything going on."

"Yeah. It surely is a lot," she agreed.

Noah pushed his spare glasses back up his nose. "How's your project going, by the way?" he redirected to Abigail's relief. "I mean, I wouldn't expect you to finish the book yet since you have it and your bookmark's about three hundred pages in, but do you like it?"

"Actually, yeah. It's not bad." Abigail smiled a little bit at the embarrassed flush in Noah's complexion from his rambling. "I like it a lot more than I thought."

"Do you have a favorite character yet?"

"Um, I don't know," Abigail replied with a shrug. "Do you?"

At this, Noah grinned. "I've always liked Samwise Gamgee. His friendship with Frodo is what saves the entirety of Middle-earth."

"Hey! Don't spoil the whole series for me!" she wailed.

The two of them suddenly burst out into the most laughter Abigail had experienced in quite a while. She was unsure of why such joy flocked to her like a herd of sheep in search of their shepherd, but it was not something she would close the gate on. Abigail felt a warmth lift her heart out of its chains of worry and self-destruction for just a little bit. It was a foreign feeling, but not an unwelcome one.

Noah's cheeks remained a rosy red by the time the two settled. "I won't spoil it, but you'll appreciate the ending," he sincerely informed her.

"I really hope so. It's long enough, anyway," Abigail teased, which was unlike her.

"It is." Noah's smile was still on his face. He nervously tapped the floor with a tip of his shoe and then composed himself. "...So, see you at lunch?"

Abigail appeared puzzled until she realized they had already arrived at her locker. "Yeah, of course," she answered. "See you then."

"Text if you need anything."

"I will."

Abigail watched as Noah reluctantly turned around and walked towards his own locker. Something tugged at her heartstrings that was not there before. While around Noah, Abigail was happier, which was a seldom emotion to feel when in a situation like hers. Abigail did not want him to leave. She knew he would stay if she asked him to, but she felt as if he had done way too much for her own good. Noah had a life as well—why would he waste it with her?

That particular thought followed her through her next two classes. Abigail was unable to sit still, much less concentrate. Her brain ran on overdrive. Without Keagan, she found it much harder to regulate. Two overwhelming minds were often able to cancel out each other with more chaos. Abigail did not know someone with a more chaotic personality than the one and only Keagan Lopez.

As if it was on cue, the very second that Abigail left her AP Chemistry class with Jade, who did not say very much, the former's phone began to ring. Abigail fumbled with her one free hand - the other occupied by her school supplies - and pulled out her phone from her back pocket. Her eyebrows furrowed in confusion at the unknown caller identification. She hesitantly accepted the call and held her phone up to her ear.

"Uh, hello?"

"Hey, Abi! It's Keagan."

Abigail smiled. Jade looked at her with her beautiful cyan eyes. "Who is it?" she asked.

Instead of answering Jade's question, Abigail exclaimed, "Hey, Keagan! How are you? I thought your mom took your phone away."

"Oh, she did." Keagan's voice was now loud enough to be heard by both girls without being on speakerphone. *"I ran up to the store as soon as she left for work or a hot date with a rich guy - I don't know which one - and bought a burner. She brought my phone with her. Can you believe it? What an invasion of privacy!"*

Abigail and Jade walked to each other's lockers to put their supplies away while on the phone. Abigail scowled due to Keagan's vent. "She did?" she inquired. "That's so dumb. You'll literally be eighteen next week."

"I know! I wonder if she'll even celebrate because apparently, I'm grounded until November first. She didn't forget my birthday this year like last time because I screamed it at her."

"That's literally so stupid," Jade commented.

"Yep! Wait, is that Jade?"

Abigail handed the phone to Jade, who confirmed, "Yep, it's me. How are you doing, Keagan? We miss you."

"I miss you too!" Keagan complained loudly. "Wait, can you put me on speakerphone?"

Abigail took her phone from Jade and pressed the speakerphone button. "Okay, Keagan, you're on speakerphone."

"Cool! So, I wanted to tell you all what I'm doing. Is Brielle there?"

As if she had heard her name, Brielle dashed down the hall. Her auburn hair flew as she darted around groups of people and loners alike. Brielle had a wide smile on her face when she noticed her two - well, three - friends together with Abigail's hand in the center of them holding her phone. Her "Harry Potter" glasses were about to fall off her face as she stumbled over towards Abigail, Jade, and Keagan on the phone.

"Well, she is now," Jade chuckled cheerfully. "Hi, Brielle."

"Hi, guys!" Brielle chirped.

"Hey, Brielle! I miss you!" Keagan exclaimed.

"I miss you too!"

"So, does everyone want to know what I'm doing?"

"Yep!" Abigail, Jade, and Brielle chorused simultaneously.

"Okay." Keagan paused for a dramatic effect. Her three friends leaned over the phone in anticipation. "I bought some early birthday presents for myself at the store."

Abigail's eyes lit up. "Ooh, what are they?"

"Well, you're currently on speakerphone over here because I may or may not have purchased a large quantity of hair dye and an electric razor."

"Oh, my God. Are you dying your hair again?" Jade asked excitedly.

"Yep!" There was a slight rustling on the other end of the line. "I'm also giving myself an undercut. My mom's gonna be pissed, but I don't give a f-"

"Keagan, you're on speaker," Brielle reminded her. "People can hear you."

"Oh, right! Are you guys in the cafeteria yet?"

"We just got there," Abigail replied as the three walked through the double doors and began to wait in line.

"*Ooh! Get me food!*"

Jade deadpanned, "You're on the phone."

"*So?*"

"Oh, I can share some of my lunch with you if you want," Brielle offered.

"*I was just kidding! I got food on the way home from the store, but I'll eat it later. My hands are covered in hair dye.*"

The group of four, even though one of them was absent, broke out into a bit of laughter. Abigail found herself smiling as she purchased her usual meal of chicken tenders and fries, but her joy was not as present as it was with Noah. She wondered to herself why that was so. It was weird. Despite being in some sort of relationship with both Ryder and Landon at different times, she never felt that way with them. Noah was different.

Abigail continued to ponder as they joined Noah and Ryder at their usual table. Abigail drifted over to where Noah was seated and took the chair next to his while Jade sat across from her with Brielle at her right and Ryder on the other side of his sister. All of them agreed to put Abigail's phone in the center of the table so Keagan would be able to contribute to their conversation.

Abigail scratched that thought. Keagan would be steering the conversation like she usually did. "*You guys! I just finished dyeing my hair and it looks really good.*"

"That's cool," Noah responded with his smile evident. "What color?"

"*I'll make it a surprise.*"

"How's the undercut coming along?" Abigail asked her.

Her response was the electric razor clicking on. A loud buzzing noise sounded on the other end of the line.

"...Be careful."

"*Don't worry, I will!*"

Abigail faded out of the conversation when Jade, Brielle, and surprisingly Ryder, filled it. She felt as if there suddenly was no room for her at the table anymore. A sense of guilt flooded her conscience. If she had not been in the wrong place at the wrong time, Keagan would never have punched Landon and gotten expelled along with a restraining order put against her. She would not have been grounded for her birthday. Abigail admired how positive Keagan sounded over the phone, but she knew she was hiding unshed tears.

The numerous times that Keagan expressed her discomfort for being at her house for most of the time brought Abigail to her knees with agonizing emotions. Keagan expressed how her mother made no effort to help educate her or find another school for her. Instead, she needed to do so on her own. Abigail, Jade, and Brielle all offered to help Keagan with her education, but she declined, saying that they all had other things to focus on.

She kept sneaking glances over at the table where Landon would usually sit, but for an unknown reason, he was not present. Abigail had not seen him for more than five seconds for quite a while. In fact, it had been since Keagan "assaulted" him in the hallway nearly two weeks prior. He had not spoken a word to her. Instead, Abigail caught his occasional look in her direction with either a small smirk or even a wink. Abigail had no idea what he meant by those gestures other than his triumph over tearing her apart.

A gentle tap on her shoulder brought her out of her imagination to view Noah with a compassionate look in his brown eyes. "Is something wrong?"

Abigail hated how vulnerable her voice sounded. "I miss Keagan."

"I know," he agreed softly. "But you don't know that she won't be allowed back before the school year's over."

"She literally has a restraining order against her. Landon's lawyer is a really good one, and I'd know, because..." Abigail broke off her statement.

Noah's eyebrows lifted. "...Wait, really?"

"I said too much," she rushed out.

"You know you don't have to talk about it if you don't want to," he reminded her of something he already shared several times. "Right?"

"Yeah, I know. It's just really hard without her. I feel awful even though it's not my fault."

Noah tried to offer an encouraging smile. "You can let go of the blame because it's not yours to carry. I've done that, and it's really helped."

"You have?" she questioned with surprise.

"Yeah, but I don't really want to talk about it right now. With that being said, I hope you know that you can talk to me if you need anything. Okay?"

Abigail nodded. "Yeah, thank you." She glanced over at her other friends and stood up from her seat. "I need to get some air."

"Are you okay?" Jade asked.

"What's going on? Is Abi okay?" Keagan shouted as if her voice was quiet.

Brielle frowned and picked at her salad. "You've hardly touched your food."

"I'll be back in a couple minutes, but yes, I'm fine," Abigail assured them. "I'd tell Keagan not to touch my food if she wasn't on the phone."

"Hey!"

Abigail chuckled quietly and then turned around. She walked briskly out of the cafeteria, weaving around tables housing large and small groups of people alike. Abigail was overwhelmed from everything hitting her at once. She was aware Keagan's expulsion was not her fault, but she could not help blaming herself for it.

"You can let go of the blame because it's not yours to carry."

Noah's words echoed in Abigail's mind. She knew he was right, however, believing it was more difficult than she wanted to admit. Each step weighed on her like a pile of bricks was in her backpack. Abigail felt her thread of sanity unraveling and detaching itself from the spool. It was only a matter of time until there was nothing left to cling on to. Her mental stability was slipping through her fingers.

Abigail reached her locker and leaned against it. She held two fingers up to her neck to check her pulse, which was racing. Her breaths were deep and burned her throat like wildfire. Her hands were shaking, and her fingertips were throbbing from the small scabs and tears searing through the top layer of skin. She slowly began to calm down, but even that fate was turned against her.

"You look awful antsy." A snarky voice to her left made her skin crawl.

Abigail refused to meet his eyes. She straightened up and made herself as tall as possible. Her heart rate accelerated to a mile a minute solely due to his presence. Abigail had no one to protect her this time. Keagan was expelled, Noah was in the cafeteria, and her friends were using her phone to talk to the former. She had no means of contact. It had completely slipped her mind and now, she felt like an idiot.

"Are you not going to talk to me?" The voice grew closer. He frowned as Abigail shrunk down to her shoes. "After all we've been through? Six months of our relationship is written off just like *that*?"

He snapped his fingers loudly, which made Abigail flinch. "We haven't kept in touch since June," Abigail's tone trembled as she seethed. "I don't *ever* want to see you again."

"The court case doesn't count, Sweetheart," Landon retorted with a sugary drawl. "The last time we properly spoke without any interruptions was in May."

"Do you think I care?"

"You're just as resistant as I remember," he mused, getting too close for her preference. Her idea of "close" was in a two-mile radius. "You still don't know how to listen to me."

Abigail bit her lip hard enough to taste blood. "I want you to leave me alone," she told him firmly.

"Why should I? You never did so to me."

"Because that was what you wanted."

"You know, you're right," Landon recalled. "We never spent a day apart, Abigail. How come you keep trying to avoid me? We were in love."

"If you think our relationship was love, then you're sick in the head," she spat. The metallic taste in her mouth and Landon's statement nearly made her want to puke in his face. *"I'd say I was afraid of you, but I don't want you to have that power over me."*

Landon set his hand on the locker next to Abigail's and leaned against it. "You told me you loved me."

"Because you forced me to," Abigail gritted out. "You need to leave."

"But I have a proposition for you. I'm not leaving until you hear what I have to say," Landon asserted to Abigail's dismay.

She thought her teeth would crack if she clenched them together any more. "...What is it?"

"I bet you miss your friend quite a lot. Keagan...is it?" he innocently asked.

"You've already done enough damage, so leave her the hell alone."

Landon held his hands out in front of him in surrender. "Woah, I'm not going after her. In fact, I'm suggesting the opposite."

"Excuse me?" Abigail snipped menacingly.

"I'm willing to lift the restraining order against her. As you know, I have a skilled lawyer and Keagan will be able to return to Hillwell High as soon as tomorrow," Landon explained.

At first, she was about to sigh in relief, but stopped in her tracks. *"It's way too good to be true. Come on, Abigail—you're smarter than that."* Abigail glared in his direction. "There's a catch to this and I know it. You can't let her off that easily."

"You know me too well. You need to do something for me first."

"What are you implying?"

"Well, I've been thinking, Abigail," Landon stated, shifting his position towards the middle of the hallway. "I've missed you since you left me last May. It's caused me a lot of pain over the past few months. I was never able to gain closure with you. So, I decided that you owe me a small token of farewell."

Abigail's heart leapt to her throat. "And what would that be?" Her voice dangerously trembled as she spoke.

"A kiss would be appropriate."

"No, I can't. I refuse," Abigail quickly denied.

"But why?" His question was as smooth as silk. "It would be a win-win situation. Keagan would return to school and graduate like her mother wants, I would leave you alone, and everything would be going your way."

"It isn't that easy."

"You're right. If you do this for me, you must promise that you'll never tell anyone about it. I don't want any more lawsuits on my hands."

Abigail almost shuddered at the wink that came right after. "What would happen if I don't do this for you?" she had the nerve to inquire.

"Well, everything would remain the same," replied Landon simply. "Your friend would probably have to drop out of high school. Her mother would be very disappointed in her and would probably reprimand her, punishing her beyond belief. And as for you...it would be all *your fault*. Your friends would hate you for what you did to Keagan. You will have torn Keagan apart and then yourself along with it."

"It would be all your fault."

Abigail's head was spinning around Landon's particular statement. For a very long moment, it drowned out Noah's advice that was given to her mere minutes before her encounter with the very boy she wanted to avoid. What he said was true, though. It would be all her fault if Keagan had to drop out of school and her mother would hate that. Abigail was unable to live with that immense guilt for years to come.

So, that's what finally led her to agree. "...One kiss? That's it? Keagan will return to school and you'll leave me alone?"

"Yes. I'll give you my word." Abigail didn't miss the triumphant glint in his eyes.

"You promise...?"

"I promise."

"Then...I'll follow your proposition as long as you keep to your word," she hesitantly said.

Landon smiled. "I thought so."

Before Abigail was able to comprehend what was going on, Landon's lips were on hers. Rather than being soft and gentle like she had hoped - what she had experienced from him several times before - his kiss was rough and intruding. Abigail struggled to breathe as her respirations became shallow from panic.

Her hands rested on his chest and she attempted to push him away, but instead, Landon shoved her against the locker behind her without breaking their contact. Abigail winced as the combination lock dug into her spine and the cool metal was against her neck. Her head throbbed from the impact. The world around her blurred, but not in the special, intimate way. Instead, Abigail was trapped.

Abigail decided his "token of farewell" had gone too far once she felt his icy fingers travel under her hoodie, her shirt and then against her skin. Her entire body trembled as his hand rose higher and higher on her body while her mouth was being unwillingly occupied. Abigail was disgusted and repulsed by his touch. She felt like she was really going to puke. He was not going to stop, so she did the only thing she could think of. While his hands were occupied with her, she gathered two fistfulls of his shirt and spun him around so his back was against the lockers instead of hers.

At an instant, Landon's lips broke away from Abigail's, but he was unable to escape her clutches. His surprise was his weakness. Abigail's fists gripped his shirt tightly and he was pressed against the wall of metal containers just like she was. Abigail's mouth curled into a snarl that she was unfamiliar with.

"Don't you *ever* touch me again," she growled in his face.

Then, she let go. Her shoes squeaked against the tile as she sprinted away from the boy who had tainted her view of life. Abigail wiped off her lips as well as she could with the back of her hand. Her skin felt like bugs were creeping and crawling all over it. Her hands were shaking with anger and fear. This was the first time she had been able to stand up for herself. The remaining adrenaline she had pumped itself through her veins but was slowly running out.

Thankfully, Abigail had reached the cafeteria before she was able to break out into a panic. She stuffed her hands into her hoodie's pouch. Abigail fought to compose herself as she walked closer and closer to her friends' table. Luck was on her side for once, since no one seemed to be quizzical when Abigail returned and sat down next to Noah again.

"Hey, Abigail," Jade welcomed her friend back to the table. "Are you feeling better?"

"Yeah, I am. Thanks." Abigail forced a smile on her face when five pairs of eyes looked at her hopefully.

"Hey, Abi! Everything okay?" Keagan exclaimed from the phone in the center of the table.

Abigail nodded, but then remembered Keagan couldn't see her. "Yeah, everything's fine," she choked out composedly. "Thanks, Keagan."

"Anytime!"

Abigail stared down at her lunch, which was hardly touched. She was not planning on being able to finish it, but for the sake of her friends, she picked up two fries and stuffed them in her mouth. Mixed with the blood from her interior bleeding lip, the food was unappetizing. Abigail forced herself to swallow and continue eating her meal.

She hardly noticed Noah's uncertain complexion from next to her. His lunch was about halfway finished, but he did not appear interested in it either. Instead, once Abigail looked his way, he stared down at his lap like it was something interesting. Eventually, he made himself look up and meet Abigail's eyes. Somehow, he knew something was wrong. Despite Abigail expertly masking her pain, there was something off about her that he could not ignore.

"Are you sure everything's okay?" he quietly inquired.

Abigail's lips were pressed together in a tight line. "It will be," she reassured him. "Don't worry about me. I'm just fine."

Noah looked like he wanted to probe further, but he knew where the line between nosiness and pure concern lay. In no way, shape, or form did he want to cross them. There was something going on with Abigail and he did not want to pry. Noah was worried about her, especially in her current state. He decided to keep himself quiet despite his racing mind.

Little did he know, Abigail was relapsing in her inability to keep herself together. It was only a matter of time until she completely shattered. Even though she was human, she felt like a piece of crumbling glass ready to break any moment.

Especially since it had been handled.

18

"...IT WOULD BE ALL YOUR FAULT."

ABIGAIL'S HANDS GRIPPED THE STEERING WHEEL TIGHTLY AS SHE SAT IN the parking lot of Hillwell High. Her knuckles turned white due to the tight grip on the rubber.

Cars surrounded her at every angle—forward, left, right, and slowly crawling behind her own gray vehicle. Abigail felt like the interior of her own would be crushed any second. The walls closed in on her like they always seemed to do. She was trapped in her own mind. Her exterior crawled with rubbish no matter how many times she scrubbed her skin raw in the shower she had as soon as she arrived home the previous day.

She hated how she believed everything and everyone was out to get her. Abigail knew she was overly paranoid, but it was something she was unable to help. She made herself get out of her vehicle with her backpack slung over her shoulder. Her usual sunglasses were on her face, shielding the world from her glossy brown irises, ready to spill over.

"Okay, Abigail. You can do this," she encouraged herself. *"Everyone's counting on you to be there for them."*

With that thought, she began to saunter towards the intimidating coral brick building. Abigail weaved around parked cars and vehicles waiting for her to cross each pathway while they were searching for empty parking spaces. Her straight hair bobbed loosely behind her. She didn't care enough to tie it back that morning. Abigail straightened the collar of her denim jacket. Despite most of her skin being covered by a pair of black leggings and a fitted white tank top, she felt exposed.

Abigail forced herself to be confident despite the swarm of tingling bugs crawling on her from Landon's prior touch. She kept her head held high as she walked through the double doors of Hillwell High School. Crowds of people suffocated the halls as usual. Abigail's black high tops made little noise while she paraded through her peers like she had everything in the world in reach of her clutches. She needed to show a certain someone what she was made of.

She was feeling a bit better about herself once she realized Landon was nowhere to be seen while on her way to her locker. Abigail obtained her supplies for British Literature and then shut the metal door. Something - or someone, more rather - caught her eye. Her sunglasses nearly fell off her face and clattered to the ground. Instead, she slowly slid the eye accessory off of her face and held it limply in her hand.

In front of her was a familiar petite young woman with black, knee-high heeled boots that made her at least four inches taller. She wore a maroon pleated skirt along with a black leather jacket over a complimenting Rolling Stones t-shirt. On top of her head, rather than green roots, red highlights graced silky raven hair styled to the right side. She wore no makeup, but her natural beauty easily shone through the piercing gray eyes facing in Abigail's direction.

"Holy...," Abigail muttered when her friend approached, flanked by Jade and Brielle.

"Hey, Abi!" Keagan chirped like nothing altered her appearance at all. "What do you think? Mom was pissed when I showed her my hair, but I love it."

Abigail's lowered jaw curved up into a smile. "Oh, my God."

"Is it too much? I found these giant boots on sale for fifteen bucks at the store yesterday and just *had* to get them. I kind of spent a lot of money other than the hair dye." Keagan frowned and adjusted her jacket.

"No, not at all. I'm just surprised that you're...back so soon."

"I know! Can you believe it?" she exclaimed excitedly. "Normally, there'd be a hearing for a restraining order to be lifted, but maybe his lawyer pulled a few strings. I can't believe he lifted the order--and only after two weeks too. I don't know how that'd be possible, even with a great lawyer. Do you know why he'd lift it?"

Abigail's grin subtly dropped. "I have no idea," she lied through her teeth.

"Is something wrong?" Brielle asked in her normal quiet voice.

"Yep, everything's fine." Abigail widened the gap between her lips.

Jade's eyebrows furrowed. "You look a bit nervous."

"Nervous?" Abigail giggled—albeit anxiously. "Why would I be nervous? I'm just surprised Keagan's back so early."

"Me too." Keagan's eyes widened with realization. "Ooh! Did I show you my undercut yet?"

Abigail shook her head, relieved that the subject was changed. "Not yet. What does it look like?"

Keagan did not hesitate to whirl around on her elevated heel. At Abigail's eye level was the underside of her already short hair styled in a buzz cut. Several lines crisscrossed along the buzzed area in a net pattern. Abigail admired how steady her hand must have been to shave that part of her head so perfectly. She remembered her phone call with Keagan while she was doing just that.

"Tada!" She cheered like a young child. "What do you think?"

Abigail plastered on a smile when Keagan whirled around. "It looks great. I love it."

"Thanks, Abi! I'm so glad to be back. My mom made my life hell."

"I'm glad you're back too. I missed you."

As Abigail expected, Keagan flung her arms around her in one of her signature hugs. "I missed you so much, Abi!"

"I missed you too." Abigail hugged her back, smiling despite the pit in her stomach.

The sinking feeling in the depths of her abdomen did not go away even when Keagan and Abigail were walking towards British Literature side by side. Keagan was relieved to be back at Hillwell High. She looked poised, confident, and most importantly, at home. Abigail listened to her heels click against the tiled floor. Some of their peers stared judgingly in their direction, but Keagan paid them no mind. She knew she looked good.

Abigail felt the crawling feeling return to her skin. In fact, it had never left, but was pushed away by the temporary joy of reuniting with one of her best friends. She pulled her denim jacket tighter around herself. Making a deal with Landon was worth it, right? Even if she was very uncomfortable with every step she made deeper into Hillwell High, Abigail knew Keagan was happy. It was a sacrifice she was always willing to make.

While upon the journey to the ill-fated classroom, Keagan gently elbowed Abigail in the upper arm. "While I've been imprisoned at home, you've kept me up on every event that I missed except for one," she noted. "You haven't said a word about Noah."

"Noah?" The name fell out of Abigail's mouth.

"Yeah. You know, average height, brown hair, funky looking glasses that disappeared a week after the dare? Does that ring any bells?"

"I know who you're talking about," Abigail deadpanned. "I just didn't think it was that important to bring up."

Keagan's eyebrows waggled teasingly. "Have you two been texting? I know you were at my house a couple weeks ago," she revealed something Abigail already knew.

"Yes, we've been texting...but not often."

"Are you sure?" Keagan egged her on. "I bet he'd be over-the-moon if he saw a notification from you. Maybe you'd be the same."

Abigail frowned at that. "We've been texting on occasion, and he's a very nice person to talk to," she admitted.

"*Just* to talk to?"

"Keagan, can we drop it, please? I don't feel comfortable talking about this right now."

Keagan's eyes grew a millimeter in size. She didn't mean to over-step Abigail's firm boundaries. "Oh, I'm sorry. Yeah, of course."

"It's okay," Abigail replied, setting her sunglasses on the top of her head.

Without another word, Keagan and Abigail walked into the British Literature classroom. The two of them were greeted briefly by Mr. Wright; by "greeted," he gave them a glance and a short nod in their direction before returning to writing on the whiteboard. Abigail kept her eyes locked on her shoes to avoid any unnecessary eye contact until Keagan elbowed her for a second time. It seemed urgent due to the several pokes, so she snapped her head in her friend's direction.

"What?" she hissed just in earshot.

Keagan glanced towards a certain desk and then back at Abigail. "So, he's been sitting with you, huh? That's adorable."

Abigail followed Keagan's eyes to view Noah in his new usual seat, which would be next to her own. His nose was stuck in the latter end of *The Fellowship of the Ring*. Brown hair was almost in his eyes. Noah's glasses were sliding down his nose like they normally did while he was reading or doing something requiring his gaze tilted downwards. Abigail slowly looked back at Keagan, who had a wide grin on her face. Her cheeks burst into flame.

"Yeah, he has. I've been lonely without you here," Abigail confessed meekly.

All she got in response was a wink from the pair of gray eyes looking in her direction. Abigail sighed and tucked her books tighter in the crook of her elbow.

The two friends awkwardly approached the middle of the class-room where Noah was seated. When he heard the duo of footsteps, his gaze snapped up to meet their own. Noah pushed his glasses back up the bridge of his nose and stuffed a bookmark in his J.R.R. Tolkien novel.

"Oh, sorry," he hurriedly apologized, standing from his chair. "I can move."

Keagan dumped her supplies on Abigail's desk. She pushed Noah back down in his seat. "Noah, sit," she instructed like he was a dog. It did not fail to make Abigail laugh. "I'll sit on the other side of her."

"Okay...?" Noah flopped back down in his seat.

"Good boy."

"That's...weird."

Abigail snorted and sat down at her own desk, depositing her friend's things where they belonged—on Keagan's desk. "She's been at home for two weeks," Abigail explained to the confused Noah. "She always says weird stuff, so it's been building up."

"She's right." Keagan collapsed into her seat.

"In that case, I won't judge," Noah shrugged. He offered the two girls a smile. "Welcome back, Keagan. I like your hair."

"Thank you! Did you see my undercut yet?!"

Before Noah even had a chance to verbally respond, Keagan whirled around to reveal the particular part of her hair that she was very proud of. When she turned back towards him, she looked to be lighting up the entire classroom.

"It looks very nice."

"Thanks!"

Keagan opened her mouth to say something else, but Mr. Wright chose that very second to address the class. "Good morning, class," he stated in his usual monotone voice. "I trust that all of you have been diligently reading because the deadline for *The Fellowship of the Ring* is next Sunday at midnight. I expect you to return to class that Monday with thorough knowledge regarding this piece. For now, though, let's get started with today's lecture."

The class fell silent while Mr. Wright began talking about certain topics in British Literature that Abigail did not feel like discussing. Abigail kept her eyes on her books piled up on the desk in front of her. On one side of her was Keagan, hiding her phone in her lap and playing a certain game, and on the other, Noah either had his nose in his book or in the direction of the whiteboard as Mr. Wright wrote more things down. Abigail felt inclined to take notes, but her mind raced a mile a minute.

It didn't stop—not even after three complete lectures and thirty minutes in the cafeteria. She was seated with her five friends; Keagan on her left and Noah on her right along with Jade, Brielle, and Ryder across the table. Rather than join in with their conversations and relief that Keagan had returned to the group - and so quickly too - Abigail remained silent. She felt numb at that point, especially since she knew there was nothing she could do about the situation.

"So, guys," Keagan announced happily. "My mom said I'm not grounded anymore, so we can continue doing the weekly movie nights at my house! Is tomorrow night at seven okay for everyone to watch *The Two Towers*?"

"Sure!" Brielle agreed.

"Fine with me." Ryder was second.

"That sounds great." Noah was third.

"I want to get out of the house, so yes." Jade set her reply on top of the others.

Keagan expectantly looked at the last remaining member of the table. "Abi? How about you?" she asked.

"That's fine." Abigail quickly glanced up from her phone and nodded. She looked back down at the screen a second later.

Keagan frowned. "Abi, is something going on with you? You look distracted."

"I'm okay," she fibbed. "I didn't sleep well last night, so I'm really tired."

Abigail's excuse was the truth, but not the entirety of it. She slowly put her phone down and pretended to be completely fine. Instead of concentrating on her lunch, which was once again untouched, her eyes drifted elsewhere. Abigail was well aware of her anxiety crawling up her throat along with the goosebumps covering her arms and legs. Hillwell High was perfectly warm, but somehow, a boy she couldn't care less about gave her the chills.

While her friends were distracted, Abigail caught herself glancing over at Landon's usual table. There he was, seated with his friends like he had not done anything wrong in the slightest. His optimistic eyes and dusty brown hair were innocent. He was just an average teenage boy, but he was something more to Abigail. He was a constant fear. Her mind flitted back to his proposal yesterday.

"No, I can't. I refuse," Abigail *quickly denied.*

"But why?" His question was as smooth as silk. "It would be a win-win situation. Keagan would return to school and graduate like her mother wants, I would leave you alone, and everything would be going your way."

"It isn't that easy."

"You're right. If you do this for me, you must promise that you'll never tell anyone about it. I don't want any more lawsuits on my hands."

Abigail almost shuddered at the wink that came right after. "What would happen if I don't do this for you?" *she had the nerve to inquire.*

"Well, everything would remain the same," replied Landon simply. "Your friend would probably have to drop out of high school. Her mother would be very disappointed in her and would probably reprimand her, punishing her beyond belief. And as for you...it would be all your fault. Your friends would hate you for what you did to Keagan. You will have torn Keagan apart and then yourself along with it."

Abigail felt disgusted since she agreed so easily to Landon's deal. For one, she did not know whether he was telling the truth. She was surprised that he was held to his word. Keagan had returned to school and everything within her life was normal starting that morning. Except, it actually wasn't normal. Abigail felt violated in every way from Landon's actions yesterday.

Her eyes were still on his table when his own pair met hers. Abigail's breath hitched fearfully in her throat due to his innocent, yet knowing stare. Landon's eyebrows furrowed while Abigail's raised. The former's lips slowly drew into a smirk while the latter's pressed together into a tight line. Abigail was frozen in place. Landon was able to see all the way to her crumbling soul beneath her frail shield of confidence. Abigail decided one thing then and there.

It was too much.

Abigail blinked herself blurrily away from Landon's piercing eyes. "I need to go home," she said to no one in particular.

"Are you okay?" Brielle asked.

"No...I mean, yes...I mean, I don't feel well. I need to go lay down," Abigail stuttered frantically under her breath.

"I can take you to the nurse's office," offered Jade gently.

"No. I-I need to go home."

Keagan carefully tapped her on the shoulder. "Want me to drive you home?"

"I'll drive myself," she insisted.

"Are you sure?"

Abigail nodded stiffly. "I'll see you all later."

Prior to anyone else's reactions, she shot up in her seat. Abigail paid no mind to the concerned expressions on her friends' faces while she bolted out of the cafeteria. She missed Landon's keen brown eyes following her every move until she disappeared from sight. Abigail was unaware that Noah considered following her out, but he knew she needed her space. It was important to her, so why would he violate it? That principle was imperative to him too.

Abigail rushed to her locker and slung her full backpack over one shoulder. She ignored how odd she looked to the occasional bystander in the hallway. Instead of caring about them, she cared about her safety, which she feared was less prevalent in Hillwell High.

She was unable to think straight as she dashed out of the large coral brick building and to her vehicle. Abigail fumbled to unlock her car, her keys nearly falling out of her hands twice. Abigail slid into the driver's seat and threw her backpack into the passenger's side. She slammed the door behind her and inserted the key into the ignition. Before she knew it, she was speeding out of the parking lot and towards one of her only safe spaces she knew of.

Home.

Abigail found herself at the same place she was that morning. Her hands gripped the steering wheel so tightly that she felt her heart beating in her palms. Her head ached with the immense amount of stress that had been put on her shoulders. She didn't feel safe in Hillwell High anymore, not even with her friends to keep her company; not even with Noah, who had proved to be someone she could rely on.

The moment she parked her car in the driveway in front of her, she dashed into the house. Abigail even left her backpack behind as she frantically unlocked the front door and locked it behind her. Her high tops carried her up the stairs and into her room. She locked that door as well and pressed her spine against it as a barrier.

Slowly, she slid down the wooden door until she was seated on the floor and her knees were to her chest. Abigail shakily unlocked her phone and sent a message to both of her parents with several typos due to her nerves.

"Had to come home since I wasn't feeling well."

A sudden surge of anger propelled Abigail to hurl her phone across the room. She winced as it hit the wall with a *crack* and fell onto her bed below. Then, Abigail let out something that she had been holding in for quite some time.

She screamed.

It was bloodcurdling, her lungs throbbing and aching. Her heart pounded its way out of her chest. Tears clouded her vision and this time, she didn't hesitate to let them spill down her rosy cheeks. Abigail hated to lie to everyone she cared about, especially when she was struggling, but she had no choice. It was eating her alive from the inside out.

Ultimately, she let herself break down into loud sobs. Salty teardrops mixed with her mascara and snot running out of her nose as she coughed and wailed. Her entire body trembled with the effort to keep herself together, but what was the point anymore? Abigail decided to let herself go and to let out her emotions as noisily as possible.

No one could hear her, anyway.

19

"NINE-ONE-ONE. WHAT'S YOUR EMERGENCY?"

THE HUMAN BODY OFTEN FUNCTIONS LIKE A TIMEPIECE. ABIGAIL KNEW by now that this rather obscure observation was true.

Both the human mind and a timepiece can distinguish the concept of time from reality. Every hour, every minute, and every second that passes indicates that the lifespan of each of these things are approaching their demise. Both the human body and a timepiece possess hands. As time goes on, the pair of hands for each of these beings gradually slows down until eventually, the hourglass has run out of sand to spill.

At the tender age of seventeen and three months, Abigail's life seemed as if it had already withered away into dust. It surely appeared as if she had to grow up very quickly in the past few months. Abigail had a reality check that fateful day that her life changed forever. She never had to fear for her safety - or even her life - before. Abigail was not naïve anymore.

"Time is free, but it is priceless."

That phrase swam through the strong current of her mind as Abigail was seated on a comfortable couch that seemed to take up half of the small room. A clock on the wall to her right ticked loudly. The air in the room was almost suffocatingly thick. Time ticked by quicker than Abigail wanted it to—even quicker than her racing heart. Abigail was wasting it sitting in that cramped room where the walls appeared as if they would crash down on top of her at any given moment.

A woman sat across from her in a chair. Abigail had memorized her blonde curls and positive mindset by now. Her occasional strokes of her pencil against the clipboard in her nondominant hand was like nails on a chalkboard. Abigail got used to the intimidating feeling the woman on the other side of the room gave her. In fact, she was not as scary as she used to be.

Time was still ticking, though. Abigail and the young woman were beginning to get uncomfortable. Neither of them said a word. The tension between them grew thicker. Eventually, the young woman spoke with her usual kind smile on her face.

"So, Abigail," she began softly. "Is there anything else you'd like to discuss during the remaining few minutes of our session?"

Abigail stiffly shook her head. She refused to meet her therapist's gaze. "No. I can't think of anything else."

Kristy frowned and set her clipboard aside. "You look a bit tense," she noted. "I want you to know that this is a safe space for you to discover what's bothering you and then we can work out solutions to better the situation."

"I understand that, but really, nothing's bothering me," she lied through her teeth.

Her therapist pulled some of her honey blonde curls behind her ears. Kristy eyed Abigail's body language. With her legs crossed tightly at the ankles, her eyes darting anywhere in the room except Kristy's eyes, and her fingers picking at the threads around a hole in her jeans, there was no doubt that Abigail was closed off. Kristy knew Abigail was hiding something, but it was not her place to pry into a mind that did not welcome her.

Instead, she tried a different tactic. "How is everything with your friends?" Kristy asked optimistically. "I recall you telling me that they helped you study for that placement test a month ago."

"Yeah, they did," Abigail replied, seeing no point to Kristy's comment. "Things are going okay, I think."

"I only brought up the placement test because they really care about you, Abigail. If there's something wrong when it comes to them, I bet you'll come to an understanding."

"There's nothing wrong. We're getting along just fine."

"Hm, I see." Kristy's eyes drifted elsewhere before coming up with another topic. "How's it going with that boy you've mentioned a few times? Noah, right?"

Abigail tensed at the mention of him, but not in a bad way. "Oh, um, it's fine," she stammered a little bit. "We've been keeping in touch a lot more."

"Is that a good thing?" she gently probed.

"Yeah, I think so." Abigail started to ramble. "It's hard for me to trust guys, as you know, but I feel like Noah might genuinely care about me. After all, he helped me with passing that test when he really didn't have to, and he checks up on me a lot. He texted me a lot yesterday after...never mind."

Kristy cocked her head to the side when Abigail trailed off, but she decided to keep her wise mouth closed. She knew her client's limits, so instead, she smiled. "I see. That sounds very nice of him. Do you think Noah's presence in your life is affecting you in a positive way?"

"As far as I know...yeah. He hasn't done anything to upset me."

"Not yet," Abigail added on fearfully.

"I'm very glad that you have someone in your life like that," Kristy truthfully stated. "And Abigail, it's okay to trust someone as long as you have boundaries."

"I *do* have boundaries. They're to not let anyone in unless I already know them really well," she deadpanned.

Kristy smiled slightly. "It's okay to let someone in, but you need to "let yourself in" first," she advised. "Life often gives you risks that you need to take, but are they often worth it? Of course-"

"-Not," Abigail finished.

"You don't know that."

"Neither do you."

The therapist's smile faltered, but it grew with enough time to spare. "That can be something you can work on for our next session. You can trust yourself, Abigail, because sometimes, you're the only ally you've got. In this situation, however, you have other people. Do you understand that?"

Abigail hesitated. She knew what Kristy was trying to say, but it was not helping. "I do."

"That's good, then," Kristy sincerely replied. She stood from her chair. "That's what I would like you to focus on for the next few days. Listen to yourself and try to let yourself in. You can't help yourself if you don't allow it."

"I'll keep that in mind."

Abigail hazily got to her feet, muttering a quiet "Thank you" to her therapist. Her entire being was a blur. The ticking clock on the wall was almost hypnotic. She did not feel entirely present as she got herself situated and standing. Kristy noticed Abigail's emotionally tired state. If she was with any other client, she would have asked again if there was anything else they would like to talk about. This was Abigail, though. Kristy knew better than to pry. In contrast, she called out a different request as Abigail was about to leave.

"Hey, Abigail? One more thing."

The girl in question spun on her heel and looked Kristy in the eye. "Yeah?"

"Don't sell yourself short," the therapist advised her. "Trust your instincts. If you need anything, you can contact me at any time. It doesn't matter when. Okay?"

"...Okay."

The glimmer in Kristy's eyes did not fail her again. "I'll see you Tuesday," she reminded her. "Have a great weekend and remember that."

"I will," confirmed Abigail with a nod.

Abigail's head was spinning by the time she left Kristy's office and then the premises of the Journey to Joy: Counseling and Wellness Center. She no longer looked at the delicate lettering above the front door as if something she despised. Instead, Abigail ignored it entirely. She had enough in front of her to look at. It sent her mind into a spiral of doubt and anxiety.

The teenager had to admit that her sessions with Kristy were helping, even if it was simply a room full of silence for her to collect her thoughts. That had occurred during her last few sessions. It was a relief to feel at peace, even if it was just for an hour at a time. She kept quiet during several of her sessions, only answering questions when she was probed to. Abigail hated lying to her therapist, but it was something she felt like she had to do in order to keep herself safe.

The entire drive from the Wellness Center to her home was in silence. Abigail didn't even play her usually loud music. Instead, she let herself think. She seemed like a horrible person in her mind's eye--lying to her friends, her therapist, and even her family about how she was really coping with life. To them, she was fine. To herself, she was a suffering, blubbering mess, sobbing into the wee hours of the night with a pillow over her face to muffle her shivering cries and soak up her tears of grief for her own self-esteem.

Abigail knew she was hopeless. In just over forty-eight hours, she let herself become stripped down into almost nothing. It was just like she had done before. Instead of going to who she loved the most, she kept to herself. Abigail let herself suffer alone, which might not have been the healthiest option, but it seemed like the only one.

As soon as she arrived at the interior of her home on Little Creek Landing, Abigail dashed up the stairs and into the bathroom. She locked the door and stripped herself of her clothes from that day, throwing them in a messy heap in the sink. Without wasting any time, she turned the knob in the glass stand-up shower. Abigail watched as water poured out of the showerhead. She waited briefly until the water was warm—hot enough to boil the crawling sensation off her skin.

Abigail stepped into the shower and let the droplets of steaming water cascade down and off her trembling body. Her head was tilted upwards, and her face received most of the stream. It was excruciating, but necessary in her opinion. Abigail had done this twice before, regardless of her morning showers. After school for the past three afternoons, she felt like she was disgusting from even his eyes raking up and down her body. She hated it enough to torture herself.

Painful memories once again pieced themselves together in Abigail's exhausted mind as she reached for the body soap on the shelf next to her. She lathered up her hands and began scrubbing the skin on her arms.

"Abigail, do you want this or not?"

"Landon, leave me alone."

Abigail moved on to her chest and down her stomach, reaching under every crevice in her frail body that had had enough.

"You've been giving me mixed signals for six months, Abigail. You know what you want. Stop lying to me."

"I told you no. I don't want this."

Her hands shook as she received more soap from the dispenser. Abigail applied a thin layer of soap to her legs, which were wobbling with the effort to keep her upright. As she scrubbed harder, her skin became redder and redder.

"You've been teasing me this whole time. Six months of this bullshit and this is what I get? I want something in return for your misdirection."

"No, Landon... Please, don't do this..."

Finally, her face was covered up with a small amount of soap. Her fingers burned against her own skin once she realized they were not hers...they were Landon's.

"You don't understand what you want, and now, I don't want to give it to you. I'll give you something else instead."

"No, please don't. Stop!"

"Shut up, shut up, *shut up!*" Abigail screamed at the top of her lungs.

Everything went silent. The echo of Abigail's desperate wail reverberated from the glass of the shower and the walls of the bathroom. It grew quieter and quieter until eventually, it stopped. The only sound remaining in the room was the water from the showerhead hitting the tiles underneath her feet. The soap Abigail applied to her body slowly rinsed off and collected in the drain in the center of the gray tiles.

Abigail's hand trembled as it fumbled to turn the water off. She was instantaneously shrouded in nothing but the cold. Water dripped down her face, hair, and down her legs until it hit the floor. She reached for a towel and wrapped it around herself. She didn't even bother washing her hair. In fact, Abigail had no idea what the shower was for other than to settle her thoughts. This time, however, it did the opposite by letting them resurface.

She was numb as she slowly walked from the bathroom to her room, tossing her dirty clothes in the hamper on the way. Abigail gathered a set of mismatched pajamas - an oversized Queen shirt and a pair of red checkered pants - and pulled them onto her body. She let the towel rest on the floor as she laid down on her bed, staring up at the ceiling. The fan above was somehow entertaining. It kept Abigail occupied with something other than her cruel imagination.

"Come on, Abigail. You know you can't hide this forever," she reminded herself with a pang.

That little voice inside her head was right. Abigail knew from experience that she needed to tell someone before she fell apart. Her heart throbbed inside her chest at the thought of letting someone else in. Who would it be, though? Her parents were out of the question for now, as was Keagan. She did not want her to feel guilty about what happened. She also knew that Jade or Brielle might notify Keagan. Everyone in the group was close.

That left one person.

Abigail instantly retaliated against that thought. "No. I'm *not* contacting him," she spoke to no one except herself.

She laid back and stared at the fan blades slowly spinning overhead. Abigail didn't really have another choice. Was she going to do it? If she did, would he have any interest in coming to her aid? Why wouldn't he?

"Don't sell yourself short," Kristy had said. *"Trust your instincts."*

Not letting herself think about it anymore, Abigail muttered a quick "Screw it" under her breath and texted him.

Meanwhile, on Precipice Way, the street adjacent to Little Creek Landing, a teenage boy was seated at the table in his kitchen with his laptop in front of him. It was not the most practical place in house number two fifty-three, but it would have to do for the time being. Noah's foot tapped against the floor while he worked tirelessly on an essay for British Literature. It was difficult to do so while his twin sisters were in the next room over playing a video game on the television.

"Lucy, I could've beaten the boss if you didn't run in front of me," Lacy told her sister.

Lucy glared at the girl seated next to her on the couch. Her light blonde curls bounced when she turned her head. "I was trying to protect you, you dummy! You're almost out of hearts. Eat something."

"I ran out of food!"

"Ugh, fine." It appeared as if Lucy shared some of her own. "Be more careful."

"What's going on in there?" Noah asked with genuine interest.

"We're trying to beat the Ender Dragon in *Minecraft*, but Lucy keeps messing me up when I'm about to kill it," Lacy whined.

Lucy frowned. "You're about to die. You literally have half a heart left."

"But-"

Both girls looked at the screen when something caught their attention. "No!" the two of them shrieked in unison.

Noah abruptly stood up, alarmed. "What? What's going on?"

"We both died from the Ender Dragon!"

"If you want, I can help you try to beat it another time. I need to finish this essay before Ryder picks me up for the movie night," Noah offered, then asked, "Is your spawn point near the stronghold?"

"Yes. I put all of our items in chests near our spawn point in the stronghold," Lucy supplied. "Unlike *somebody*."

Lacy was livid. "Hey!"

"That's good. How about you two take a break?" Noah suggested, sitting back down at the table in front of his laptop.

The twins looked at each other and then shrugged. "Okay," replied Lucy.

Noah typed some more on his laptop. He heard his twin sisters enter the kitchen. One sat on his left and the other sat on his right at the table. Noah pretended to pay them no mind. He knew Lacy and Lucy were curious girls, so it was no surprise to him when both of them were peering over his shoulder at the screen.

"What's the essay about?" Lucy inquired.

"It's about the *Lord of the Rings* trilogy." Noah smiled at the topic. "I have to compare the series to an event in my life."

"That sounds interesting," noted Lacy. "Do you know what event you're comparing it to?"

Noah's grin grew even larger for a split second. "Yeah, I do."

"Are you gonna tell us?" When Noah shook his head, she tried again. "Please?"

"Lacy," the other twin protested. "It isn't our business. Just let him work on his essay."

"Thank you, Lucy," Noah sighed in relief.

Silence ensued in the kitchen and Noah began to type on his laptop some more. He was in deep concentration, blocking out his surroundings. His way of being able to focus on his homework was almost destructive. Once he began an assignment, it seemed to him that he needed to finish it as soon as possible. He often wondered how he wasn't burnt out yet.

"Noah?" Lacy tried to get his attention.

"In a minute, Lacy. I want to finish this paragraph."

"Noah?"

"Just give me a second."

"Noah?"

The boy in question's head snapped up to meet his younger sister's gaze. "What is it?" he exhaled deeply.

"Your phone made a ding," Lacy informed him.

Noah stopped what he was doing and picked up his phone. His eyebrows scrunched together and then lifted at the contents of the text message he had received. The sender was not a surprise, but what she had requested most definitely was.

"Hey. I know it's last minute, but is there any way you could come over? I want to talk about something important and it shouldn't be over the phone."

"Is something wrong?" Lucy's brown eyes were filled with concern.

"Sure, I can come over. What's your address? I'll be there in a couple minutes," he texted back without thinking twice. He looked at his sisters' identical expressions. "Hopefully not. A friend just wants to talk to me about something."

"Is it Ryder?" Lacy asked. "You two have been hanging out a lot lately."

Noah blinked at the sudden question. "No, actually. They're...a different friend."

"Is it that girl you're always texting?"

Lucy elbowed her sister in the stomach. "Lucy!" she hissed. "You weren't supposed to tell him that we knew."

"...Sorry."

Their older brother looked at Lacy and then Lucy. "Yes, it's her," he answered truthfully.

"Do you like her?"

"Lacy, stop," Lucy protested.

Noah's phone dinged again. He looked at the new message from Abigail. *"Thank you so much. It's twenty-three Little Creek Landing."*

"Look, you two, I have to go." Noah stood from his chair and shut his laptop. He called up the stairs to Jenny. "Mom! I'm going out earlier than I thought!"

"Be careful, Noah!" Jenny replied loudly. "Be home by midnight!"

"I will!" He ruffled Lacy's hair and then moved on to Lucy's. "I'll see you two later. Good luck with beating the Ender Dragon. I'll help you tomorrow, if you want."

"Okay!" the twins chorused.

Noah smiled at them before grabbing his phone and wallet. He scurried out the door and down the driveway. He knew exactly where he was going since he had walked the Highland Heights neighborhood several times while in transit to and from school. Noah half-walked, half-ran down the sidewalk. He was aware of the abnormality of Abigail's request, which was what worried him.

Eventually, he ended up in front of twenty-three Little Creek Landing. Noah recognized Abigail's gray Honda Civic parked in the driveway. Not many lights were on that he could see. The house was a regular size for the neighborhood, being two stories. It appeared to be cozy from the inside out. Little did he know what was occurring beyond the exterior.

The teenage boy did not waste any time. He walked up the porch stairs and rang the doorbell. He listened as the chime made its way through the house. It did not take long for a pair of footsteps to approach the front door. The sight on the other side was not what Noah was expecting at all.

An exhausted Abigail stood at the other side. Her hair was dripping wet, hardly wrung out from the shower she had minutes before. Her mismatched pajamas screeched a new abnormality for the usually put-together girl. Big brown eyes met Noah's with dark circles underneath them that he somehow missed at school earlier that day. She looked like she didn't even care how fatigued she appeared to be.

That was why Noah bit his tongue when he was going to ask if she was alright. "Abigail, I-...what's wrong?" he stuttered out off-guardedly.

"Just come inside." Abigail didn't mean to snap. "Please."

Noah did not think more than he had to. He stepped inside the house and around Abigail, who shut the front door behind him. Her fingers were knotted together in front of her as she walked through the house and into the living room. Noah followed without a word. He was afraid of shattering what was already cracked inside of the girl in front of him.

"I'm sorry about this being last minute," Abigail apologized, sitting down on the sofa. "I hope I wasn't interrupting anything."

"You weren't." Noah sat down next to her, but not too close. He left just enough space between the two of them to deem comfortable without being awkward. "I'm just concerned. Actually, concerned isn't a strong-enough word. I'm worried about you, Abigail."

Abigail looked as if she was smaller than she was already. Her knees were pulled up to her chest and her arms were wrapped around her legs. "I know. That's why I wanted to talk to you about something, because I know you care."

"I do. I have all day...or night, more rather." Noah's words collapsed on each other from the tension of the room.

Luckily, his fumble spurred the smallest of smiles on Abigail's face. "Thank you," she gushed shakily. "But my parents will be home around dinnertime, so this hopefully won't take long."

"That's fine too."

Abigail paused. Her eyes glazed over with a sudden panic. "Okay, but what I'm about to tell you might surprise you. It might even disgust you and change how you think of me."

"I told you I'm willing to listen to anything. This counts," Noah assured her. "I seriously don't think it'll change my view of you."

She smiled slightly at that, but it quickly faded away as flashbacks, both new and old, began to resurface for the millionth time. "As you might know, Landon and I used to date," she started to explain. "We were together for just over six months starting in January, and we both were really happy. At least, I was happy...or I thought I was."

The room was silent other than the air conditioner whirring in the distance and the fan blades swirling gradually overhead. Noah's eyes were fixed on the broken girl about a foot away from him. His heart tugged already with sympathetic pain. He wanted to be there to comfort her, or - dammit - hug her if she needed it, but it did not seem like the right time.

"We saw each other almost every day, and when we didn't see each other, we were on the phone constantly. Landon always seemed content, and I was happy because I was making him happy. That all changed when he started being forceful towards me since he wasn't getting what he wanted from me like I thought he was. I remember the day he made me tell him I loved him."

"Abigail, tell me you love me. Now."

"Please let go of me."

"I'll let go of you when you say it."

"Let go. Please"

"It's only eight letters, three words, and three syllables. I swear to God if you don't say it right this second, I'll-"

"Okay, okay. I love you."

- "He didn't say it back. He never did, and I was too naïve to notice. That was the first instance he grabbed me physically and held me against his will until I did what he wanted. He'd push me, shove me, sometimes even slap me, but I thought it was all for my own good. I thought he loved me. This went on for three months and I dealt with it. I didn't tell anyone, not even my parents, Keagan, Jade, or Brielle. Then, on May twenty-ninth of this year, it got to a new low." -

"Abigail, we've talked about doing this for months. Now, you're backing out? Pathetic."

"I thought we had an agreement that if I didn't want to, we wouldn't."

"But I want this."

"Stop it, Landon"

- "He wanted to take something from me that wasn't meant to be his. I wasn't ready to give a crumb of my innocence to him, and he almost manipulated me into doing so." -

"Abigail, do you want this or not?"

"Landon, leave me alone."

- "He said I was messing with him and giving him mixed signals for the entire time we were dating, making him believe that I wanted something that I really didn't. Because he said these things, I thought it was my fault." -

"You've been giving me mixed signals for six months, Abigail. You know what you want. Stop lying to me."

"I told you no. I don't want this."

- "He made me blame myself for how he felt and what he thought I wanted when it was all one huge lie." -

"You've been teasing me this whole time. Six months of bullshit and this is what I get? I want something in return for your misdirection."

"No, Landon... Please, don't do this..."

- "I wouldn't do what he wanted, so..." -

"You don't understand what you want, and now, I don't want to give it to you. I'll give you something else instead."

"No, please don't. Stop!"

- "He beat me. I ended up with a broken wrist, a concussion, two cracked ribs, bruises all over my stomach and legs, whiplash, and a dislocated shoulder. That wasn't the worst part, though." -

"Please don't do this!"

"I need to teach you a lesson so next time, you'll listen to me. Understand?"

"You're sick! Let me out of here! Let me out!"

- "He locked me in the pitch black basement of his house. My phone was in his room, so he sent texts to my parents saying I was staying at his house and that everything was okay." Abigail's eyes, which had been welling up with tears, blinked and sent two little waterfalls spiraling down her cheeks. "I was there for two days. Nobody knew. As soon as he let me out, I ran home and called the police from the home phone. My parents were at work." -

"Nine-one-one. What's your emergency?"

"I was just attacked and kidnapped for two days in my boyfriend's basement without food or water. Please come quick! I'm injured and I-...I-..."

The phone fell to the floor with a sickening crack.

"Ma'am? Ma'am! What is your location? Ma'am!"

"I fainted after that from the pain. I woke up in the hospital with my parents by my side. Luckily the operator was able to track my call and send an ambulance. I told my parents everything and they filed a lawsuit against Landon. He got five years in prison, but since his lawyer's very good, he got out on parole. He went on a damn vacation during the first couple weeks of school while I was suffering."

Abigail roughly wiped her reddening face from the tears cascading down it. "Then, two days ago, he approached me and made me kiss him so he'd lift the restraining order against Keagan.

He manipulated me into thinking it was my fault...again. I did it because I thought everyone would hate me if I didn't and I put myself first."

"No one would hate you," Noah choked out, fighting his own tears. "I surely don't. I think you're very brave."

"That's why I'm so scared of every guy who comes my way. That's why I was so nervous around you while you were tutoring me. That's why I-..."

"Abigail...," Noah trailed off when she broke down into a fit of strangled sobs. Frankly, he had no idea what to do other than choke back the thought of her being frightened of him. "Can I hug you? It's okay if you don't, I just-"

She cut him off by leaning over and flinging her arms around his neck. Noah was caught by surprise again but did not hesitate to reciprocate the gesture by hugging her gently towards him. Abigail cried hysterically against his chest. All Noah could do was to embrace her and let her release the pent-up emotions she had stored for who knew how long.

"I'm so sorry," he mumbled tightly. "I knew something was going on, but not this serious."

Abigail sniffled and tilted her head upwards. Her red-splotched eyes were glossed over with shiny tears. "...You did?" she squeaked.

"I pieced it together," he explained timidly. "During the third week of school, I saw you run out of the Precalculus classroom and not come back to school until the next day. You looked scared, and I tried to figure out why that was, but then I realized there was a new student entering moments before you escaped. That's why you wanted to transfer to AP Calculus so badly, wasn't it? To get away from him?"

Abigail nodded.

"Then, Ryder and I were walking down the hall and saw you and him by the lockers that time...you know, when I slammed into him? That was Ryder's doing, by the way. He pushed me into him and ran."

Abigail let out a breathy laugh at that. Noah smiled a little.

"At that point, I knew there was something specific going on between you two. I had a good idea of it, but I didn't know it was this bad. I'm just glad you're okay."

"You're not...angry at me?" Her voice trembled as she inquired.

Noah's face contorted into a glare "Why would I be mad at you? I'd rather beat Landon's face in and throw him in a garbage disposal for what he did."

Abigail's eyes widened at that.

"But we should be smarter about this," Noah finished sensibly.

"...We?"

"Of course," he replied. "He can't just get away with this with no repercussions. I want to help you if you'll let me."

Abigail was uncertain. "Are you sure?"

"Why wouldn't I be sure?"

"You mean it?"

Noah smiled, gently setting a hand on her shoulder. "I mean it," he pledged. "But one thing first."

The smile that was about to glimmer upon her lips faded away. "What is it?"

"Don't be mad at me, but I think you should tell your parents about this. They'll be able to help you like last time."

"Oh, um, I don't know..."

"It's your choice, but they're not going to hate you for it if that's what you think," he assured her calmly.

Abigail sniffled. Her tears had mostly stopped by that point. "I'll think about it. They'll be home any minute-"

She was about to finish when she heard two pairs of dreaded footsteps walk up the porch steps. Abigail knew it was the two people she wanted to avoid at that moment. She cringed and began messing around with her damp hair as a distraction. The inevitable happened before she had a chance to do anything about it. The front door opened, and Abigail's parents stepped in. She knew the bottom was about to drop when they discovered a boy in the living room.

"Hey, Abigail!" Harold Bartley greeted his daughter cheerfully. "How come the front door was unlocked? You know it's the rule, especially when it's dark-"

Abigail's father stopped in his tracks once he reached the living room. "Uh, Abigail? Who's this?" he asked skeptically.

"Um...this is Noah," Abigail responded nervously. "He's one of my friends. Sorry about not asking if I could have him over. It was last-minute."

"Abigail, I-"

At that very second, Lillian Bartley entered the room. She had a much friendlier expression on her kind face. "Hi, Noah. I'm Lillian and this is Harold," she introduced the two of them. "What brings you here on such late notice, and at six o'clock at night?"

"Um, Mr. and Mrs. Bartley, I don't mean to intrude, but Abigail needed my help with something," Noah cautiously elaborated.

"Abigail, have you been crying?" Harold's eyes narrowed protectively.

"Yes, Sir, she has, but-" Noah started, but he was interrupted by Abigail.

Once the words left her lips, they were out for the world to hear. Abigail regretted them at first, but she knew that after everything was explained, it would be for the best in the long run.

"Mom? Dad? Can I talk to you both? It's important."

20

"THANK YOU, THANK YOU. I GOT IT FROM FLYNN."

"DAD, I TOLD YOU THAT I WAS GOING OVER TO KEAGAN'S HOUSE yesterday." Abigail asked in dismay. "Can I not go now?"

Harold sighed. "Abigail, Dear, it's not that we don't trust you. We're very worried about you, especially after what happened on Wednesday."

"But you can trust Keagan, Brielle, and Jade."

"Will that Noah boy be there?"

Abigail hesitated. She knew she needed to tell the truth. "Yes, he'll be there. So will Brielle's older brother, but you've met him. He's nice, and besides, he always hangs out with Brielle," she replied.

"I think it would be best for you to stay home," her father reasoned. "You were just bawling your eyes out thirty minutes ago. I can see how tired you are."

It was true. For the better of her mental - and physical - health, Abigail forced herself to notify her parents of what was occurring behind the walls of Hillwell High. Through the blubbering mess of her words, her parents finally realized how much she was struggling. She told them about transferring to AP Calculus, the ice cream parlor incident, the restraining order against Keagan...all of it. It spilled out of her mouth like a waterfall of tears.

When both of her parents started to tear up, she did too, Abigail realized she was glad Noah was not sitting next to her. The teenage boy decided to give the family of three privacy and head outside, much to Abigail's relief. Her heart was torn, though. For a moment, she thought it would have been easier if he was by her side for moral support. Her parents loved her dearly, though, which made the difficult conversation a little bit easier.

Abigail broke down for the second time that evening, sobbing on the sofa between her mother and father. The two of them embraced her in a much-needed hug, which soaked up her pain and made it bearable. Lillian and Harold vowed once again to do their best to protect their daughter from the young man they all hated the most in the world.

Now, Abigail was perched on the kitchen counter with her father preparing dinner. "I'm really tired, but I think seeing my friends will help," she tried to negotiate.

"Wouldn't you be too fatigued to drive?" Harold asked.

Abigail shrugged. "Brielle's picking me up. I texted her asking and she said that was okay with her."

"Would her brother be with her?"

"Yes, and Noah, too, probably, but-"

Harold denied, "I don't think that's such a good idea."

"Please?" Abigail was close to begging. "I'll text you and Mom every hour so you know I'm alright. I'll be with Keagan and Jade too. You like them, right?"

"Yes, I do, but-"

"Oh, Harold, just let her go," Lillian interjected to her daughter's relief. "Having her cooped up in the house all night would probably make her feel worse."

"Lillian, I-" Abigail's father started to protest.

Lillian gave him a stern look. "Let her be with her friends. They're a positive influence on her and they won't let anything happen."

"But-"

"It'll be fine. Okay?"

Harold sighed stressfully. "...Okay."

"Thank you!" Abigail rushed over to her parents and barreled into them with a hug. "Brielle will give me a ride home."

"Let us know when you're coming home," Lillian told her kindly.

"I will. I'm going to wait on the porch steps for her. She should be here any minute."

"Be careful," Harold worried.

"I will."

"Love you!" Both parents chorused as Abigail opened the front door.

Abigail turned around and smiled. "I love you too."

She then shut the door behind her. Abigail walked down a couple of the porch steps before sitting down on the top one. She unlocked her phone and began scrolling through it to pass the time. She couldn't care less that she was dressed in the same mismatched pajamas as before, sitting in front of her house under the darkening sky. Abigail didn't care about a lot of things anymore. Attire certainly was not one of them.

A sudden voice from her right startled her right off the stairs. "Everything okay?" When Abigail jumped, it hurriedly apologized. "Oh, God, I'm so sorry. I didn't mean to scare you."

"...It's alright," Abigail replied hesitantly from the sidewalk.

"You know, hiding in a bush is certainly a new scene for me."

The corners of Abigail's lips quirked upwards into a small smile. "Noah, I didn't tell you to hide in a bush in the front yard."

"You asked me to stay outside," he reasoned. "Figured I might as well hide."

"I didn't think you'd actually do it."

Noah appeared triumphant. "Well, I did. I also texted Ryder to see if they can pick us both up here if that's okay."

"Yeah, that's fine," responded Abigail. She appeared rather awkward sitting on the sidewalk with a boy in the bush across from her.

"Are you hurt? You know...from the tumble off the stairs."

Abigail examined her hands and elbows, which she had landed on. "I'll be fine. Just a few scrapes."

"Are you sure?" Noah appeared concerned.

"Yeah, I'm fine." A pair of headlights coming into view and turning into the driveway prompted Abigail to change the subject. "Looks like they're here."

Abigail typed out a text to her parents and walked over towards the car's left side with Noah in tow. She waved to Brielle as she walked past her window, who eagerly waved back from behind the steering wheel. When Noah walked around the other side, he noticed Ryder sitting next to his younger sister. The taller of the two siblings looked to be a bit nervous. Noah guessed it was due to his younger sister driving their vehicle for once. Abigail and Noah got into the opposite sides of the vehicle and shut the doors behind them almost in sync.

"Hey, guys!" Ryder exclaimed once everyone was in the car.

"Hi," Abigail and Noah said in unison. The two of them looked at each other in surprise and then at their seatbelts to buckle them.

Brielle's giggle could easily be heard from the driver's seat. "How are you two?" she asked in her usual sweet voice.

Both replied with variants of "I'm okay" and then asked Brielle and Ryder the same question. Noah frowned at Abigail's answer. It was obviously a lie.

"I'm excited for the movie," Brielle commented brightly as she maneuvered the vehicle out of the driveway and onto the road. "Abigail, have you seen it?"

Abigail shook her head, which Brielle saw through the rear-view mirror. "I haven't seen it, but Noah here tells me it's good."

"I did?" Noah blankly questioned.

Abigail elbowed him in the arm. "Shh. Just go with it," she whispered. "I'm trying to make conversation."

"Oh...oh!" Noah recalled a slight fib. "Yeah. I'm excited for her to see the Battle of Helm's Deep. It's awesome."

Brielle's smile was wide as it reflected the mirror. "It is! Helm's Deep is my favorite battle in the movie trilogy except for the Battle of the Morannon."

"Huh?" Abigail blinked.

"Don't ask me," Ryder chuckled. "I know nothing about this stuff."

"It's the final battle," Brielle explained while stopping at a stop sign. "I don't want to spoil anything, but you'll see when we watch the third movie."

Abigail forced a smile. "Sounds good."

Other than the engine of the car whirring and the occasional sound of the turn signal turning on and off, the vehicle went silent. Ryder turned on the radio after about a minute to make the experience much less awkward. Abigail scrolled on her phone while contemplating a certain idea that she had. After at least three minutes of thought, she reopened her text thread with Noah and typed out a message to him.

"I'm going to tell Keagan, Brielle, and Jade about what happened with Landon on Wednesday."

Noah's phone chimed. He picked it up and read the notification. His eyebrows lifted, mirroring his surprised response. *"Are you sure? It doesn't have to be this soon, or at all."*

Abigail quickly typed back, *"They can help stop this mess. I know they all will have great ideas...but I don't know if I want to tell Ryder."*

"I'll handle Ryder. You tell who you're comfortable with."

"I don't mean to leave him out, but I just don't know him as well as everyone else."

"That's understandable," Noah replied to her text.

When Abigail finally looked up from her phone, Noah caught her eye. He mouthed the question "Are you sure?" once again. Abigail nodded and put her phone away.

In the front seat, Brielle and Ryder were talking about something that the former was learning in her book club. Abigail was not really listening, to be honest. Neither was Noah. The latter was an empathetic person. Little did Abigail know, once he exited her home so she could speak with her parents in peace, he let the tears roll down his cheeks for a few minutes. Noah hated to cry, but he knew it was necessary for many reasons.

Abigail's mind wandered briefly until a thought occurred to her. "Wait...should we have invited Jade?" she fretted guiltily. "She must be driving herself and we're all here together. I hope she doesn't feel left out."

"I offered, but she said no,'" Brielle stated, her mood dropping.

"Oh," she exhaled. Abigail wondered what was going on with Jade.

That was the end of the conversations in the O'Brians' vehicle. Abigail grew oddly silent, as did the other three passengers. Luckily, they were nearing Keagan's neighborhood. Abigail watched the speedometer over Brielle's shoulder to entertain herself. Noah looked out the window at the houses passing by. Ryder kept switching channels on the radio. Some of them were static, but most were pop or rap. Frustrated with the lack of song choices, he turned the radio off, leaving the car in silence.

Brielle parked the car on the curb in front of Keagan's house. Abigail noticed Jade's car already in the driveway. It appeared as if she had been there for at least a few minutes due to her person being vacant from the driveway. Abigail, Noah, Ryder, and Brielle got out of the car and walked down the driveway towards the front door. Abigail briefly sent a text to her parents notifying them of her arrival.

Before Noah was able to ring the doorbell, the door swung open. It startled all four of them nearly off the porch. There, in the doorway, was Keagan, holding her particularly excited Yorkshire terrier, Flynn, in her arms. She had a wide smile on her face.

"Hey, guys! Welcome!" Keagan's gray eyes were bright and her red-streaked pixie cut was vibrant. She looked at Abigail. "Nice pajamas, Abi."

Flynn barked happily in agreement, his tail wagging a hundred miles an hour.

Abigail blushed with embarrassment. "Thanks."

"Come on in!" Keagan opened the door the rest of the way. "Jade's already upstairs. She got here like ten minutes ago to help me set up the snacks and things."

"Is she okay?" Brielle inquired without thinking.

Keagan gave Brielle a puzzled look. "I think so. Why wouldn't she be?"

"...I don't know."

The five of them - including Flynn - made their way through Keagan's house after the front door was shut by Ryder. The house was quiet except for Flynn's occasional yips and Keagan's commentary as the group of five walked up the stairs and into "the lounge". Keagan seemed to be in a very happy mood. Abigail liked and disliked it, her reasoning being that she was happy her friend was happy, but she would regret it when her smile was turned upside down.

Seated on the couch was Jade. She had her hand in a family-sized bag of potato chips and her other was holding onto the remote. She was flipping boredly through the bonus features of the second movie of the *Lord of the Rings* trilogy: *The Two Towers*. When Jade noticed everyone else's presence in the room, she set the remote down and stuffed her handful of chips into her mouth. She waved at them, but her face fell a little bit when she saw Noah.

Abigail definitely noticed it that time. She gave a friendly wave back. "Hey, Jade," she greeted her. "How are you?"

"Good," she mumbled with a bunch of chips in her mouth. She then swallowed them. "Keagan, I got the movie all set up."

"Oh, good!" Keagan plopped down on her usual seat in the corner of the couch.

In order to avoid any conflict, Abigail chose the seat on the couch next to Jade. Noah sat on the opposite side of her while Brielle and Ryder decided on the cushions on the other side of Keagan. Jade offered Abigail a pleasant smile, which she returned. Flynn, who was oh-so excited, sat down on Keagan's lap, but he barely fit. Keagan smiled at her loveable dog as he curled up on her lap and she picked up the remote.

"Everyone ready? This movie's also long, but it's just as good as *The Fellowship of the Ring*," Keagan assured them happily.

Murmurs of "Yes" and "I'm ready" emitted from the group. Keagan eagerly pressed the play button on the remote and sat it down.

The movie began and hardly anyone spoke for quite a while. Abigail twiddled her thumbs anxiously in her lap. She had already notified Noah of her plan, which meant she had to do it in her eyes. She was committed now. There was no going back. Noah was counting on her, and she needed to take this step. Once it was over, the better she would feel.

Abigail listened to Brielle's occasional fact and Keagan's commentary in complete silence for over half of the movie. She soon decided that she couldn't be quiet anymore. Abigail was ripping herself apart from the inside out with the anticipation she felt. Her brown eyes traveled over to Noah's, which were locked on the television screen. As if he sensed her gaze upon him, his own darted over to her. Abigail gestured with her eyes over towards her friends. The gesture was almost telepathic, but Noah understood, nodding.

Noah turned towards Ryder, who was seated the furthest away from him. "Hey, Ryder," he said to get his attention. Ryder's eyes snapped in Noah's direction. "Want to get more snacks?"

"Huh?" Ryder was confused. "We have plenty, though. Besides, we're almost to the Battle of Helm's-"

Keagan cut him off. She noticed the uncomfortable look on Abigail's face. "Yeah, how about you get some more chips?" she suggested. "There's loads in the pantry. You can't miss it."

"Uh, okay?"

"Let's go, Ryder." Noah stood up from his seat.

Ryder looked at Brielle, who was also puzzled. He shrugged and then followed Noah out of the room. Abigail thought she saw a quick thumbs-up from Noah, but maybe it was just her vivid imagination. By now, Keagan had paused the movie and three pairs of worried eyes looked in Abigail's direction. Abigail squirmed in her seat as Brielle reached over towards the table to pick up the remote. She paused the television. This was it, Abigail realized.

"What's going on, Abi?" Keagan asked softly. "You look nervous; I know it."

Abigail resisted the urge to gnaw on her fingernails from anxiety. "You guys won't get mad at me if I tell you I've been hiding something from you...right?"

Brielle's eyebrows shot up. "Why would we get mad at you?" she inquired. "We're your friends and we love you. If you're hiding something, it's for good reason."

Jade remained eerily silent at that, but she and Keagan nodded.

"I agree with Brielle," the latter stated honestly. "You can tell us what's going on if you want, but if you don't, it's okay."

Abigail's stomach turned circles upon itself until she spit out, "Landon did something to me last Wednesday."

"What?!" Keagan, Brielle, and Jade exclaimed loudly.

"Did you ever wonder how your restraining order got lifted so quickly?" Abigail swallowed down a lump of anxiety as she asked Keagan, who nodded in reply.

She took a deep breath before confessing, "Landon approached me in the hallway on Wednesday when I went out to get some air during lunch. He told me that if I did something for him, he'd lift the restraining order against Keagan as well as leave me alone."

"...You didn't do it, did you?" Keagan's hopeful face fell.

"I asked him what it was, and he said I had to kiss him," Abigail continued, choking it out. "I agreed, and he kissed me, but it was more than that. He trapped me between the lockers and touched me under my shirt. He wouldn't let me go until I grabbed his shirt and whirled him around into the lockers. I ran after that."

Abigail could barely look up at her friends for several seconds. When she did, though, she noticed Brielle tearing up, Jade angrily fiddling with her clenched fists, and Keagan...was staring into space. Abigail noticed the fury in the pair of gray eyes closest to her gaze. At once, guilt flooded her system. She knew she shouldn't have told everyone, especially Keagan.

Or should she have?

Keagan threw the clenched fist of her right hand into her left. "I'm going to kill him," she muttered darkly. "I'm so stupid. I shouldn't have punched-"

"Don't blame yourself," Abigail pleaded with her friend.

"I didn't think it would cause this much trouble for you, Abi," Keagan persisted. "I'm so sorry."

"No, no... don't be sorry. It was my decision."

"But-"

Abigail leaned over and embraced the petite girl in a tight hug. It hardly took long at all for Brielle, who wiped away a stray tear, and the quiet Jade to join them. For once, Abigail felt protected within the arms of her friends. She could tell Keagan was nearly in tears, which was why she held her the tightest. Abigail assumed herself as the villain of this story when she could not have been further from it.

"Please don't feel bad," Abigail reiterated against Keagan's hair. "It's over and done with. I'm okay and it's over."

Keagan sniffled but had a determined look on her face. "No, it's not. We're going to end this and get him the hell away from you.

"...He said he'd leave me alone."

"You don't believe all the nonsense coming out of his mouth, do you?" Jade asked her first question of the conversation.

Abigail released herself fully from the hug the four of them shared. "He did lift Keagan's restraining order though."

"That was probably a diversion," Jade mused thoughtfully. "He wanted to manipulate you into giving him what he wanted. He only kept his word so you'd believe him, but he'll probably try something else soon."

"I know, but-" Abigail was interrupted by a snap of two fingers.

"I've got it!" Keagan determined loudly enough for Flynn, who was sleeping, to wake up and jump off the couch. "...Sorry, Flynn."

Flynn sat down on the floor by Keagan's feet. She sat down next to the dog and began to soothingly pet him on the top of the head.

"I'm really sorry, Buddy," she apologized.

"Keagan, what was your idea?" prompted Jade.

"I didn't mean to scare you, Flynn, I was just trying to get my point across."

"Keagan."

"Do you forgive me? I really didn't mean to startle you."

"Keagan!" Abigail, Brielle, and Jade chorused at a loud volume.

"What?" Keagan blubbered while scratching Flynn behind the ears. "Oh, sorry. I was so caught up in apologizing to Flynn that I didn't tell you guys my idea."

All three of them gave her exasperated looks.

"Alright, alright!" Keagan held up her hands in mock surrender. "But it just occurred to me that Hillwell High is being monitored by security cameras. That's what confirmed me punching Landon. If you were in the hallway, then the cameras must've gotten you two on tape. You could go to the Principal's office and accuse him. There's no way it'd be denied!"

There were murmurs of agreement and excitement among the group of friends. Abigail was still unsure, though, which made Keagan think harder

"But wait, I have something else. I call it the "secret sauce"," Keagan leaned over into Abigail's ear and whispered a suggestion.

"Oh, my God. Keagan, you're a genius." Abigail's face slowly stretched into a smile.

The small girl dramatically bowed. "Thank you, thank you. I got it from Flynn."

Flynn tilted his head to the side. All four of the girls began laughing at the poor dog who had no idea what was going on.

"Seriously, though," Keagan redirected, "On Monday, we should go down to Principal Bryant's office and request the footage. Then, once he's convicted and everything's taken care of, we'll use the "secret sauce". We'll get him once and for all! Are you all in?"

Keagan put her hand - palm facing downward - out in front of her. Jade and Brielle were quick to put their hands on top of Keagan's, but Abigail stayed still. Three pairs of eyes, one gray and two brown, eyed her hopefully. It was all up to her, now. Did she want to get rid of Landon after what he had done to her? That question seemed obvious, but Abigail was hesitant to let go. Eventually, she placed her hand on top of Brielle's, which was on the top of the pile.

"We got this!" Keagan declared confidently despite Abigail's worry. "Don't worry about a thing, Abi. We'll take care of it."

"...Okay."

Brielle and Jade agreed, however, Abigail was still wary. At that moment, there was a knock on the door to "the lounge." Keagan hopped to her feet and was about to open the door, but she stopped in her tracks. She turned to Abigail.

"Does Noah know?" she questioned in a hushed tone.

Abigail nodded. She felt a grin appear on her face that matched Keagan's, which grew larger with her friend's answer. She opened the door and let Noah and Ryder inside. Noah entered first with a large transparent bowl of barbeque chips under his right arm. Ryder, however, was empty-handed. He looked as puzzled as ever, but Noah shot him a look that seemed to tell him to not ask questions. Ryder shut the door behind him.

"Hey, everyone." Noah sat down on the couch next to Abigail. "It took a while, but we found the chips." He set them down on the table.

"No, it didn't. You told me to talk about baseba-" Ryder was promptly elbowed by Brielle before he was able to finish. "...Uh, yeah. It took a while."

Brielle, Jade, and Keagan giggled a bit at Ryder's awkwardness. Meanwhile, Abigail was seated on the couch, twiddling her thumbs nervously. A gentle tap on her shoulder prodded her back to reality. Abigail blinked up from her hands knotted together in her lap and at Noah, whose eyes were locked on her. She almost let her vulnerability take over, but it didn't stand a chance.

"Are you okay?" he whispered with a concerned expression.

Abigail caught herself nodding. She did feel a little bit better. "Yeah, or at least I will be. We have a plan."

The corners of Noah's lips tugged upwards at that. He decided not to say anything else about the matter. Abigail already had a difficult enough day. She had felt all of the emotions she wanted to feel for a long while.

Meanwhile, Keagan grabbed the remote off the table and pressed the play button to resume the movie. She had a knowing smile on her face when she glanced over at Abigail and Noah, but she had no plans to ruin the moment for either of them. Instead, she turned her eyes eagerly towards the television.

"Okay, let's watch the Elves and the Rohan people kick some Orc butt."

21

"I'D LIKE TO HEAR WHAT THIS IS ABOUT."

DESPITE THE THREE YEARS AND TWO MONTHS SHE SPENT HERE, Hillwell High School never, and never will be, the same for Abigail.

There she was, surrounded by the usual swarms of people hustling and bustling to enter the large building with coral brick. Rather than joining them, Abigail's worn black high tops were rooted to the concrete beneath her feet. The sun was high up in the air with tufts of cumulus clouds fogging the blue above them. It was almost as if the sky was mocking her. While Abigail felt like a rainy day on the inside, the weather on the outside couldn't have been more perfect.

It was an abnormally warm day for the Midwestern town of Hillwell. Abigail noticed small beads of sweat running down her back underneath her band t-shirt. She wore her usual pair of light washed jeans with a hole in the knee. Abigail's gold-tinted sunglasses were perched atop her head and over her long straight hair that was worn down around her shoulders.

Abigail took several deep, steady breaths as she waited. In through her nose, and out through her mouth, she respirated to keep herself calm. She kept her hands firmly in the small pockets of her jeans. Her eyes were glued to the large, propped-open doors in front of her. Abigail felt herself tremble with each breath. What if she was making a huge mistake?

She was unable to contemplate that thought for more than five seconds because of her rather spontaneous and petite friend jogging towards her. "Hey, Abi!" she exclaimed between two deep breaths. "You're standing in the middle of the sidewalk."

"I know," Abigail deadpanned.

"Well, I just thought I'd tell you," Keagan rambled. "Wait, what?"

Abigail smiled a little bit. "Never mind."

"What's going on?"

The two teenagers spun around to view Jade and Brielle walking side by side. The former was the one who produced that query. Keagan offered them a friendly wave as they approached despite the demeanor of the other three. Jade and Brielle appeared neutral on the outside while nervous on the inside, but Abigail was a completely different story. She was visibly crumbling from the stress placed on her back.

"Not much," Keagan supplied in a matter-of-fact tone. "Does everyone know what the plan is?" she asked.

The three of them nodded at that.

"Are we actually skipping class?" Brielle inquired a bit anxiously.

"Just the first block," Jade assured her. "We just need to make sure that Principal Bryant listens to us and that might take a while."

Abigail was rocking back and forth on her heels. "I don't know about this."

"Abi, no offense, but how aren't you sure about this?" questioned Keagan in disbelief. "We can get rid of him. First, we just need to convict him."

"What if it backfires?"

"It won't."

"What if we miss something important in British Literature?" Abigail was busy making excuses by this point.

Keagan smirked. "We won't."

"...How?"

"We've got Noah in there paying attention to the lecture for us,"

Keagan reminded her triumphantly. "He'll let us know if we miss something and he'll fill us in after."

Abigail's lips flattened into a thin line. "Oh."

"It'll be fine," the petite girl stated. "You've got all of us to back you up."

"Promise?" her voice wavered as she asked.

Keagan smiled genuinely. "I promise. Are you ready?"

"I guess so."

The four of them walked through the double doors of Hillwell High. Abigail would never get used to the overwhelming number of students crowding the hallways and classrooms. Abigail would normally be walking towards her locker, but instead, she, Keagan, Jade, and Brielle were walking towards the Principal's office.

The room in question was always intimidating. No one among the students of Hillwell high School desired to sit in the chair across from Principal Bryant's. That was exactly what the foursome were going to do, though. Abigail's heart was pounding in her chest with each step she took. Everything around her blurred. Even as students left the halls to attend their classes, Abigail felt like she was drowning from the prior sea of them.

Abigail, Keagan, Jade, and Brielle stopped in front of the door to Principal Bryant's office. Every single one of them was hesitant. Abigail slowly removed her right hand from her pocket and lifted it towards the door. She looked at her friends, who all gave her a nod and smiles of encouragement.

Three knocks on the door broke the silence surrounding the four girls. Unfortunately for them, one of the people they wanted to avoid cracked the door open with a frustrated expression on her middle-aged face.

"What do you four want?" Vice Principal Coleman snapped, her eyes slitted.

Abigail gulped down an anxious lump. "Um, hi," she stuttered out. "We'd like to see Principal Bryant about something, please."

"It's urgent," Keagan added on.

Rather than answering Abigail's request, Vice Principal Coleman glared at Keagan. "I thought you were expelled, Miss Lopez," she commented.

"Principal Bryant revoked my expulsion last Thursday, but I guess she didn't tell you about that," Keagan snipped sweetly.

"You're treading on thin ice, young lady."

"Could we speak to Principal Bryant?" Keagan redirected. "It's very important and it can't wait until later."

Vice Principal Coleman looked back at the woman sitting at her desk and repeated the question to her. After a wordless nod from her superior, she rolled her eyes and opened the door the rest of the way to allow the four teenagers inside. Abigail, Keagan, Jade, and Brielle walked past Vice Principal Coleman - Keagan offering her an innocent smile as she went by - and stood in front of Principal Bryant's desk.

"Good morning, girls," Principal Bryant expressed in a much friendlier tone than her assistant who seemed as if she had a stick up her...area of waste disposal. "I understand that you would like to speak to me about something important?"

"Uh, yes, Ma'am," Abigail replied. "I wanted to report-"

"I'd like to hear what this is about," Vice Principal Coleman remarked.

Principal Bryant adjusted her glasses and smiled apologetically at the four teenagers sitting in front of her. She then fixed her gaze on her associate. "Mrs. Coleman, could you please deliver these files to the copier? I need five copies of each."

Vice Principal Coleman's face fell as she looked at the large stack of papers being handed out to her. "Certainly," she snapped.

She snatched them from her and walked out the door, letting it close loudly behind her. Abigail watched dumbfoundedly as the Vice Principal, who was clearly an adult, was acting less mature than a first grader.

Principal Bryant waited for the Vice Principal to leave before she continued, "I'm sorry about that, you four. What would you like to report?" she inquired kindly.

After a deep breath and three encouraging looks, Abigail choked out, "I'd like to report Landon Woods for harassing me verbally and sexually in the hall last Wednesday."

"...I see." Principal Bryant was caught off-guard. "Abigail, I'm so sorry that happened to you, and it must be hard to think about, but could you please explain exactly what occurred?"

Abigail decided there was no use in fighting the vivid memories that haunted her as she spoke, "It was during lunch, and I had left the cafeteria to get some air."

Abigail reached her locker and leaned against it. She held two fingers up to her neck to check her pulse, which was racing. Her breaths were deep and burned her throat like wildfire. Her hands were shaking and her fingertips were throbbing from the small scabs and tears searing through the top layer of skin. She slowly began to calm down, but even that fate was turned against her.

- "Landon approached me. He knows that his presence alone makes me uncomfortable, and for a good reason." -

"You look awful antsy." A snarky voice to her left made her skin crawl.

Abigail refused to meet his eyes. She straightened up and made herself as tall as possible. Her heart rate accelerated to a mile a minute solely due to his presence. Abigail had no one to protect her this time. Keagan was expelled, Noah was in the cafeteria, and her friends were using her phone to talk to the former. She had no means of contact. It had completely slipped her mind and now, she felt like an idiot.

- "He started provoking me about not talking to him. If you didn't know, we used to be in a relationship." Abigail's voice shook. "Landon was very pushy. In June, there was a lawsuit about it. He sexually assaulted me. He was convicted but got out easily on parole." -

"Are you not going to talk to me?" The voice grew closer. He frowned as Abigail shrunk down to her shoes. "After all we've been through? Six months of our relationship is written off just like that?"

He snapped his fingers loudly, which made Abigail flinch. "We haven't kept in touch since June," Abigail's tone trembled as she seethed. "I don't ever want to see you again."

"The court case doesn't count, Sweetheart," Landon retorted with a

sugary drawl. "The last time we properly spoke without any interruptions was in May."

"Do you think I care?"

"You're just as resistant as I remember," he mused, getting too close for her preference. Her idea of "close" was in a two-mile radius. "You still don't know how to listen to me."

- "Landon was often forceful with me. He was the one who requested the restraining order against my friend, Keagan, for punching him to defend me. After he was talking about how I never listened to him - because he was forceful - he offered to lift the restraining order." -

"I'm willing to lift the restraining order against her. As you know, I have a skilled lawyer and Keagan will be able to return to Hillwell High as soon as tomorrow," Landon explained.

At first, she was about to sigh in relief, but stopped in her tracks. "It's way too good to be true. Come on, Abigail--you're smarter than that." Abigail glared in his direction. "There's a catch to this and I know it. You can't let her off that easily."

- "I told him it would be too easy, and he said I was right. He said I had to do something for him first, and that something was a kiss." -

"You know me too well. You need to do something for me first."

"What are you implying?"

"Well, I've been thinking, Abigail," Landon stated, shifting his position towards the middle of the hallway. "I've missed you since you left me last May. It's caused me a lot of pain over the past few months. I was never able to gain closure with you. So, I decided that you owe me a small token of farewell."

Abigail's heart leapt to her throat. "And what would that be?" Her voice dangerously trembled as she spoke.

"A kiss would be appropriate."

- "I only agreed because he told me it would be all my fault if Keagan didn't graduate high school due to her expulsion. He also said if I did this, I wouldn't be able to tell anyone." -

"It isn't that easy."

"You're right. If you do this for me, you must promise that you'll never tell anyone about it. I don't want any more lawsuits on my hands."

Abigail almost shuddered at the wink that came right after. "What would happen if I don't do this for you?" *she had the nerve to inquire.*

"Well, everything would remain the same," replied Landon simply. *"Your friend would probably have to drop out of high school. Her mother would be very disappointed in her and would probably reprimand her, punishing her beyond belief. And as for you...it would be all your fault. Your friends would hate you for what you did to Keagan. You will have torn Keagan apart and then yourself along with it."*

- "Before I was able to do anything else other than agree without wanting to, he pushed me up against the lockers and kissed me roughly. He trapped me against the metal and put his hand up my shirt." -

"Then...I'll follow your proposition as long as you keep to your word," she hesitantly said.

Landon smiled. "I thought so."

Before Abigail was able to comprehend what was going on, Landon's lips were on hers. Rather than being soft and gentle like she had hoped - what she had experienced from him several times before - his kiss was rough and intruding. Abigail struggled to breathe as her respirations became shallow from panic.

Her hands rested on his chest and she attempted to push him away, but instead, Landon shoved her against the locker behind her without breaking their contact. Abigail winced as the combination lock dug into her spine and the cool metal was against her neck. Her head throbbed from the impact. The world around her blurred, but not in the special, intimate way. Instead, Abigail was trapped.

- "After a while - I don't know how long - I decided I had enough." Abigail's body trembled harder at the memory. "I grabbed his shirt and spun him around so I had the upper hand." -

Abigail decided his "token of farewell" had gone too far once she felt his icy fingers travel under her hoodie, her shirt and then against her skin. Her entire body trembled as his hand rose higher and higher on her body while her mouth was being unwillingly occupied. Abigail was disgusted and repulsed by his touch. She felt like she was really going to puke. He was not going to stop, so she did the only thing she could think of. While his hands were occupied with her, she gathered two fistfulls of his shirt and spun him around so his back was against the lockers instead of hers.

At an instant, Landon's lips broke away from Abigail's, but he was unable to escape her clutches. His surprise was his weakness. Abigail's fists gripped his shirt tightly and he was pressed against the wall of metal containers just like she was. Abigail's mouth curled into a snarl that she was unfamiliar with.

"I told him to never touch me again and fled," Abigail concluded breathily. Her palms were sweating. Keagan had reached over and grabbed her hand sometime during her story, which she was squeezing the warmth out of. "So far, he's kept his promise, but I'm afraid of him. I was expecting just a little peck on the lips, but he took it way too far."

Principal Bryant had not blinked once during Abigail's recollection of events. She cleared her throat to compose herself. "Thank you for being thorough with your explanation," she responded as compassionately as she was able. Principal Bryant's eyes landed on her friends. "Are you three here to attest to her claim?"

"Yes, Ma'am," Keagan confidently answered along with Jade and Brielle nodding. "We aren't witnesses, but Abi - Abigail - told us about this last Friday evening. We see no reason for her to lie about this, especially since Landon has a history of harassing her in the past."

"I understand that," Principal Bryant sympathized, "But, I need to be absolutely sure. Do you have any proof of this occurring? If I were to ask Mister Woods about this, would I have a fair reason to refute his opposing viewpoint?"

Keagan smiled to the Principal's surprise. "We do, actually. Do you happen to have footage from the security camera pointed at locker number one thirty-three in Hallway B? It would have occurred about halfway through lunch on Wednesday."

"I'm sorry, girls, but every Sunday evening at eleven fifty-nine, the cameras are wiped clean to reset for the next week. The footage from the previous week is unavailable," Principal Bryant apologized sincerely.

Abigail's face fell along with the rest of her friends'. She knew this plot to get revenge on Landon was a huge mistake. Having it fall apart right before her very eyes was heartbreaking. She had no idea what to do at that point. Keagan gently squeezed her hand with sympathy, but Abigail ignored it due to the tears pricking behind her eyes. Jade's gentle hand was placed on her shoulder. Abigail was frozen solid.

However, Brielle did not join the pity party. Instead, she approached the large desk and the woman sitting across from them. "Principal Bryant?"

"Yes, Brielle?" The Principal instantly drew her gaze towards the auburn-haired girl.

"I happen to notice that Hillwell High uses security cameras from iSpy Surveillance Services." This caught everyone's attention. "I did some research on their products this weekend and if your cameras are connected to a computer as a base - which in this case, they have to be - then a copy of the week's footage is automatically saved. Would you be okay with me viewing the archive? It can be hard to find and I know how to do it."

Principal Bryant's glasses nearly fell off. "Um, I think that would be alright, but let me unlock the computer first."

The four of them watched as Principal Bryant typed on her computer that was on the desk. Principal Bryant stood up from her chair once the computer was settled and beckoned for Brielle to sit down, which she did. Abigail, Jade, Keagan, and the Principal watched as Brielle periodically clicked through several files. Her eyebrows furrowed after another click, then complete silence.

"What is it?" Keagan asked after at least a minute of quiet passed.

"Come here. I found it." Brielle's words caused everyone in the office - including the Principal - to crowd around her and the computer. "This is at eleven forty-two on Wednesday morning.

Abigail had to blink a couple of times at the screen. There she was, her long black hair, brown eyes, and maroon hoodie clear as day. Approaching her with dusty brown hair and a smirk was the very boy she despised. The camera's footage was nearly crystal clear. Brielle hesitated before clicking the play button.

The events, just like Abigail described them, played out for the Principal to see. When Landon approached Abigail with a kiss and a bit more, Abigail closed her eyes and covered them with her hands. When she peeked through her fingers, she noticed Keagan fuming, Jade stiff with anger, and Brielle's hands trembling. Brielle paused the video directly after the scene unfolded and all four of the teenagers looked at Principal Bryant.

The Principal swallowed thickly and beckoned for Brielle to stand, which she did. "Thank you for notifying me of this." Principal Bryant sat back down in her chair. "I will be calling Mister Woods down to my office as soon as I'm able to. For now, please be patient. I will be in contact with you, Abigail."

"Thank you," Abigail exhaled.

"You're welcome," Principal Bryant replied politely. "I hope you all have a good rest of your day. Keep me updated if something else happens."

"I will."

Abigail couldn't have gotten out of that office quickly enough. She led the pack of her friends. Brielle shut the door behind them. Once the Principal was out of earshot, Abigail let out a loud sigh of relief. Keagan, Brielle, and Jade practically tackled her in a group hug, which she gratefully returned. Abigail's entire body was trembling with anxiousness over what she had just done. What if it put her in jeopardy once again?

"You did it, Abi," Keagan congratulated her. "We're so proud of you!"

Abigail smiled a little bit. "Thank you, but it isn't over yet."

"You're right," Jade recalled gleefully. "We still have the "secret sauce" to make sure he's gone for good."

"What do we do now?" Brielle worriedly asked.

Keagan ruffled Brielle's hair. "You're the smarty-pants who saved our butts in there with the security footage," she teased. "You figure it out."

Brielle frowned at that.

"Kidding!" Keagan's red-highlighted hair bounced along with her. "But it's quite obvious now."

Abigail fiddled with a long piece of her ebony hair. "And what's so obvious?" she inquired with her eyes fixed on her shoes.

Keagan would have rested her elbow on Abigail's shoulder, but she was at least four inches too short to. Instead, she placed her index finger under her chin and lifted it up to meet her blazing gray eyes. Abigail wondered how one young lady could have so much confidence in one single stare. It was breathtaking.

"Now, Abi," Keagan drawled, "*we wait.*"

22

"AND ANOTHER ONE BITES THE DUST."

Abigail thought she was about to faint.

One foot struggled to pass the other as she darted aside to return a volleyball over the net in front of her. Back and forth, she sprinted to serve, pass, and spike the ball. It seemed like she was the only active player on her team consisting of all females.

Abigail knew she hated her PE class, but when she was the only person participating on her team, it was somehow worse. What made it even more awful was that the class was separated by boys and girls, and most of the girls happened to dislike physical activity as much as Abigail did. Unfortunately, that did not mean they could sit on the sidelines and let one girl do the work.

That one girl happened to be Abigail.

What made matters almost insufferable was the fact Noah was positioned across the net from her. If Abigail failed to feel awkward before, she was feeling the aftershock now. Abigail was dressed in her usual gym clothes, consisting of an old t-shirt and a pair of athletic shorts. Her long hair was tied back in a high ponytail. Everything was different except for her black high tops that squeaked against the floor of the gym with nearly every step.

Mrs. Watson, the PE teacher, blew her whistle to get her class' attention. "Okay, class. Another volley from the top."

Abigail noticed that the volleyball was in Noah's possession. She watched as he fumbled around with it before somehow popping it up in the air and over the net. Like she had expected the ball was hurtling towards her, but Abigail was ready. She knotted her fingers together, squatted slightly, and prepared to return the ball. Her hands seared with pain as the slightly weathered volleyball came in contact with them. The small creases and tears dug into her skin, but she succeeded in passing the ball back over the net.

She watched as Noah stumbled forward to retrieve the ball and succeeded. He passed the volleyball to another teammate who returned it over the net. Abigail was somehow unable to remove her eyes from him. Even though he probably looked very uncivilized to the other students when it came to the rules of volleyball, she found him amusing, or even endearing.

Abigail continued watching as Noah flung himself to his right to return the volleyball over the net to another of Abigail's teammates. She, unbeknownst to her, was standing numbly while the rest of her team took her place for once. The game continued on without her. Mrs. Watson did not seem to notice Abigail's lack of participation. In fact, no one did until...

Smack!

The black-haired girl's knee buckled when a hard, round object collided with the side of her head. Abigail tumbled to the ground and hit her shins on the hardwood gymnasium floor. She grimaced at the thought of unexplainable bruises - this time, from embarrassment - appearing on her body.

It was not something Abigail hadn't experienced before.

Abigail blinked her vision back into focus to discover that the majority of her PE class was gaping or giggling at her. Her cheeks flushed with humiliation from the scene she had just caused. She hardly noticed Noah's outstretched hand, which she hesitantly took once she reoriented herself with the room around her. Abigail straightened herself up and abruptly let go of his grasp, which was foreign to her, but a gentle kind.

"Are you okay?" Noah asked authentically. "That ball hit you pretty hard."

Abigail subconsciously rubbed the point of which the ball hit impact. "Uh, yeah," she stammered. "I'm okay."

Mrs. Watson didn't seem to notice what had happened. "Okay, class. That concludes today's session. See you all tomorrow," she exclaimed in her loud, nasally voice.

Abigail did not waste any time walking with wobbly steps over towards the bleachers of the gymnasium, where she had kept her water bottle. She popped it open and took a long sip. The water was heavenly against the parched walls of her throat. Abigail hastily gulped down half of the bottle before readjusting the lid on top.

She didn't bother with changing back into her regular clothes. It seemed as if Noah was the same, since he was also taking a sip of water from his own bottle and lazily looking at his phone. Abigail was certainly unsurprised when Noah approached her again. Neither of them said a word as the rest of the class began funneling out the door and into the hall. This was an occurrence that was rather common.

Come to think of it, Abigail was hardly left alone anymore ever since the Landon incident.

Abigail had not seen much of Landon for the past week. Ever since she and her friends reported him to Principal Bryant, she had noticed his presence start to diminish among the halls of the school. Even during lunch, he was not at his usual table. Abigail thought this was very strange, especially due to his loud presence in her life. It was odd not having him there--a good odd, but an unusual one, none-theless.

She walked behind the rest of the class along with Noah by her side. Abigail gripped her water bottle tightly as if she was about to drop it. She knew it was from anxiety, but how was she supposed to say that?

Instead of formulating a well-thought-out question, Abigail blurted, "Have you seen Landon anywhere for the past week?"

"I can't say I have," Noah replied with a shrug. "Why?"

"It's just that," Abigail sighed, "ever since we reported him to Principal Bryant, I haven't really seen him anywhere. It's scary, to be honest with you."

Noah offered her a sympathetic expression. "It'll be fine," he assured Abigail. "Who knows? What if he was suspended for what he did? Maybe even expelled?"

"I don't think that would be the case."

"Why not?" Noah inquired while the two walked down a quieter hallway. "Keagan was expelled directly after Landon reported her."

Abigail shook her head dismissively. "I don't think that's the case, because one: Landon issued a restraining order against her; and two: what she did to him was much worse than what he did to me."

Noah stopped in his tracks. "Are you kidding me?"

"...What?" Abigail halted beside him.

"Don't you dare invalidate yourself like that," he firmly told her.

Abigail's face fell. She had never seen Noah angry. "What do you mean?" she stuttered obliviously.

"Just now." Noah's brows furrowed. "Didn't you *just* say that what he did to you wasn't nearly as bad as what Keagan did to him?"

She slowly nodded.

Noah explained wildly, "That's not true. She punched him and stuff to defend you. He...he *manipulated* you! You were hesitant to do what he wanted because you thought it would be for Keagan's good. He used that to his advantage and h-he...he assaulted you for no reason. I'm not going to forget what you told me he did. If I had my way, he'd be six feet under our shoes."

"But...but..."

"But what, Abigail?" he questioned. "You can't deny that he's been horrible to you. He deserves all of this and more. Hell, he deserves to be in jail right now."

"Noah, *please*."

"Can you listen to me? Please?"

Abigail nodded again.

Noah gently set his hand on her shoulder. Abigail surprised herself by not needing to suppress the urge to flinch away from his touch. Instead, she looked him directly in the eyes with her lips in a tight line. Her brown eyes were not fearful, but so...vulnerable. Noah seemed to understand this. He kept his tone clear and precise.

"Promise me that you won't invalidate yourself like that," he spoke almost pleadingly. "You've been through a lot of shit lately and you don't deserve any of it. I can only imagine how this has affected you mentally and emotionally. I've been through some shit too, but right now, this is about you. Do you understand me?"

"I understand," Abigail replied shakily with her water bottle clutched tightly in her hands in front of her.

"Can you promise me?"

Abigail hesitated, but then: "I promise."

Neither Abigail, nor Noah noticed a pair of footsteps dashing towards them until a familiar petite young woman was standing in front of them. Slowly, both of their heads turned to face Keagan. The red highlights in her hair were vibrant along with her cropped black tee and ripped jeans. She had an awkward look on her face.

"Would this be a bad time to barge in and say Landon's been expelled?" she asked sheepishly.

Abigail nearly fell over. "Excuse me?"

"You haven't heard?" Keagan inquired in disbelief. "He was expelled this afternoon. Principal Bryant showed him the tapes this morning and he couldn't come up with an excuse, so she finally expelled him. He tried to get his lawyer involved, but the school didn't allow it."

Noah tapped Abigail on the shoulder. "See?" he asked with a sheepish grin.

"Oh, my God," Abigail stammered.

"I know!" Keagan barreled into Abigail with one of her bone-crushing hugs. "It's amazing, isn't it? He's finally gone after so long."

"Keagan. It's only the start of November."

"Yep! Best birthday present ever!"

Abigail and Noah smiled at the thought of Keagan's eighteenth birthday being the previous day. She had not done anything that seemed special. Keagan had remained in her room with Flynn on her lap binge watching one of her comfort shows. She hadn't even invited any of her friends over. Like she had said during lunch, she needed some "me time" and was not going to get it any other day. She said the best part was that she locked her mother out of her room.

"I'm just...so relieved," Abigail expressed breathily. "He's gone. It's over."

Keagan eyed her with a raised brow. "Not yet. We still have one more thing to take care of, but first, let's celebrate."

"Celebrate?"

"Yeah, of course! Why don't we hit the ice cream shop? I'll get Jade, Ryder, and Brielle so they can join us. I'm not sure where they went."

Abigail hesitated. "Oh, um...I don't know."

"I seriously doubt that he'll be working since school just got out," Keagan reasoned authentically. "If he is, we'll just leave and go somewhere else."

"I think that's a good idea," Noah added on. "But we can do whatever you want, Abigail."

Abigail was unsure, but nodded, nonetheless. "Okay. Let's go."

"I'll meet you two there," Keagan chirped before she dashed away, probably to find the three vacant members of their group.

Abigail lamely lifted a hand to wave to her friend, but she was already gone. Her cheeks pinkened at the amused look Noah gave her. The rosy glow did not disappear even when they both made a pit stop at their respective lockers to obtain their things. Abigail remained quiet as they roamed the halls and eventually exited the building.

Before either of them knew it, they were both seated in Abigail's car. Abigail had made a cautious effort to turn her music down before Noah entered. She learned from past experience that he had sensitive ears. Either that, or her music was simply deafening. The latter was the most likely, Abigail thought, as she began to pull out of her parking space and drive down the road. She hated how crowded the Hillwell High parking lot was at the end of the day.

"Are you sure you're okay with going to this ice cream place?" Noah asked Abigail whilst she was driving downtown.

Abigail kept her eyes on the road even though she knew Noah's were on her. "I'm okay with it. It's the only ice cream shop in town."

"I just didn't know he worked there. That's all," he elaborated.

"Yeah, unfortunately," replied Abigail with a sigh. "After I passed the placement test to get into AP Calculus, we decided to go there to celebrate, but he was working the counter."

"I'm sorry."

"It's okay." Abigail refused to meet his eyes even as she stopped at a red light.

Noah blinked in disbelief. "No, it's not."

"...It will be."

Other than the soft music ebbing from the Honda Civic's radio, the car fell into silence. Before Abigail or Noah knew it, they had pulled into the parking lot of the Ice Ice Baby ice cream parlor. Once again, Abigail rolled her eyes at the sign above the doorway. Noah looked at it with wide eyes.

"Did they seriously name the ice cream shop after a song with a borrowed bass riff?" Noah questioned incredulously.

Abigail nodded, shifting the car's gear to park. "Yep. The original's much better."

"I agree."

"You know," she continued with a growing grin, "after that riff was copied and had a single note added, the writer couldn't be considered *somebody to love.*"

"Oh, my God."

Abigail knew exactly what he was talking about but decided to play dumb. "What?"

"I had no idea that you're the *queen* of puns," Noah snickered.

"Were you *under pressure* to make that one up?" Abigail retorted playfully. "Because that was pretty bad."

"Hey! Yours was worse!" he fretted.

"I'm about to have a *sheer heart attack* from your complaining."

"Okay, *don't stop me now* because *I want to break free* from this car," teased Noah as he dashed out of the vehicle, shutting the door behind him.

Abigail rolled her eyes and followed him. "And *another one bites the dust.*"

"Stop it!"

"It's not my fault you got all of my references. You have taste."

"Yeah, but-"

"You two look like you're having fun," a familiar voice sounded from a couple of yards away.

Abigail and Noah turned at the same time to view Keagan with Brielle, Ryder, and Jade next to her. She gave them a friendly smile and a wave, which they returned. Abigail couldn't help but notice that Jade's face fell a little bit once she met her eyes. She was worried about her friend. It seemed like whatever was going on was serious.

"She was bombarding me with Queen puns," Noah joked and pointed an accusing finger in Abigail's direction.

Abigail smacked his finger away. "You started the whole conversation."

"Let me guess," Ryder butted in, "it started with the "Ice Ice Baby" sign. Right?"

"Yep," Abigail and Noah chorused.

"Because the main riff was stolen. Right?"

"Borrowed," Brielle corrected.

Ryder rolled his eyes. "Right."

"Come on, guys!" Keagan encouraged the five people in front of her. "Let's go get some ice cream—my treat!"

"Oh, um, I can pay for mine," Brielle quickly offered.

"Don't be silly," the petite girl assured her. "Now, come on! My triple scoop mint chocolate chip in a waffle cone bowl with chocolate syrup and a cherry on top won't be waiting all day."

"Really, Keagan? Why so specific?" Noah asked her.

Keagan elbowed past him. "It's the best kind. Get your priorities straight."

"...Alright, then."

The group of six walked towards the stupidly named ice cream parlor without much of another word from anyone other than Keagan, who was furiously debating that a triple scoop mint chocolate chip in a waffle cone with chocolate syrup and a cherry on top was the best flavor of ice cream in the world. Brielle opened the glass door and held it open for everyone, even after Ryder insisted he would hold it for his younger sister.

Abigail remained towards the back of the group. Noah walked next to her. She once again noticed Jade's neutral expression. It was not like her to be so upset when something so wonderful happened. Abigail felt as if there was something really wrong.

Now, she had two problems left: how would she figure out what's going on with Jade and execute the "secret sauce" - Keagan's idea - to get rid of Landon for good?

23

"WE WERE WORRIED ABOUT YOU."

ABIGAIL WAS STANDING IN FRONT OF A BUILDING SHE KNEW ALMOST TOO well. It was not any ordinary building despite looking like one of such. With one story, cream shingles, a maroon roof, and a mat on the front porch saying "Welcome!" that seemed too energetic, it was a picture-perfect home in the middle of a neighborhood that could have been used in a movie shoot.

Birds chirped in the distance. Abigail noticed a small nest of blue robin eggs perched on a low branch in one of the trees in the freshly cut lawn. The sun shone high overhead, giving the entire property a living glow. Simply standing in the premises made Abigail feel slightly more alive.

She knew this place all too well. Abigail was there when the youthful resident of house number twelve on Riverwalk Road. In fact, it was in the neighborhood beside her own. Abigail had many fond memories in this place. She would arrive at this very doorstep several years ago with stuffed animals, dolls, or any other toys that she was ecstatic to share with her playmate on the other side. Abigail laughed with her, cried with her, and the two of them walked through life by each other's sides.

Now, she seemed further away than ever. When a text was sent to

Abigail during her AP Government class that afternoon requesting her arrival, she couldn't turn it down. Now, she was finally able to uncover what exactly was bothering one of her oldest friends. For the past couple of months, she had seemed quite off.

The anticipation was killing her, so Abigail decided not to wait any longer. She walked up the three porch steps, which Abigail had done hundreds of times before. Her outstretched finger hovered over the doorbell. Why was she so nervous to ring it? It was not a new occurrence to her. The blonde on the other side was one of her oldest and best friends.

"Come on, Abigail. Stop being stupid," she reprimanded herself.

Abigail swallowed down a lump of anxiety and rang the doorbell before she was able to stop herself. About ten seconds later, the door opened to reveal a man Abigail had seen countless times over the years. He had fair brown skin with dark hair and a mustache that was neatly trimmed. He looked nothing like his daughter, who was pale with light blonde hair and stunning cyan eyes as opposed to his brown pair.

Abigail had heard the story many times. Her friend never knew her biological parents. In fact, she grew up in an orphanage for the first three years of her life. A man who had recently been divorced over an affair his wife conducted decided that the only way to fill his broken heart would be to give a young child a home. So, he did, and that was the man standing right in front of Abigail. He had been a much better father than most. His choice not to remarry did not deflect that quality one single bit.

"Oh, hello, Abigail!" The man greeted her kindly. "Jade's up in her room since that's who I imagine you're here to see."

Abigail smiled at him. "Yeah, she invited me over. Thanks, Mr. Summers."

"You know how many times you've been over here," he replied, opening the door the rest of the way and standing to the side. "You can call me "John." Mr. Summers is too formal for someone I can consider a second daughter."

"Oh, okay...John...," Abigail fumbled with a laugh. "Thank you."

"You're very welcome. Let me know if you need anything."

Abigail looked at him as she walked past him and towards the stairs. "I will. Thank you!"

Her black hair swished behind her as she dashed up the stairs that could have had footprints fitting her shoes from how many times she had run up them. Abigail stuffed her clammy hands into her pockets while she walked the familiar route towards Jade's room. Even when Jade was at her lowest, Abigail never felt this nervous. She felt so far away when her oldest friend was on the other side of the door she now looked at.

Abigail took a deep breath, folded her right hand into a fist, and knocked on the door three times. When there was no answer at first, she exclaimed, "Hey, Jade! It's Abigail."

Sure enough, Abigail heard footsteps and the door opened to reveal Jade. Her light blonde hair was oddly matted near the scalp and her beautiful cyan eyes were bloodshot. She had changed from her school attire she wore to Hillwell High into an oversized shirt and pajama pants. Abigail took in her appearance with wide eyes. What looked to be a perfectly poised teenage girl earlier that day was now crumbling at Abigail's feet.

"Hey, Abigail." Jade smiled, but it looked like she was a marionette with the corners of her lips being forced up with strings. "Come on in."

Abigail stepped into the room that hadn't changed since they were kids. The walls were painted an off-white. A full-sized bed rested in the corner of the room with a baby blue comforter and white and gray pillows on top. The occasional stuffed animal laid on the mattress. There was a white desk opposite of the bed along with a dresser and a bookshelf on the adjacent wall. A closet was on the remaining wall. Abigail chose to sit on the bed. Jade followed behind.

"Is everything okay, Jade?" she asked cautiously.

Jade shrugged incredulously. "I guess we'll find out."

"...What do you mean?"

"Aren't you wondering why I asked you to talk?" inquired Jade shakily. "I'm sorry for texting in the middle of class. I figured before we did the "secret sauce" thing - God, I hate that name - I could talk to you."

"I'm curious, but I'm worried about you," Abigail confessed. "You come first, even before the "secret sauce." Also, I agree," she joked to lighten the mood. "I hate that name too, but you know Keagan."

Jade smiled, rendering Abigail's attempt to do so successful. "Yeah, I agree." Her face fell. "I guess I need to explain why I've been weird lately."

"Only if you want to."

"You deserve an answer."

Abigail hesitated but nodded. "If you insist."

Jade was uncertain as well, however, she had invited Abigail into her home for a reason, and she was not about to waste her time. "I don't know how to say this," she stumbled.

"It's okay," Abigail assured her gently. "Take your time."

"I've taken enough time if you consider two months to be plenty."

Abigail blinked at least twice. "...What?"

"Okay, I'm going to cut to the chase," Jade insisted firmly.

"What are you talking abo-"

"I'm *jealous!*"

Abigail froze. What could she possibly have that Jade was jealous of? Abigail had nothing of the sort that Jade would envy her for. At first, she thought she was bluffing, but when she saw the vulnerable and guilty look in her eyes, Abigail knew it was the truth. There was no way that Jade would be able to weave around the strong wall of trust they had built around their friendship. She thought harder until an idea hit her.

"Wait...are you jealous of-" Abigail started, but she was interrupted.

"No, I'm not jealous of you." Jade shook her head. What she said next nearly startled Abigail off the bed. "I'm jealous of *Noah*."

Abigail's mouth opened and closed like a goldfish. "You're *what*?"

"Jealous of Noah," she choked out without meeting her eyes.

"Why would you be jealous of N-"

"Listen. Can you hear me out?"

Abigail nodded cautiously. She watched as Jade clasped her fingers together in her lap. Her eyes dully stared down at her connected hands. Abigail stared unblinkingly in Jade's direction. She had no idea what to think until she eventually spoke up.

"Over the summer, I've been having a hard time with myself...mentally," Jade started with uncertainty.

Abigail scooted closer to her supportively.

Jade smiled a little bit. "Since you were struggling so much with what happened with Landon, I didn't say anything. I was questioning myself for months. In September, I finally figured out the answer."

"Can I ask what that is?" Abigail asked timidly.

"I'm getting to it. The main thing is that I've been questioning my sexuality," Jade mumbled almost incoherently. "I needed to find an explanation for how I felt, and I don't want to label myself, but I'm pretty sure you know where this is going."

Abigail stood stock still. "Jade, if you think I won't support you in this, then you clearly don't know me," she expressed.

"I know, but I told you that I'm jealous of *Noah*. Have you fit the pieces together yet?"

The thought was fresh in Abigail's mind, but she was not so quick to release it to the girl sitting next to her. Abigail knew that once she heard it from Jade's lips, she would be sure, but she kept her mouth closed. Jade was waiting for a proper answer, which Abigail half-heartedly supplied with a shrug and an "I don't know."

Jade sighed and took a deep breath. "Abigail, I like you," she admitted before she could stop herself. "I figured it out over the summer-" Jade held up a hand to silence Abigail, "-and I'm certain that this is what I'm feeling. I'm sure you've noticed that I've been acting a bit like a jerk, especially around Noah."

Abigail nodded, having nothing to say.

"That's why. He likes you - hell, probably even loves you - so much and it's been going over your head this whole time," Jade ranted breathily. "I know the most we can be is friends, but I need to be honest with you. I've been hiding it for too long."

"But I-..."

"Trust me. I know you're fond of him too," she noted. "I just thought you needed to know, and another thing..."

Abigail watched blankly as Jade leaned over and opened the drawer on her nightstand. She was unsure what exactly Jade was doing until she saw the object in her hands after the drawer was closed. Her eyes widened at Jade and she opened her mouth to speak, but Jade beat her to it.

"Do you remember when Noah lost his glasses?" Jade waited until Abigail nodded. "He tripped, and I was the person who caused it. I took his glasses because I saw him as some weird form of competition for me after you did the dare. I thought that if something important was taken from him while you were present, he'd blame you in some way. I dared you because I thought it would backfire and everyone would stop talking to him. I didn't think it would get this far, and for that, I'm really sorry."

Abigail looked at her silently before she was able to choke out, "I-...Jade...I really don't know what to say. Out of all things, I wasn't expecting this."

"I'd understand if you don't want to be friends anymo-"

"That's not what I'm saying at all, Jade!" It was Abigail's turn to interrupt. "You've been nothing but honest with me today and that takes a lot of guts. Sure, stealing his glasses was not the best thing to do, but I know you were going through a hard time, and... I forgive you."

Jade's eyebrows shot up. "Are you serious?"

"I'm serious," Abigail confirmed authentically. "I'm not mad, but when I give these-" She gestures towards the glasses in Jade's hands, "-back to him, I want to tell him what happened. I promise I'm not going to out you. I'm just going to say that someone I know took them and then gave them back. Is that alright with you?"

"Yeah, that's okay with me." Jade smiled and handed Noah's glasses to her friend. "Thanks, Abigail."

Abigail tenderly retrieved the eye accessory, returning the favor. "You're welcome, Jade."

Her black hair fell in front of her eyes, which caused her to pull it back. Abigail looked at the pair of glasses delicately clutched in her hands. She didn't think they were obnoxious anymore, especially after she had gotten to know the boy behind them. Abigail internally swore at her prior mindset, which had grown and developed so much in the past two months. Her mind was spinning around itself at the thought of how one simple thing could be broken down into a complex storyline.

The sound of Jade clearing her throat spurred Abigail to look up. "Um, do you think you're ready for the...thing?"

"What thing?" asked Abigail innocently.

"The "secret sauce.""

Both of them cringed at the name. Abigail laughed quietly, "Oh, uh, yeah."

"I hate that name too," Jade repeated playfully. "But seriously, are your parents meeting us up there in a bit?"

"Yeah, they are. They said they'd be there around five."

Jade checked the time on her phone. "Well, it's getting close to five, so how about we head out now?"

"That sounds like a good idea," agreed Abigail.

Jade stood from the bed and Abigail followed close behind. Abigail kept Noah's glasses delicately enclosed in her right hand as the blonde in front of her dashed down the stairs with her hot on her tail. The sound of their footsteps prompted Jade's father to look up from the newspaper he was reading at the kitchen table. Mr. Summers - or John, as Abigail often neglected to call him - was an old-fashioned man to say the least.

"Are you two leaving already?" he asked with raised eyebrows over the title: *Hillwell Tribune.*

Jade nodded. "Yeah. We thought it'd be better to get it over with.

"Just be careful. Okay?"

"Okay," both girls chorused, Abigail's voice being much quieter and fearful.

John waved to Jade and Abigail with a sympathetic smile on his face. The two teenagers waved back as Jade grabbed her car keys and opened the front door. Abigail followed behind her and gave John one last wave before shutting the door behind her. She walked towards Jade's vehicle and the two entered it. Jade turned on the engine and pulled out of the driveway.

Abigail said nothing and resorted to watching the town of Hillwell pass by. Jade kept her eyes on the road while she drove. The radio, set to a random alternative pop station, was on a low volume as the girls rode along in near silence. Despite Abigail's phone blowing up with "good luck" texts from her friends, including Keagan, Brielle, Noah, and even Ryder, she did not feel motivated enough to go through with her plan.

Before long, Jade parked her car in the parking lot in front of a large building. It looked to have at least two floors. To say the least, the dark brick structure along with several vehicles with black and white exteriors and blue lights on the top was intimidating. Abigail and Jade walked down the sidewalk leading up to the large double doors with a bold lettered sign stating: "Hillwell Police Department."

Jade looked at Abigail, stopping in front of the entrance. "Are you ready?"

"I think so," Abigail exhaled with a trembling tone.

Abigail pushed open one of the doors with a grunt. The two girls walked inside of the police station, which looked much homier on the inside than it did on the outside with gray carpeting, black chairs, and matching glass coffee tables. In one seating area sat Lillian and Harold Bartley, who were waiting anxiously for their daughter. Abigail caught their eyes immediately as she dashed over to them.

"Mom, Dad," she panted. "You're here early."

"We were worried about you," Abigail's mother sadly replied.

Abigail sighed. "I'm okay."

"Does that mean you're ready for...," Harold trailed off., "...you know?"

The teenage girl fiddled around with her black hair between her fingers. She hesitantly nodded and looked at her father. "I'm ready."

With that, Abigail, aided with her parents and Jade, who was like a sister, walked towards the front desk together. A woman in her forties sat behind it with curly red hair. To Abigail's distaste, she was chewing pink bubble gum, and loudly too. The woman adjusted her thick glasses and looked up from her computer when she heard the group of four approach.

"May I help you?" she asked in a bored tone.

Three pairs of eyes latched onto Abigail, who averted eye contact. With a deep breath, she forced her brown gaze to meet the secretary's from behind the desk. Abigail's hands shook, but she stored them tightly in her pockets. Slowly, her lips parted to create a sentence.

"Hello. Where can I file a restraining order against a minor?"

24

"I GUESS THAT'S WHAT HAPPENS WHEN YOU HAVE TRAUMA."

"It's very nice to meet you, Noah! I'm glad we could get to know you after all the chaos has ensued. Thankfully, we won't be seeing You-Know-Who ever again."

"Voldemort?" Abigail asked herself with a grin.

Her brown eyes darted over to view the nervous boy sitting next to her. Noah's right leg was bouncing up and down under the table. His eyes were focused toward his lap, but once the chirpy female voice across from him came into earshot, he looked up. Across from him was Lillian Bartley with a friendly smile on her face. Noah fought to return it, and his attempt was successful...for the most part.

"It's a pleasure to meet you too, Mr. and Mrs. Bartley. Me too. I'm really glad Landon and his family have decided to move from Hill-well," Noah replied in a stiffer tone than he meant to. *"Come on, Noah! The least you can do is not look like a moron, especially after you were at Abigail's house without their permission."*

Next to Lillian and across from Abigail was Harold, who looked like he wanted to be anywhere but here. His stoic expression was a drastic change from his goofy personality. Lillian obviously kicked him from under the table since he flinched and muttered an "Ow." Abigail smiled a little bit, but Noah's heart was pounding.

Harold smiled the grin that Abigail was used to. "So, how did you two meet?" he asked to make conversation.

Abigail and Noah looked at each other before the former decided to answer, "It's a long story, but basically, Jade dared me to take his glasses off his face. I have no idea why."

"Oh, really?" Lillian questioned, starstruck. "That's a bit peculiar."

"We were playing truth or dare at lunch on the first day of school and it just came up," Abigail explained awkwardly.

Noah politely and hastily butted in, "We're also in the same British Literature class as well as PE. We've been working on a Literature project for the past six weeks."

"The *Lord of the Rings* one?" inquired Lillian.

Prior to Noah's opportunity to respond, a brunette waitress adorning a red apron with the words *Express-O Café* on it approached. She had a pearly smile and a name tag that said "Meg" in cursive lettering. "Are you four ready to order?"

"I think so...," Abigail's mother trailed off until her husband, daughter, and Noah all nodded. "Yes, I believe we're ready."

"Okay. What would you like?" Meg flipped open a small notebook and grabbed a pencil that was resting behind her ear.

"I'd like a grilled chicken sandwich with no tomatoes, please," Lillian requested.

"Are fries okay for the side?"

"That's fine."

Harold shrugged when Meg looked at him. "I'd like the same thing she's getting."

"Are fries okay?" Meg scribbled the next order down on her notebook.

"Yes, that's great."

Meg finished writing down the parents' orders and then looked at Abigail, who said, "I'd like the chicken tenders, please."

"Would you like any dipping sauce?"

"Um..." Abigail thought it over. "No, thank you."

Noah always noticed that when she was thinking hard, her lips pressed together in a tight line and her irises drifted towards the ceiling. He found it quite endearing and he did not even realize he had been watching her contemplate her order until the waitress - Meg - cleared her throat and asked him what he would like. His gaze flew over to her.

"Uh, I'd like the grilled cheese, please."

"Are fries okay with that?"

Noah nodded a bit awkwardly. "Yeah, that's fine. Thank you."

"Your food should be ready shortly," Meg stated before briskly walking away.

Noah turned to Lillian, resuming their previous topic. "Yeah, we've been working on the *Lord of the Rings* project. It isn't due until January, though."

"Oh, I see," answered Lillian, intrigued. "How is that going?"

"Well, we aren't exactly working on it *together*," Abigail countered, giggling way too much than she was used to from anxiety. "Although, we did study AP Calculus together for a while."

"You're in AP Calculus?" Harold spluttered. "But I thought-"

Noah's head snapped to meet Abigail's panicked gaze. "You didn't tell them?" he asked in a hushed voice.

"...It didn't cross my mind," Abigail whispered back. She had realized what she did.

"What's going on, Dear?" Lillian was eyeing her daughter along with her husband.

Abigail hesitated. *"Come on, Abigail. You can't get yourself into a bigger hole by telling the truth instead of lying,"* she reassured herself. "Landon was in my Precalculus class, and there were no other classes available, so I asked to be moved up to AP Calculus to avoid him. Jade, Keagan, and Brielle tried to help me, but they couldn't, so I asked Noah, who's in that class, to help me. I took a placement test at the end of September and got into AP Calculus."

"So, that's why you randomly had an AP Calculus textbook." Harold had an eureka moment. Lillian kicked him under the table again; his expression was concerned. "Why didn't you tell us any of this, Abigail? We could've helped you."

"I...I was scared," Abigail fumbled. "I knew you two were really busy with work and I just wanted to handle it myself, so I did. Everything worked out and now I have better credits for college."

Her parents frowned. "You know you can tell us anything," Lillian spoke softly.

"I know, and that's why I'm being honest with you now. Do you remember those nights I pretended I was going out with friends?" Her parents nodded. "I was studying with Noah to pass the placement test."

Noah could not keep quiet anymore. "Mr. and Mrs. Bartley, I didn't know that this was kept from you. If I had known, I-"

"It's alright," Lillian replied despite Harold's protesting expression. "Thank you for being honest with us. Most of all, thank you for helping protect our daughter."

Noah's complexion was reddened with embarrassment. Abigail fought back a wide smile at her mother's words. What she said was true. Noah had protected her from who was after her both physically and mentally. He held her as she cried. He listened as she spoke. He spent much of his free time helping her avoid the young she feared most.

The teenage boy smiled and adjusted his glasses. "You're very welcome," he earnestly expressed. "Over the past couple months, Abigail's become a wonderful friend to me."

Noah neglected to mention how oddly painful the word "friend" was once it left his lips.

"I'm very glad to hear that."

Harold took a sip of his water with a lemon slice in it. He decided to change the subject. "So, Noah—what do your parents do?"

"Oh, my mom works as a psychologist at the Journey for Joy: Counseling and Wellness Center," Noah responded nonchalantly.

Abigail's eyebrows raised at that. "That's where I go for therapy twice a week," she commented.

Noah looked at her with a confused expression. "Oh, really?"

"Yeah," she replied, surprisingly not as anxious to mention the topic as she thought. "After you-know-what happened, I started going on Tuesdays and Fridays. It didn't help at first, but now it does. I have a very nice therapist."

The boy next to her grinned softly at that and looked as if he was about to say something, but he was cut off by Harold's slight interrogation, "So, what does your dad do?"

Noah completely froze. The cup in his hand nearly fell to the floor as his hand started to tremble. Abigail noticed this abrupt change in Noah's demeanor with worrying eyes. Noah blinked several times to better his composure. Abigail's eyes darted down to his shivering hands under the table and without thinking twice, she slipped her own into his grasp. The boy stiffened at the gesture but welcomed it. His fingers closed around her warm, comforting hand.

Noah took a deep inhale through his nose and allowed himself to embrace the moment he was in by informing the family, "My dad passed away in July. Cardiac arrest."

"Oh, my God," Harold stumbled over himself. "I'm so sorry. I didn't mean to bring up a painful topic for you."

"I'm very sorry for your loss," Lillian sympathized solemnly.

"Yeah, I'm sorry too." Noah shook his head. "It's okay. You didn't know."

Abigail didn't need to say anything. Instead, she gave his hand a gentle squeeze, to which he returned. Noah conjured up a small, but authentic smile, to which Abigail did the same. The two remained as such for no more than three seconds before Meg returned with all their orders balanced on a single black tray. As she passed them out, each member of the table expressed their gratitude. Abigail kept her hand in Noah's for a little while longer until she needed it to consume her meal.

Once the family began to eat, Abigail's mother decided silence was not the best option. "So, do you have any siblings, Noah?" Lillian asked to lighten the mood.

"I do." Noah perked up a little bit. "Their names are Lacy and Lucy. They're twins who just started the fifth grade."

"You have siblings?" Abigail asked, dumbfounded.

"Yeah," Noah shrugged. "They're a couple of handfuls, though."

"Could I maybe meet them sometime?"

A smile returned to the boy's face. "Yeah, of course. Would you like to meet them later?"

"I'd love to." Abigail was immediately ecstatic.

Other than more casual conversation, the group of four ate their lunch in silence. Abigail fought the urge to say something awkward as she devoured her chicken tenders and fries like she usually did in the Hillwell High School cafeteria. Instead, she focused on the sacred object she held comfortably in her pocket. Noah did not say much other than "Yes," "No," or other miscellaneous answers to the generic questions from Lillian and Harold. Frankly, Noah felt like he was being interviewed for an exclusive article in the *Hillwell Tribune*.

As Abigail continued to eat her lunch, a text popped up on her phone, which was resting with the screen facing upward on the table. She instantaneously knew it was from a group chat that she, Keagan, Jade, and Brielle shared. Abigail put down the rest of the very last chicken tender she was holding and picked up the phone to properly read it.

The first notification was from Keagan, and it read: *"How's your little date going?"*

"She said it wasn't a date," Brielle countered next.

"But Noah's meeting her parents!"

"We're probably bothering her," Jade reasoned fourthly.

Keagan sent a plethora of devil-faced smirking emojis along with: *"That's the plan!"*

Abigail smiled amusedly. She resisted the urge to show the screen to Noah, who was having a bit of trouble talking with Mr. and Mrs. Bartley. Instead, she typed out a message to her three friends.

"Brielle's right, and it's going well. I'll tell you three about it when I get home."

She put her phone away and redirected her eyes to those sitting at the table. To her surprise, her father had already asked for the check despite Noah's protests to pay for his and even Abigail's meal. Harold simply smiled and muttered "Nice boy" to his wife, who smiled with a pointed look at him.

Lillian stood from her chair once Meg returned with their receipt and all of the plates were cleared from the table. She prodded her husband to follow behind her, which he eventually did once he noticed the expression on her face.

"Abigail, your father and I are going to head home if you're okay with that," Lillian stated in her usual sweet tone.

"We are?" Harold blurted.

Lillian gave him another look as Abigail blinked at them. "Oh, that's fine," she responded with a nod. "I'll drive Noah home soon."

"Text if you need anything," her father reminded her.

"I will. Promise."

"We'll see you later." Lillian gave the both of them a delicate wave at the same time she was practically dragging her husband out of the restaurant.

"Once again, it was very nice to meet you," Noah called after them.

Lillian smiled over her shoulder. "You too, Noah!" she exclaimed.

With that, Abigail and Noah were left in silence at the table that was formerly bubbling with chatter, mostly from the "grown-up" side of the table. Neither of them had anything to say for quite a while, even when they eventually walked out of the bustling restaurant - it was quite busy, even for a Saturday around lunchtime - and stood outside. Abigail stood facing the parking lot with her keys in hand while Noah was next to her. None of them spoke a word until Abigail uttered an inquiry.

"Should we go?"

Noah looked at her as if he was thinking the same thing. "Maybe."

Abigail pressed a small button on her keys and her gray Honda Civic unlocked with a click and a flash of the headlights. She got into the driver's seat and Noah did the same with the passenger's seat. The two of them brought their doors to a close in near-perfect harmony. Abigail turned on her vehicle and pulled the seat belt over her lap, which Noah had done seconds before. Her already-programmed music ebbed softly through the speakers as Abigail drove out of the parking lot down the familiar route towards their neighborhood.

Noah kept quiet, but he could not do so for long. He twiddled his thumbs in his lap and kept his gaze towards the passing colors of the flourishing world around them. It was like the earth itself was mocking him by being so beautiful when his soul was so crushed. The guilt weighed upon him like a thousand tons. The agony was a thousand cuts among his skin.

Eventually, he spilled himself out all over Abigail's healing conscience. "I'm sorry that I didn't tell you about my dad. In truth, my family is still mourning."

"Why would you apologize for that?" Abigail asked incredulously. "I knew something was going on from the moment I got to know you, but it was none of my business."

"You told me about what happened to you. Now it's my turn."

Abigail muted the music that was playing as background noise. "Do you really want to? It's your choice, you know, just like it was mine."

"I think I'm ready, unless you want to wait," Noah considered nervously.

"No, I'm okay with whatever you choose."

Noah hesitated but spoke anyway as his eyes were locked on the outside world. "We used to live across the country near the beach. We were a happy family with my dad around. He was the best father that my sisters and I could ever ask for, along with being the best husband my mother could ever have--her words, not mine. There was one problem, though: he was a heavy smoker."

"Hey, Dad!" A small Lacy bellowed. "Can you put the cigarette away and play Minecraft with us? I hate the smell, but I need help beating the boss."

"Give me a minute, Honey."

Lacy gave him five and a half minutes, and then, finally, the flame was extinguished.

- "No matter what we did, we couldn't get him to stop. It bothered my mom as well as my sisters and I, because we were very worried about him smoking at least a pack a day. It was how he coped with stress. Even though he knew it was harmful to him, he never stopped." -

"Dad, you know those things can hurt you, right?" A nine-year-old Lucy asked as she worked on her homework.

The middle-aged man sitting at the kitchen table blew out a puff of smoke and adjusted his glasses with particularly thick frames. "I know, Sweetie, but it's harder than that."

- "We all begged for him to go to the doctor once he started experiencing chest pains and discomfort, along with several other things. He later got a diagnosis of coronary heart disease and began taking medicine for it. Nevertheless, he continued fueling his addiction." -

"Please, stop doing this," Jenny pleaded with her husband. "You're killing yourself slowly."

"I'm taking the medicine. I'll be fine."

"That doesn't matter!"

- "My mom told him that he would eventually succumb to the flame of his strong will, and inevitably, he did. I found him on the floor of the kitchen." -

"Dad? Dad! Wake up!"

The body on the tiled floor was motionless, cold, utterly lifeless. The glasses formerly on his face were crumpled on the ground, cracked, and dead.

"Please!" Tears cascaded down the teenage boy's face. He ran his fingers through his matted brown hair. "I'm still here! We're still here! Don't leave us!"

"I tried everything to keep him here with us. I attempted forcing his medicine into his mouth, chest compressions and CPR once I couldn't find a pulse, and I called nine-one-one the very first chance I got," Noah confessed shakily. "He died right in front of me and there was nothing I could do about it."

Thankfully, Abigail's car was parked in Noah's driveway since she was watching him with tearful eyes. "Oh, my God, Noah. I'm so sorry."

"We had a funeral for him and then two weeks later, my mom decided that she couldn't live there anymore. We all packed up our things and left. We wanted to live somewhere we could completely start over, where no memories of the past could reach us, but the fragments are still there. I feel guilty about it, even though it's not my fault. I feel like I could've done something else to resuscitate him, but that's not how it happened."

Abigail slid her hand into Noah's sweaty, clammy one again. "It really wasn't your fault," she sniffled empathetically. "Nobody deserves to go through something like that."

"I know," Noah replied, gripping Abigail's hand. "We're slowly recovering from this, but I'm just trying my best to help my mom and sisters. I've been having nightmares about this nearly every night. Those glasses that I lost were his, and I was very attached to them. I guess that's what happens when you have trauma."

"I guess so." Abigail half-heartedly smiled when Noah did. "But...I have to ask: have you tried speaking to a professional? I didn't think it would help me at first, but it does now."

Noah shrugged. "I did, and it didn't work for me, but I think trying it again would be a good idea."

"We can get through our struggles together," proposed Abigail. "How does that sound?"

"You know...," Noah briefly considered. "I'd like that."

"Me too."

Abigail turned the key sideways in the ignition and pulled it out. The car switched off and both of them exited it. Abigail locked the car behind them and watched as Noah was slowly walking towards his porch. He figured Abigail had followed him down the smooth concrete sidewalk, but he was mistaken when she stayed behind.

"Noah, wait."

Noah instantaneously stopped and turned around to view Abigail fumbling around for something in her pocket. "I wanted to give this to you, but I couldn't figure out a good enough time for it," she explained.

"What are you-" Noah began, but when he noticed the pair of thickly rimmed black glasses in Abigail's hand, he began to stutter. "O-Oh, my God—where did you find those?"

Abigail looked at the seemingly useless glasses, then to the boy who appeared to be nearly in tears. "A friend of mine told me they took them, but they gave them back recently. I promised them that I wouldn't disclose their identity, but they will give you their apologies from me."

"You have no idea how much it means to have them back," Noah blubbered. Abigail wasted no time handing the glasses to him.

"Honestly, I think I do."

Noah blinked back the unfamiliar salty droplets ready to fall onto his flushed cheeks. "This might sound stupid, but it feels like I have a part of him back," he confessed.

"I'm really glad," Abigail sincerely expressed.

Instead of putting his glasses on at once, he flung his arms around an unexpecting Abigail, who flinched a little bit at first. She offered him a delayed response and gingerly wrapped her arms around the boy who was doing his best to keep himself together. Abigail noticed this with a frown. She tapped him on the shoulder and mumbled in his ear.

"It's okay to cry, you know. I'm here."

"I know," muttered Noah, who eventually broke apart to put his glasses on his face, "but, my sisters are waiting. They want to play *Minecraft* or something. I'll cry later."

Abigail gently smiled up at him. "Okay, but if you want someone to cry to, my ringer's on."

"I'll keep that in mind," Noah assured her while returning the gesture. "Would you like to meet my sisters? I bet they'd love to know that I actually have a friend other than Ryder."

"Sure," giggled the girl across from him.

Without any warning, the front door flung open directly before Noah was able to curl his fingers around the knob. On the other side stood two girls, one being slightly taller than the other. Abigail noted that to be the only visible difference since the two were dressed alike, had the same blonde curls, and brown eyes. Abigail thought she was seeing double.

"Noah! You've been outside for five minutes!" Lacy wailed. "You promised you'd play *Minecraft* with us—wait...who's this?"

Two pairs of brown eyes stared at Abigail. Noah laughed, "This is Abigail. She's a really good friend of mine."

"Ooh, *'friend,'* huh?" Lacy's eyebrows waggled until Lucy elbowed her in the stomach. "Hey!"

"Lacy, be nice," hissed Lucy between a gritted jaw. She then smiled widely. "Hi, Abigail! I'm Lucy, and this is my sister, Lacy."

Abigail waved a bit shyly. "Hi."

"By the way, your hair's really pretty—and so are your nails! Did you paint them?" Lacy chirped happily.

Abigail blushed and looked down at her fingernails. They were slightly longer than they had been the entire semester and painted a robin egg blue--courtesy of Keagan. "My friend painted them, yeah. Thank you, Lucy," she gushed.

"Would you like to play *Minecraft* with us?" Lucy offered. "We're about to start a new survival game to try to beat the Ender Dragon!"

"Her parents might want her home-" Noah started, but he was interrupted by Abigail.

"I'd love to."

Noah did a double take. "Really?" he asked at the same time as the twins.

Abigail nodded enthusiastically. "Yeah. I'll text my parents and let them know I won't be home until later."

Noah nearly didn't believe her until she pulled her phone out of her pocket and sent a quick message to both of her parents. She put her phone back in her pocket and smiled authentically at the three siblings. Rather than being afraid, she was excited. It was a very nice change.

"Okay, I'm ready," she exclaimed to the twins' delight. "Show me where we can beat the Ender Dragon."

"Yay!" Lacy and Lucy chorused and dashed inside.

Noah stayed back while Abigail paused. She set her right foot onto the floor of the foyer seconds before her left. She looked at Noah and a grin automatically spread across her face. Rather than appearing dull, her eyes were bright and had several twinkles among their chestnut irises. Instead of a sense of dread drowning her once Noah shut the front door, her heart pounded with joy at the sight of the two ecstatic twins leading her to the living room.

"I'm ready for something new," Abigail decreed to herself, *"and I'm not afraid anymore."*

The young girl had been through a lot during the past six months. Her life took her to hell and back on the journey to find her inner bravery and uttermost joy. Because she decided to take that first step on the path to recovery, she was a new person.

Little did she know, once she walked through the doorway to her next chapter, she gave Noah the key, and she was more than okay with that.

EPILOGUE
JANUARY

"How do you think you did on that paper?" Keagan asked once she caught sight of Abigail.

Abigail swept a loose piece of her black hair behind her ear. Her ponytail was slowly falling from its perch on the top of her head. "I hope I did okay. I've been worrying about it ever since I turned it in this morning."

"I bet you did fine," Keagan assured Abigail.

"What's going on?"

Abigail and Keagan whirled around to see Jade, Brielle, and Ryder approaching in a line with Jade heading it. Both of them waved at the trio, who returned the favor with friendliness and genuine grins.

"We were just talking about the paper due today," Keagan explained.

Ryder appeared as if his eyes were about to fall out of the sockets. "We had a paper due today?"

"No, Silly," Brielle teased her brother. "It's for British Literature. You aren't even in that class."

"Oh."

Brielle and Jade didn't even try to stifle their laughs. Ryder visibly pouted while his sister and one of her best friends chuckled at his blunder. It hardly took long at all for Abigail to join in. Ever since the middle of the Fall semester, she found herself smiling more and more. It was definitely a pleasant change.

Brielle's laughter quickly died down when she noticed a particular person's absence. "Wait, where's Noah?"

"I don't know," Abigail shrugged. "He left PE a few minutes early and I haven't seen him since."

"I hope everything's okay," Brielle worried out loud.

"He probably needed to go home early to watch his sisters," explained Abigail, even though she knew the real reason...or did she? *"Or, he had to leave for therapy...but, wait. That's on Wednesdays. Today is a Monday."*

"I'm sure that's what it is. From what I've heard, those two are a handful," Keagan shrugged, leaning against a random locker without a care.

Her black hair styled in a pixie cut now had baby blue highlights rather than red. It had been a last-minute decision during Christmas break in order to try something new. Her mother had not given her anything for the holiday, so she marched herself right up to the store and bought more hair dye. Needless to say, she surprised everyone when the break was over.

A phone chimed, reverberating throughout the hallway. Abigail, Keagan, Jade, and Brielle all checked their phones, but it turned out to be Ryder's. Brielle looked at her brother as he read the notification that popped up. He unlocked his phone and then sent a reply before looking up at his sister and friends.

"That was Noah," he answered a nonverbal question from all of them. "He said he had to go watch his sisters since his mom has a late shift tonight."

"Oh," the four girls chorused the elongated word.

For some reason, Abigail did not find herself believing Noah completely. It was an oddity if he sent a message to Ryder notifying him where he was without doing the same for Abigail. She was not paranoid like she used to be, but she couldn't help beginning to raise a red flag in the back of her mind. She knew she was overreacting, but it was something she could not control.

Abigail tightened the ponytail on the back of her head. "I think I'm gonna head out," she excused herself. "I'll see you all tomorrow."

"Bye, Abi!" Keagan could not let her leave without one of her signature bear hugs. Abigail eagerly returned it.

"Bye, Abigail!" the rest of her friends dismissed her kindly.

Abigail waved to the three girls and one boy smiling in their usual kind way. She then turned around on her heel and began walking the familiar route towards her locker. She hadn't bothered changing back into her regular clothes after PE since she would just be going home anyway. Abigail ignored the smell of sweat clinging to the back of her t-shirt and in her socks as she strode down the desolate halls. It appeared as if everyone was in a rush to arrive at home.

She inputted her combination into the lock on her specific metal compartment and it clicked open effortlessly. Abigail unweaved the lock from the handle and opened the locker door. She began to pack her books safely into her backpack when a light force landed on her shoe. Abigail's gaze darted downward and towards a couple of sheets of folded notebook paper that was on her left foot. Confused, she picked it up and began to read.

NOAH HOWELL

Professor Wright
British Literature
9 January 2018

ABIGAIL GAPED at the heading with wide eyes. This was Noah's essay that was due earlier that morning. How did it get into her locker? She was about to go into a complete panic until she read a small note in the top right corner.

·   ·   ·

P.S. THIS IS ANOTHER COPY. I turned in my official essay this morning, but this is the handwritten version meant for you.

-Noah

"MEANT FOR ME?" Abigail asked herself in disbelief.

She did not ask any other questions, but instead, started to read the essay that was placed in her locker for no apparent reason. Why would Abigail need to read Noah's British Literature paper? She was about to find out as she leaned against a locker next to her own, slid down it, and held the paper in front of her while she sat.

THE LORD of the Rings trilogy is a whirlwind of action, mystery, and magic warped into one thousand, one hundred, and thirty-seven pages. Rather than being tied together with one spine and engulfed by one cover, the series is separated into three parts: the exposition in the first, rising action in the second, and then the climax, falling action, and resolution in the third and final volume. The trilogy is a path of twists and turns. Some portions lead to overgrowth and uneven chaos while others are smoothed out and shrouded with sunlight. There is one thing that each part of this path has in common, though: all of the routes have an ending, but it is undetermined whether it will be fruitful or lead to utter destruction.

I've learned a valuable lesson in my seventeen years. Despite my life being short, I believe I have lived through quite a lot in this time. For most of my youth, I lived near the beach with my wonderful family: my mother, my father, - whose relationship was as good as gold - and my twin sisters. As you would know out of all people, Professor Wright, every story has a deeper and darker meaning etched between the lines. There is hardly ever purity among the pages. Instead, there is pain, fear, and darkness. While in the midst of my picture-perfect life, my family's ties were slowly falling apart from my dad's smoking problem. He developed coronary artery disease and eventually died at my feet. We moved away as quickly as we could after the funeral and my entire world changed. Everything fell apart, but luckily, I had someone enter my life who was unknowingly picking up the pieces.

When I first started at Hillwell High during my senior year, I didn't know a soul. At least I didn't until a certain girl - who will remain anonymous - entered my life out of the blue. At first, I found her quite amusing, but as I got to know her after she requested a frantic favor, I realized there was much more to her than what meets the eye. Behind her hair that was always in front of her heart-shaped face and those striking brown eyes, I discovered that the world inside her head was shattered like mine, but in a different way. Used. Abused. Tainted. Flawed. Scarred. Deemed unworthy of love. I saw it with my own eyes. I noticed how her anxiety was taken out on her nails, gnawed to the bone. I noticed how she flinched whenever someone would touch her, even if it was a comforting hug. I noticed it all, and I knew what I had to do.

The broken pieces of my recent past were used bountifully to patch up her own wounds from the battle she was consistently fighting. It refused to cease. It was so difficult to watch her crumble into pieces like my father did, so I fulfilled every single request of hers, whether it be spoken or mute. I was there for her whenever she needed a helping hand against the demons turning her life into a living hell. The more time I spent with her, the more I realized that I had developed feelings that were indescribable in every way. I knew they were unobtainable, especially after what she had been through, and I needed to respect her boundaries no matter what. That was the difficult part of the past semester—I couldn't live what I thought to be my truth, because sometimes, it fails to work out. It's as simple as that.

You're probably wondering: what does this have to do with the Lord of the Rings trilogy? Since I was a little boy, I loved the action scenes that the movie trilogy had to offer, such as the Battle of Helm's Deep in The Two Towers and the Battle of the Morannon in The Return of the King. It wasn't until I grew older when I started to discover what the movies were really about: friendship, love, and the battle between good and evil. We fight the battle between good and evil waged in our minds on a daily basis.

You see, Professor Wright, my favorite character of the trilogy has always been Samwise Gamgee because of his undying devotion and support towards his best friend, Frodo Baggins. Even as Frodo grew closer and closer to insanity with each moment that he wore the Ring around his neck, Sam remained by his side. Gandalf gave Sam very simple instructions, which were:"Don't you leave him, Samwise Gamgee," and the hobbit replied, "I don't mean to." I hope with all of my heart that I've been a "Samwise Gamgee" to the "Frodo Baggins" I've gotten to know. She deserves a friend - or even more - ebbing kindness, love, and respect more than anything. I hope to be the "Samwise Gamgee" in her life because - unless she wants me to - I'm not going anywhere.

BY THE TIME Abigail reached the end of Noah's essay, she felt tears pricking behind her eyes and spilling down her cheeks. Even though her own essay had been about something similar, describing events during the past six months and comparing herself to Frodo Baggins, his essay took the cake for being the most meaningful.

Now, she understood exactly why he had left early—to place this paper - which was much more of a confession - in her locker for her to find. She knew exactly what to do at that point. Abigail hoisted herself up and slung the strap of her backpack over her shoulder. She hastily wiped away the stray tears falling down her face and sprinted towards the familiar double doors leading to the exterior of Hillwell High School's grounds. Abigail flung herself into her car, which was thankfully parked somewhat close to the doors, and abruptly drove off.

It hardly took any time at all to discover what - or who - exactly she was looking for. He was walking on the right side of the road on the sidewalk. Abigail was able to recognize him from the back at least a couple hundred feet away. Even as Abigail parked her car by the curb, climbed out of it, and ran up to him, he did not turn around. It wasn't until she wrapped her arms around him in a tight hug that he turned around and acknowledged her, returning the gesture affectionately.

"...I'm guessing you read what I left you," Noah bluntly stated, hence Abigail's giggles against his chest.

"You sure know how to overshare to a teacher," she snickered.

A smile grew upon Noah's face. "I hope it wasn't too much, but I wanted you to know a bit more about my side of the story," he explained, looking down at her.

Abigail met his eyes. "It was perfect."

"Oh, praise the-" Noah appeared relieved.

"But I have something to tell you."

Noah paused at once. His heart threatened to leap its way out of its chest while he waited for Abigail's contradiction to her statement seconds ago.

"I know you have feelings for me...and I can safely say that I reciprocate them, but to be completely honest with you, I'm not ready for anything like that yet," she admitted softly. "I don't want to disappoint you, but I need to take this one small step at a time."

Noah brushed a tendril of her hair behind her ear. "I'd hope that you've learned by now that something like that would never disappoint me."

"I know. I'm just...not ready," repeated Abigail worriedly.

"I understand, and we can go at whatever pace you'd like. If that means remaining friends, then I'm all for it. Just let me know."

The beautiful smile that Noah adored was back on Abigail's lovely face. "I will."

"Promise?"

Her answer was certain. "I promise."

Abigail and Noah remained in each other's arms for a little while. It was the only shelter Abigail needed at that very moment in time. She had herself, she had her family, her friends, and Noah, which was more than enough. Her mind finally cleared when she realized everything was going to be okay...at least for now.

Abigail caught herself wondering...what would have happened if she never looked past the seemingly ugly black glasses upon Noah's face? What if she never discovered the beautiful boy who was hiding behind the lenses?

She didn't have to know, but one thing was for sure: her story would've been a hell of a lot different. Abigail was more than happy with how it turned out.

ACKNOWLEDGMENTS

I would like to express a huge thank you to those who have stood by my side while I follow my dream to be an author and a freelance writer.

Even though college has me busier than a bee, I have left some of my time to write and create a series that touches my heart in more ways than one.

Thank you to my parents, who have been nothing but supportive as I drive myself down the road of uncertainty.

Thank you to my sister for proofreading this book and assuring me that it was worth the six months that it took for me to prepare to publish.

Thank you to my Uncle Rob who has been one of my biggest inspirations to this date and has helped me with my books.

Thank you to my friends and anonymous buyers/reviewers who have shown Huntington Avenue so much support and rated both of them five whole stars!

Most of all, thank you, God, for giving me fingers to type, a mind to create, the health to keep myself upright, and my hands to hold the finished product. Without Him, I wouldn't be here right now.

To all of you, thank you. I love you all.

ALSO BY CASSIDY STEPHENS

Huntington Avenue: Part One

Nearly perfect grades, a loving family, and being a guitar prodigy seem to be attributes of the ideal teenage life, right? In his case, there was a debilitating catch.

Zachary West - a blind teenage boy - had no clue what he was getting himself into when he stepped foot into Oceanview High School. After recently moving to the suburbs of Kitty Hawk, North Carolina, the seventeen-year-old desired a chance at the normality of being a teenager. Being homeschooled for the past eleven years after a traumatic accident caused his condition was a nightmare for an optimistic extrovert.

Soon enough, and consequent to a couple of encounters with resident hothead, Jaylen Hunt, Zach crosses paths with the bully's long-term girlfriend—Kelsey Davis. In contrast to what her peers might assume her personality to be due to her boyfriend's nature, Kelsey was a sweet soul who made the best out of every situation. Her life seemed to be perfect, but everything changed when the teenage girl noticed Zach's intriguing sight impediment. She wanted to learn more about it.

As questions, an unlikely friendship, and possibly more begin to arise, life continues to wreak havoc for the both of them. With Jaylen and his close friend, Lyla Walker, becoming a problem, Zach and Kelsey find themselves growing closer together and further apart from the people they had been familiarized with.

Would Kelsey flip her life around for the unique boy on Huntington Avenue who needed a friend, or would she remain with the people who might not have been the best for her?

Huntington Avenue: Part 2

Supportive friends, an eligible love interest, and an opportunity to obliterate the concept of blindness seem to be the dream of Zach's, right? Unfortunately, it was more of a nightmare.

Following an unexpected confession of lies, concealed emotions, and an unconsented first kiss from Kelsey at the airport, Zach had no idea what to think of his life crashing down upon him. He finally had the chance to regain his eyesight after eleven years of confining darkness. Kelsey had proved to be his light and guide throughout his adjustment to his new home and school. There was nothing distrustful about her...until the airport incident.

For the duration of the two teenagers spending some much-needed time apart—Zach being in Florida for his procedure and Kelsey remaining in Kitty Hawk, tensions begin to rise between the latter and her significant other: Jaylen. The relationship between Kelsey and her "so-called" best friend, Zach, caused too much insecurity in the seemingly confident teenage boy. He wanted their friendship to end as quickly as it came about, but it was easier said than done—oh, how much easier.

While several attempts, lies, and pure toxicity tear Kelsey and Jaylen's "golden" relationship to pieces, Zach attempts to readjust to society. With the help of his friends, family, and trust issues, it was nearly a walk in the park. Alas, a recurring string of nightmares, confidential information becoming jeopardized, and dishonesty sprouting from Zach and Kelsey's new chapter of romance kept the situation from remaining peaceful.

Would a simple mistake drive Kelsey and Zach apart for good, or would the two of them work through their struggles side by side?

Made in the USA
Middletown, DE
02 December 2021

54054533R00166